D0350204

EXIT

Also by Belinda Bauer

Blacklands
Darkside
Finders Keepers
Rubbernecker
The Facts of Life and Death
The Shut Eye
The Beautiful Dead
Snap

EXIT

BELINDA BAUER

Atlantic Monthly Press
New York

First published in Great Britain in 2020 by Bantam Press
an imprint of Transworld Publishing

Typeset in 11.75/15pt Minion by Jouve (UK), Milton Keynes

Published simultaneously in Canada
Printed in the United States of America

First Grove Atlantic hardcover edition: February 2021

ISBN 978-0-8021-5788-1
eISBN 978-0-8021-5790-4

Atlantic Monthly Press
an imprint of Grove Atlantic
154 West 14th Street
New York, NY 10011

Distributed by Publishers Group West

groveatlantic.com

21 22 23 24   10 9 8 7 6 5 4 3 2 1

To Sarah Adams – my kind, clever, patient,
one-in-a-million editor.

Part One

The Job

The key was under the mat.

As usual.

Felix Pink found the predictability comforting – even if the predictable outcome was death.

'Here we go then,' said Chris, putting the key in the lock.

Chris talked too much but Felix never said anything about it. He imagined it was nerves. He himself had stopped being nervous a long time ago. Now he cleared his throat and adjusted his cuffs, and followed his accomplice inside.

The house smelled of the dust that coated the inside of pill bottles. They often did.

They stood in the hallway and Chris called, 'Hello?'

There was no sound apart from a clock ticking somewhere. Not a real clock, Felix could tell, but some battery thing that ticked a small, fake tick to make people think they were getting olde worlde value for money.

He noticed a piece of paper on the third stair, folded into a little tent, like a place card at a wedding.

UPSTAIRS

He picked it up and showed it to Chris, who started up the stairs. Felix took a moment to fold the paper several times and put it in his briefcase, then he gripped the banister. He was naturally cautious but, when there was a job to be done, it became a conscious effort.

Chris was waiting for him on the landing.

'Hello?'

'Hello.' The answer was small and weak.

In the big front bedroom there was a man in bed. He was propped upright by pillows and facing the bay window, which revealed a view of a similar window across the road.

'Rufus Collins?' said Felix.

The man in the bed nodded weakly.

'I'm John and this is Chris.'

Mr Collins nodded again, as if he knew why they were there – and then closed his eyes.

Felix had chosen the name John because he thought it sounded competent. Margaret had had a doctor called John Tolworth who had seemed competent for quite a long time. It wasn't his fault that he'd been beaten by death.

In the end, it beat them all.

He didn't know Chris's real name. It was for the best.

There was a chair beside the bed and Felix sat in it and put his briefcase on the floor beside him. There was no room on the night-stand, what with all the pills and tissues.

The cylinder was already there. Dull grey metal, like a little aqualung, attached by a length of clear tubing to a plastic face mask that lay under the man's chin. A tired-looking piece of elastic looped from the mask around the back of his neck and over his ears, making them fold down a little. One bony hand covered the mask protectively, as if someone might steal it.

'I'll get another chair,' said Chris and left the room.

Felix looked down at Mr Collins. He was old, but probably no older than *he* was, which was seventy-five. But this man was sick, and that made all the difference, and he looked a hundred. His yellowy skin so stretched across his cheeks and brow that it looked ready to split. His breath rattled in his throat as if he needed to cough but just didn't have the strength.

Chris puffed in with a small wooden armchair and put it down at the other side of the bed with a loud clump.

Mr Collins's eyes opened and his hand clutched at the mask.

'Sorry,' said Chris.

The sick man closed his eyes again.

And then they waited.

The house was so quiet that Felix could hear the clock fake-ticking downstairs. Now and then cars shushed by outside, and Mr Collins breathed. Every breath was different from the one before, as if he was discovering breathing each time anew and trying to work out which way was best. Some breaths were short and gaspy, some long and wheezy. The little rattle was the only constant.

Felix folded his hands in his lap like a priest, and waited.

'How long have we got?' said Chris, and looked at the door.

Felix had a watch but he didn't look at it. 'There's no rush,' he said.

It was true. It was often like this. It rarely happened fast. Occasionally it didn't happen at all . . .

It would or it wouldn't.

They could or they couldn't.

The ultimate outcome was, of course, inevitable, but in the short term an Exiteer had to learn to be patient.

Felix had always been a patient man. He had actually toyed with calling himself Job instead of John, but Job would have invited interest in a way that John never did. And interest was to be avoided at all costs.

But, like Job, he waited. They both waited.

An hour.

Two.

Felix had to guard against sleep. He found it hard to sleep at night but often dropped off during the day. But never on the job. He studied the bookshelf and recalled the plots of those books he had read. Dickens. Tolkien. He remembered his wedding and tried to recall every guest. Chris did a Sudoku, with a pair of bifocals gripping the tip of his nose for dear life. Felix had never got on with bifocals. The optician, Mrs . . . Something, had told him his eyesight was good for his age, which was some comfort. He'd lost a button on his cuff. Annoying. But he always kept spare buttons, so probably had one that would suit . . .

He swallowed a yawn out of deference to the sick man, but missed the feeling of his respiratory system being flushed out. He'd read that when the iron lung was first introduced, patients would die even though they were breathing, because no allowance had been made for the occasional sigh. Just breathing was not enough. He hoped it was a true fact. You had to be so careful nowadays.

Children passed outside. Home time. Strangely Felix recalled it better now than he'd ever done. The long trudge. The heavy bag. The mock fights that sometimes turned to real ones. Looking down at his scuffed shoes and scabbed knees, with his belly gurgling for tea . . .

Quietly, Felix put his briefcase on his knees.

Mr Collins opened his eyes and looked at him.

'Do you mind if I eat?' Felix asked him politely.

Mr Collins looked vaguely amused. 'You go on,' he whispered.

'Can I get you anything to eat or drink?'

Mr Collins shook his head almost imperceptibly.

Felix took out a red tartan thermos flask and tinfoil block which, when unwrapped, revealed his sandwich. It was strawberry jam on white bread – a childish preference he'd never managed to shake off, despite his age and gravitas.

He'd lived through rationing.

The man in the bed watched him eat his sandwich and sip his tea.

The children faded to silence.

The clock pretended to tick.

Chris's chin drooped on to his chest and his mouth fell open.

Felix finished his sandwich and his tea, then shook a clean tissue from his pocket, wiped the little cup dry and screwed it back on to the top of the thermos. He folded the tinfoil into a neat square for future use. He put both back into the briefcase with the soiled tissue, and quietly closed the lid.

Before he could click it shut, Mr Collins lifted the mask to his face.

'Thank you,' he murmured, and died.

They held the debrief at a nearby café.

There wasn't much to talk about, but Chris ordered a ham and cheese toastie, a slab of coffee cake and a large cappuccino.

Felix had already eaten, of course, but ordered tea to keep him company.

As they waited for the food to arrive, Chris said, 'I'm not doing this any more.'

He looked as if he expected a fight, but when none was forthcoming he went on, 'It's all got too much for me. All this death.'

Felix stirred the teabag in the pot. 'Well,' he said, as if about to pass comment, but then he didn't. Just left *Well* hanging there between them.

The truth was, he didn't blame Chris. Of course, he was disappointed that he was leaving, because it meant he'd have to get used to somebody new. He also felt Chris was giving up on important work. There weren't enough of them as it was. Geoffrey was always saying so in the rambling, late-night phone calls he sometimes made to Felix's home.

We need more like us, Geoffrey often said. *Good men prepared to step up to the crease. Because if we don't do it, who will? Tell me that, Rob. If not us, who?*

Geoffrey often called him Rob. Felix often thought Geoffrey might be drunk, but he didn't blame him if he was. Geoffrey had

Parkinson's and had to use sticks and sometimes a wheelchair, so Felix felt he probably had the right to be drunk whenever he could hold a glass to his lips without spillage.

He'd never met the man, of course. Didn't even know where he lived. The Exiteers were very careful about anonymity. Geoffrey encouraged the use of pseudonyms, and was always telling Felix never to speak to anyone on the phone claiming to represent the Exiteers.

Protects us all, Rob, he'd slurred. *A secret shared is a secret halved.*

It was Geoffrey who'd named them the Exiteers.

Like Musketeers, you see? he'd told Felix on more than one occasion. *All for one and one for all. After all, not everybody can afford to go to Switzerland.* And Felix had wondered if that meant that *Geoffrey* couldn't afford to go to Switzerland.

A bustling pepperpot of a woman with her hair in a golden bun put their food on the table, and Felix blinked out of his own thoughts and back to the café.

'What do you think?' said Chris, as if he wanted to be talked out of it, but Felix refrained from trying. Exiteering was all about rights, and that meant Chris had the right to leave the group, just as their clients had the right to leave life – without judgement or question, or attempts at persuasion to the opposite view.

Also, if Chris wanted to give up, then Felix felt he was possibly no longer the right person to *be* an Exiteer.

Was not *steadfast.*

Being steadfast was no longer fashionable but it was a quality Felix had always admired. He liked to think he'd been a steadfast husband to Margaret. Even after she had left him alone with their memories.

Even after that.

Steadfast.

'John?'

'Yes?' Felix was blank for a second, then remembered that Chris had asked him what he thought about him leaving the Exiteers.

So he cleared his throat and said, 'I understand completely,' and Chris nodded gratefully, as if Felix had actively supported his decision. Chris took a huge bite of his toastie, and a long string of melted cheese looped from his lower lip and draped itself down his navy tie.

Felix twitched but managed to stop himself from wiping it away. Chris was not his son.

Chris finished his sandwich without further cheese incident, and then ate his cake and drank his cappuccino.

They were encouraged to take public transport to jobs to avoid their cars being captured on CCTV, so they walked to Bristol Temple Meads station together and Chris shook his hand and said *Good luck, John*, and Felix said something similar back, and then Chris walked off to get his train home. Felix thought he lived somewhere near Winchester, but wasn't sure.

He walked the two miles to the bus station and got the coach back to North Devon.

Mabel was waiting in the hallway to glare at him, and there was a puddle by the back door.

Served him right, he supposed. He looked at the clock. He'd been gone for nine hours. Next time he'd ask Miss Knott next door to have her. Miss Knott was always interrupting their walks to engage him about Mabel, as if she were a Crufts winner and not a scrubbing-brush mutt with breath that could strip paint.

He opened the door to the garden and Mabel gave him a withering look that said it was too late *now*, before stalking slowly outside.

He cleaned up the widdle using yesterday's *Telegraph* sports section and a bottle of bleach. After washing his hands, he put his briefcase on the kitchen table and removed the thermos, then washed it out and turned it and its accompanying plastic cup upside down on the rack to dry. He unfolded the foil that had wrapped his sandwich, shook the crumbs from it and wiped off a spot of jam with the J-cloth. Then he folded it back into its square and smoothed it into the second drawer down, along with more of its kind and a collection of paper and plastic bags, elastic bands and string.

Finally he took out the silver cylinder of nitrous oxide and the clear plastic mask, and wiped them clean of . . .

anything

. . . and put them in two separate shopping bags. Tomorrow he would take the cylinder with him and drop it in a bin near the library, where he needed to renew a book about the migratory routes of seabirds. The day after that he would put the mask and tubing into somebody else's recycling bin.

Felix always disliked getting rid of the evidence. It all felt rather *grubby*. What the Exiteers were doing was not illegal, of course, he had made very sure of that. So long as they didn't actively help the clients. Didn't encourage them. Didn't supply the cylinder of nitrous oxide – or what Geoffrey called 'the instrument of death'. So long as they just sat there and witnessed the end of life, then everything was fine. The client died quickly and without pain, and the family could be assured that their loved one had not died alone, without themselves being implicated in their death. Everybody got what they wanted. Sometimes insurance companies were cheated of a few premiums, but as unnecessary lingering and suffering were prerequisites of their contractual fulfilment, Felix's conscience was crystal clear. Even so, it would have been foolish to leave anything lying around that might prompt a suspicious mind to ask awkward questions about what had at first appeared to be the wholly expected death of a terminally ill patient. And Felix Pink had never been a foolish man.

He opened the corner cupboard. His own nitrous oxide cylinders were behind the dog food. He had secured them from the same tame dental surgeon that Geoffrey had recommended, after the third or fourth Exit he'd attended. Mrs Casper – a sweet-seeming woman with motor neurone disease. By then Felix had seen enough to know how easy, how kind an end it brought to life. He bought a fresh cylinder every so often, just to be sure it was all in working order. One day he'd need it, and it would be there. Sooner rather than later, he hoped. Although not before Mabel, of course, because in these days of Bichipoos and Poodledoodles, nobody wanted to adopt a scruffy old mongrel – especially a scruffy old mongrel who enjoyed sliding her face through fox poo.

But when Mabel was gone, *then* his time would come . . .

Mabel had had Lamb and Vegetables last night, so he thought she should probably steer clear of red meat tonight. Tuna Surprise, perhaps, or Chicken Terrine. He held the can at arm's length so he could read the ingredients on the Chicken Terrine and was disappointed to find that it contained only seven per cent meat products. *Meat products.* That left the door open for some of those seven per cent not even being *chicken.* Felix speculated as to what meat could be so much less than chicken that the makers would just call it 'meat' rather than tell it like it was and trumpet it on the label.

Mabel nudged his calf with her nose.

'All right, all right,' he said. He tipped the Tuna Surprise into her bowl and put it on the little plastic mat that saved the floor from spills.

By the time he'd straightened up with due deference to his hip and had glanced down again, Mabel had eaten the Tuna Surprise and was looking up at him expectantly. He ignored her and went slowly up to their bedroom to put away his navy mac. It would be the last time he wore it this year, unless there was a sudden cold snap.

He stood for a while with the doors open, surveying his wardrobe with a pragmatic eye.

Felix Pink's days of buying clothes were over. He had bought his last three-pack of Y-fronts a year ago, and the socks he had now

would see him out. It was a strange feeling – that he would be outlived by his socks.

Although it had already happened with other things, of course.

The last house.

The last car.

Felix wondered how finely he might judge it. How low he could
go. The last can of shaving foam? The last jar of jam? He sometimes wondered whether his dying thought would be of a half-pint
of milk going to waste in his fridge.

He had three suits – tweed, navy pinstripe and black – and five
shirts: four white and one in a muted country-check. For outdoor
pursuits, supposedly, although he only ever wore it in the garden.
Two pairs of slacks, one grey, one brown, three ties and three pairs
of shoes – to whit: brown brogues, shiny black funereals, and some
misguided loafers, which he never wore because loafers of any type
were anathema to him.

He hung the navy mac on the rail, next to a short beige zip-up
jacket.

Felix was at peace with most of his wardrobe, but the beige zip-
up jacket still bothered him. Margaret had bought it from Marks
& Spencer years ago, and he'd been secretly appalled. Felix was no
adventurer, but he had never dreamed that he would wear such a
staid thing. Such an *old man* thing. He'd seen old men in that very
jacket for decades. Often with matching flat cap and walking stick.
He had a hazy recollection of his father in the same jacket, and
quite possibly his grandfather. The fact that Margaret had apparently felt the jacket was suitable attire for him at the age of sixty-four
had come as something of a blow.

The trouble was, he now wore it all the time! It was warm but
not hot. It machine-washed, and dried in a jiffy, looking like new,
and it went with everything else in his wardrobe, somehow making the smart look casual and the casual look smarter. On principle,
Felix had spent ten years looking for something more suitable to

replace it with when it finally wore out, but it never *did* wear out, and he was far too much a man of his generation to dream of discarding something when it was still entirely serviceable, even if he had an existential crisis every time he wore it.

He closed the wardrobe door, went downstairs and watched the recording of that afternoon's *Countdown*.

Mabel barked to let him know that she needed help getting on to the sofa.

Margaret had never allowed Mabel on the sofa, but once she was gone Felix had thought, *Why not?* He creaked to his feet to lift the dog on to the neighbouring cushion, but before he could even bend down, she jumped up, scurried behind him and plopped herself down on his warm patch.

'Off there, Mabel,' he said sternly, but she ignored him.

'Oi,' he said, and poked her. 'On your own seat.'

Mabel feigned death in every respect but a rolling eye, and Felix sighed. This was *why not*. Just one more thing Margaret had been right about. Mabel was a very determined dog and never gave up this particular battle. The only thing that prevented her winning it every time was his physical ability to pick her up and move her. Felix suspected that if Mabel had possessed the same power, he would at this very moment be watching *Countdown* from the garden, with his nose pressed against the living-room window.

He left her where she was and instead went into the kitchen and sat down to finish the jigsaw.

He'd always fancied himself a solver of puzzles, so had plumped for a very challenging two-thousand-piece snowscape featuring reindeer, called *Frozen Waste*. And what a waste it had become . . . The reindeer were not a problem. They were virtually complete. The snow, however, *was* a problem. Felix had four corners and most of the edges, and several random patches of white snow or blue sky that had fallen into place more by luck than by judgement, but most of the snow and tufty yellow grass remained in the box in a

tantalizing tundra. Felix had been building the jigsaw for coming up
to six months now, and rarely found homes for more than a couple
of pieces a day. He had completely overreached himself, but he hated
to give up.

He picked up a tuft. It looked like a hundred other tufts but he
knew it was the same tuft that had haunted him for weeks. He had
examined every possible option for it minutely, leaning over the
picture on the box with a magnifying glass so that he might match
every tiny detail – the scrappy brown grass, the smooth white snow
at the base – and yet this tuft seemed to belong to another puzzle
altogether. Nonetheless Felix spent fifteen minutes brooding over
it before putting it aside for tomorrow and picking up some sky
from the sky pile. Pale blue, featureless, with three ins and an out.
He didn't know what the proper names for the ins and outs were,
or even if they *had* proper names, but that's what he called them.
Ins and outs. Not that it mattered: they were all in the wrong place,
or were the wrong subtle shade of blue.

The box said AGE 8+. Felix snorted.

The phone rang and he tutted and frowned at the clock. It was
after nine, so it could only be Geoffrey. Even *before* nine he rarely
got calls from anyone except telemarketers, and they were mostly
robots now. Felix almost missed the good old days of hanging up
on real people.

'Rob?' said Geoffrey. 'Chris is giving up!'

'So he told me,' said Felix.

'It's too bad,' said Geoffrey. 'We can't afford to lose people.
We've got so much work to do.'

'Have we?' said Felix, rather surprised.

'Of course. We're inundated.'

'Inundated?'

'Indeed,' said Geoffrey. 'We get twenty calls a week.'

Felix was surprised by the low number that Geoffrey considered *inundation* – especially as he knew not all of those would be

deemed suitable clients. The Exiteers existed to support people with terminal illnesses and for whom pain meant their lives were no longer bearable. Geoffrey had told him long ago that they were not in the business of enabling anyone who was 'just a bit fed up'.

Felix was disappointed that there was so little demand for their services, but then they were hardly advertising in the Yellow Pages. Theirs was a hush-hush operation accessed only by cautious word of mouth. It ran on instinct, trust and secrecy, and the fact that there were only twenty calls a week must mean there was a far wider need.

So he tempered his disappointment and asked, 'And how many Exiteers are there?'

'Seven,' said Geoffrey. 'Six now.'

Now Felix was truly surprised. He'd had no idea there were so few of them. He'd never dwelt on a number, but if he'd been pressed he'd have guessed at a hundred like-minded people dotted all around the country. But obviously he'd have been very wrong. Somehow he had always imagined himself to be a small part of a much bigger network. A cog in a reasonably sized machine. Not a battleship or a jet fighter, of course, but a steam traction engine, perhaps, or a church clock. It was rather disappointing to realize that he was more of a spring in a pop-up toaster.

Plus he felt a little miffed at being called Rob, if Geoffrey had the names of only seven precious front-liners to remember.

Six now.

But then he realized that even if Geoffrey *did* remember his name, it would be John, which wasn't even the right name, so he took offence and forgave it all in the same moment. Felix was good at that. He'd had such big things to be upset by in life that it had become much easier to forgive the little ones.

Geoffrey sighed. 'You'd be surprised how hard it is to find new volunteers. Many, many people support what we do, but very few actually want to do it. And many of those who *do* want to do it are just not . . . suitable.'

'I can imagine,' said Felix.

'Indeed,' said Geoffrey. 'You just can't be too careful with this sort of thing.'

'Of course,' said Felix. 'So with whom will I work now?'

Exiteers always worked in pairs. Geoffrey said it was for emotional support, but Felix – ever the accountant – imagined it was so that nobody stole anything. Nearly all of his work had been done with Chris. Only on his first case had he been paired with a sprightly middle-aged woman called Wendy, who'd apparently died herself shortly thereafter. Geoffrey had told him she'd choked on a sweet during a yoga class, which Felix felt was so bizarre that it must be true.

'I'll take care of it,' said Geoffrey, 'and let you know.'

'Thank you, Geoffrey.'

'Night, John.'

Felix put the phone down and then called through to the lounge, 'Garden, Mabel!'

The Loving Wife and Mother

Felix always wore his best suit to visit his wife and son. The navy pinstripe, with a white shirt and the blue-and-green Argyll tie Margaret had bought for him the last time she'd remembered Christmas.

Best bib and tucker. That's what she'd call it. You didn't hear that any more – or any of the old sayings. And the new ones were just f-words.

It was a perfect April morning. Sunny, but not too hot, and with a gentle breeze. Felix had bought flowers from the corner shop. They were yellow tulips and nice enough, but wrapped in layers of plastic and brown paper when all they really needed was a good old bit of garden twine to hold them together.

He opened the boot, took out his thermos flask and the fold-up camping chair and trudged up the hill.

Margaret and Jamie were buried side by side on the slope over-looking the whole town and, beyond that, the estuary. It was a lovely spot. Felix had paid for the original double plot close to the oak tree many years ago, but when Jamie died they had buried him here, and Felix had negotiated to purchase a third plot alongside the other two. The would-be occupant of that plot had recognized that behind Felix's odd request was a man in want, while he him-self was only a man in grudging need, and so had made an absolute killing on the deal, but Felix didn't mind. He had enough money and little left to spend it on.

Now he took comfort in knowing that when he died he would take his place once more beside his wife and son.

He stood at the foot of the graves while a blackbird showed off in the nearby hedge.

'Hello, Margaret,' he murmured.

The blackbird answered him with a long, happy lungful, but Margaret's headstone only said:

LOVING WIFE AND MOTHER

Felix wished he'd chosen a different inscription. He'd seen this one in countless obituaries, and so – at a time of flux – it had felt safe to him. But increasingly he thought it made it sound as though a wife and mother was *all* Margaret had been, and that was very far from the truth – although it was only since her death that Felix had truly understood that she had been the sun, and he and Jamie just two little planets in her orbit, held in place by her gravity, lit by her light, and basking in her warmth.

Everybody had loved Margaret. They'd loved her kindness, and her wisdom, and her humour, and they'd deigned to like him too, just for being with her.

But when she'd started to leave him, her friends had left as well, until Felix had been entirely alone with Margaret. And then entirely alone without her, and by the time she had died, he'd been so exhausted that he could barely think. Her slow demise had been like a steamroller trying to run him down while he staggered from kerb to kerb, trying to dodge the inevitable. Often it felt almost as if *he* had died too, because all that was left now was a pale shadow of himself, hanging like limp lace at an airless window.

Without you I am nothing. That's what he *should* have had set in stone.

At least they'd done right by Jamie . . .

TAKEN TOO SOON FROM THOSE
WHO LOVED HIM DEARLY

Dearly had been Margaret's decision. Felix had never seen *dearly* on a headstone before and felt that it was rather showy. They'd argued about it. Rowed, actually. Now he thought of it, it had been the only proper row he and Margaret had ever had. The only time she'd got really angry about anything. But, of course, every time he looked down at the words now, he knew she'd been right, and that *dearly* was not only essential but was, in fact, the most important thing on the stone – and that he'd been unbearably stupid to think or say otherwise.

Margaret had been right about everything. He was still learning that every day. Whenever he was stuck or confused, Felix would ask himself, *What would Margaret do?* And the answer would come to him as if she was right there, whispering in his ear. Young and sensible Margaret, of course. Not old, sad Margaret, whose reason had deserted her and whose memory had gone and who would clutch his arm and say, *Promise me! Promise me you'll look after Jamie!*

And he could only say *I promise* because she didn't know that their son was already dead.

Felix emptied last week's carnations into the hedge, then washed and refilled the plastic vase with water he'd brought in a bottle, and arranged the new tulips. He folded the wrapping into a square and placed it under a stone so it wouldn't blow away. He'd take it home with him. Recycle it. Two different boxes, of course. Both inconveniently big, both made of plastic. And then a lorry belching diesel fumes would come along and do its bit to save the planet . . .

He unfolded the folding chair and sat down.

The cemetery was filled with new life. The trees sang their rustling songs, and little animals and birds scurried in the verge, while every sparrow and tit seemed to be carrying wisps of grass or a downy feather. A bumblebee droned by heavily, as if it were in the wrong gear, and the blackbird hopped out of the hedge again to show Felix a strand of orange baler twine.

Felix smiled and closed his eyes. This place soothed and restored him. Gave him the strength to carry on. One day he hoped it might give him the strength to give up.

Seagulls called overhead. Immediately he thought of fishing with Jamie. Watching his son curl a strip of mackerel on to a hook, so scared he would pierce his tender little fingers . . . *I can DO it! Let me DO it!* Felix chuckled under his breath. They'd caught nothing, of course. How could they? Jamie had been so excited that he'd reeled in every ten minutes to check the bait. It would have defeated the most suicidal of fish.

His smile faded. It was hard not to slide from those memories into much harder ones: from the boy to the young man whose slow death had sunk the fragile raft of faith they had all clung to for two miserable years, adrift on a sea of false hopes and platitudes from doctors whose best was never going to be good enough. They'd all known it, but never spoken of it. Instead they'd chatted and played canasta on Jamie's hospital bed, or sat silently while he slept, growing smaller with every exhalation, until he barely raised a bump in the blanket.

In his room they'd always been bright with optimism.

They'd saved the cracks for the car park . . .

Nobody ever spoke of the relentless *parking* that was demanded by a relative in hospital with a prolonged illness. Twice a day, every day, in the dystopian concrete multi-storey that smelled of urine and smog. The constant change for the ticket machine. The long queue at the barrier. The forgetting where the car was. Was it this row? This level? This *car park*? The only time Margaret had broken down during that whole long nightmare was once when they couldn't find the car. She had finally bent over and wept on somebody else's bonnet while he'd stood beside her, uselessly rubbing her back and clutching the keys to nothing.

At the funeral, Felix had ached to punch the vicar.

God didn't care for them. Only they cared for each other. He and Margaret had cared for Jamie, and then he had cared for Margaret when she could no longer care for herself, and now he didn't have anyone to care for except Mabel.

And nobody cared for him.

The First-timer

The new Exiteer called herself Amanda.

She was sat outside a little café on the square in Bideford, close to where Felix got off the bus. There was a nip in the air, but it was bright and breezy. Perfect weather for the beige zip-up jacket, in fact. Felix introduced himself and Amanda shook his hand. She had only just started a glass of hot chocolate, and so he ordered a pot of tea.

She was startlingly young and he wondered how they'd found her. He himself had been recruited by an elderly woman who worked at the funeral parlour where Margaret had been laid out. Elspeth, her little black name badge had read. White hair. Blue eyes. Kind mouth.

I'm sorry she suffered so, she'd said, and Felix had nodded at the withered corpse of his wife and said, *Death was a relief to both of us.*

He couldn't quite remember how the conversation had turned from Margaret's death to the Exiteers, only that when it had, he had not recoiled. Elspeth had alluded to a group who supported the right to die and said she'd 'leave that thought' with him – along with her card.

Felix had thought about it for six whole months, because he was not the kind of man to leap before he'd looked, and then looked again – and then possibly commissioned some sort of risk-assessment report. Caution was as much a part of him as Margaret or Jamie or a jam sandwich.

But finally he had called Elspeth. *I'd like to be an Exiteer*, he'd said, feeling as if he were applying to be Batman. But Elspeth hadn't laughed. She'd told him where to meet her, and by the end of a civilized tea in Banbury's he'd been approved. By what formal psychological standard, he had never been sure. He suspected it was none. But Elspeth seemed to be a very intelligent woman, and he'd had confidence in her good judgement.

Felix hoped that somebody like Elspeth had checked Amanda out properly, but, really, somebody should have warned him that she was quite so young.

'Have you done this before?' he said as soon as the waitress walked away.

'No,' she said. 'Have you?'

He nodded. 'Many times.'

'How many?' she said. 'Times. I mean, how many times?'

She was nervous. He'd been nervous too, before his first time.

'Twenty-seven.'

She widened her eyes at him. 'That's a *lot*.'

She made it sound as if he were some kind of serial killer, and she must have realized that because she blushed, making her look even younger than she already did. He estimated twenty-five, even allowing for an exaggerated judgement of youth from his own remote perspective of seventy-five.

'It becomes easier,' he said. 'Not that it ever becomes pleasant.'

Amanda nodded at her hot chocolate going cold in its tall glass. Most of the cream had already sunk into the muddy liquid.

'Do you mind my asking,' he said, 'how old you are?'

'Twenty-three,' she said. Then, anxiously, 'Is that OK?'

'Of course it is,' he said, although it was even worse than he'd thought. 'All you need to remember is that ours is a passive role, not an active one. The most important things we can offer our clients are kindness and calmness. We give them the support to leave this world without pain or fear. When we do that, we have done all we can.'

She nodded, then frowned and said, 'What if I panic?'

Felix appraised her. She had straight, dark eyebrows that made her look sensible, so on the basis of her brows alone, he said, 'You won't.'

'What if I get . . . emotional? What if I cry?'

'Is that likely?'

She frowned, although her forehead was still so new that the lines it made were shallow and fleeting. 'If I feel sad I might.'

'Well, it's all right to *feel* sad,' said Felix, 'but I'd strongly discourage any overt display of emotion while we're actually with the client.'

'Like what?'

'Wailing,' he said. 'Rending of garments . . .'

She surprised him by getting the joke. When she laughed her whole face lit up and she barely looked twenty.

He really hoped Geoffrey knew what he was doing.

'Why do you . . . do this?' she asked.

Felix took the lid off the pot and peered at his tea. He stirred it a little and replaced the lid. 'I think everybody has their own reasons.'

'My nan died of cancer,' she said, as if he'd asked her. 'First one kind and then another, and then another after that. It took her two years and the last few months were just, like, totally *horrible*.' She stopped and looked at the people bustling past, shopping, chatting, walking dogs. 'I wish I'd known about this then.'

She dropped her spoon in her chocolate with a dull tinkle and he could tell she wasn't going to finish it.

Felix nodded. He felt a bit better about her now.

'Shall we go?' he said.

He insisted on paying, and left a tip on his saucer. Twenty per cent. Margaret had always over-tipped and he'd always been irritated by it, but he did it now in her memory, and always enjoyed his own mini-largesse.

'OK,' said Amanda, and suddenly looked older again. As she

reached for the bag slung over the back of her chair, Felix noticed her hand was trembling.

'You'll be fine,' he said kindly.

She gave a smile, but it was small and tense and didn't linger.

The key was under the mat.

Of course it was.

Felix thought sometimes of the living he might make if he were a burglar instead of a retired accountant.

Inside, a small black-and-tan dog yapped at them, then stopped and smelled Mabel on his trouser leg.

'Good boy,' said Felix, and the dog wagged and trotted into the front room.

'This feels so wrong,' whispered Amanda, looking around nervously.

Felix nodded. Letting himself into a stranger's house always did. Although he found the frisson of risk not unpleasant.

There were photos on the wall of the stairwell. Old black-and-white ones. It always made Felix sad to see photographs of people he didn't know, and to wonder where the pictures – and the people – went after they were forgotten.

The house didn't smell of pill bottles, but it was a bit of a mess. Not dirty, but untidy. There was a man's sock on the floor.

'Hello?'

The dog gave a single yip but there was no human response.

They went to the bottom of the stairs and immediately Felix could hear the laboured breathing – like a marathon runner trying to suck air through a straw.

People who were dying made all kinds of noises – grunts, farts, groans – but the fight for air was the one that always stuck with Felix. The one that invaded his dreams, and woke him, sweating and gasping.

This was as bad as he'd heard.

'Mr Cann?'

No answer. Only that dreadful gasping.

He looked at Amanda. She had gone pale. 'I don't . . .' she said. 'I don't . . . think I can do this.'

'Of course you can,' said Felix. 'You'll be fine.' He gave her a reassuring smile, gripped the banister, and led the way before she could argue. He didn't look back, but he could feel her follow his lead.

The gloom deepened as they climbed, and as Felix's head rose above the level of the landing, he could see why. There was only one door open off the landing – the back bedroom at the top of the stairs – and even in that room the curtains were drawn.

Before he'd mounted the last step, Felix could see the man in the bed.

He walked quietly into the room. 'Hello, Mr Cann?'

The dying man looked bad. He was propped up on his pillows, his eyes closed, his brow furrowed and his teeth gritted with the effort of staying alive long enough to die.

'Mr Cann?'

There was no acknowledgement. Felix bent closer and could see that despite the struggle of breathing, Charles Cann was asleep. Whatever illness he had, it had shrouded his true age in mystery: he could have been fifty or eighty. His face was crumpled paper, his hair grey and straggly, his body painfully thin. There were dark smudges under his eyes and, even by the meagre light, Felix could see that his skin and lips had a blue mottle to them which spoke of a lack of oxygen. He looked as if he was slowly suffocating in his own bed.

Felix glanced down at the big old-fashioned dresser. It wasn't covered with the usual detritus of pills, tissues and books. Instead there were cigarettes, with a photo on the pack of tarry black lungs. *People never thought it would happen to them.*

The brushed-steel cylinder of N_2O had pride of place.

Good.

And held down by a small gold carriage clock was a form. The standard waiver.

I, Charles Cann . . .

Felix knew what the rest of it said by heart.

. . . being of sound mind but terminally unsound body, do hereby declare my intention to take my own life to avoid a painful and undignified death, as is my right under British Law. I further declare that, in order to relieve the burden on my loved ones, I have enlisted the services of the Exiteers, who will witness my death, but who solemnly undertake not to encourage or assist my demise in any way – or to provide the instrument of death – as to do so is unlawful. I have given attending Exiteers permission to remove all evidence of my suicide in order to spare my family the trauma of the choice I am making by signing this document. In the unlikely event of an official investigation into my death, I hereby absolve the Exiteers of any culpability.

The signature was spidery. Frail.

'Charles?' said Felix gently. 'Mr Cann?'

Then he said it more loudly, and the man opened his eyes groggily and raised a weak hand.

'Mr Cann, we're the Exiteers. I'm John and this is Amanda.'

Amanda was at the foot of the bed now, and raised a hand in a small salute at the man, who half returned it. He frowned and opened his mouth and then closed it again, apparently too exhausted by the effort.

'Don't speak if it's difficult,' said Felix. 'We've just come to sit with you.'

There was a small armchair next to the dresser, and an uncomfortable-looking stool propping open the door. Felix gestured Amanda to the chair and picked up the waiver and put it in his briefcase. There was an envelope too, with WILL written in the same watery handwriting. He didn't open it, just put it in his case with the waiver, and snapped it shut.

'There,' he said. 'Now, there's no rush, all right? You take your time.'

He put his briefcase at the end of the bed, and perched on the stool. It was as uncomfortable as it looked, but Felix had a hunch that this wasn't going to take long. Charles Cann looked as if he would soon be gone, with them or without them. His bluish eyelids drooped, then he coughed and opened his eyes and scanned the room as if looking for something important.

He cupped his hand over his nose and mouth and whispered, 'Plea—'

He wanted the mask.

Felix looked at the dresser and frowned. He couldn't see the mask. It should have been around the man's neck or in his hand before they even got there. Geoffrey always explained that very carefully to the clients, but Felix couldn't see the mask at all.

He looked at the N_2O cylinder and followed the clear plastic tubing from the valve as it ran across the walnut top of the dresser . . .

Then his stomach flipped nervously.

Mr Cann had dropped the mask.

When Felix leaned to one side he could see it dangling between the bed and the dresser, twisting gently a few inches above the carpet.

Out of reach.

'Plea—' Mr Cann grunted. Then again – the word becoming high and thin as it squeezed from his airless throat. '*Plea—!*'

Amanda looked at Felix, but he shook his head. There was nothing they could do. Nothing legal, anyway. She flushed and bit her lip. Felix's fingers knotted together in his lap. Uncomfortably so.

Mr Cann's pale, veined hand flapped at his side on the bedspread, seeking the mask that should be there. His breathing was a squeal now. His head twisted and his chest started to pump up and down out of all proportion to the amount of air getting through to his lungs. It was horrible to watch and Felix wished fervently that Amanda's first job was not so hard.

She might not come back.

It's not always like this, he wanted to tell her. But it would have to wait. First they had to get through this. All three of them.

Mr Cann looked at Amanda, and then at Felix, as if wondering why they weren't helping him. Felix gritted his teeth. He was here to help the man; the man needed his help; but he couldn't help him. Not with *this*. *This*, he had to do himself.

And Mr Cann tried. Hard. He grunted. He strained. He gasped. He reached and reached and flopped back on his pillow as if exhausted. Then he made one last effort and his desperate fingers hooked the tubing . . .

It pulled the gas cylinder on to its side with a *clunk*. Then it rolled off the shiny wooden surface.

With the reflexes of the young, Amanda caught it before it hit the floor, and lifted it up, mask swinging beneath it—

'*No!*' Felix stumbled off the stool and she flinched.

'*What?*'

But it was too late and Felix bit back his warning. Mr Cann had caught the mask as it dangled over him, and clamped it hard to his face. Now he sucked greedily at the gas as if it were saving his life, instead of ending it.

The agonized breathing stopped almost immediately. His eyes closed . . .

Another deep breath.

'*What?*' said Amanda again, panicking. Felix put his finger to his lips to silence her. Hearing was the last sense to fade, and he didn't want Charles Cann dying to the sounds of a squabble.

'Nothing's wrong,' he murmured calmly. 'Everything's just right. Everything's wonderful.'

Mr Cann's hand twitched twice on the mask, then loosened a little and – after a moment – lolled on to his chest, his fingers curled like those of a sleeping baby. Felix and Amanda stood either side of the bed, silently united in the anticipation of another breath.

It never came.

The dog scratching itself downstairs was suddenly the loudest noise in the house.

Slowly, Felix bent down and touched the side of Charles Cann's neck. The skin was warm, but the artery was motionless under his fingers.

'Is he dead?' whispered Amanda. And when Felix nodded that he was, she burst into tears.

Felix was surprised, but said nothing. There was nothing to say. She would cry and then she would stop. And then they would catch the bus down the hill to Bideford and drink more tea or hot choco-late and talk about how life goes on, and she would feel better, even though it never sounded entirely convincing to him.

He opened his briefcase and placed the bottle and the mask next to his unmolested sandwich, then clicked it shut once more – relieved that in the end it had all happened so fast, for Mr Cann's sake. He straightened up and cleared his throat. *It's time to go.* That's what the clearing of the throat meant. But Amanda wasn't hearing. Or stopping. She was *proper bawling*, as Margaret used to say when Jamie was little. He handed her his handkerchief.

'Was that wrong?' she sobbed. 'I just caught it and he grabbed it and now he's dead and I feel terrible!'

'We're not here to assist physically in any way,' said Felix patiently. 'We're only here to lend moral support.'

'I know! But he couldn't *reach* it! And he *wanted* it! Because he couldn't *breathe* . . .'

'Not breathing is really the goal,' he said, hoping to lighten the mood a little, but it just set off a new round of sobbing.

Amanda reached for the dead man's hand, but Felix stopped her arm gently.

'Best not to, now that he's gone,' he said, and she nodded and then, to his surprise, turned and hugged *him* instead – her head buried in his chest and her embrace pressing his arms to his sides.

'I'm so sorry,' she wept. 'I just . . . I mean . . . I didn't know it was going to be so . . . *sad*.'

'There, there,' he said awkwardly, feeling like a Victorian father trapped by an unwanted public display of affection. He might have patted her on the back, but his arms were pinioned.

Probably for the best.

Amanda took her time finishing her cry, then blew her nose and sighed and looked up at him. 'I'm sorry,' she said.

'That's perfectly all right,' said Felix, although he really didn't think it was, and hoped she would never do it again. He'd speak to Geoffrey. Maybe he could work with another man in future. Or just somebody older. He looked at his watch. They really should be going.

'I've never seen someone actually die before. Not even my nan.'

'Of course. The first time is always difficult.'

His first time hadn't been, though. An old woman who was so weak that the difference between life and death had been hard to distinguish. When his fellow Exiteer had confirmed that she was dead, Felix had felt oddly uplifted by the experience. It had been *so different* from watching his wife and his son die, and his first thought had been that he wanted to see it again – just to know how kind death could be. As if he might blur his old memories with new ones.

Amanda wiped her eyes and blew her nose again. Felix noticed her mascara had run and looked down at his chest. There was a dark smudge on his beige jacket.

'What happens now?' she said.

'Now we leave,' he said.

'Just go?'

'Yes. We'll go and have a nice cup of tea and a chat.'

'What about his . . . his family?'

'When the family get home they will find Mr Cann has passed away and call a doctor. The nitrous oxide does not show up in post-mortem toxicology reports, so the coroner will record it as a death from natural causes. His family will not be implicated in messy legalities. The insurance company will pay up, as they absolutely should. And it will be as if we were never here.'

Amanda nodded, looking down at the man. 'He does look better,' she sniffed.

It was true. The mottle had left the man's skin, and the lines of desperation on his face had relaxed, making him look closer to fifty than eighty.

'Do we just . . . *leave* him?'

Felix nodded. He understood that almost overwhelming urge to *arrange* things – to close eyes, to wipe away dribble, to tuck in hands or feet – to make things look *nice*.

'We don't tidy up,' he explained. 'We've done our bit. Now somebody else will come and do theirs.'

Amanda nodded again.

'You did very well,' Felix said kindly, although really she hadn't. But they could talk about that at the debrief.

'Thank you,' she said. And then added, 'So did you.'

She was sweet. But she had to understand how even touching the gas cylinder could have compromised them – that it tipped witnessing and supporting death into assisting, which was strictly illegal. It was a technicality, of course, but it was important that the error should not be repeated.

Downstairs the little dog yapped and broke a sombre silence.

'Right then,' said Felix, in a tone that any British person would know meant, *Let's go* – and Amanda *was* British, so she left the bedroom and he opened his right arm to usher her ahead of him as they started down the stairs.

There was a sound.

They both stopped and Amanda looked up at him. 'What was that?'

Felix's head was still above the level of the landing. He looked around at the open door behind him. Mr Cann was as they'd left him.

Motionless.

'I don't know,' he said. 'I'll check.'

Felix had witnessed twenty-seven deaths and the gas had never not worked. It was invariably lethal in the concentration used as long as there was minimal leakage – and Charles Cann had clamped the mask hard to his face and taken at least two deep, gasping breaths of it.

Nonetheless, he returned to the room and once again sought a pulse at the man's throat.

He was still dead.

BANG!

Amanda and Felix both flinched and turned to look at the door at the opposite end of the landing.

'Somebody's in there,' whispered Amanda.

Felix put down his briefcase and crossed the landing in three strides. He stood for a long moment, then took a deep breath and pushed open the door.

In the front bedroom an old man was leaning out of a bed by the window, trying to reach a walking stick that had apparently fallen on to the wooden floor. He propped himself on an elbow, glared at Felix and grumbled:

'You took your time!'

Felix froze.

Took in the gaunt, grey face, the frail body, the bedside table filled with pills . . .

Then he stepped backwards out of the room and pulled the door smartly shut behind him.

Amanda was at his shoulder now. 'What is it?' she said, but Felix couldn't speak because all the words he'd ever known seemed to be whirling around inside his skull like bingo balls.

The ones he needed finally dropped slowly from his numb lips.

'We killed the wrong man.'

The Wrong Man

'*What?*'

Felix cleared his throat. 'We killed the wrong man.'

'*What?*' she said again, and Felix *was* going to repeat his line, but then realized they could be here all day saying the same two things to each other and still not quite grasp what had happened, or how. Only one thing was clear: accidentally assisting a man who had planned to die by providing him with an instrument of death was a technicality.

Doing the same thing to a man who had *not* planned to die was something else entirely.

'The wrong *man*?' Amanda said, not moving. 'What do you—?'

'Ssh!' He glanced at the bedroom door.

'But how do you *know*?' she whispered.

And he hissed back, 'Because the man in *this* room is expecting us.'

Amanda gasped at the closed door, and then turned to stare down the landing at the inanimate mound that had been a living human being just minutes before.

'But how—?'

'I don't know.'

Amanda stared at the front bedroom door again, as if she could see through it, and through the wall beyond that, and into the road outside.

'*Shit!*' she said, and slow horror dawned on her face.

And then he heard it too.

Sirens.

For one long, thrumming moment Felix might have panicked.

Then he said, 'You have to go.'

'Go?'

'Yes. You have to *go*,' he said again, more urgently this time. 'Just go home and forget this ever happened.'

'What?' she stammered. 'But what will *you* do?'

'Don't worry about me,' he said. 'I'll take care of everything.'

Felix had no idea what *everything* might entail. All he knew for sure was that Amanda was twenty-three with her whole life ahead of her, while he was seventy-five, with most of his behind him. Mathematically, it made no sense for her to be involved.

'Hurry now,' he said, but she was looking at him, open-mouthed, wide-eyed. Dazed. Felix put a hand on her back and propelled her firmly along the landing and down the first few stairs.

She grabbed the banister and turned to look up at him. 'But what about you?'

'I'll be fine,' he said. 'You just go.'

'OK.' Her eyes swam with tears. 'Thank you,' she said, and then she hurried on down the stairs and out of the front door.

The dog had come into the hallway to watch her leave – and now looked up at Felix, waiting for his next move.

But Felix didn't have a next move.

He looked again at the body of the man he'd believed to be Charles Cann. Then he walked slowly downstairs and sat on the sofa.

This was the worst thing that had ever happened to him.

As soon as he had the thought, Felix rejected it, but, an instant after that, he knew it was true.

Jamie's death had been tragic. Heart-crushing. *Unbearable.*

But it had not been his fault.

This *was*.

Amanda had handed the man the mask, but it was *his* fault. He'd assumed she would react the way Chris would have reacted. But it was her first time and the man was dying badly, and she'd panicked. In hindsight, it all seemed very obvious that something had been likely to go wrong. He should have planned for disaster, taken charge, sat on that side of the bed, warned her more forcefully – done *something* – before the point of no return . . .

Numbness crept slowly over Felix Pink. A merciful detachment. His old life was over, and now he was just going to sit here and wait for someone to come along and show him the way his new life was going to be.

He took off his watch. It was nothing special – just a quartz Sekonda he'd been given when he'd retired, and probably worth a pound for every year he'd given to the company – but there was no reason to have it scratched by handcuffs. He zipped it safely into the inside pocket of the beige jacket. There were two of those – one on each side – and they were very useful. He kept his reading glasses in the other one.

The sirens were closer now. Soon they would be here. Felix wondered what being arrested was going to be like. What they would say. What *he* would say. Would they have guns? Should he put his hands up? Like a cowboy? He hoped they wouldn't make him lie on the floor to cuff him. He wasn't sure he'd be able to get up again, because of his hip. He had been on the list for a replacement for over a year now and it wasn't getting any better . . . Although he supposed that the policemen would just help him up if he got into difficulties, so maybe he shouldn't worry about that aspect of his imminent arrest.

The sirens wailed.

Felix straightened his tie with a trembling hand, and cleared his throat in preparation. He brushed at the mascara smudge on his beige jacket, but it didn't come off. He tutted and wondered if it ever would. It would be ironic if he had to throw the jacket away now, all of a sudden, and before he had identified a worthy replacement. Although where he was going he probably wouldn't need the beige jacket for quite some time. Or *any* jacket . . .

The little black-and-tan dog jumped up beside him on the sofa, then sat and scratched its ear with a noise like a flag in a high wind. Felix wondered if it had fleas. He stood up quickly and with a wince, and brushed his trousers down briskly. He didn't want to give Mabel fleas—

Then he froze.

Mabel!

Who would let Mabel out if he didn't go home? Worse, who would feed her? Nobody knew he wasn't there. Nobody knew he wouldn't *be* there. And even if they did know, nobody had a key. By the time word filtered back to his neighbours that he had been arrested, Mabel could be dead!

The sirens groaned and faded. Through the window he saw the blue flashing lights swing into the road.

Coming for *him*.

But he couldn't be arrested. Not *yet*. Not until he had made sure Mabel would be all right.

With a twinge in his hip that made him suck air through his teeth, Felix hurried through the house and out of the back door. The little black-and-tan dog rushed out with him, barking and excited to be out.

'No!' Felix said. 'Inside!'

He limped back to the door and waved an urgent hand at the dog, which was sniffing around some rusty paint tins.

'Here, boy! Here, boy!'

The dog cocked its leg on an old wooden ladder.

Felix heard the car doors slam. He picked up the dog, and deposited it unceremoniously inside the house, then closed the back door and lurched down the garden as fast as he could go.

The garden was so dense with brambles that it was only after he'd rounded an old greengage tree at the end of it that he realized it was completely enclosed by a solid wood-panel fence, silver with age, as tall as he was – and without a gate.

Felix put his hands on the top of the planking, clambered awkwardly on to an old plastic garden chair, and peered over the fence to the safety of the fields beyond. Even on the chair, the fence was armpit-high. He'd never be able to climb it. Not even for Mabel.

His bid for escape was over.

Felix looked back up the garden. The house was almost hidden from his view by brambles and the tree, which leaned drunkenly between him and the back door. But through the branches he could see the hi-vis jacket of a policeman, checking the back of the house. He hadn't seen him. Yet. Felix glanced skywards and thanked Margaret for dressing him in beige. But it would only buy him seconds. Once the policeman turned and came down the garden, there was only so much a beige jacket could do to hide a full-grown man against a garden fence, and then he would be captured.

Felix turned and shook the top of the fence as if he could pull or push the whole thing over.

And that's exactly what he did.

With a rotten crack, an entire six-foot panel of fence flopped flimsily towards him like a big wooden blanket.

For one surprised moment, Felix was the only thing holding it up. Then he lowered the panel quietly to the ground, and hobbled over it to freedom.

It wasn't until he got off the bus in Barnstaple that Felix Pink realized that, in all the confusion, he had left his briefcase on the landing.

The Worst Job Ever

Calvin Bridge stared at the body in the bed and wondered for the umpteenth time why he'd become a policeman.

He'd always loved the *idea* of being a police officer. Something about being good, when everybody around him was bad. But being a cop had turned out to be about more than just being good. There was also a lot of paperwork involved. And a lot of getting up early and going to bed late. And *thinking*! There was an awful lot of thinking. Calvin wasn't stupid, but constantly thinking about things – like crime, for instance – required a lot more effort than he'd imagined it would. Not that he was lazy. Far from it! He jogged five miles three times a week, and once had even been persuaded by his girlfriend, Shirley, to go into plainclothes and become a detective. Calvin had gone along with it because going along with things was in his nature, and because his uniform did take a lot of fiddly ironing. But after a single horrible murder case, he had been relieved to give up detective work.

And Shirley.

He didn't regret either decision. He could do what he liked at home, and at work he was happy bumping along the bottom of burglary and public-disorder offences and shoplifting – most of which were committed by a hard core of about a dozen addicts and alcoholics, or by Tovey Chanter, who was neither, but who outstripped both in his sheer enthusiasm for wrongdoing. Anyway, the point being that there was rarely a crime committed in Bideford for which Calvin Bridge didn't have a good idea of where to start.

And now . . . *this*.

They'd been called to a possible break-in – his favourite kind of case, because only occasionally did a possible break-in turn into an actual break-in, but it still gave him a chance to switch on the old blues and twos and put his foot down. And even when it did turn out to be an actual break-in there was rarely anyone still in the house to have to deal with by the time they arrived. Not unless the perp was on drugs and too dazed to run.

Anyway, this *was* an actual break-in. And then had quickly turned into something much more sinister . . .

His colleague, Jackie Braddick, had banged hard on the front door, while he'd snuck round the back in case anybody was dangling out of a kitchen window.

Nobody was.

Calvin had tried the back door and it had opened, and a little black-and-tan dog had squeezed between his shins and trotted out into the overgrown garden.

Calvin had called, *Hello?* but nobody had answered. However, the back door being unlocked seemed suspicious, so he'd drawn his baton and walked quietly through the house. Downstairs first – the kitchen with dirty dishes in the sink, and the dining room, where a hole in a window breathed on the curtains.

Calvin had noted there was no glass on the floor, which meant it wasn't a recent break, so had moved on. He'd peered into the living room, with the coffee table piled high with crap that didn't belong there, and then he'd opened the front door for Jackie and followed her upstairs . . .

And now here he was, standing guard over a corpse while Jackie was in the front bedroom, comforting a confused old man who kept saying that *he* was the one who ought to be dead. Said he'd woken and seen a tall, white-haired figure at his door, like the angel of death, who'd disappeared without a sound – and taken the wrong soul with him.

It's all my fault, he kept saying. *It's all my fault.*

Calvin sighed. *Worst job ever . . .*

It was a private game he and Jackie played to mitigate the daily assault on their persons and senses. A stoic attempt to turn a no-win situation into a dubious kind of victory for one of them, at least. Like when Jackie had had a tooth knocked through her lip by a runaway donkey. And a drunk in a minidress had once shat on Calvin's shoe. Both previous winners. The loser bought the first drink the next time they went to the pub. Except that today they were both playing the same game, so unless one of them had to deal with bodily fluids or violence between now and the end of their shift, today would be a tie.

Still, plainclothes were on their way and, once they got here, Calvin could stop thinking about the dead man in the bed. He wasn't crazy about corpses, so he looked forward to getting back in the car and driving to Bideford police station and having a cuppa with the lads and maybe a bit of Sergeant Coral's wife's terrible fruit cake. But until then he had to think about things *here*. The tip-off and the unlocked back door and the yappy little dog and the briefcase on the landing, and the poor old boy in the front room and the corpse in this one, presided over by a big black oxygen cylinder on a trolley that stood solemn guard beside the bed. It was hard to see how they all fitted together, but even his limited experience told him that it was inevitable that somehow they would. That at some point all the dots would join up to form a recognizable picture of what had happened here and why.

He heard the front door open, and peered over the banister to call, 'Up here!'

Calvin hoped it wouldn't be DCI Kirsty King. They'd worked together during his short spell in plainclothes, but once had been enough for Calvin – the case had gained her a commendation and him a nervous tic. Calvin had appreciated DCI King's down-to-earth thinking and inclusive approach. Even though he'd been young and inexperienced, she had treated him like a man who'd had something to contribute. And to his surprise Calvin *had* contributed! He'd exceeded both their expectations, and she'd told him she felt he had a real future in plainclothes. And then, when it was all over, he'd proved her wrong by immediately requesting a return to uniform. She'd never said so, but Calvin knew he'd disappointed her.

But luckily the detective wasn't King. It was an officer he didn't know – a young bloke with neat hair and a corduroy jacket with leather elbow patches. He looked like a scientist.

'Hello,' he said. 'What's going on?'

As he walked up the stairs, Calvin brought him up to speed. 'PC Bridge, sir. Responded to a call about two possible intruders. Male and female. No sign of forced entry. The tip said two suspects went in the front door. Back door was unlocked. And we've got a body in this room and a male resident in the front bedroom.'

'What?' said the detective, glancing over his shoulder towards the front room.

'Old man, sir. Very confused. Says he should be dead. I think he's a bit . . . you know . . .' Calvin's finger circled his temple to officially diagnose the old man as nuts.

Still the detective stared at him blankly.

'A body?' he said. '*Whose* body?' The young man's eyes darted past Calvin to the bed and he said, 'Dad?'

Oh shit.

Calvin realized his mistake with a mixture of horror and defensive irritation. Why hadn't plainclothes got here sooner? What was taking them so long? Now he'd screwed up big time and it was all their fault!

Right on cue, he heard the front door open and DCI Kirsty King call, *Hello.*

'I'm sorry, sir,' Calvin told the panicky boffin. 'Would you mind coming downstairs with me?'

'But I have to . . . Can I just?'

He tried to peer around Calvin, who spread his arms. 'Just for a minute, please, sir.'

The man hesitated, then turned, and Calvin followed him.

Not a Crime

Reggie Cann wasn't a detective or a scientist. He turned out to be something in computers. Calvin guessed that made the leather elbow patches ironic. Now he sat on the sofa, with a cup of tea Calvin had made, shaking a little. 'I can't get my head round it,' he kept saying. 'I only came home for lunch.'

Kirsty King nodded, her elbows on her knees as she leaned forward sympathetically in the easy chair. DC Pete Shapland perched a little more awkwardly in a less-easy chair and took notes. Calvin watched from the hallway while overhead were the creaking floor and muffled voice of his partner, Jackie Braddick, keeping the old man calm. He'd kept trying to get out of bed, but although she was young, Jackie had the cheerful smile and iron will of an NHS nurse, and so far the old chap had been compliant with her, and her alone.

'Where do you work, Reggie?'

'CompuWiz. In Bideford.'

'I know it,' said King. 'Up in Old Town, right?'

He nodded.

'What time did you leave this morning?'

Reggie shrugged. 'About eight fifteen. It's not far.'

DCI King started. 'OK, we had a call mid-morning saying there were intruders in your house.'

'Intruders?'

'A man and a woman.'

He frowned. 'I don't know who that could be.'

'No? Does anyone else have a key to the house?'

'No. Just me and Albert.'

'Your father?'

'Yes,' nodded Reggie. 'But he doesn't go out much. And Skipper hasn't been outdoors for months.'

'That's your granddad? Charles?'

'Yeah, Charles. Skipper, we call him.'

'He tells us he has cancer?'

'Yeah. Lung. Late stages, the doctor says.'

'I'm sorry,' said Kirsty King.

'Yeah,' nodded Reggie, but he wasn't thinking of that, Calvin could tell. 'Who called you?'

'A woman. She wouldn't give her name.'

King took her phone from her coat pocket and fiddled about with it for a moment, then held it up for Reggie to hear the recording.

It was muffled, but obviously a woman, and with a strong local accent.

There's people in the house opposite. The bay who lives there went to work and these people have gone in and—

Do you know the people, ma'am?

No, they're strangers. An old man and a girl. And they looks a bit dodgy.

How did they get in?

In the front door, but they didn't knock or ring the bell and I don't know them—

What's your name, ma'am?

I'm not saying. I don't want some nutter after me, you know? But I think you should send someone over here because I never seen 'em round here before and I don't think they should be in that house . . .

She turned off the recorder. 'Do you recognize the caller?'

Reggie Cann shook his head. 'No, but it is quite crackly.'

'It is,' said King. 'But from the information given I'm assuming it's one of your neighbours . . . ?'

'Could be Jean across the way, I suppose. She's super-nosey.'

'What number is that?'

Reggie looked blank for a moment, then shook his head. 'I don't know. The house with the gnomes.'

He sat back in his chair and rubbed his face.

'Sorry to put you through this right now, Reggie,' said King kindly, 'but obviously we need to gather as much information as possible as quickly as we can in this situation.'

He nodded. 'Yes, of course. I get it.'

'Thank you,' King said, and went on, 'From the call, it sounds like whoever came in had a key, doesn't it?'

'There's a broken window, ma'am,' said Pete Shapland helpfully, and Calvin winced for him.

'That wasn't done today,' King said, without looking. 'No glass on the floor.'

Pete reddened.

'Who else has a key to the house, Reggie?'

'Nobody.'

'Not a neighbour? A relative?'

He shook his head.

King went on. 'Who cares for your grandfather while you're at work?'

'Well, Dad was, mostly. He doesn't work because he's got emphysema.' He stopped and grimaced. '*Had* emphysema. But most days he gets up and comes downstairs to watch TV or whatever . . . Make soup or something.'

'So normally he'd be out of bed?'

'Yeah. Most days he gets up.'

'But not today?'

'Suppose not.'

'And you do what you can before and after work?'

'That's *all* I seem to do,' said Reggie. 'Work at work and then work at home. I mean, a Macmillan nurse comes in a couple of times a month, but I do pretty much everything! Dad says he helps, but it's not help. Like, he'll make a meal but he won't clean up. Leaves everything out on the side or in the sink and thinks he's done me a favour. Or Skip'll try to get up and come downstairs and I'm like, *Just stay in bed for fuck's sake – you're dying of cancer!*'

He stopped and there was an awkward silence. He sighed deeply. 'Sorry. It's just, I come home for lunch and my house is full of police and my father's dead . . .'

'Of course,' said King. And then, after a moment, 'So nobody else comes in to help? Social services?'

'No,' said Reggie. 'The cleaner will make them a sandwich or something.'

'The cleaner?' Kirsty King somehow resisted looking around at the chaotic room. 'Does she have a key?'

'I leave one for her.'

'Where?'

'Under the mat.'

King didn't roll her eyes but even from his post in the doorway Calvin Bridge could tell she wanted to. But she could roll her eyes all she liked. It wouldn't change the fact that this was Devon and people left their homes and cars unlocked, and keys under doormats.

'What's her name?'

'Hayley.'

King glanced at Shapland, who wrote it down. 'Do you know her last name?'

Reggie frowned. 'I don't know. I just got her from a card in the Co-op.'

'That's all right.'

But Reggie was distracted. 'I never even asked . . .' he muttered. Calvin knew it was the shock, surfacing inappropriately.

'Doesn't matter,' said King. 'When does she come?'

Reggie took a moment of staring at nothing to remember. 'Mondays and Fridays.'

'So yesterday?'

Today was Tuesday. He nodded.

'Do you have her number?'

'Yeah, sure,' he said, and took out his phone and scrolled through while they all waited. Finally he showed it to King, who jotted it down, then tapped the briefcase that lay on the coffee table.

'Is this yours?'

'No. Why?'

'It was on the landing,' said King, and opened it. She was wearing shiny latex gloves and took out the items one by one. 'So . . . we've got a thermos flask, and a . . . sandwich, and we've got *this . . .*'

She took out a slim steel cylinder with a rubber mask attached. 'You know what's in this?'

'Uh . . . Oxygen?'

'It's not a guessing game.'

'Sorry,' he said. 'Then no.'

'It's almost certainly nitrous oxide,' she said.

'What's that?'

'N_2O. Laughing gas.'

'Oh. OK. Don't dentists use that?'

'Yes. In low concentrations, nitrogen is used as an anaesthetic. But kids fill balloons to huff it, and in high concentrations it's lethal. Fast, painless and untraceable. Unless you leave it at the scene, of course.'

'I don't understand.'

'Your grandfather – Skipper – told us *he* was supposed to die today.'

'I don't understand,' said Reggie.

'It seems he had planned to commit suicide.'

'*Suicide!*' Reggie looked about wildly at Shapland and then at Calvin, as if King must be joking and one of them might wink. Nobody did.

'Seems he'd been in contact with a group who support the right to die. He says they call themselves the Exiteers.' She watched Reggie's face carefully.

'Never heard of them,' he said. 'I mean . . . he's been sick for so long and I know it's getting on top of him. You can't blame him, can you? I mean . . . but bloody hell!'

'So you don't know anything about this?'

'No! He never said a thing!'

'What about these?' She unfolded two documents on the coffee table in front of him.

'What are they?'

'His will and what looks like a waiver.'

'Skipper's will?'

'Yes.'

'Where was it?'

'Also in the briefcase.'

She tapped the document. 'Is that your granddad's signature?'

'It looks like it, yes. But I've never seen Skipper's will. Didn't know he'd made one.'

'Well, he's very old,' said King, 'and he does have terminal cancer.'

'I just never thought about it, I suppose.'

King moved her finger to the waiver. 'Have you seen this before?'

'No.'

'It appears to be a waiver absolving the Exiteers from culpability in his death.'

Reggie read it, then nodded.

'And that's Skipper's signature too?'

'It looks like it. As far as I can tell, yes.'

'So as you can see, the Exiteers say they do not provide the instrument of death. In this case, the nitrous oxide. Do you know where Skipper got it from?'

'No. Have you asked him?'

'We will be speaking to him in a minute,' she nodded. 'Was there anything unusual about this morning, Reggie? Anything different?'

'Not that I can think of. I had breakfast and fed the dog and said goodbye to Skip and went to work.'

'You didn't say goodbye to your father?'

'He was still asleep.'

'Are you sure?'

Reggie nodded. 'He breathes *loud*.'

'I see there's an oxygen tank in his room. How long has he been using that?'

'About a year,' said Reggie. 'Has it upstairs and downstairs.' He gestured across the room to where a large black tank stood on a trolley beside the sofa.

'Reggie, can you think of any reason someone would want to hurt Albert?'

'No.' For the first time, Reggie Cann looked truly upset. He stopped talking and King handed him a tissue so he could wipe his eyes and loudly blow his nose.

'I'm sorry,' she said. 'We have to ask the question.' She waited for him to compose himself and when he appeared to have done so, she went on. 'But if you don't feel anyone would have wanted to hurt your father then it could be that these Exiteers simply made a mistake. Somehow gave the gas to the wrong person and then panicked and left this case behind. What do you think? Is that possible?'

'I suppose so,' he shrugged. 'I don't know *how*, though. I mean, it's a pretty bloody big mistake to make!'

'It is.' King nodded and closed her notebook. 'Thank you, Reggie. I'll be back to speak to your grandfather in a minute.'

She got to her feet and Reggie looked up at her anxiously. 'Is Skipper in trouble? I mean, it's not a crime to kill yourself, is it?'

'No, it's not,' said Kirsty King. She hesitated, then said, 'But, of course, *he* didn't die . . .'

Calvin and Pete followed DCI King outside.

'What do you think?' said King quietly.

'I think his cleaner's ripping him off,' Pete snorted. 'Place looks like it's been burgled!'

King raised her eyebrows and turned to Calvin, who hesitated. He felt bad that he'd broken the news of Albert Cann's death to his son the way he had, and decided to cut him some slack. 'I think he's very shaken up.'

'Understandably,' King nodded, 'but we'll check his story anyway. I don't think the old man arranged this by himself.'

She looked at her watch. 'First things first – let's try to find the caller. The techs should be able to triangulate it but it would be nice if we could get a head start from an eyewitness. You and Pete knock up the neighbours. There's only a few houses so it shouldn't be hard to narrow it down. Start with Jean over the road.'

There were only six houses in Black Lane – three either side. The house directly opposite boasted a picket line of gnomes standing shoulder-to-shoulder along the front edge of the lawn. There had been no attempt to arrange them in suitable locations. Those that fished, fished for ants, those that dug, dug pavement. One focused a telescope into the pointy ear of his neighbour.

'I'll take the gnomes,' said Pete, as Calvin had known he would, so he went to the immediate neighbours. The squat woman who opened the door looked vaguely familiar.

'Oh,' she said. 'Hello, Calvin!'

It took Calvin a moment before the penny dropped. 'Hello, Mrs Moon!'

Just a few hundred yards from this very spot, Marion Moon's husband, Donald, had climbed over a gate in a lay-by and stepped on to a murdered woman's face.

'How are you and Mr Moon?'

'Can't complain, Calvin, and yourself?'

'Can't complain.'

'We heard you broke up with Shirley.'

Calvin blinked in surprise. That was the thing he hated about being a copper in a small town. People he hardly knew knowing things about him that he'd rather they didn't.

'Got a couple of quick questions, if you don't mind, Mrs Moon?'

Her face clouded over and she leaned in and whispered, 'Police business?'

He nodded.

'Because Donald's not up to it,' she went on. 'Standing on that woman, you see? It knocked him for six. And then just as he was getting back, one of the sheep broke his leg and that knocked him for *another* six and he had to retire and sell that little bit of land we'd kept because it was all too much, and move here, and Donald doesn't like being in the town, you see, and his nerves are terrible, and he's just getting over a chest infection, so I don't think he's up to much.'

'Of course,' said Calvin, reeling from the litany of disasters that had befallen Donald Moon since he'd stood on Frannie Hatton's face. It was too tangled to even start to unravel, so he just pressed on, lowering his own voice in consideration of Donald Moon's nerves. 'We had a call from a lady earlier today about two people who were seen going into the Canns' house. Was it you who called?'

'Not me,' said Mrs Moon. 'I didn't see anybody.'

Calvin considered for a moment, then asked, 'Might I ask Mr Moon if he noticed anyone?'

Marion pursed her lips.

'It's really very important. I wouldn't ask otherwise.'

She sighed, and Calvin followed her through a dark hallway and into the back room, where Donald Moon sat in a chair by the window with a pair of binoculars in his lap. He'd lost weight and looked ten years older than he had three years ago.

'You remember Calvin, Donald!'

'Calvin?' Donald Moon looked up vaguely. 'No.'

'From the police. Remember?'

'Oh, the police,' he said, and didn't smile.

Calvin put on his best cheerful voice. 'Hello, Mr Moon, nice to see you again.'

'Mm,' said Donald.

'Sounds like you've had a bit of a tough time of it since we last met.'

'Could say that.'

'Sorry to hear it, sir. But I wondered if you might be able to help me. There were a couple of strangers around the street this morning,' Calvin said carefully. 'Did you see or hear anything odd?'

'No.'

'Not through the old bins?' Calvin gestured at the binoculars.

'They're for the birds,' he said, and his wife smiled anxiously at Calvin.

'We can't have sheep now, you see? So Donald looks after the birds.'

'Got to look after *some*thing,' the old man said grumpily and turned and lifted his binoculars to his eyes to look down the long garden.

'Well, thank you anyway, Mr and Mrs Moon. It's good to see you again.'

Marion saw Calvin out. 'You must excuse him,' she said at the step. 'He hasn't been the same since all that happened.'

'I'm not surprised,' said Calvin. Donald Moon had been a simple farmer who'd dutifully reported a gruesome find – whereupon he and his wife had become collateral damage in the quest for a serial killer. He'd been questioned about Frannie Hatton until he'd broken down, and then he and Mrs Moon had wept again as the police had torn apart their old farmhouse on the cliffs. They'd had to, but it had all been for nothing. Donald Moon had had nothing to do with the crime. No wonder he looked guarded now. He would probably never trust the police again, and Calvin couldn't blame him.

'Is everything all right next door?'

Calvin knew he should fob Mrs Moon off with police-speak, but felt he owed her some honesty, so he told her that Albert had died.

'Oh dear!' she gasped. 'Poor man. Was it his lungs?'

'We're not sure what happened,' hedged Calvin. 'How well do you know the Canns, Mrs Moon?'

'Not well,' she said. 'We only moved in eighteen months ago. We knew they were sick, of course. Albert and Skipper. Reggie told us. But he's a lovely boy. Looks after them a treat *and* works full-time. And Albert wasn't an easy man, you know?'

'What do you mean?'

'Just not easy. He and Donald had words soon after we moved in. Over who was supposed to repair the fence between us. It's their fence, you see? But it was rotten and their little dog kept coming through and doing his business in our garden. Donald fixed it in the end. With his bad leg and all. But then Albert got sick and we didn't see him much after that.'

Calvin nodded. 'Did you ask Reggie to fix the fence?'

'No, no. We could see he was snowed under. I don't know what they'd do without him. And when we moved in he helped me move furniture about while Donald was in plaster. I gave him some scones to take home and he brought the plate back all washed and dried and everything. Oh dear. Poor Reggie. And now you think these two people might have something to do with it?'

'Yes,' said Calvin, 'but you mustn't worry about it, Mrs Moon.

We don't know yet what happened but it looks like a one-off in very specific circumstances.'

She nodded, regaining her sensible demeanour. 'I don't think I'll tell Donald,' she whispered. 'He hardly gets out any more. Down the garden to feed the birds and that's about it, and he hasn't even done that for a week, so he won't notice anything's amiss next door for a good while.'

'That's probably best,' nodded Calvin. 'Would you have any idea who might have called the police? It was a woman.'

'There's Jean over the road where the gnomes are. She's very nosey.'

'Yes, thank you. My colleague is speaking to Jean.'

'Other than that the only women are me and Mrs Digby next door.'

Calvin thanked her and said goodbye, and moved on to the next house, where Mrs Digby – a very old woman on a walker – took for ever to reach the glass front door. Then, when she made it, she couldn't hear Calvin, even when he shouted.

'I'LL FETCH MY HEARING AID!' she finally yelled, as if it was something that had to be toted about by Sherpas instead of worn in her ear. Calvin almost told her not to bother, and then – after another five minutes of fruitless conversation on the doorstep – wished he had.

Calvin saw Pete knocking on the door of the middle house and called over, 'Any luck?'

Pete shook his head.

Calvin crossed the road. The last house in the row had a *No Parking* sign on the wall, a *Keep off the Grass* sign on the grass and a *No Cold Callers* sign on the door. When he knocked, a flurry of angry barking surprised him and he took a small, wary step backwards. Calvin wasn't scared of dogs but this one sounded big and he'd once been bitten by a Dalmatian. The owner had said it was just playing, but Calvin had seen the intent in its white-walled eye.

The door cracked open on a chain, and the dog stopped barking.

'Yes?'

The man was middle-aged, with a monobrow. Calvin glanced down but couldn't see the dog.

'Good afternoon, sir, I'm PC Bridge from Bideford. Just asking neighbours about an incident in the street. Wondered whether you'd seen or heard anything unusual.'

'What kind of incident?'

Calvin sidestepped. 'Somebody called in a report of two suspicious visitors to the Canns' home earlier today. Was that call made from here, sir?'

'No,' said the man. 'Not me.'

'It was a woman who called. Could that have been your wife?'

'I don't have a wife any more, thank God.'

'OK,' nodded Calvin, relieved for womankind. 'Could I take your name and a phone number, please, sir? In case we have any further questions?'

'Bob Wilson.'

Calvin jotted it down.

'Like the goalkeeper.'

'Yes? Who does he play for?' Calvin wasn't a big soccer fan.

'Bob Wilson!' said Mr Wilson tetchily. 'Arsenal, 1963 to 1974!'

'Before my time, I'm afraid, Mr Wilson,' smiled Calvin, but Mr Wilson was in no mood to forgive Calvin his age. He gave a big *tut* of contempt and said his phone number fast, as if he might also catch Calvin not knowing the numbers between one and ten.

'Well, thanks, Mr Wilson. You just give us a call if you remember anything.'

'I haven't *forgotten* anything!' he said angrily, and banged the door loudly in Calvin's face.

He blinked at the door for a moment, then knocked again.

The dog barked, just as hard as the first time – sounding ready to tear his throat out. But when Mr Wilson answered, it stopped again.

'What?' said Wilson angrily.

Calvin looked down at the man's legs. There was no dog. No real dog anyway.

'Nothing,' said Calvin.

He turned away and took a shortcut across Bob Wilson's grass.

Waiting

It was two hours past Mabel's lunchtime walk, and Felix still hadn't been arrested, so finally he jingled the lead, clipped it to her collar, and took the spare key from the hook. Then he closed the front door behind him with a Post-it note stuck to it at eye level.

Dear Officer. Walking the dog. Not armed. Back soon. F. Pink.

Miss Knott was weeding next door.

'He*llo*, Mabel!' she always said. 'And how's my favourite girl?'

Felix always suspected that Miss Knott would like him to respond to such greetings in Mabel's voice – *Bit RUFF today, Miss Knott, and how are WOOF?* – but he refused to summon up the required foolishness.

'Good afternoon, Miss Knott.'

'And how are *you*, Mr Mabel?' Miss Knott smiled.

I killed a man today.

'Quite well, thank you, Miss Knott.'

'Going anywhere exciting?'

To prison, in all probability.

'Just around the block.'

'Lovely,' she said. 'It's a nice block, isn't it?'

Felix didn't know what to say to that. The block was no nicer than many and no worse than most. Mostly residential with a mix of terraces that opened straight on to the pavement, and semis that had driveways and little front gardens. There was a corner shop with a bucket of overpriced flowers on the pavement and a rack of postcards that showed pictures of pretty places that were quite near, but not quite here.

'I like looking at the other people's gardens,' Miss Knott went on. 'Don't you?'

Felix never noticed other people's gardens but he said 'Mm' to be polite, as she prattled on gaily, 'I like to give them marks out of ten.'

'Oh,' he nodded. And then he said, 'Actually, Miss Knott, I've been meaning to give you my spare key' – as if he'd moved in a month ago, not forty years.

Miss Knott looked surprised. 'Are you going away?'

Felix winced at her unwitting turn of phrase. 'It's only for emergencies,' he said. 'I'm thinking of Mabel being stuck indoors, you see, if something should happen to me.'

'Oh, I'm sure it won't,' Miss Knott said sweetly, and then added, 'But that's a very good idea, isn't it, Mabel?'

It's GRRRRReat!

Felix didn't say that. He just handed Miss Knott the key. He didn't tell her that he expected she would be using it quite soon because he was wanted by the police and would shortly be dragged off in handcuffs. That would only complicate matters.

'Thank you, Miss Knott,' he said, and was relieved that the transaction was over. He didn't like to ask people for favours. People might think they were friends.

'Not at all,' said Miss Knott. 'And please, do call me Winnie.'

See what I mean? thought Felix, but he just said, 'Of course.'

'Perhaps I should give you my key as well.'

Really, this was spiralling out of control. Felix heartily wished he'd given his key to somebody else, but the thing was, there *was* nobody else. Not since their friends – or the friends Margaret had graciously shared with him – had drifted out of his life. Miss Knott, however, had never stopped visiting, and had cried hard at both funerals, and continued to hand-deliver a Christmas card to him every year, so Felix cleared his throat impatiently and said, 'If you like. For emergencies.'

'Of course,' she said. 'I'll pop it round.'

'Just put it through the letterbox,' he said. 'Well, we must be going.'

'Goodbye, Mabel,' said Miss Knott, and giggled – which was an oddly pretty sound to come out of such an old woman – and gave them a little wave of a trowel as they went on their way.

Felix waited until he was out of earshot before looking down at Mabel and murmuring, 'Mad as a hatter.' But Mabel gave him a sidelong look that made him feel rather judged, and he proceeded more humbly with his walk.

He hoped Amanda was all right. He hoped she wasn't wracked with guilt. He'd misjudged the situation, so it was only right and proper that he should take the blame.

Except he *hadn't* taken the blame. Instead he'd fled the scene of the crime to feed his dog.

Felix blushed at the memory. In the heat of the moment it had seemed like a perfectly reasonable thing to do. Now it seemed like a cowardly plummet from the moral high ground he'd claimed so grandly when he'd told Amanda that *she* must leave and *he* would take care of everything.

So now he was . . . *wanted*.

Felix Pink hadn't expected to be a wanted man when he'd left home this morning. He'd expected to go to Abbotsham, oversee a man departing this life with quiet dignity, and be home in time for tea. Instead Amanda had panicked and the wrong man had died, and he'd had to escape from police by breaking down a garden fence. After seventy-five years of law-abiding citizenship, Felix hated to think of all the laws he'd broken, all since breakfast. Goodness only knew what Margaret would say!

Felix hoped that the man they had killed by mistake had been an ass, whose family were not sorry he was dead. And although he recognized the selfishness of this idea, he felt so stupidly cheered by it that he let it run about freely in his head for a bit, enjoying itself. The positivity was infectious. Maybe the whole thing would come to nothing. The police must know where to find him, and yet here he was, free as a lark, walking Mabel and chatting to neighbours as if he hadn't killed a man at all.

Mabel stopped suddenly to widdle on a weed growing against the Martins' garden wall, and Felix sighed as his silly fantasy fragmented and blew away. He had created a new reality and he needed to accept it. He'd given Miss Knott his key now, so Mabel would be all right. And if he couldn't get hold of Geoffrey tonight . . . well then, tomorrow he'd just have to go to the police anyway, and explain his mistake.

Although he wasn't sure how . . .

'Hurry up, Mabel,' he said with a tug, but the little dog hadn't finished snuffling and dug in her heels. Felix didn't press the point. He knew from experience that Mabel's weight increased exponentially the harder he tried to drag her away from any point of interest.

While he stood there waiting for her to set off again, he looked at the Martins' flowerbeds. It was early May but the tulips were still spectacular. A living, breathing firework display of orange, pink and red brilliance, with daphne scenting the air and velvety camellia petals scattered over the small patch of lawn.

Felix gave the Martins' garden an eight.

He called Geoffrey for the third time since he'd arrived home.

No answer.

Felix frowned at the telephone. He really wanted to make sure they were on the same page regarding Amanda's involvement. He was sure Geoffrey would support the promise he'd made to

Amanda that he would take care of everything because, although he was still hazy as to what *everything* might entail, he was reasonably sure it didn't mean ratting on her to the police.

Felix shuddered. *Ratting on her.* He'd been a criminal for less than a day and already he was using the vernacular.

He dialled again. Again there was no answer, so he made preparations to hand himself in.

He went around the house and switched off all the appliances apart from the fridge-freezer, then watered the houseplants, with double rations for the gerbera at the top of the stairs that always drooped pathetically at the first sign of drought. If he wasn't back soon, that would be the first to go. He furled a Post-it note into the neck of a milk bottle – *No milk until further notice, thank you. F. Pink* – and put the bottle on the step.

He tried Geoffrey again, but the phone just rang and rang.

He was becoming concerned. Geoffrey had once told him that he rarely left the house, but apparently he'd left it now. Or had fallen over and was unable to reach the phone. Felix hoped that wasn't the case.

He glanced at his watch. It was just gone three. There was still time before he should head to Bideford, so he sat down at the kitchen table and leaned over the jigsaw, picking up the awkward tuft.

But then he just held it between his thumb and finger and stared blankly at the reindeer.

There was one more thing that had been bothering him all day. It had seemed insignificant in comparison with everything else that had happened, and so he'd tried to push it out of his mind. But now he found that the more he tried to ignore it, the more he couldn't.

There had been a moment – a single split second – when the horror of his blunder had hit him. And in that frozen moment at the bedroom door, Felix Pink's life had flashed before his eyes.

It was a cliché, and he felt a little foolish that it had even happened to him, but now that he had time to think about it, the most
worrying thing about it was that it had been so . . .

So . . .

Felix grimaced.

It had been so . . .

boring.

There. Boring. He'd thought it now and couldn't take it back.

Felix *was* boring. Deep, deep down, he'd always suspected it.
Feared it. He'd just never admitted it – even to himself – before
this very moment. But he'd *always* been boring. He'd been a boring child and a boring teenager. The middle of three, with an
athletic brother and a genius sister. He'd been average at school
and at work. Not bully or bullied. Neither bright nor dull. Neither
lonely nor popular. On the fringes of everything – unable to lead
and slow to follow. Always somewhere in the middle, and making a pretty poor fist even of that. Felix had never missed death
by inches or experienced a religious epiphany or had a eureka
moment. There'd been no crazy hallucinogenic trips, no mountain-
top sunrises, no stolen kisses or dumb near-misses. He'd spent
three years at university without dabbling in sex, drugs *or* rock 'n'
roll, before finding his spiritual home in accounting. Risk-averse
and lumpen, it suited his nature. Independent thought was not
required and flair was frowned upon – and Felix had been more
than capable of not bringing them to the table.

Even Jamie had once called him boring. He was just a teenager
and had quickly laughed and made it sound like a joke, but Felix
had known . . .

And Margaret?

Well, he had the beige zip-up jacket to remind him of what Margaret had thought of him . . .

He remembered the mascara smudge and hoped it would come
out. He had some upholstery cleaner in the utility room. That

would probably do the job. It had worked on the living-room rug where Mabel had had a little accident. Although, of course, the rug was dark red with a faux-oriental pattern, and his jacket was a single, pale colour, so it would require a bit of luck to—

Felix blinked in surprise. *See?* What was *wrong* with him? Worrying about mascara on his jacket at a time like this? He'd *killed* a man, for God's sake!

And he was painfully aware that it had immediately become the most interesting thing about him.

The phone rang and he flinched.

'John?'

'Geoffrey!' said Felix. 'Are you all right?'

'Not bad, thank you,' said Geoffrey. 'Only thing is, I've been arrested for murder.'

Geoffrey's Day Out

Despite being arrested for murder, Calvin thought that Geoffrey Skeet seemed to be enjoying his day out.

He and Jackie had been careful with the wheelchair, and considerate when helping Geoffrey haul himself from it and into the back of the police car. Calvin thought he could have carried him from the house to the car if he'd had to, the man was so thin.

Then – because Geoffrey obviously didn't get out much – Jackie had taken the scenic route from Exeter to Bideford, down pretty lanes and through tunnels of trees, and then across what people still called the new bridge over the Torridge, even though it had been there thirty years. It gave a glorious view up and down the river – of sailing boats and bright little trawlers leaned over in the swirling mudflats, and grand houses with gardens that sloped all the way down to the water, and of the Old Bridge further upstream, tripping across the river in twenty-four uneven arches.

Geoffrey had enjoyed the scenery and the progress, and chatted about the past – his and theirs – and marvelled to find that he'd once taught European history to Jackie Braddick's father, who now owned half of Appledore, despite having had no interest in the Hapsburgs. Then Calvin had let slip that he'd grown up in Tiverton, where Geoffrey had also spent time in his youth, and he'd kept trying to name somebody they both knew – although without much success.

'Different generations, I suppose,' he'd said more than once, while Calvin had nodded in the rear-view mirror.

Then when they'd reached the police station he'd noticed Tony Coral was wearing a South West Steam Society lapel pin, and they'd got talking about locomotives and gauges and signage, and the tragic conversion of branch lines into ghastly tarmac tracks filled with dogs and bicycles instead of rolling stock, and how eBay had become a *bloody minefield* for honest, decent grisers trying to preserve an enamelled bit of railway history.

Calvin and Jackie went to report to DCI King and left Tony asking whether Geoffrey wanted tea or coffee or another slice of his wife's leaden fruit cake.

King picked up the Cann file and headed for the interview room. 'Does he seem worried?'

Jackie shrugged. 'As an orphan at the circus.'

There were four of them in the cramped Victorian cell-cum-interview room, with village-hall plastic chairs pushed aside for the wheelchair, and an old wooden desk that held a digital recorder. In one corner of the room was a television; in the other was a camera pointing at Geoffrey.

DCI King glanced at Calvin and Pete, then cleared her throat and began. 'Geoffrey Skeet, we were given your number by a Mr Charles Cann, also known as Skipper, of Black Lane, Abbotsham.'

Geoffrey said nothing.

'Mr Cann says he spoke to you several times in your capacity as the organizer of the Exiteers regarding arrangements for his proposed suicide.'

Silence.

'Is that true, Mr Skeet?'

Geoffrey looked at her and then sighed regretfully. 'I don't mean to be rude,' he said, 'but I have no comment.'

'Well, we have no reason to doubt Mr Cann's version of events.'

Silence.

'He says you told him that two people would be there today to witness his suicide.'

Silence.

'Given that, doesn't it seem logical that, when two people arrive at his home this morning, they would have been sent by you?'

Geoffrey sighed. 'No comment.'

DCI King took a piece of paper from a case file and laid it on the table between them. 'We found this at the scene.'

Geoffrey patted his pockets until he found his reading glasses, and cleaned them thoroughly on the end of his tie, and then put them on so he could see what she was showing him.

'Do you recognize it?'

Geoffrey took off his reading glasses and lay them on the table. 'I really can't comment.'

'It's a waiver,' said King. 'Releasing the Exiteers from any culpability in the death of a client – in this case, Mr Charles Cann.'

Geoffrey said nothing.

'There's also this will,' she said, flattening said document on the table. 'Have you any knowledge of this?'

'No comment.'

Kirsty King shrugged. 'Mr Cann says you advised him to buy nitrous oxide from a dentist called Mr . . .' She glanced at her notes. 'Williams. And that you gave him precise instructions on how to use it.'

'No comment.'

'Where does Dr Williams practise?'

'I really can't comment.'

King watched him for a long beat, then lifted an old leather briefcase on to the table. 'This was left behind too,' she said, and clicked it open. 'And these . . .'

She removed the thermos, the N_2O cylinder and the foil-wrapped sandwich, and laid them out in a neat, if random, row.

'Do you recognize any of these?'

Geoffrey put his glasses on again. 'Is that a sandwich?'

'Yes.' DCI King peeled back the foil.

'Strawberry jam?'

'Yes.'

'In that case,' said Geoffrey, 'no comment.'

King pursed her lips at him. 'This is not a joke, Mr Skeet. It's your right not to answer my questions, but I'd very much appreciate it if you'd remember that a man has died.'

'You're right,' said Geoffrey. 'I apologize. I'm a little nervous, that's all. This is all very new to me.'

'I understand,' nodded King.

'May I have a glass of water, do you think?'

'Of course.'

Calvin fetched it. Geoffrey thanked him and took a careful sip. His hand shook a little as he did and he smiled thinly at them. 'Parkinson's,' he said. 'I spend most of my life spilling things down my shirt.'

King remained stony-faced. She tapped the briefcase. 'These items were left behind in the Cann house. The older Mr Cann – your client—'

'Alleged client.'

'Alleged client . . . says that this morning he put the cylinder beside his bed with the attached mask within easy reach, along with his will and this signed disclaimer, which he says was provided to him by you. He says he was expecting somebody from your organization to witness his suicide.'

Geoffrey said nothing.

'However, Mr Cann says he woke later to find the cylinder, will and waiver removed from his bedside and a stranger in his room. When he asked what was going on, the man left without a word. Somebody had already called the police but by the time we got there, the intruders had escaped. Sadly, a man was already dead. The wrong man.'

She let the words hang there for a moment.

'Not Mr Charles Cann . . .' She tapped the will with a short, no-nonsense fingernail, '. . . but his son, Albert.'

Geoffrey's eyebrows flickered upwards, and King nodded, as if she agreed wholeheartedly with his surprise.

'So,' said King, 'what went wrong?'

Geoffrey frowned as if he was trying to work that out. 'No comment,' he said very slowly.

'Have you spoken to the people involved?'

'No. Comment.'

'Has anyone in your organization made this kind of mistake before?'

'No comment.'

'This waiver shows that you understand how carefully your operatives have to carry out their duties to stay the right side of the law.'

Geoffrey didn't look at it.

'But of course,' King said, 'the waiver is meaningless unless the person who signed it is the person who actually . . . you know . . . *dies.*'

Silence.

'So where does that leave you?'

He did not reply.

'Then I'll tell you,' she said. 'Up to your neck in it.'

He did not reply.

DCI King sat back in her chair and observed him coolly. 'You're not helping yourself, you know, Geoffrey. You think you're protecting the people who attended this scene, but refusing to reveal their identities amounts to an obstruction of justice at the very best. Accessory to murder at worst. Albert Cann used oxygen for emphysema. It was right there in his room next to his bed. Huge big tank. Anyone who was there must have seen it. Anyone with common sense would have understood that it might lead to confusion. They would have double-checked. *Should* have double-checked. To have not done so is criminally reckless at best.'

Geoffrey said nothing.

King leaned back in her chair with a sigh. 'The trouble is, Geoffrey, you're the only suspect we have right now, and unless you help us to identify anyone who may be more culpable, I'm afraid you're *it.*'

Geoffrey smiled faintly.

'What's funny?'

'Nothing,' he said. 'It's just, they say that on TV police dramas and then the suspect always breaks down and tells the police everything they want to know. I just wondered whether it ever works in real life.'

'Often,' said King, 'but only because it's true.' She smiled. 'You know what else often works?'

'What's that?'

'A search warrant.'

The Discrepancies

'I'm so sorry, Geoffrey!' Felix was mortified. 'Where are you?'

'Bideford police station.'

Felix squinted at his watch, but his arm wasn't long enough to read the time without his glasses. 'I'll be there as soon as I can and tell them this is completely my fault, then they'll let you go.'

'Don't you worry about me, John, I'm fine. I'm doing the old *no comment* thing at the moment. The only trouble is, I don't really know what it is I'm not commenting on.'

So Felix took a deep breath and told Geoffrey exactly what had happened. After he finished speaking there was a long silence.

Then Geoffrey said quietly, 'The police think it was deliberate, John. They're talking murder.'

'What?' he said. '*What?*'

'A man died . . .'

'But . . .' Felix was dazed. 'It wasn't deliberate! It was just a terrible mistake!'

'Well,' said Geoffrey cautiously, 'it does sound as if there are some discrepancies.'

'Discrepancies?'

'Between your version of events and theirs.'

'But how can there be? I did everything by the book. I mean, I checked his name, and the cylinder and the will and the waiver were right there next to his bed—'

'Well, Charles Cann told the police they were beside *his* bed.

But, of course, they found them in your briefcase, so that's impossible to establish for sure. And apparently the poor fellow who died – *Albert* Cann – had emphysema or some such and used oxygen and they think he may have confused that with the nitrous oxide.'

'But there was no oxygen in the room,' said Felix. 'People use those great big cylinders on wheels, don't they? I couldn't have missed it.'

You weren't looking for it . . . a little voice niggled in his head and Felix thought back to the bedroom – small, stuffy, with big old brown furniture and a gloomy carpet. But no oxygen tank. Not that he could *remember* anyway . . .

He thought of Albert Cann. The laboured breathing, the mottled skin. The poor man *had* been suffocating right in front of them. The way he'd looked frantically around the room for the mask, and how – when he'd found it in his lucky hand – he'd clamped it so hard to his face, and sucked so greedily . . .

Desperate for life, not death.

'My God . . .' Felix felt reality shift around him and settle into a new, far less comfortable position. He sat down heavily on the little telephone seat in the hallway of his home, feeling numb.

'Now don't worry, John,' said Geoffrey kindly. 'I'm sure there's a good explanation for all of this. You just lie low. I've got your back on this, one hundred per cent.'

'Lie low? But I have to tell the police what really happened!'

Geoffrey hesitated, then said sombrely, 'I think that until we know more about what went wrong, that might be rather dangerous for all of us.'

Felix nodded, trying to think against the tide of shock. 'Just promise me you'll keep that girl out of it, Geoffrey. She's got her whole life ahead of her.'

'Absolutely,' said Geoffrey. 'No point in bringing her into it at all.'

'Thank you,' said Felix. 'I only—'

'So anyway . . .' Geoffrey cut across him brusquely, as if he suddenly had company. 'I need somebody to feed my cat.'

'Your *cat*?'

'Do you have a pencil?'

Felix was discombobulated by the sudden conversational swerve. He frowned at the little pad they always kept by the phone but was still thinking about the man in the bed, sucking death through the mask that Amanda had handed him, and the pad . . . the top page had Margaret's writing on it – *Jean lunch Thursday?* – and Felix had been loath to tear it off and throw it away, so he had folded it back and used the pages underneath . . .

'. . . Exeter,' said Geoffrey, and Felix realized that Geoffrey had given him his address and he'd missed it, so he asked him to repeat it and wrote it down, feeling as if he was going a bit mad. Writing down a cat's address, while thinking of Albert Cann gasping and dying and the little gold pencil with the tassel, and Jean coming for lunch on Thursday . . .

'Geoffrey—'

'His name is Buttons,' said Geoffrey, and the line went dead.

Felix placed the receiver back in its dock with barely a sound. Then he just sat and stared at the address without seeing it.

Deliberate?

The police must be wrong. The will had been right next to the bed. And the waiver too. And there was no oxygen in Albert Cann's bedroom. He was sure of it.

Wasn't he . . . ?

Felix was a fair and thorough man and so he sat and examined his own memory – walking it carefully through the day's events, from the moment he had taken the key from under the mat, right up until the old man in the bed had said those fateful words . . .

You took your time!

Felix took his time again now. Didn't hurry. Wanted to make sure he wasn't missing anything. But at no point did his memory stumble over what he already knew to be true. There was no catch, no revelation, no cloudy area where he realized he'd mixed things up and needed to revise his version of events. Nothing came to him now that had not been part of the experience then, or that might have happened in the wrong order.

Felix knew he was right. But he also knew he was old . . .

He frowned down at his hands on his knees. They were big square gardening hands with sparse hair on the knuckles, and knobbly in places they hadn't been the last time he'd noticed. Although the last time he could remember really *looking* at his own hands, he'd glued his thumb to the fuselage of an Airfix Spitfire and his mother had made him soak the whole lot in a bowl of warm water for half an hour, while the RAF decals floated sadly off the wings . . .

These weren't the same hands. These were an old man's hands! And yet here they were at the ends of his arms, all rough and wrinkled.

His memory was rough and wrinkled too – with hills and gullies that might hide truths or lies. He vividly remembered hanging this woodchip just after they'd moved in – the dry roughness and the smell of the paste – but sometimes he forgot to put out the recycling. Often, in fact. And only last week he'd missed a doctor's appointment. And gone out twice to the corner shop for milk and come home both times with Margaret's string bag full of everything *but* milk. Including okra, which he had no idea how to cook and no desire to eat, so why on earth would he buy it?

The truth was, Felix *had* started to forget things. So if he had forgotten something about this morning would he even *know*? Would he remember that he had forgotten? Or would the forgetting be complete?

The thought was frightening – that maybe all his future held for him now was forgetting his past.

Would he forget Margaret one day?

Jamie?

The thought alone scared him.

And now something new scared him too.

Until now Felix had been quite sure of one thing – that when he was arrested the police would believe his version of events, because the evidence would support it. That he'd only have to tell them the truth to make them understand how the tragedy had unfolded.

But what if his truth was wrong?

What if some bit of evidence he'd missed or forgotten supported another truth entirely?

Then, killing the wrong man and fleeing the scene of the crime might not sound understandable *at all*.

It might just sound like murder.

Another Bite of the Cherry

Calvin Bridge didn't like the Cann case.

For a start, it made him consider his own mortality. Calvin already considered it more often than was probably healthy. Or logical, given that all four of his grandparents were still alive, with Dermot Bridge leading the way on ninety-nine not out.

But Calvin had never felt quite like one of the family. He'd never looked much like his dark-haired brothers and sister, and he didn't think like them at all, and so had always felt that being confident about sharing their life expectancy was a luxury he should not presume to afford. Therefore he was only too aware that he might have a limited time to get a proper life under way, and that he'd already had one false start with Shirley. He hadn't had a proper girlfriend since then, and he was nearly twenty-seven. Which was pretty much the same as being nearly thirty. Which was only ten years from being forty, and *then* he might as well just admit defeat and slide downhill towards the grave.

So, obviously, this case had raised the spectre of death in his mind once more.

Then yesterday he had been further unsettled by Geoffrey Skeet's innocent musings on Tiverton folk they might have in common. The old man had thrown names out there every now and then as they'd taken the winding route between Exeter and Bideford: Tigger Jackman and Derek Trott and Cynthia Curley and Paul Minster . . .

Most of the names Skeet had mentioned were unfamiliar to Calvin, but one of them was not.

Cynthia Curley was his mother.

Geoffrey Skeet had said it with a question mark, and Calvin hadn't even blinked before shaking his head.

I don't know her.

And Geoffrey Skeet had moved on to another memory without him, while Calvin had sat in cold, dark dread.

Cynthia Curley had been in and out of prison for theft and handling stolen goods for much of his life, and Calvin Bridge couldn't think how Geoffrey Skeet might know her. Calvin had worked too hard at leaving his history behind him to let some random suspect in the back of a cop car open it up like a scab to be picked over by colleagues. Or – worse – leak out into the wider community, so that every little thief he collared felt he had the right to ask him why he wasn't arresting his *mother* for *real crimes*, instead of *him* for pinching a six-pack from Morrisons, or shooting up in the doorway of the White Hart.

Calvin Bridge loved his mother but, at the moment of truth, he'd denied her like Peter.

'All right, Calvin?'

He flinched as DCI King dropped a file over his shoulder and on to the table.

'Yes, ma'am.'

'Bollocks,' she said.

Calvin blushed deeply. *How does she know?* Was he really that transparent? Maybe he should come clean. If only he could trust her to—

Then he looked around and realized that King wasn't talking to him – she was talking to the vending machine.

The Bideford police station vending machine was the biggest thief any of them knew. It routinely took their cash and gave nothing back. Worse, it taunted them while it did so – uncurling its spiral arms to proffer chocolate or a sandwich . . . and then refusing to hand over the treat, sometimes leaving it well short of the ledge, other times grabbing its ankle and dangling it over the drop, like a mob debtor off a roof.

Calvin had lost dozens of coins over the years, and always just sighed and hoped for better luck next time. But Kirsty King was made of sterner stuff. Now she thumped the glass sharply and when that didn't work she grabbed the machine by both shoulders and shook it, whereupon it choked up the Twix she'd paid for, and a bag of Quavers she hadn't.

She dropped the Quavers on the table in front of Calvin. 'Your lucky day,' she said, and sat down.

'I paid for these a week ago,' Calvin mused as he opened the snacks. 'Skeet cracked yet?'

'No comment,' she shrugged. 'Bloody annoying. He's obviously covering up for the men on the ground.'

'Or women,' Calvin said.

'Or women,' she agreed. 'I've sent Pete back to Black Lane to see if anyone has any CCTV of the scene, and I'll have another bash at Skeet this morning, but he's not going to give us anything, if I'm any judge of character.'

Calvin nodded and DCI King looked at him carefully. 'Talking of which, everything all right with you?'

'Yes, ma'am,' he said, wide-eyed.

'You sure? You've got a face like fourpence.'

That stung. Calvin liked to think he had a face like Ryan Gosling.

King regarded him coolly down the double barrel of her Twix, and Calvin was filled with a mixture of irritation and admiration at her powers of perception. He did his best to look cheerful.

'Honest,' he lied. 'I'm fine.'

She raised her eyebrows, but when he didn't fill the void, she said, 'Good,' and pushed the file across the table at him. 'Because you're on the case.'

'Oh!' he said, looking down at the Cann file.

'Anything wrong?'

So much! thought Calvin, but said, 'No. It's just . . . I suppose I have mixed feelings about euthanasia, that's all.'

'You have mixed feelings about an illegal act?'

'Yes. Well, no, obviously. But—'

King winked at his discomfort. 'Don't worry, Calvin. This is assisted dying, not euthanasia. It's a thin line, but don't let it confuse you – this case is not some grand ideological battle. The people involved here are amateurs. Clumsy amateurs. On tightropes. That's why people like Geoffrey Skeet need to be prosecuted. He's not a doctor. He's not a philosopher or a guru. He's a retired history teacher playing God. Worse than that, he's outsourcing it! Without training or oversight or repercussions if things go wrong. And, trust me, it's only ever a matter of time before they do.'

'Yes, ma'am,' said Calvin.

'There's not much in the file,' she went on, nodding at the folder. 'And there doesn't look to be anything nefarious in Charles Cann's will. No dodgy codicil naming Skeet as a beneficiary or anything.'

Good, thought Calvin. Despite DCI King's legal logic regarding the Exiteers, he couldn't help feeling some sympathy for Geoffrey Skeet's moral stance, and was glad not to have been disappointed by his motives.

Yet, anyway.

King went on, 'Obviously, with his disability, Skeet wouldn't have been directly involved in the death, but he's almost certainly the only way we're going to get to the perpetrators, so I'll apply for ninety-six hours if I have to, so we can squeeze him as long and as hard as we legally can.'

Calvin only nodded and DCI King looked at him more closely. 'This is another bite of the cherry for you, Calvin.'

'Yes, ma'am.'

'Good.' DCI King smiled at him. 'I've got Pete on to the British Dental Association to try to track down this Dr Williams and we'll start by checking Reggie's story.'

She got up and headed out, leaving Calvin staring down at the thin brown card folder on the table in front of him.

86923 CANN, Albert

He didn't open it. Unconsciously, he slid his hands off the table and made them into nervous fists on his thighs.

'Let's *go!*'

Slowly he rose, picked up the folder and trailed out after King.

Calvin Bridge didn't *want* another bite of the cherry.

Especially if it meant being involved with anyone who might discover that he was his mother's son.

Buttons

If Geoffrey hadn't been arrested for a crime *he'd* committed, Felix would never have agreed to feed his cat.

Feeding somebody's cat was very different from feeding their dog. A cat had to be found before it could be fed, and yet was never where it should be when you needed it to be there. Feeding somebody's cat was like trying to plan a mini-break in Brigadoon.

Having said that, a large ginger cat was already sitting on Geoffrey's doorstep when Felix got to Exeter around eleven the next morning, so the first part of the task was a breeze.

There was only one free parking space a few doors down and, because he didn't plan to be long and it seemed to be a nice enough area, he didn't even lock the car or wind up his windows. Margaret would go mad. *Reckless*, he could hear her say.

He was sure it would be fine.

The house was part of a red-brick terrace. Geoffrey's peeling front door bore a rustic wooden nameplate that read *Dunloanin'*, which made Felix smile. At least Margaret had been lucid when they'd paid off the mortgage. Enjoyed that moment of release . . .

He looked under the mat and the milk bottles, but there was no key. Geoffrey hadn't said there would be, of course. Hadn't said anything about a key before hanging up, so Felix stepped to the right and knocked next door.

The neighbour had a key and said she'd happily have fed

Geoffrey's cat, if only he'd asked. She seemed rather miffed that he hadn't, so Felix soothed her feelings by telling her that he'd owed Geoffrey a favour and had insisted on undertaking the task.

He opened the door and Buttons ran ahead of him into the gloomy interior.

The house was stuffy, and smelled like many others Felix had let himself into over the past few years – medicinal. That was Geoffrey's illness, he guessed. There were other, bigger clues to his Parkinson's – a stairlift in a fetching shade of Elastoplast, and a pair of crutches leaning against the wall behind the front door.

He went into the kitchen and opened cluttered cupboards until he found a box with a dozen pouches of cat food in it. He emptied three into a bowl and put it down, then filled a bigger bowl with Go-Cat kibble, and an even bigger bowl with water.

'Here, Buttons . . .'

He turned, but the cat had disappeared.

You see!

Felix looked around irritably, then relaxed when he noticed there was a catflap in the back door. Good. The cat could come and go as it pleased and eat when it fancied and, with all the food and water he'd just put down and a willing neighbour happy to take over the reins, Felix wouldn't have to worry about it again. Geoffrey would surely be home soon. It must be evident to the police that, in his condition, Geoffrey could have had no direct involvement in the death of Mr Cann.

Feeling pleased that feeding the cat had proved far less trouble than he'd imagined it would, Felix headed back to the front door. As he did, he glanced into the front room, which contained a sofa and a television and a little desk against the window, with a huge computer monitor on it, and a stumpy black filing cabinet on the carpet beside it.

Felix stopped. Then turned and stepped cautiously into the room. He felt a little naughty doing so. This was beyond the scope

of his permission. He'd been asked to feed Geoffrey's cat and he'd
done that. Now he should be leaving.

But the little filing cabinet . . .

Felix put on his reading glasses and peered at it. Each of the
three drawers had a handwritten card in the label window.

A–F

G–M

N–Z

Felix glanced behind him as if he might be observed, then
opened the top drawer. There were dozens of hanging files, each
labelled with a name tab. He picked out one at random.

Austin

Inside the folder was a standard waiver form with the name and
age of a Mrs Joyce Austin of Kidderminster. That was outside his
patch. Felix was exclusively West Country. He'd been as far as St
Ives and Bristol, but no further. He had no idea who might handle
Kidderminster.

Behind the waiver there was a will, and Joyce Maureen Austin's
signature was scrawled across the bottom of both documents.

Geoffrey had explained to him that the waiver was designed to
protect the Exiteers as they walked a thin line to stay on the right
side of the law. And keeping a copy of the will was to show that no
Exiteer had profited from the death of the client. Felix thought
that was a very good idea.

He put the Austin file back where he'd found it and flicked to
the Cs.

Cann.

There was nothing in the brown card folder. There wouldn't be,
of course. He had left the will and the waiver in the briefcase on
the landing. Along with all the other evidence that would probably
convict him in the end . . .

Quickly he shut the folder and put it back in the drawer.

He opened the other two drawers and hurried through them,

here and there recognizing the names of people he'd helped to ease from life into death.

Garth. Herman. Keith. Pares. Powell. Rhys. Rodgers. Standish.

He wasn't looking for anything really, but he found it anyway. The last name tab was Younger, but there was another folder behind that – although it did not have a tab on it. Felix took the folder out and opened it. Inside was a single sheet of paper, and on it was a list of names and phone numbers. It was only when his eyes were drawn to the fact that the fifth name on the list – *Chris* – had been crossed out, that Felix realized it was a list of Exiteers. Indeed, there he was – *John*, the third one down – and right at the bottom was *Amanda*.

Amanda – who could easily verify or correct his own memory of events.

Felix looked around the room and located the telephone. Without hesitation, he dialled her number.

Hello . . .

'Hello, Amanda, this is—'

. . . can't take your call right now but I won't be long, so please leave a message after the beep and I'll call you back ASAP! Especially if it's a happy one! Bye for now!

Felix felt foolish that he hadn't realized it was a recording, and waited for the beep.

Beep!

'Hello?' he said. 'Amanda? This is Fe— John. From the . . .'

He stopped. He hadn't thought about what he was going to say. He probably shouldn't mention the Exiteers, or Mr Cann, or Abbotsham. Or anything that might indicate to a third party who might hear the message, what all this was about. He adjusted as best he could with, '. . . house. John. From the other day in the house. Where we went together. You remember. I wonder if you would mind ringing me back, please . . .' Again he had to think on his feet. 'Not on this number, though. On my home phone number . . .' He gave it slowly so that she would have time to get a pen and jot the number down. Then he remembered. 'I'm not there at the moment, but I will be back . . .' He stretched his arm out in front of him and squinted. 'Some time after—'

Beep!

He'd run out of time.

Felix was sweating lightly. He patted his brow with his handkerchief. He thought about calling back and doing the whole thing better, but once had been stressful enough. Oh well. She had his number. When she called he would reassure her that he had no intention of involving her in any investigation. All he needed from her was corroboration to put his mind at rest, so that he could go to the police completely confident in his own memory of events.

He hung up and looked again at the list of names in his hand. A dozen in total, but six crossed out, including poor Wendy, so he imagined those were other former members. Apart from himself and Amanda, the four left were Rupert, Delia, Connor and Jim. They were probably all fake names like his own. But the numbers were apparently real enough.

Felix frowned at the paper. The wills and the waivers had always seemed a very good idea when Geoffrey had explained them to him. But suddenly he couldn't help thinking that leaving such a paper trail was a very *bad* idea. Geoffrey was always banging on about how cautious they must all be, and yet here he was with a cabinet full of evidence in plain view in his front room.

The thought slowly occurred to him that maybe *this* was why Geoffrey had asked him to feed his cat. He must have known that his neighbour would have happily done it. Did Geoffrey *mean* him to let himself into his house and go through his filing cabinet? Was *feeding the cat* some sort of code for concealing evidence?

It made Felix go shivery inside just to think of doing anything so . . . *criminal.*

Although it *would* be sensible . . .

Slowly he folded the list of Exiteers into quarters and tucked it into the inside pocket of his beige jacket. He placed the empty folder back in the drawer and closed it. Then he took out his hanky for the second time in five minutes and wiped down the filing cabinet. Then opened the drawers – again using the handkerchief – and swabbed the little plastic file-name tabs too, paying particular attention to Austin and Cann.

Covering your tracks.

Felix ignored the sly little voice in his head. He finished wiping the Cann tag, but then unclipped it entirely and slipped it into his pocket, leaving only an empty brown folder. He stood up. Walked to the doorway, then turned and looked around from there . . .

The filing cabinet was a magnet to his eyes.

It was silly to leave it there. He was sure Geoffrey would agree.

He went back over and picked it up. *Tried* to pick it up. It was only as tall as his knee but was surprisingly heavy. He certainly couldn't carry it out to the car – not without drawing unwanted attention by dropping it or putting his back out. So he pushed it instead, sliding it across the carpet until it was away from the computer and beside the sofa. Then he went into the kitchen and opened one of the cupboards he'd opened earlier when he was looking for cat food. It was the tea towel cupboard. Geoffrey was apparently something of an aficionado, and there must have been forty tea towels, folded in two neat piles. Felix thumbed through them and chose one printed with the safari Big Five on it because he couldn't imagine anyone wanting to dry their hands on a buffalo.

In the front room he draped the tea towel over the the filing cabinet, which hid most of it and made it look much more like a little side table. Felix stood back to admire his work, then put a pot plant on it as well, to discourage the curious even further. He did feel a little rude for rearranging Geoffrey's room but felt it was prudent, given the circumstances.

Then he closed the front door behind him and breathed a sigh of relief at a job well done.

He returned the key to the neighbour, who said she would keep an eye on Buttons until Geoffrey got home, then walked towards his car – his own keys dangling from his finger.

''Scuse me?'

A woman's voice. Felix turned to look at the road. A car was slowing beside him.

A *police* car.

Felix got such a fright that he actually staggered a little. He tingled all over with shock, then went horribly cold.

'Yes!' he said. 'Hello. Hello. What?'

The driver was a woman. There was a passenger too. A younger man. Neither was in uniform.

'Are you leaving, sir?'

'What? Where?'

She pointed to his hand. 'Are you leaving? In your car?'

Felix stared at his car keys for a minute and finally interpreted what she was saying to him. She wanted his parking space. That was all. That was all!

'Yes, sir,' he said. 'I'm leaving now. I'm going home.'

'Thanks,' smiled the woman, and put her indicator on.

He'd called her 'sir'! He'd panicked. Should he explain? No, she'd see him sweating . . .

Felix hurried to his car with the little plastic *Cann* file tag feeling like a lump of lead in his pocket.

He got in and mirror-signalled-manoeuvred out of the spot as quickly as he could with the wheel slipping through his sweaty palms. As he pulled away, he glanced in his mirror to see the police car overshoot the space and then swing backwards into it in a single deft arc.

Felix was so unnerved by his close call that he drove home on autopilot, unaware of anything as piffling as traffic or directions, so anxious was he about his sudden descent into the criminal underworld. Yesterday he'd killed a man. Today he'd removed what might be vital police evidence, and hidden more, and then narrowly avoided being caught red-handed. He was so distracted by his own crimes that he found himself swinging into his driveway as if he'd reached it by time travel.

And so it was only when something terrifyingly quick and silent leapt over his shoulder and disappeared along the side of the house like a furry orange rocket, that Felix realized that – somehow – he had also stolen Geoffrey's cat.

Old Times

DCI King drove to Exeter, while Calvin held on to the dash, just like old times.

He was wearing his only suit. It was navy blue, and he hadn't worn it since being on plainclothes duty with King, more than two years before. He hoped she didn't recognize it.

They got lucky with parking – somebody was just leaving.

Geoffrey Skeet's house reminded Calvin of his grandfather's home. It smelled of school dinners and underlay, and the dingy walls of the hallway were hung with blue-faded prints of warships and kittens. There was a stairlift. DCI King folded down the seat and sat on it and fiddled with the controls. 'Always wanted a go on one of these,' she said, but they couldn't get it to work, so they went into the front room where there were ugly, overstuffed chairs and a rickety desk bearing a computer monitor so giant that it cut light from the bay window. Dusty ornaments elbowed for space in a looming dresser. Every available surface was covered with either big outdated technology or something that ought to be in a drawer. But when Calvin opened a drawer he found it was already stuffed with things that ought to be in a bin.

'Concentrate on finding anything that connects Skeet with the Exiteers,' said King. 'Names, numbers, literature, posters, you know . . .'

'Yes, ma'am,' said Calvin, then put his hands on his hips and turned a slow circle in the middle of the cluttered room. 'This is going to take for ever,' he sighed.

'Found it!' said King, and Calvin looked around to see her kneeling at the open drawer of a squat black filing cabinet, with a tea towel over her arm like a maître d'.

Calvin hurried over.

'Looks like these could be clients,' King said. She plucked a folder from the top drawer and read the name on the tag. 'Raymond Arlow. Ring any bells?'

'No, ma'am.'

'Nor me,' she said. 'But there's a waiver in here exactly like the one we found at the scene. *And* Mr Arlow's last will and testament.'

King rifled through the A–F drawer. 'No Cann file, but I imagine that's only because we've got the will and the waiver back in Bideford.'

'Well, that was easy!' said Calvin.

'Yeah,' she said slowly. 'It's good when it happens like that . . .'

But Calvin could tell she was thinking something completely different. 'Something up, ma'am?'

DCI King sat back on her heels and scanned the room. 'It just feels a bit . . . *too* easy.'

'It *was* hidden under a tea towel,' he pointed out, and she laughed, and he blushed and said, 'Sorry, I just mean, it wasn't right out in the open.'

She smiled. 'No, you're right – it *did* have a tea towel on it.' She stared at the tea towel, then at the cabinet, then at the tea towel again. 'But that makes me almost more suspicious than if it didn't. It's almost as if he wants us to feel we've found something he was trying to hide, and so maybe we'll stop looking.'

'What else do you think there might be?'

'Well, there doesn't seem to be any record in here of Exiteers' names and numbers, for a start.' She flicked quickly through the cabinet before sitting back on her heels again. 'That makes no sense. He must have that somewhere.'

'I just keep all my contacts in my phone,' Calvin shrugged. 'Did Skeet have a phone with him?'

'An ancient Nokia,' she said. 'Leatherette case and everything. It was so bad Tony Coral thought it was good.'

Calvin smiled. The desk sergeant was so retro he was almost back in fashion.

'How are you with computers?'

'Not terrible.'

She jerked a thumb at the monitor. 'See if you can fire up that dinosaur. I'll have a look upstairs.'

Calvin got on his hands and knees to switch on the suitcase-sized grey box under the desk. He hadn't seen a computer like this since he was a kid, when his brother Victor had had one with a dicky fan that hummed so loudly that nobody could watch TV at the same time. Not that they'd wanted to watch TV of course; they'd all been huddled around the monitor – agog at the text-only web page revealing itself at the speed of a quill pen.

This PC wheezed into life in just the same old way, and the keyboard was just as grubby and over-used, with the E rubbed completely off. It was so slow that he had time to take apart the gummy mouse and clean it on the buffalo tea towel before the computer had finished booting up.

He poked around for a while but there didn't seem to be much on the system. Not even a browser. There were ancient versions of Word and Outlook Express and a few folders containing random files. Nothing seemed to be password-protected and as soon as he opened the email program, messages started to arrive.

After about twenty minutes, Kirsty King came downstairs and stood at his shoulder, so he showed her all he'd found. 'There are a couple of personal emails in the inbox but they're about railway stuff. Some old eBay receipts . . . but most of this is spam and even the stuff that's not hasn't been read since March.'

DCI King tapped her teeth with her forefinger while she thought. 'Who has a computer and doesn't read their email?'

'Nobody,' he said. 'Not even pensioners. And I didn't need a password either.'

'Strange.'

'Another tea towel, ma'am?'

'Maybe,' she nodded. 'Fooling us into thinking we've found all there is to find . . .' She sighed. 'I think we should assume we're looking for another phone and computer. The real ones.'

Calvin watched her think.

'Right,' she finally said, 'let's search again, every room, systematically. There *must* be something here. The files in the cabinet link Geoffrey to the work of the Exiteers, but he obviously knows his way around the law, which probably means we're going to *have* to connect him to whoever went into the Cann house to make a case against him.'

'Yes, ma'am,' said Calvin. 'And what if we can't?'

'If we can't,' said King, 'we'll have to let him go.'

Amends

Geoffrey had told him to lie low, but lying low – even *thinking the words* 'lying low' – made Felix feel like a fugitive from justice.

Which he was, of course, so he really should be lying low . . .

He'd been up since six, and had spent most of the morning perched nervously on the hard bench in the hallway next to the phone, waiting for Amanda to return his call.

On his knees, the front page of the *North Devon Journal* shouted *Police investigate 'suspicious' death of OAP*. There wasn't much more to the story. Felix knew because he'd read it twenty times. Mr Albert Cann had been found dead at his home in Abbotsham and police were appealing for anyone who had seen any suspicious activity to come forward. An anonymous neighbour had allegedly said the usual thing about never thinking this kind of thing could happen there, and that was all there was.

It was a strange feeling, to know more about a story in the paper than the paper did. Than *anybody* did, apart from Amanda, or whatever her real name was.

Of course, he didn't know everything. He knew what *he*'d done, and that was about it. What had happened before or after he and Amanda had been there was a mystery to him. He had made a terrible mistake, but hoped there was a good reason why. He just hadn't found it yet.

He kept unfolding and refolding the list of Exiteers he'd stolen from Geoffrey's house. He wanted to call them all, but wasn't sure what to tell them or how they might help. He also didn't want to tie up the phone in case Amanda rang.

Which she didn't.

At nine, Felix stuck his Post-it note back on the door and took Mabel with him to the corner shop, although she had no desire to leave the house – at least not via the front door. She had spotted a ginger intruder lurking in the back garden and since then had been transfixed at the French windows – her wet nose leaving slug-like trails of intent in its quivering wake.

At the shop, Felix bought cat food, frozen peas and two pints of milk. On the way home he gave the gardens marks out of ten, but few had really got going yet, and mostly they scored threes and fours. A few pots of old daffs here, a desultory row of pansies there. Weeds everywhere. It wasn't an impressive line-up. Until he got to the Martins, of course, where once again Mabel stopped for an investigation of the low wall, which seemed to be some sort of doggy noticeboard.

While he waited, Felix reduced the Martins' score to a seven because the grass hadn't been cut since his last assessment. Maybe the Martins were on holiday and that's why the place was starting to look a little neglected. The tulips would start to go over in a day or two, which made him think it would be a shame if there was nobody home to appreciate them.

So he picked one – leaned over the wall and plucked a single pink tulip, not yet fully unfurled from the bud. It was just perfect, and Felix threaded the fleshy stem through the ring on the zip of his beige jacket and walked on, feeling oddly . . . *unfettered*.

Miss Knott was opening his gate.

Felix cut her off. Blocked her way and glanced nervously at his own front door. Even from here the Post-it note was eye-catching . . .

'*Hello*, Mabel,' smiled Miss Knott. 'How's my beautiful girl?'

Mabel wagged her stumpy tail.

'Hello, Miss Knott,' said Felix guardedly.

'Been somewhere exciting?'

'No, no,' he said, holding up Margaret's string bag. 'Just the shop.'

'Very handy, isn't it?'

'Oh yes,' he said. 'Very.'

'What a lovely tulip.' She nodded at his jacket.

Felix looked down at it. He felt rather bad about picking the flower now. Especially as all he'd done was worn it for the last leg of his walk. He would remove his jacket in the house and hang it on the hook in the hallway, and by nightfall the bloom would droop and die and its dusky petals would wilt. It seemed rather a high price to pay for half a block of swagger.

So he pulled it from his jacket and held it out to Miss Knott.

'Here,' he said. 'You have it.'

Miss Knott looked at him as if he were playing a trick on her. As if she might reach for the tulip, and it would squirt water in her face.

'Are you sure?' she said.

'Of course,' he reassured her, and Miss Knott smiled and took it and said, 'Thank you,' and Felix said, 'Don't mention it,' and then there was an awkward silence before she suddenly reached for his chest and said, 'You have a . . .'

Felix drew back from her hand and frowned down at his jacket. The dark blob.

'Oh yes,' he said, 'it's mascara.'

'Oh.'

There was another, much more awkward, silence, and Felix wished she would go. What if the police came to arrest him now? It would be so embarrassing. He willed her to go.

But instead she held up a key. 'I brought you my front door key.'

'Oh,' said Felix.

'You said I should bring it round.'

'I did,' he said, and tried to take it, but his hands were restricted by the dog and the shopping, and Miss Knott bent a little and tried to place the key in one of his hands, and then the other, and they both jerked their arms like marionettes before Miss Knott eventually slid the key into the pocket of Felix's beige jacket.

'There!' she said, flustered.

'Thank you!' he said, flustered.

Then he said his peas would thaw, and Miss Knott said goodbye to Mabel and he hurried up the path and took the Post-it note off the door, and went inside.

Honestly!

Felix stood behind the front door for a moment, feeling as if he'd been buffeted by a high wind. His top lip had broken out in a light sweat and he had to totter through to the kitchen before he could put the shopping and the dog lead down, to blot it with his hanky.

After he'd put the shopping away, he labelled Miss Knott's key and hung it on a hook, then finally spooned a little mound of cat food on to a saucer and left it outside the back door, much to Mabel's outrage. His plan was to lure Buttons out of the shrubbery, then grab him, put him in a box, and take him back to Exeter before Geoffrey got home and found him gone.

Felix put an egg on to boil, and buttered some bread and cut it into soldiers. He checked the answering machine but Amanda hadn't called so he called her again. Again, she didn't pick up, and he started to worry that she was never going to. He wouldn't blame her. She was young and obviously frightened of being dragged back into an unpleasant tangle when she'd already escaped it so cleanly. He understood. After all, he was trying to do the same—

He straightened up and frowned at the very idea.

No!

He wasn't trying to *escape* the tangle. He was just trying to *understand* the tangle before attempting to untangle the tangle. They were two completely different things.

Weren't they?

Felix stood at the stove and felt a growing sense of unease.

Geoffrey – a disabled innocent – was at this very moment languishing in police custody, while *he* was standing here staring at a small brown egg bobbing and dancing, with his soldiers lined up dutifully on a side plate, ready to be dipped and to die.

He should really be doing something more. Something better. Something . . . *else*.

But *what*?

Felix didn't know.

What would Margaret do? he wondered – and had the answer in a flash.

Margaret would not be boiling an egg and waiting for someone to call her back. Margaret would take the bull by the horns, find out what had gone wrong – and do her best to make it right.

Felix didn't know what had gone wrong, and he couldn't bring Albert Cann back from the dead. But there *were* things he could do to make amends.

And he could start by fixing the fence.

Without further ado, Felix switched off his egg and pardoned his soldiers and drove back to the scene of the crime.

The Fence

A bbotsham was a twenty-five-minute drive from Barnstaple.
Felix made it in forty.

This is not like me, he thought nervously all the way there. *This is not like me.*

He kept glancing at his toolbox on the passenger seat. He hadn't used his tools since Margaret got sick because that had taken up all his time. Before that he'd been quite the handyman – always repairing this or improving that. So much so that Margaret used to call him Fixit Felix. *Watch out, here comes Fixit Felix!* Or *Stand aside, Jamie, and let Fixit Felix have a go . . .*

His tools had been there waiting for him in the garage exactly where he'd left them nearly a decade earlier. It had felt good just to carry the toolbox to the car.

From Bideford he drove up the hill into Abbotsham and turned right into Black Lane. As he approached the Cann house he slowed down – and then saw a young man in the driveway, buffing the windscreen of a little red sports car. He didn't look up, but Felix had lost his nerve anyway, and went past. Fifty yards up the road the street narrowed to a mere lane again, bordered by high hedges, and winding vaguely towards the cliffs and the ocean.

Felix pulled the Rover into a field gateway and took a moment to regroup. He wanted to fix the fence, not engage with anybody. But now there was this young man in the driveway. Felix didn't know if he was a member of the family or a neighbour – or possibly even a police officer. He only knew he couldn't go in while he was there.

Felix glanced at his watch, then put the Rover into gear. He performed a five-point turn between the hedges and drove back down Black Lane.

The little red car had gone . . .

The key was not under the mat but the door was slightly ajar so, after a moment of dithering, Felix knocked.

No answer.

Inside he could hear a television blaring.

'Hello?' he called.

No answer.

Mabel hopped up on to the step and shouldered open the door and Felix hurried after her, trying to hiss at her to stop and come back, but she didn't. Instead she snuffled around the skirting and then wandered into the front room, where the little black-and-tan dog trotted over to her with its tail aquiver.

Felix peered around the doorway. A young woman sat on the sofa with a tube of Pringles resting on her tummy. She was watching that show where a rude chef shouted at Americans.

'Hello?' he said cautiously.

She looked up, startled. 'Oh!' she said. 'Hi.'

She was buxom and pretty in a way that many local girls were – round-faced and rosy-cheeked. Felix thought she might be eighteen, but her shortish blonde hair was held out of her eyes by a little rainbow clip, like something a child would wear.

'I'm . . . Felix,' he said after a brief hesitation, during which he debated calling himself John and got so confused in his own head that he decided just to go with the one name he was sure to remember.

'Hiya,' she said with a slightly puzzled smile. 'I'm Hayley.'

'Hello, Hayley,' he said. 'I've, um, come to fix the fence.'

'I didn't know it was broken,' she said.

'Yes,' said Felix. 'A bit of it fell down. Because it was rotten. Apparently.'

'Yeah?' she said. 'Are you from social services?'

'Hm,' said Felix. He hated to lie, but the truth was not an option. 'Do you live here?'

'No,' she laughed. 'I'm the cleaner.'

Felix's eyes flickered around the messy room and the girl reddened. 'I know,' she said. 'I do try, but I feel so tired 'cos I'm pregnant, see?'

She pointed at her tummy.

'Ah,' he nodded but didn't look. No need.

'To be honest,' she went on, 'all I want to do now is eat Pringles and cry.' And to demonstrate the point, her chin wobbled and her eyes flooded with tears and she gave a big ready-made sob – as if it had been threatening to burst out of her for a while, like a bubble in mud.

'Now, now . . .' said Felix. Margaret had had a terrible time carrying Jamie – cried and cried, as though she'd known from the start how sadly it would end.

He offered Hayley his handkerchief and she pressed her eyes and blew her nose and then used it to wipe the Pringles off her fingers for good measure.

'Thanks,' she sniffed, holding it out to him.

'You keep it,' said Felix. Time was you could lend a lady your handkerchief, certain in the knowledge that she would have the decency barely to pat her brow before handing it back unsullied by anything more than perfume and gratitude.

Those times were obviously gone.

The girl nodded her thanks and then tapped her knee at Mabel. 'What a cute little dog! What's his name?'

'Mabel.'

'Oh!' She laughed. 'Hello, Mabel.' And Mabel gave her best wag – the one she reserved for anyone who looked like a promising source of grease.

Felix looked around the chaotic room. He supposed that this was what happened when you did away with National Service.

'Let's give you a hand,' he said, and began to tidy up.

He started by taking all the dirty crockery and cutlery through to the kitchen, while the girl got up and ran a sink full of hot water. Felix found a bin bag which he took into the front room and filled with rubbish. Old newspapers, wrappers, random bits of plastic. Anything that wasn't obviously rubbish he divided into flat things and lumpy things and put them in two rough piles on the coffee table. The first was made up of bills and junk mail. Most of the bills were addressed to Albert Cann and remained unopened – even the red ones. The thought of not opening a bill immediately was anathema to Felix, and it took all his self-restraint not to open them himself, but instead he stacked them in a neat pile. The other pile was more random – DVDs, computer bits, plastic action figures, dirty clothing and, weirdly, a brick with an elastic band around it.

Felix stared at the brick, wondering why it was there and which pile he should put it in, if any. 'Do you think they want to keep this?'

'It's been there ages,' shrugged Hayley. 'And there's an elastic band on it.'

'I know,' said Felix doubtfully, because somehow the elastic band did make it seem like *more* than a brick, so he left it on the coffee table and carried on cleaning.

They took two bags of waste out of the room before Felix felt they'd broken the back of the mess.

Hayley smiled at him. 'Thank you. That's so nice of you!'

'Not at all,' said Felix. 'Happy to help.'

'It looks so much better already!'

'A place for everything,' he nodded, 'and everything in its place.'

She looked at him wide-eyed. 'Oh my God, that's totally true! You're, like, the Yoda of tidying up.'

Felix wasn't sure what a yoda was so he just smiled vaguely, then rubbed his hands together. 'Better get to work.'

'Do you need any tools or anything? Reggie has some in the shed.'

'Who's Reggie?'

'You know,' she said, and lowered her voice, 'Albert's son.'

'Of course,' he said, as if he'd only forgotten. That must be the young man with the red car.

He told Hayley he had his own tools, and then left her with her crisps and her painfully loud TV, and went to get them from the car. He carried them around the side of the house and down the back garden.

Everything was just as it had been two days ago, except now Felix had more time to look around him. He glanced up at the window that he presumed belonged to the bedroom where Albert Cann had died, and thought of the desperation, and the panic, and the shock of opening the other door—

'Come on, Mabel,' he said briskly.

The garden was full of shrubs and flower beds, but all submerged by huge sprays of wild brambles that fountained fifteen feet into the air and narrowed the garden by the same margin on both sides. The shrubbery was still there – somewhere underneath. Felix could tell because here and there a rhododendron poked a desperate blossom through the undergrowth, or a rose waved while drowning in thorns, but most of the shrubs had long since become mere trellis for the well-armed invaders.

Mabel was excited by the newness of it all. She found notices to read on an old wooden ladder and more on a cluster of flowerpots. She chased a wren under the ramshackle shed and a pigeon up the greengage tree, then she led the snuffling way through the long grass and past an old cold frame with broken windows to where the gap in the fence beckoned like a portal to another – much better kempt – existence.

Felix got to work repairing the breach. The stakes at the bottom of the broken panel were rotten – as he'd expected they would be. He hadn't had any stakes handy in the garage or in his shed, but he did have several lengths of two-by-four, and now sawed one end of each into a rough point that might be more easily driven into the ground. These he set about attaching to the existing posts with plentiful screws, having first sawn off the rotten ends flush with the bottom of the panel.

It didn't take long to improvise four new stakes and to screw them sturdily to the posts, and when the panel was ready to be fixed in place, he levered it upright and leaned it against its neighbour, then stepped into the field holding a plastic garden chair and a mallet, and pulled the panel into place behind him, tilting the chair to wedge it upright while he worked. He hammered the new stakes into the ground with such ease and accuracy that he was sorry there was nobody there to witness his skill. By the time the stakes were properly seated so that the panel sat flush against the grass and perfectly square to its neighbours, Felix was so warm that he had to hang his beige jacket over the fence.

It took him nearly an hour, and when he had finished he wiped his brow on the sleeve of his jumper and surveyed his handiwork.

Not bad! And he hadn't enjoyed anything so much for ages.

Then he realized he'd fenced himself out of the garden.

'Ha!' he snorted. 'Old fool!' And was pleased that nobody but Mabel was watching after all.

He'd been this side of the fence before, of course, but on that occasion he had just hobbled blindly across the field until he'd reached a random hedge and then a gate and then a lane and then a bus stop. It was all a bit of a blur. But now he wanted to get back *into* the garden, not away from it. He looked around him. The neighbours had a similar high wooden fence along the bottom of their property, interrupted only by a gnarled apple tree next door that leaned over it, hung with half a dozen bird feeders and nesting boxes. Scores of sparrows and tits and chaffinches fluttered and swooped around them, arguing furiously over this nut or that sunflower seed.

Despite his predicament, Felix took a moment to enjoy the sight. He'd always liked birds. He should get a feeder. He *would* get a feeder – as soon as he'd caught Buttons and taken him safely home to Geoffrey. That reminded him of why he was here and what he was doing and that he still needed to get back into the Canns' garden.

He peered back over the fence but it was too high to climb, and so he stood on the chair, but even then it only raised him chest-high against the fence. If he'd been fifty, he might have managed it, but at seventy-five, even the small optimistic hop he tried made the garden chair wobble precariously and he clutched at the fence, and Mabel barked furiously at him, as if they'd never met. It made Felix wonder if she really only knew him from the knees down.

'Don't be a silly old dog,' he chided her, but she was determined to alert the planet to his presence, so he clambered off the chair and looked around. The front of the Cann house faced the neighbours and – beyond them – the sky that hung over the grassland that led to the sea, but the views from the back were much prettier: small, bright green fields dotted with sheep, sloping gently down into a shallow coombe and up the other side towards Bideford.

Felix's sense of smell had been declining for years but there was enough nature here even for him to draw in the scent of all-purpose greenery and the soil below it, while – now that he wasn't bumbling about on the fence and the chair – the birds had returned to the apple tree en masse, and filled the air with their cheerful squabbling.

Felix wiped his hands on his trousers. He would just have to

walk around the end of the row of houses and hope to find a gate
he could climb over.

He lifted the plastic chair back over the fence and was about to
drop it into the garden when the cleaner threw open the back door,
ran as far as the shed and shouted at him, 'Hey! Skipper's fallen
over!'

Felix froze.

'Oh dear,' he called, non-committally.

But she yelled, 'I can't get him up alone!' And then waved her
arm at him and disappeared back inside – apparently expecting
him to follow post-haste.

Felix didn't move. Just stared at the house through the brambles
and didn't know what to do. It was in his nature to help, but he'd
imagined things would happen at his own pace. This was too
fast. Too soon – and he felt panicky at the prospect of seeing the
old man again. How could he look him in the eye and admit what
he'd done? He just wasn't *prepared* for it.

In his head, Margaret said crossly, *I thought you'd come to help.*

Felix sighed. With a horrible sense of foreboding, he pulled the
chair back to his side of the fence and looked around him with a
more urgent eye.

A branch of the apple tree curved gracefully down over next
door's fence. Felix placed the plastic chair underneath the lowest
point of the curve. He climbed up carefully and gripped the
branch – and was instantly transported through time. When had
he last touched a tree? When had he last *climbed* a tree? My goodness, it must be sixty years! And yet it felt so familiar. That rough,
dry bark, the creak of the wood as he tested his weight, and the
flurry of birds rushing to leave as he rocked their world.

Felix pulled the branch as low as he could and lifted one leg
towards it. The chair wobbled precariously and he quickly put his
foot down again, quaking inside.

This was never going to work!

But Mr Cann needed help. And Felix had come here with the express purpose of helping him, so it would be a very poor show if he let something as simple as a tree get in his way.

He tried again. He threw one arm over the branch and then his right leg. It wasn't easy: he hadn't lifted his leg this high for years. Something creaked and he couldn't tell if it was the tree or his hip. But he wedged his right knee on to the branch. And then over the branch. And suddenly the branch shifted and his left foot was no longer in contact with the garden chair and he was definitely *in the tree*, with his cheek and chin pressed against the bark. He moved his head minutely and looked down. From the ground the branch had been head-high but from the branch the ground looked a dizzying distance away, and Felix clung on for dear life, scared to move for fear of unbalancing himself and dropping to earth like a floppy monkey pierced by a poisoned dart.

But the whole point was to move . . .

Slowly he inched forward and didn't fall. So he took a deep breath and did it again. *Hurry up!* said Margaret, and Felix finally accepted his fate and hurried up. If he made it, good. If he didn't, well, the girl knew where to look for his body, and Mabel was microchipped and so somehow she'd find her way to Miss Knott, he was sure.

Actually it wasn't so hard. The further he went, the more confident he felt. He'd done this before – a long time ago, of course – but his brain knew that was true, and reminded his hands and his arms and his legs and his feet that this was all perfectly possible, and then waited patiently for them to catch up.

Before he knew it, Felix was watching the top of the fence edge beneath him, and impending triumph strengthened his grip. There was a small wobble when he banged his head on a nesting box and another when a nut feeder swung into his ear, but other than that all went quite smoothly and less than five minutes after starting this latest adventure, Felix shuffled his hips sideways and let his legs drop from the branch. He had planned to dangle by his arms, judge his distance and land on his feet, but as soon as his legs left the branch, they just yanked the rest of him out of the tree and he fell.

Six inches.

The ground surprised him so early that his knees buckled and he staggered into the trunk, and threw his arms around it to steady himself.

I'm OK. I'm OK!

Nobody cared, of course.

Slowly Felix released the tree from his embrace and brushed himself down and clapped his hands on his thighs to rid himself of bits of moss and bark and bird poo, and then straightened up and hurried up the neighbour's garden with a new sense of purpose. If anyone confronted him now, he'd tell them firmly that he was on a rescue mission and to stand by in case they were needed. If they tried to stop him . . . Well, he would simply brush them aside.

Felix Pink had climbed a tree, and *nothing* was beyond him.

'Up here!'

The stairwell was much brighter than the last time Felix had been here. As he got to the landing he realized it was because all the doors upstairs were open. At the door to Albert Cann's bedroom he stopped as if struck, and felt a cold shiver run down his back.

There was an oxygen cylinder. Not a small one either, but a large black tank like an aqualung, with big industrial-looking valves and loops of tubing and a mask, all on a sturdy metal trolley so the user could wheel it about from room to room. Exactly the kind of thing a man who suffered from emphysema might need.

It had not been there before. Felix was sure of it.

Wasn't he?

'Hello?' the girl called. 'In here!'

Slowly Felix moved past the room where he'd killed the wrong man and went into the front bedroom, where the right man was sitting on the rug beside the bed with his back to the door. Hayley was supporting him – her knees braced against his back.

'What were you even doing out of bed, Skip?' she grumbled. 'You shouldn't be up without help. You've got cancer!'

'Bollocks to cancer,' the old man grunted defiantly. 'Day I can't get to the head alone . . .'

The girl looked over her shoulder at Felix. 'We'll take an arm each. You're lucky Felix is here, Skip. I couldn't do it by myself.'

'Who?' Skipper squinted around, dazed, but Felix edged sideways to stay behind him.

'From social services,' she said. 'Come to fix the fence.'

'What fence?' said Skipper.

'The garden fence!' She rolled her eyes at Felix. 'Can you get his other arm?'

Felix approached cautiously from the rear, and helped Skipper off the floor and to his feet. It wasn't too hard; he weighed nothing, and Felix could feel his sharp ribs against his arm, right through his pyjamas.

'Where's my stick?'

'It's broke,' said Hayley. 'Don't worry, we'll get you a new one. We'll just get you back in bed for now, all right?'

With arms linked, they all started towards the bed. Then Skipper stopped and said he still needed to *go*, and so the three of them performed a bumbling U-turn in the middle of the room, like a badly rehearsed chorus line.

'Thanks,' said Hayley as they reached the door, and smiled at Felix to let him know she could take it from here, so he disengaged from the old man's elbow and watched them make their way slowly out of the room together.

Felix looked around.

Charles Cann.

Skipper.

He had knocked stuff off the dresser as he fell. Holding on to the edge of the old oak furniture, Felix creaked down and picked up a pair of reading glasses and a pill bottle. The spectacle lenses were very thick and he held them up to read the label. They made the print huge and distorted.

MORPHINE SULFATE ER

It took him back with a sad jolt. Jamie had been prescribed the same painkillers near the end. Thank God. He set the bottle and the glasses on the dresser and bent again to pick the walking stick off the rug. It was L-shaped now. Poor old chap could have broken a hip. Or worse.

Fresh from his triumph with the fence, Felix wondered whether the stick might be repaired, so when he left Abbotsham, he took it with him.

Felix sat in a traffic jam. He craned to see what the hold-up was, but there was nothing to see apart from a line of cars that wound down the hill from Old Town, around the Pannier Market and continued down Bridge Street towards the Quay.

Two cars ahead he could see a little red coupé. A lean and a squint told him it was the same one he'd seen outside the Cann house earlier today. With the same young man at the wheel. Reggie Cann.

Felix immediately felt panicky.

Don't be daft, he told himself firmly. *He doesn't know you.*

Even so, two cars' lengths seemed very close, and he glanced about, in case he might be able to swing out of the queue of traffic and get away from the red car. But he'd already passed the only available turn into Buttgarden Street and they were all now edging down Bridge Street, which was one-way and narrow, and so steep that there were handrails for pedestrians to cling to during an ascent. He was forced to stay behind the car. He watched it warily.

In a book – a spy thriller – the driver's door would open and the young man would get out and walk towards him.

With a gun!

Felix shivered and told himself that this was Bideford, and so that was impossible.

But then, hadn't he killed the wrong man when everything had pointed to it being the right man? *That* hadn't seemed possible either . . .

He swallowed a little lump in his throat as they edged downhill in convoy. When the red car reached the foot of the hill, it turned left into the car park opposite the Town Hall. When he reached the same spot, Felix would drive straight ahead – over the old bridge and home to Barnstaple.

Except that he didn't.

Instead he followed the red car into the car park. Found a space and parked. He watched the young man get out of his car and walk to the ticket machine – then got out of the Rover and did the same. Even queued a few yards behind Reggie Cann at the machine but couldn't think of how to introduce himself, or even whether he should. Felix didn't really know what he was doing. Was he going to apologize? Or demand answers? The idea of revealing who he was and what he'd done made him feel all fluttery inside. Who knew what he was getting into? He should watch the young man for a little while. Try to get a sense of who he was and what he was like, before making a move.

But this time he *would* make a move. He felt more in control than he had earlier. More resolute. If he wasn't going to at least *try* to find out what had gone wrong in the Cann house, then he had no excuse not to turn himself in immediately and hand that responsibility over to the police, whatever Geoffrey said.

So Felix put the ticket on his dashboard and cracked a window for Mabel, then hurried after the young man with a little thrill at his own derring-do.

It must be the tree, he thought, *making me brave.*

Allhalland Street was only a car's width wide, and filled with quaint little shops. But the young man didn't look in the windows. He knew where he was going and walked briskly enough so that Felix grimaced with every stride. They crossed the High Street and went on to Mill Street, past the supermarket, and then down an even narrower street on to the quay. Felix wished they could stop. He was out of breath and his hip tweaked constantly. He didn't know what he was going to say, even if he had the guts to say it, so this might all be a big waste of time.

But he persisted, and fifty yards along the quay Reggie Cann slowed as he came to a little pavement café. Despite the breezy weather, plenty of hardy customers were prepared to dine *al fresco* in their coats and scarves, and he picked his way between the tables and chairs dotted about under the trees.

Felix stopped under a tree at the perimeter. He had caught up with his quarry, and now had no excuse not to approach him. He must simply introduce himself, apologize and take it from there. If things went well, he might discover valuable information. If they went badly . . . well, there were plenty of people around who would probably come to an old man's aid if things got out of hand.

Felix felt Margaret at his shoulder and took a deep breath. It was now or never.

Reggie Cann bent and kissed the cheek of a girl at a table, and Felix turned sharply and hurried away.

The girl was Amanda.

The Big Spender

Calvin drove DCI King to Old Town to check Reggie Cann's alibi.

CompuWiz was a nondescript shop in a short row opposite the fire station and between the narrow terraced houses. It was a ten-minute drive from Abbotsham – only five from the police station.

A little bell rang as DCI King opened the door, but it still took a few minutes before anyone emerged from the gloomy interior, so she and Calvin had plenty of time to look at the mysterious electronic components in the dusty glass cabinets and the small selection of used laptops in the window.

'Right?' said the fifty-something man who finally did appear with stubble, glasses and an Asteroids T-shirt that curved space–time around his belly.

'Are you Daz?' King said, showing him her ID.

Daz sneered. 'I'm always telling you lot, I don't *buy* stolen gear, I don't *sell* stolen gear.'

'We're not here about stolen gear.'

'Oh,' said Daz.

'We're here about Reggie Cann.'

'Is he OK? Went to lunch the other day and never came back.'

'He's fine.'

'Oh good,' Daz said, 'because he's in the middle of a Mac and I don't have a bloody clue about Macs.'

King nodded. 'What time did he get here on Tuesday?'

'Tuesday? Um, eight thirty-ish? Usual time, I think.'

'And what time did he leave for lunch?'

'About twelve? I'm not a Nazi about it. Is something wrong?'

'Does he usually go home for lunch?'

'Yeah. He only lives in Abbotsham and he's too cheap to buy a pasty. What's the big deal?'

'His father died,' she told him.

Daz frowned. 'His father's dead? Are you sure?'

King cocked an eyebrow at him. 'The doctor seemed sure.'

'I just mean . . . I thought his *grandfather* was sick.'

'He's sick too,' King said. 'They're both sick. *Were* both sick. One still is.'

'Well,' Daz said, and puffed out his cheeks. 'That's a bit shit.'

'Yes, it is,' King said. 'What did Reggie tell you about his grandfather?'

Daz shrugged. 'Just that he was sick. Cancer, I think, although maybe I'm wrong. Seems like everybody's got cancer nowadays, don't they? I've probably got it – just don't know it yet!' He laughed.

King waited for him to stop. 'How about his father? Did he talk about him?'

'Not so much,' said Daz.

'Did he ever talk about either of them wanting to die?'

'To *die*? No. Not that I can recall. I mean, he'd talk about how hard it is looking after them and all that. The old man, specially. Like, you wouldn't let a dog suffer that way for so long, would you?'

'Reggie said that?'

'No,' shrugged Daz. 'I'm just saying – you'd put a dog down, wouldn't you?'

They thanked him and left – and drove back to the police station in silence.

*

At lunchtime, Calvin headed up the hill to the bookies. He had
had the bitter misfortune to win his first ever bet on the horses. In
honour of his younger brother, he'd had a one-pound each-way
bet on a 33–1 shot called Lucky Louis at Worcester. The horse had
romped home, and Calvin's fate was sealed. Now, nearly ten years
on, he had a flutter almost every day, and it was only his paranoia
about getting into debt that kept him from becoming a complete
degenerate.

As it was, he spent many a lunchtime at the Ladbrokes on Bideford High Street, frowning at the newspapers tacked to the walls,
and scrawling optimistic Yankees on to the little pink slips, then
crumpling them up for less heady Trixies, then discarding those
for still-dubious doubles, before finally handing over his cash at
the counter. That cash was received by Dead Mike, who was so
thin and grey that every breath sounded like a resurrection, or by
Sylvie, who had worked in the same shop since the early nineties
and knew every loser in town by name – and a few by what they
liked for breakfast. In a shop full of men, she'd once been an object
of some interest, but those days were long gone, and now she wore
her red uniform scarf knotted tight under one ear to keep her
chins in check. She still flirted occasionally, apparently on the
basis of having a monopoly.

Women didn't come into the bookies.

Bookmakers could sponsor pretty girls in sashes at sporting
events until the cows came home, but Calvin had never seen
another woman in Ladbrokes apart from Old Greybeard, who sat
bundled up in an anorak and wellington boots, come rain or come
shine, and never spoke to anyone, except now and then to tell Dead
Mike she'd take a price.

Calvin didn't think she counted.

The core membership of the shop was about a dozen deep.
Mostly unemployed or self-employed. A few were *actually*
employed – probably by some poor bastard who fondly imagined

they were somewhere else, doing something else. King of the regulars was Dennis Matthews. Den to those who knew him, Denny to those who thought they did. Matthews was six-four and three hundred pounds and never went anywhere without his inflatable haemorrhoids cushion.

Nobody laughed at him.

He had the red face, buggy blue eyes and tight yellow curls of a cherub who'd outdrunk his child-star status. When he sat, he spread his arms and legs to every quarter, so that anyone who found themselves sitting beside him, or behind him, or afore, must give way or risk becoming intimately acquainted with his elbow, or his giant shoulder, or his careless boot. In this way he had created a large Dennis Matthews-shaped space in the bookies, which only he was qualified to fill.

Nobody else sat in his seat. All the regulars knew that Matthews had been behind bars for assault and nobody wanted to be the reason he went back there. They kowtowed to him. They showed him the bets they were having or had had, offered to fetch him coffee from the machine, laughed at his non-jokes, agreed with his rants, and generally did all they could to avoid getting in his bad books. Even Dead Mike let him put bets on past the 'off' time. Sometimes two fences past the off . . .

Despite all this, he was an unlucky man. Nobody in the Bideford branch of Ladbrokes could compare to Dennis Matthews when it came to hard luck. When he lost, he would get up and stand in front of the big screen – so close that his nose almost distorted the pixels – and glare at the errant horse/dog/jockey, as if fury itself might turn back time. When that happened, everybody tiptoed around the shop. Many left and came back later when Matthews had gone and they could see the TV again.

Even when he won, he bitched like a loser. He should always have had more on. Or his winnings barely covered what he'd lost on the same horse over the past six months because the trainer was crooked and the jockey was crooked and the horse should be shot. There was never a silver lining around Dennis Matthews' cloud. At the start of the day he would drop heavily into his seat and grumble, *I hope I break even – I could do with the money.*

The only person who ever willingly sat beside him was a small, surprised-looking fellow called Shifty Sands.

Of course, he hadn't been christened Shifty. His parents had named him Simon. But in a town where the tide emptied the river twice a day, having a name like Sands was just asking for trouble. To be fair, he didn't *look* shifty. He was about thirty and had the wide eyes and raised brows of a man who was eager to please, although anyone who tried to cadge a fag off him as he puffed industriously in the doorway quickly discovered that that was an illusion.

Shifty smoked forty a day, so was up and down like a yo-yo in a chimney, but when he sat, he and Matthews sat together, cursing fat jockeys and wishing glue on their horses. Every four years they also cursed Olympic athletes, swimmers and cyclists, who, it turned out, were all part of the same conspiracy to steal their money. Money that was rarely well-gotten and always tax-free.

Calvin had been raised around men like Matthews – blustery alpha males with chips on their shoulders and dirt under their nails – and his deference to someone bigger and more dangerous was inbred. He and Matthews were not friendly, but they were not unfriendly either. They would nod a surly acknowledgement of each other's status as regulars, and occasionally bumped elbows at the *Racing Post* pinned to the wall when they were both considering an investment.

They'd never spoken, though.

Until today.

For some reason, when Calvin joined him to look at the latest Derby betting, Matthews dragged a finger the size and complexion of a raw Lincolnshire sausage down the list of jockeys booked to ride in the Derby.

'Thieving little pricks,' he muttered.

Calvin Bridge was an officer of the law, but he had never felt more like a man.

Which was why he made a terrible mistake . . .

The Derby had never been a lucky race for Calvin. He preferred the jumps, where outrageous misfortune occasionally gifted him a long-odds winner that would have been a loser, but for the final fence.

However, back in December he and Jackie Braddick had been called to the rival bookmakers, William Hill, down on the Quay, after one punter had stabbed another – apparently during a heated debate about *Strictly Come Dancing*.

Calvin had spoken to the alleged victim, Tomas Novak, who'd had two small triangular puncture wounds in his cheek. Bookies' pens were triangular to stop them rolling off the counters, so it didn't take Poirot to identify the weapon of choice. Despite the holes in his face, Novak had declined to name his assailant, and the shop had been suspiciously empty by the time they'd arrived, so Calvin and Jackie had deduced that any witnesses to the assault were declining too, and the whole matter had to be dropped there and then.

However, while Calvin was trying to persuade Novak to at least go to hospital, the latter had had a winning forecast on the dogs and they'd both stopped to watch it come in at odds of 26–1. Calvin had shown interest in Novak's alleged *system* and – presumably by way of compensation – Novak had looked around furtively, then whispered to him the name of the Derby winner.

This was nothing new. Men in bookies were always whispering winners into each others' ears. Calvin had done it himself on occasion – murmured the name of a horse he fancied and then, when it didn't win, he and the man attached to the ear would both pretend he'd never spoken.

But if it *did* win, then the whisperer was thanked and possibly materially rewarded with a cup of soup from the machine or a Mars bar – and moved a tiny notch up the rankings of regulars.

Calvin wasn't a William Hill man. He was a Ladbrokes man, so he didn't know Novak from Adam. Therefore, before he'd joined Jackie in the car, he had surreptitiously checked out the man's credentials with the manager. They turned out to be impeccable, as Novak's brother had once ridden in the Pardubice.

The tip's name was Rumbaba, and Calvin had had fifty quid to win at 20–1. It was a huge bet for him; he usually confined his outlay to a fiver, spread as thin as Marmite over several horses.

In March the horse had won a good mile race on the all-weather and was cut to 10–1 and when the trainer retained the excellent D. Mahony for the Derby ride, the bookies slashed the price to sixes, and then quickly to 9–2, and suddenly Rumbaba was third favourite behind only the usual Ballydoyle hotpot and the winner of the Dewhurst.

Now, with only a few weeks to go to the race, Calvin was in possession of a ticket potentially worth a month's wages, and could barely sleep. The first thing he did whenever he went into the bookies was check the ante-post Derby betting and shiver at the anticipation of a coup.

And so, when Dennis Matthews deigned to share his opinion on jockeys with him, Calvin's entire history moved him to reciprocate. And he did so with the only thing he had that might impress the big man.

He tapped Rumbaba's name and murmured, 'I've got that at twenties.'

Dennis Matthews grunted. His bulging eyes flickered up and down the list, and he pursed his cherubic lips and, after a minute or two, he slid a fresh slip from the well in the nearest counter and picked up a little blue pen and wrote on it in big careful letters:

RUMBABA. DERBY.

Calvin tried not to show how much it meant to have Dennis Matthews give him that affirmation.

But as he watched Matthews complete the slip, he nearly fainted. £500 WIN.

Calvin went clammy. *Five hundred quid?* To *win*? On *his* say-so? Worse – on the say-so of some William Hill idiot whose brother was a thieving little prick and who didn't have the good sense to move his face out of the way after the *first* stab of a bookies' pen? Calvin felt faint. What if the horse lost? Lost five hundred quid? Of Dennis Matthews' money! He had to say something. Take it back. Say he'd been joking. But if he did that, and then the horse *won*, then where did that leave him? Matthews would find out sooner or later that he'd won big on the Derby, and then it would look as if he'd just not wanted Matthews to share in the spoils.

Calvin watched Dennis Matthews hand the slip to Dead Mike with the numb horror he could only imagine feeling while watching his firstborn ride a tricycle off a cliff.

One macho moment, one childish boast and suddenly Rumbaba had to win the Derby, or Calvin Bridge knew he was in serious trouble.

The Set-up

Felix had come up the hill so fast that he could barely breathe. 'Margaret,' he panted. 'I need your help!'

He put one hand on her headstone to steady himself, the other on his heart, which had not stopped racing since he'd lurched away from the café on the quay.

Amanda and Reggie Cann.

What did it mean?

What did it mean?

If only Margaret were here! She would know.

He tried to calm down and think it all through.

If Amanda knew Reggie, then she must have known Albert was not Charles Cann. And if she had known it, then she'd lied to him. Right to his face. She didn't *look* like a liar. But what did a liar look like? Felix didn't know, but felt utterly wounded by betrayal. He'd trusted Amanda and she'd lied to him. She'd told him about her nan dying of cancer. Was *that* a lie too? Who would lie about such a thing? And when she had wept he'd given her his hanky. She still had it. A liar had his hanky! He had covered for her. Felt sorry for her. Felt connected to her by shared trauma and her mascara on his jacket. But now Felix realized that she was connected to someone else, some*way* else, and that he really didn't know her at all.

It was a set-up!

His gut lurched in response to the thought. Felix couldn't

remember the last time he'd known something in his gut – maybe he *never* had – but it was there now.

If it was a set-up, then Albert Cann's death was no accident. Somebody had *meant* to kill him.

And used *him* to do it.

Felix swayed with horror.

Then he turned away from his wife and his son and stumbled down the hill like a drunk.

The lowering sun was opening long, shadowy graves in the grass that threatened to swallow him as he lurched back to the car. By the time he got there he was shaking so hard he could barely find the lock with the key.

He opened the driver's door and Mabel jumped out, ready for her walk.

'No, Mabel, here . . . Stay . . .'

He opened the back door and bent and scooped her into his arms.

The heft was so like that of a child that for one divine moment Felix closed his eyes and wrapped himself around that warm weight, and pressed it to his chest and his cheek and thought of a boy – maybe two, maybe three – with perfect little teeth, each with a perfect little gap; a boy whose tiny bottom fitted neatly into the crook of his arm; a boy who still smelled like a baby even though he could already say all the important things.

Mummy

Daddy

Foo-ball

Felix breathed deeply.

Mabel smelled like a dog.

He opened his eyes and placed her gently on to her rug on the back seat. As he shut the door, he noticed the broken walking stick. He had forgotten it was there. He reached into the car and picked it up. It was a natural branch of cherrywood, with a pretty grain, and with the knot at the top rubbed shiny by an old man's grip. About eight inches up from the rubber ferrule at the tip, the stick had snapped.

Felix brought it closer to his face and frowned. The inside of the break was just splinters and strips of bent cherrywood holding things together. But the outside – where the inner wood had been exposed . . . there the break was straight.

Sharp.

Deliberate.

As if somebody had sawn through the stick just enough so that it would break under a load.

The load of Skipper Cann.

Felix stood and stared at the stick for so long that by the time he looked up, the red sun had been torn in half by the trees at the top of the hill.

He got behind the wheel, laid the walking stick on the front seat beside him, and drove home.

Fast.

The Pigeon

Geoffrey Skeet had been in custody now for nearly three days. Calvin had plugged in the dinosaur in the office, where it had attracted some attention.

Jackie Braddick was younger than him by only four years but had never seen anything like it. When Calvin first put the monitor down on the desk they shared, she thought it was a microwave oven, and visibly recoiled from the dot-matrix display. Tony Coral, on the other hand, put his hand on the nicotine casing as if it were the tousled head of his favourite son and said, *Ah, they don't make 'em like this any more.*

DCI King had asked Calvin to create a database of the Exiteer files on HOLMES, so it could be shared with forces around the country. It was a sensible thing to do, but Calvin was a little peeved that he'd been asked to do it. It meant a lot of scanning and form-filling, and was the kind of work a DCI usually handed off to a uniform, whereas he was supposed to be in plainclothes while working on the Cann case. Calvin didn't *want* a second bite of the cherry, but he also didn't want the cherry taken away from him in humiliating circumstances.

Even so, he knuckled down to the task, and worked through eleven files in three hours, which he thought was pretty good going, considering how boring it was. He skim-read each will as he scanned it, with an eye to red flags like large sums being left to non-relatives or the same dodgy charity, but it was all so random.

Here, a godson received a thousand pounds. There, a cousin got a grandmother clock. A neighbour was bequeathed 'my lawnmower and the contents of my toolshed'.

Calvin wondered idly what he might one day inherit. His father had moved on to a new family he seemed to like much better, so he couldn't see much return from that quarter, and his mother's possessions now consisted of whatever she was permitted to keep in her half of an eight-by-ten cell. His little brother Louis was already running both the legal and illegal incarnations of Bridge Fencing and doing a fine job of both, as far as Calvin wanted to know. Beyond that were slim pickings. He tried to think of a single item that had been in their chaotic home when he was growing up that was both desirable *and* legally theirs, but the latter was a qualification too far and he gave up.

At two o'clock he attempted to buy a cheese-and-onion sandwich from the machine, but had to settle for nicking two chocolate chip cookies from Jackie Braddick's drawer. He'd replace them at some point; they had an understanding.

Kirsty King and Pete Shapland came in just after three.

'How are you getting on, Calvin?'

'Not bad, ma'am. I'm scanning all the paperwork and checking the wills in case I can see anything obviously suspicious.'

'Bit random, isn't it?' said Pete. 'How many have you done?'

'Fourteen so far.'

Pete snorted. 'There's nearly two hundred files! It'll take for ever! Bloody waste of time if you ask me.'

Nobody *had* asked him, and Calvin avoided his eyes. Pete might be in plainclothes, but it made no difference: they were the same rank and about the same age, and he shouldn't speak to him as if he were his boss.

'You're not his boss,' Kirsty King said coolly as she rocked

Calvin's cheese-and-onion sandwich out of the vending machine. 'And it sounds like you had a more productive morning than we did. We've got a lot of witnesses to eff-all and still don't know who made the tip-off call.'

'They couldn't triangulate?' asked Calvin.

'They could only narrow it down to the area of Black Lane. The Canns don't have cameras but a couple of their neighbours do. We're going to go through the footage now, if you'd like to watch.'

Pete put memory cards into readers and set up the footage on two different screens.

They hit the mark immediately. Two people walking away from the camera, up Black Lane. A long rear shot of a tall man with a slight limp, wearing a short pale jacket – 'Looks like he could be old,' King remarked – and a slim woman with dark hair and a long coat over jeans. They turned towards the Cann house and disappeared from view. The time code said it was 10.11.

The second camera was mounted on a roof and the shot was mainly of other roofs, but they could just see the pair in the lower right quadrant. They were standing at the door of the Cann home, but were only visible from the waist down – their upper bodies shielded by the little porch over their heads.

'Is this the best angle we've got?' frowned King.

'Yes, ma'am,' said Pete. 'It's from next door.'

'The Moons?'

Pete nodded.

At 10.13 the tall man suddenly bent into frame and they all leaned forward in anticipation. But just at the critical moment where they might have seen his face, they all recoiled as a gigantic pigeon fluttered into shot and then perched on the guttering, preening itself and filling the screen.

'Bloody hell!' muttered Pete.

King frowned. 'Why the hell would you have a camera pointing at a gutter?'

'Donald Moon's a birdwatcher, ma'am,' said Calvin. 'Maybe the pigeon is the point.'

Pete ran the footage forward until the pigeon disappeared, but by then so had the man and woman.

The three of them watched and waited. A car jerked across the first screen. They waited some more. Five minutes. Ten.

Calvin glanced at the time code. 'What time was the tip-off call made?'

King said, 'Ten twenty-two,' without looking at her notes.

At 10.27 – fourteen minutes after the Exiteers had entered the house – the woman emerged from the house and walked quickly back the way she had come. Alone.

'She left without him!' said Shapland.

'Odd,' said King.

They waited, but the man did not emerge from the front door. Then at 10.31 the police car pulled up and Calvin watched himself pass through the shot on his way to the back of the house.

Nine minutes response time, he thought. *Not bad going.*

Jackie's legs disappeared through the front door.

Then nothing more.

'The bloke must have been in the house at the same time you were!' Pete said to Calvin.

'I don't think so,' said Calvin. 'We covered both doors right off the bat. I reckon he was already gone through the broken fence.'

'Should have checked the garden first,' said Pete.

'Jackie was already in the house,' said King sharply. 'You want Calvin to leave her without backup? Anyway, the suspect was probably already gone out the back.'

'What about a car?' said Calvin.

King shook her head. 'Nobody we spoke to recalls a strange car in the street that day. They could have parked in another part of the village and walked. Or caught a bus.'

Pete snorted. 'Who goes to a murder on a bus?'

'Phone records?' Calvin asked, more in hope than expectation.

'Nothing from Geoffrey Skeet,' said King. 'If he was in touch with them, it wasn't from the Nokia. His landline records will take a couple of days, but I'm not hopeful. I think he's too careful for that, or we'd have found a list of Exiteers in his files.'

'We're running out of time', she sighed, and tapped the screen with her pen. 'Without a connection between Skeet and these two suspects, all we've got is a charming old man who knows exactly how to stay just the right side of the law.'

King glanced at her watch and grimaced, then she gave Calvin a serious look. 'Go and see Hayley Pitt.'

'Ma'am?'

'The cleaner,' she reminded him. 'Cleaners hear things. See things. Find stuff out. That's why I don't have one; they give me the bloody creeps. But if someone had a motive to kill Albert Cann, the cleaner's likely to know who.'

The Cleaner

Hayley Pitt lived in a tiny terraced cottage on the main road in Abbotsham, less than four hundred yards from the Cann house.

Calvin could hear the music spilling from the house as soon as he got out of the car, and when a woman he imagined was Hayley's mother opened the door, it got even louder. Something with a throbbing bass beat that he was already too old to identify.

Mrs Pitt shouted up the stairs for her daughter with a voice like a foghorn, then smiled cheerfully at Calvin. 'She'll be down in a mo,' she said, and showed him in to the front room, which was a colourful sea of Lego bricks with a small child bobbing in it. There were great piles of laundry on every available surface – the coffee table, the chairs, the sofa – and, from the smell, it wasn't clean. Near the window was a grey parrot in a cage, squawking so loudly that Calvin winced. The carpet all around its cage was covered in seeds and bird shit.

Mrs Pitt made no reference to the noise, the child, the parrot, or the condition of the room, which made Calvin think it was all probably the norm.

'Tea?'

'Thanks.'

'HAYLEY!'

'*What?*'

'Come down here!'

'What *for*?'

'Someone to see you!'

There was some stomping, then silence, as if Hayley had started to obey and then thought better of it halfway across the landing.

'Kids!' Mrs Pitt rolled her eyes and left to make tea.

The parrot had stopped squawking and was evaluating Calvin. Calvin nodded at it and then looked at the child. It was a boy of about eighteen months, with solemn eyes, sitting on a nappy so thick – or so full – that it was like a cushion.

Calvin never knew what to say to children, so he just nodded and said, 'All right?'

The baby opened his mouth and slowly spat three Lego bricks on to the carpet.

'Shit,' muttered Calvin and crunched across the floor to check his mouth for more choking hazards. The little boy passively allowed Calvin to run his finger around the inside of his mouth, then, as he withdrew, bit down hard.

'Shit!' Calvin's eyes watered. 'Let go!'

The boy held on, glaring at him.

'Little fucker!' Calvin hissed and glanced at the doorway. Nobody was watching. He pinched the kid's nose hard, until he opened his mouth and started bawling.

'Shut it!' said the parrot in a young girl's voice and Calvin laughed, and the parrot joined in, then out-laughed him and went on cackling for ages, only stopping on a long sigh that was so human that Calvin laughed again.

'Shut it!' said the parrot. 'No, *you* shut it!'

Nobody came to comfort the baby, who quickly stopped crying and stuffed some more Lego in his mouth. Calvin let him. He examined his finger. The kid had made good use of each and every tooth he could muster.

Calvin moved an armful of girls' clothing aside so he could sit on the sofa. Underneath the laundry was a plate with the remains of an English breakfast. A gelatinous slice of egg-white, and random baked beans. He dumped the clothes on to another similar pile, balanced the dirty plate on top of that, and sat down.

'Hiya.'

Calvin turned to see a skinny girl of about twelve at the door.

'Hayley?'

'She's upstairs doing her hair in case you're cute.'

She giggled and so did somebody behind her and Calvin felt his ears go red.

'Who are you?' he said.

'Rita. Who are you?'

'Detective Constable Bridge.'

'You a copper?'

'Yes.'

Her eyes widened with excitement. 'What's she done wrong?'

'Nothing.'

Rita pulled a disappointed face and leaned backwards into the hallway. 'He says nothing.'

Calvin could just make out another girl's voice mumbling.

'Why you here then?' Rita said.

'To ask her some questions.'

'What about?'

'Someone she cleans for.'

'Who?'

'The Cann family on Black Lane.'

Rita leaned out again and there was more hushed conversation and giggling.

Rita reappeared. 'Do they want their money back?'

Gales of laughter and Rita disappeared and didn't return.

Mrs Pitt came in with a mug of tea. There was nowhere to put it, so she just handed it to Calvin. 'She'll be down in a minute. You know what girls are like. Can't come downstairs for breakfast without a face full of make-up.'

She picked up the baby and left again. The tea was awful. Calvin looked around for somewhere to throw it or leave it. Before he could find a surface big enough, there was the sound of stomping down the stairs and Hayley appeared.

She was a chubby, pretty girl with perfect skin and a short blonde bob held back by Wonder Woman clips.

'Hayley?'

I love you, Hayley! said the parrot tenderly and the girl blushed.

'Hiya.' She plonked herself down in the armchair without bothering to move the laundry.

'I'm DC Bridge from Bideford Police.' Calvin put his mug on the floor so he could take notes. 'I understand you work for the Canns in Black Lane.'

'Yeah.' She nodded. 'Been there a while now.'

'Are you aware Albert Cann died on Tuesday?'

'Someone said it in the shop.'

There was a tiny newsagent's up the hill.

'When did you last see Albert?'

'Monday.'

'How was he then?'

Hayley made a face. 'I dunno. The same?'

'The same as what?'

'Always?'

Calvin tried again. 'So what kind of person was he?'

'He's all right.' She shrugged. 'To me, anyway. Always moaning about this and that, but I brung his booze for him, and helped him with the computer and stuff.'

'What was his tipple?'

'Gin.'

'How much did he drink?'

She widened her eyes. 'A *lot*.'

Ooooo, said the parrot, full of judgement.

Calvin underlined 'lot' twice. 'And what would he moan about?'

She shrugged. 'Just the usual. Money and stuff.'

'How'd you get on with Skipper?'

'Good.' She shrugged again. 'I always make 'em both tea or a sandwich, or cereal, 'cos Albert's rubbish at cooking.'

'That's nice of you,' said Calvin.

'Yeah,' she said. 'But Skipper don't eat much anyway 'cos of the cancer.'

'How about Reggie? You get on with him?'

'Yep,' she nodded.

'And how'd they all get on with each other?'

'Fine,' she said, yawning. 'Far as I can see.'

'Did you know about Skipper planning to kill himself?'

'No.' She hesitated. 'But I seen his will.'

'Where was it?'

'By the bed.'

'His bed?'

'Yeah.'

'When was that?'

'Monday.'

'Did you discuss it?'

'He were asleep.'

'But you read it?'

She hesitated, then shrugged. 'Well, I never seen one before.'

Calvin winked at her. 'Did he leave you anything?'

'Nah.' Hayley yawned loudly without covering her mouth, and stretched, showing her belly button. Calvin tried not to smile. For some reason, her youthful apathy tickled him.

'Can you remember what else was next to Skipper's bed?'

'Not really. I mean, he's always got some water and his pills and stuff. Magazines. Photos. I don't know.'

'Not a gas bottle?'

'Like Albert's?'

'Yes, but much smaller. About this big? Silver?'

She screwed up her face. 'Oh yeah. That was there.'

'Next to his bed?'

'Yeah. Thought it was a thermos flask.'

'You ever hear of the Exiteers?'

'No. What's that?'

'It's a group that helps people to kill themselves.'

Hayley's eyes widened and for the first time she sounded interested. 'Did Albert kill himself then?'

'What do you think?' he said.

'Well, he *was* pretty sick. Took ages to go up and down stairs and stuff. Still smoked, mind! Mum works at the hospice and says she sees it all the time. Puffing away with one lung and whatnot!'

'The Canns have many visitors?'

'Nah. The doctor comes, and the McDonald's nurse.'

'Macmillan?'

'Who?' she said.

'Nothing,' said Calvin. 'What about an older man? Mr Skeet? Geoffrey?'

She shook her head. 'Don't know them. But all old men look the same, don't they?'

Calvin just nodded, because unpicking her stupidity would take too much effort.

'One old man come round from social services.'

Calvin perked up. 'When was that?'

'Yesterday.'

Calvin perked down. He was interested in visitors before Albert's death. 'Do you know of any reason anyone would want to hurt Albert?'

Hayley shook her head without thinking about it.

He closed his notebook, and then remembered something that had been bugging him. 'Hey, you know the broken window in their dining room?'

'Yeah?'

'When did that happen?'

'Christmas?' She didn't seem sure.

'Christmas?' he said.

She nodded. 'Around then. It was cold. I cut my finger cleaning up the glass and Reggie drove me home.'

'Ouch,' said Calvin.

'Weren't much.'

'You know how the window got broken?'

Hayley shook her head and shrugged expansively to show she'd reached the outer limits of her knowledge.

Calvin was disappointed. The cleaner hadn't been the oracle that DCI King had hoped for. She knew Albert was a drunk and Skipper hadn't left her anything despite all the sandwiches, and that the will and the gas bottle had been in Skipper's room on Monday. But that didn't mean they couldn't have been moved to Albert's room by Tuesday. It was only two bits of paper and a can of air, not Stonehenge. Nothing Hayley had said spoke to motive, or to anything much at all, other than the fact that she was a bit thick. The only silver lining was that the bite mark on his index finger would probably win him a pint from Jackie Braddick.

He stood up. 'Well, thanks for your help, Hayley.'

'No probs.'

No probs, said the parrot in Hayley's voice.

'He's a right joker, isn't he?'

'He's a bugger,' she agreed. 'Does all our ringtones. Drives us nuts. He's only got to hear something once and he's off, aren't you, Nipper?'

The parrot cocked its head. It regarded Calvin with a gold-rimmed eye and hissed, '*Little fucker.*'

The List

'John?'

'Geoffrey!'

'How are you?'

'How are *you*? More to the point, *where* are you?'

'I'm at home.'

'They let you go?'

'Well, I just kept saying no comment until they ran out of time. Oldest trick in the book.'

Felix was impressed by Geoffrey's quiet strength. 'I must say, you've got nerves of steel.'

'Not at all,' Geoffrey said modestly. 'They obviously had nothing to connect me to the crime scene, and you and Amanda are lying low, so I knew it was only a matter of time. They've taken my files, which is annoying of course, but at the end of the day, there's nothing incriminating in them because this is not a criminal enterprise. We don't provide the instrument of death, and we're waivered up to the eyeballs.'

'Geoffrey,' said Felix hesitantly, 'I took the list of Exiteers from your cabinet. And the Cann name tag off the folder. I hope you feel it was the right thing to do.'

'I most certainly do!' said Geoffrey. 'Very sensible.'

Felix was pleased that he'd done the right thing, but he held his breath and waited for Geoffrey to ask about Buttons. He didn't, though. Probably thought Buttons was off at a neighbour's and would be home soon.

And he soon *would* be . . .

'So . . .' said Geoffrey. 'All's well.'

'Not exactly,' Felix said seriously.

'What do you mean?'

Felix stared at the woodchip, unsure of how to start. 'Have you spoken to Amanda?'

'Not yet. Why?'

'Because,' Felix started. Then stopped. Then started again. 'Well, because I saw her with Albert Cann's son.'

'*What?*'

'Albert's son. Reggie Cann. I saw them together yesterday at a café in Bideford.'

There was a stunned silence from Geoffrey before he asked, 'What did you say?'

'Nothing. I was so surprised that I didn't say anything. Just walked away before they saw me.'

'That's not . . .' Geoffrey said. 'I can't . . . Why would she . . . ?' He kept stopping, like a car turning over in cold weather but never quite catching.

'I don't know, Geoffrey,' said Felix. 'But I have to say, it just felt . . . *I* just felt as if I'd been . . . well, set up.'

'Set up? What do you mean, *set up?*'

'I mean Amanda handed Albert Cann the mask. At the time, of course, I thought it was an accident, but now I'm not so sure.'

Geoffrey muttered something that Felix couldn't quite hear, but which could easily have been an expletive. He sounded shaken to his core.

'I assume she was properly vetted,' Felix ventured.

'Of course! Elspeth checked Amanda out. Just like you. Elspeth's my most experienced and conscientious volunteer. She'd never have approved Amanda unless her motives were absolutely beyond reproach. I believe she lost her grandmother quite recently . . . ?'

'That's what she told me,' agreed Felix. 'And obviously I want to give her the benefit of the doubt, but I just don't understand why she would be meeting Reggie Cann.'

'Neither do I!' said Geoffrey angrily. 'Most ridiculous thing I've ever heard. What *was* she thinking? The stupid, *stupid* girl!'

'I'm concerned that Charles Cann might be in danger too.'

'Why would he be in danger?'

Felix hesitated. Geoffrey had been so scathing about Amanda's contact with the family that he had no desire to share the fact that he himself had been back to the house.

'Well,' he said carefully, 'if Albert's death was not an accident then somebody wanted him dead. And that somebody might want Charles Cann dead too.'

'I don't see that,' said Geoffrey. 'If somebody wanted Albert dead, then that's what they've achieved. In fact, if somebody killed Albert, then they saved the old man's life to do it. So I don't see how he's in any danger now.'

Felix nodded down the phone silently. Geoffrey's logic was unimpeachable, but he didn't have all the facts at his fingertips. Felix didn't either, but he had more facts than Geoffrey did, and couldn't shake that uneasy feeling in his gut.

'Nonetheless, Skipper Cann is only alive because *we* messed things up,' he said, 'and Albert is dead for the same reason. So I feel that it's up to us to uncover the truth.'

'Well, I don't!' Geoffrey said – and then he sighed deeply. 'Trying to uncover the truth would only expose you, John – and if it exposes you, it exposes all of us. In an ideal world you'd be right. But this is not an ideal world and I think we just have to accept that we may never know what went wrong, and move on. Better for you and better for the Exiteers, to be absolutely frank.'

'It doesn't sit well with me, Geoffrey.'

'It doesn't sit well with me either.'

'Geoffrey, I . . . I'm not sure I can do this any more.'

'But you *have* to!' said Geoffrey. 'People *need* us. Obviously *I'm* no good to them in a hands-on capacity, stuck in this bloody chair, so what I'm really saying is, people need *you*. What good does it do those people if you go to jail? What good does it do those poor men and women who are going through such torture that they'd rather take their own lives than spend another day with their friends and families? If your search for the truth ended up with your arrest, it would only hurt the very people we're trying to help.'

'But I killed the wrong man!'

'And never will again because of it!'

Felix hesitated, then murmured, 'That's true.'

'Exactly,' said Geoffrey, and Felix could hear the relief in his voice. 'Now we need to put all this unpleasantness behind us and remember we're doing very important work. Will you do that for me, John?'

'I will,' said Felix.

But he didn't.

As soon as he'd put the phone down on Geoffrey, Felix unfolded the list of names he'd taken from his house and called the first of them.

Connor didn't answer.

Felix was relieved – then immediately apprehensive again. He'd barely started. The next name down was Rupert. A man answered after the first ring.

'Good afternoon, Rupert?'

'Hello?'

'My name is John. I'm calling from the Exiteers—'

There was a short silence, then a mysterious clattering sound, and the line went dead. Felix frowned at the handset. Either Rupert had fallen down some stairs, or he didn't want to talk to him. Almost certainly the latter. Felix thought it very rude – whatever Geoffrey had told them about being wary of strangers asking about their work.

Rupert's rudeness only stiffened Felix's resolve and he called the next name on the list with barely a pause. A woman answered.

'Delia?' he said.

'Geoffrey?'

'No, this is John.' Felix spoke fast. 'Please don't hang up. I know Geoffrey told us not to speak to anyone but him about the Exiteers, but I'm an Exiteer and I really need to speak to you.'

Delia said nothing but didn't hang up, so Felix ploughed on. 'This is an odd question, Delia, but when you've been on a case, have you ever had anything go wrong?'

'Wrong?'

'Yes,' he said. He didn't want to say *how* wrong. Not right up front. 'Anybody who . . . I don't know . . . Anything out of the ordinary? At all?'

'I don't think I know what you're talking about,' Delia said warily.

Felix sighed deeply. 'I do apologize,' he said. 'I know this is an unsettling call to receive out of the blue, but I find myself in a very strange situation and I just wanted to ask other Exiteers whether they had had any similar experiences and, if so, what they might have done about it.'

'Well, that depends on what's happened, doesn't it? And whatever it is, it's certainly not something I want to discuss over the phone. Where are you?'

'Devon.'

'I'm in Bath,' she said.

'Oh dear,' he said.

'Can you meet me halfway?'

'Yes.'

'Good. Gordano services on the M5. In the coffee shop.'

'When?' said Felix.

'Wednesday?' she said. 'Two o'clock?'

'Two o'clock,' he said. 'I'm tall with grey hair.'

'I'm not,' she said.

'Goodbye then.'

'Goodbye.'

Felix hung up the phone and adrenaline squirted him out of his chair. He paced up and down the hallway. He'd disobeyed orders. Geoffrey had told him to leave it and he'd said that he would, but he *hadn't*. He felt terribly disloyal and anxious.

And a little bit excited.

He'd just arranged an assignation in some truckers' caff with a co-conspirator. Like spies under a town-hall clock! It was heady stuff. He couldn't stand still, and limped aimlessly from room to room until he noticed that it had started to rain, whereupon he filled a bucket with hot soapy water and went out to the driveway to wash the car so that the rain would rinse the suds away for free.

When he'd finished, he went inside to find Mabel cowering in the corner of the kitchen, but didn't understand why until half an hour later when he carried his fish fingers and tea on a tray into the front room and found Buttons reclining on the sofa like Nero.

Felix set down the tray and picked up the cat.

It dug its claws into him so hard that he dared not even try to shake it off, for fear it would peel his arm right through his jumper. It was all he could do to stagger through the house, fumble the back door open, flick his arm and shout, *Out!*

Buttons hit the ground without a sound, twisted around and jumped lithely on to the kitchen table. Mabel cringed behind Felix's legs, while he glared at Buttons nervously. Then he remembered his dinner was getting cold.

He left the back door open, edged past the table with the scuttling Mabel, shut the kitchen door firmly and returned to the lounge.

But he barely saw *Countdown* or tasted his fish fingers, so jumpy was he that the cat would suddenly appear in the doorway.

Somehow in boots, and with a rapier.

The Ex

'Got the toxicology results on Albert Cann,' said DCI King.

Calvin looked up. He was two-thirds of the way through the Exiteer files and was bored to tears. For once, he welcomed a chat about death.

'There was Oxycodone in his system,' King said. 'Not prescribed by his doctor.'

Calvin and Pete exchanged frowns. Oxycodone was a hardcore opioid.

'Does the old man take it?' said Pete.

King shook her head. 'Nope, only morphine.'

'Is it what killed Albert?' asked Pete.

'No, the nitrous oxide did that. But the fact that he had it in his system at all concerns me. Oxy would certainly have made him drowsy and disorientated.'

'Hayley Pitt said Albert was a big drinker and smoker,' said Calvin. 'Maybe he had other addiction issues.'

'I wondered that, but I called Reggie and he said not.' King took a jar of olives from her top desk drawer and dug one out with a gallstone scoop she kept for the purpose. 'Any luck with the dentist, Pete?'

'Still trying,' Pete sighed. 'The British Dental Association has nine hundred dentists called Williams on their books.'

King sighed and put her olives away. 'Black suits all round on Wednesday for the funeral.'

Calvin frowned. 'I don't have a black suit.'

'That one'll have to do,' King said. 'Got a black tie?'

'No.'

'Get one. It won't be wasted. Not in this job.'

'Yes, ma'am.'

It was lunchtime so Calvin decided to go and get one now, but buying a black tie in Bideford High Street was harder than he'd thought it would be. Very few of the shops sold anything real any more. There was the bookshop, the newsagent's and a bunch of charity shops. Finally he bought a tie from Barnardo's for the princely sum of forty pence.

Then he popped into the bookies in the hope that Rumbaba had been declared a non-runner. Dennis Matthews would still lose his £500, but at least it wouldn't be his fault.

He nodded at Shifty on the step. Inside, Old Greybeard was already at the wall reading the *Racing Post*. She made space for him, but the only mention of Rumbaba Calvin could see was a brief quote from the trainer who assessed the colt's chances in buoyant terms. *If he comes round the Corner, he's got a great shot.*

Calvin shook his head. If he comes round the Corner? The Corner at the foot of a steep hill and on a bad camber? The Corner that a three-year-old horse had to be perfectly balanced, bold beyond its years, and insanely lucky to navigate? For God's sake – Tattenham Corner *was* the bloody Derby! Horses that swept around it with ease were the only ones with a fighting chance at the business end of the race.

The trainer of the favourite said the horse was 'as balanced a colt as I've ever seen' and the owner of the Dewhurst winner said he'd told every lad in the yard to stake a week's wages on their charge. Yet here was Rumbaba's trainer with *nothing*. No revelation that he'd worked the horse down hills all winter. No strategy to keep him out of trouble. No reassurances that the colt was mentally prepared for the most challenging flat race in the world.

Just a big fat IF. Like some miserable punter.

'. . . zavool,' muttered Old Greybeard.

'Pardon?' said Calvin, and she poked the report with a long yellow fingernail and repeated, 'Man's a fool. Tattenham Corner *is* the bloody Derby!'

'Exactly,' Calvin said. 'I've got that at twenties.'

Old Greybeard ran a finger across Rumbaba's form and made a noise between a huff and a snort.

'What's your tip then?'

'Don't tip no more,' she grumbled. 'Not since some fool put silly money on a horse I give him.'

Calvin raised a sardonic eyebrow. 'What's silly money?' He'd seen Old Greybeard's betting slips. She probably thought silly money was a pound on the nose.

But she didn't answer his question. Instead she glared at him. 'Have the courage of your own convictions, bay. Make your own mistakes. Anything else is just ego and ignorance.'

Calvin shifted uncomfortably. *Ego and ignorance.* Did she know about him and Dennis Matthews?

'Don't worry,' she muttered, 'you'll still get poor without me.' And she shuffled back to her seat.

Before Calvin could decide what to do next, the door opened and Reggie Cann came in.

They looked at each other in surprise.

Reggie had a black eye, a red nose and a split lip.

'What happened to you?'

Reggie touched his nose self-consciously. 'Had a bump in the car.'

'Everyone all right?'

'Yeah, yeah,' said Reggie. 'Just me, the car and a lamp post. I wasn't paying attention. Suppose I was distracted by everything that's going on . . .'

'Understandable,' Calvin nodded, but he wondered what the hell Reggie Cann was doing here, looking as jittery as hell.

As if he'd read his mind, Reggie jabbed a thumb at the door behind him. 'I only came in to dodge my ex. We broke up. I told her it's over but she can't let it go. Keeps calling me. Turned into a bit of a nut, you know?'

Calvin *did* know. Shirley had turned into a bit of a nut too, after he'd told her they weren't getting married. Admittedly, she had been right in the middle of finalizing the wedding invitations, but a week later she'd come to the station to try to embarrass him with a box of porn he'd left in her flat. Calvin had had to set Tony Coral on her: he could bore the pants on to any woman.

Even now, if she spotted Calvin from any distance, Shirley made a point of glowering at him. And if she were with somebody else, she'd turn to them and say something, and then *that* person would glower at him too, which made him feel like a bad person – which he knew he wasn't – so if he ever spotted Shirley before she spotted him, he always just hid.

Which was exactly what Reggie Cann was doing right now, so Calvin felt joined to him in a sort of brotherhood of avoidance and denial.

'Well, these things take time,' he said sagely, as if he were wise to the ways of women.

'Because women don't like to come into the bookies, do they?'

Calvin glanced over at Old Greybeard. 'No,' he said, 'they don't.'

There was an awkward little silence.

'Any progress with the case?' asked Reggie.

'If you give DCI King a call, she'll be able to update you,' said Calvin.

'Sure,' said Reggie. 'Of course. Thanks.'

'You sure you're all right?'

'Yeah, yeah. Thanks.' Reggie pushed open the door and leaned off the step.

'Who you looking for?' said Shifty.

'My girlfriend,' said Reggie.

Shifty peered off the step helpfully. 'What she look like?'

'It's all right,' said Reggie. 'I don't see her anywhere.' He turned and gave Calvin a thumbs-up and then left.

Calvin stepped outside after Reggie and watched him hurry down the hill and turn into Mill Street.

He wasn't sure he believed him about the car. Or about the girlfriend . . .

He flinched as Shifty puffed smoke and the single word *Women!* into his ear – as if the two of them were above all that nonsense.

But Calvin wasn't above it at all. For the first time he wondered if spending so much time in a place where women didn't like to go might be a bad way to find one.

He had time to have a bet, but headed back to work instead.

Halfway down the High Street he nodded to Dennis Matthews, who was lumbering up the hill with his piles cushion under one beefy arm.

Calvin fingered the black tie in his pocket and thought about death.

The Wire

The coffee shop on the M5 was a Starbucks, not the greasy-spoon caff that Felix had imagined. He ordered a tea and a slice of Victoria sponge that was so big that when it was handed to him he remarked that it was enough for six men and a boy, which only confused the girl behind the counter, who asked him if he wanted another fork.

'Oh no,' he said, but she continued to frown at him anxiously until he told her he was only joking.

'Ohhhh,' she nodded, and smiled as if she'd suddenly got it, and a little of the spy excitement left Felix as he was reminded that he was a very old man in a very young world. That was confirmed when he realized that the tea wasn't going to come in a pot, but was just a bag dropped into a mug of hottish water. He sat down and watched it bobbing on the surface like a corpse, and hoped very much that Delia was not a young woman.

He was in luck. Delia was at least sixty, and as broad as she was long, with wild grey hair, and a string of pearls so tight around her thick neck that they made her look like an escaped bulldog.

'John?' she said and then, as he half rose, 'What a huge piece of cake!'

'Six men and a boy!' he said.

'You can say that again!'

'Shall I get another fork?'

'Lovely,' she said.

Felix was relieved that she seemed more friendly in person than she had on the phone. He came back to the table with a cup of tea and a fork, which she immediately put to good use.

'Thank you for coming.'

'Well,' she nodded, 'I'm not sure it's a good idea. You could be a plant.'

'A plant?'

'Undercover police or something. Wearing a wire.'

'No, no,' said Felix reassuringly, but inside he quivered at the very idea. Maybe he should have worn a wire? Maybe *Delia* was wearing a wire!

'Are *you* wearing a wire?' he asked.

'Goodness, no!' She laughed loudly. 'Why would we want to wear a wire? We're not doing anything wrong!' Then she looked around furtively and leaned into him and hissed, 'Are we?'

'Actually,' said Felix cautiously, 'this is what I wanted to speak to you about. Things that go wrong . . .'

He looked at her meaningfully but she only shrugged. 'Things do go wrong. They're bound to sooner or later, aren't they? Sod's law.'

'Of course,' said Felix, relieved.

Delia went on. 'Back last year, I was on a job in Bath. Chap I was working with stole the ring off a dead woman's finger.'

A week ago Felix would have been shocked beyond belief. Now he just said, 'What did you do?'

'Nothing official because I didn't *see* it happen. But it was on the client's finger before she died, and afterwards it was gone. I always notice a nice ring.'

Felix glanced down at Delia's hands. They were small and delicate for such a large woman, and she wore a diamond that would have choked a horse.

'Did you tell Geoffrey?'

'You bet your bottom dollar I did! He was absolutely *fuming.* He said he'd take care of it, and he did. Called me not even a day later to say that the ring had been returned to the family.'

'And what about the thief?'

'Said he'd taken care of him too. It was the first and last time I saw him. I imagine he was, you know . . .' Delia jerked a thumb over her shoulder.

'I certainly hope so!'

'Dreadful affair,' said Delia. 'Put me off for a bit, but then, you get bad apples everywhere, don't you?'

'I suppose you do.' Felix frowned.

Delia sipped her tea. 'So what happened to you?'

'Well,' he said, and then stopped and took a long calming breath before going on. 'A few days ago I was with a new colleague – Amanda, she called herself . . .' He glanced at Delia. 'Do you know her?'

'Never heard of her.'

'Young. Dark hair. Sensible eyebrows . . . ?' He looked hopefully at Delia but she shook her head.

'Well, it's probably not her real name. Is Delia your real name?'

'Of course not,' said Delia. 'Is John yours?'

'No,' said Felix. 'Well, anyway, the thing is . . . the client was in great distress—'

'Terrible, isn't it?' said Delia. 'When that happens.'

'And he couldn't reach the mask, you see?'

'Oh dear.' Delia nodded warily as if she knew what was coming.

'It was on the bedside table and he couldn't reach it and he sort of knocked it on to the floor . . .'

'Oh dear!'

'And anyway, to cut a long story short, this Amanda panicked and before I could stop her she sort of *handed* the mask to him—'

'Well, that's not good,' muttered Delia through a mouthful of sponge, 'but it happens. She'll learn. No harm done, really.'

'Well, yes,' said Felix awkwardly. 'And no.'

She looked up at him. 'And no?'

'Yes. Because . . .'

He stopped.

'Because what?'

'Because then. Well . . . we discovered it was . . . umm. The wrong man.'

Delia stopped chewing and looked at him like a deer in headlights.

'The *wrong man*?'

'Yes,' said Felix.

'You killed the *wrong man*?'

Felix blushed hotly and looked furtively about in case anyone had heard. Delia was the first person he'd told apart from Geoffrey, but she wasn't at all understanding. In fact, she looked aghast. Appalled. Maybe even angry.

'No, no, no!' he said, backtracking. 'Not *killed*! My goodness, no – that *would* be truly dreadful. But nearly, you see? I mean, I stopped it in time, but it could easily have happened. And it made me so worried, you see? Because if he *had* died, then where would we stand? Where would *I* stand? Where would we *all* stand? That's why I called you, because it's just something I'd never thought of before, but this made me think of it. It made me think of *all* of us, and how vulnerable we *all* are if something like that *were* ever to happen. Aren't we? And that's why I wanted to know *if* – God forbid – something like that were to happen, what would we do? What would Geoffrey do? What would *you* do?'

He was babbling, so he stopped, but he'd blown it. Delia's cheerful demeanour had been replaced by a suspicious frown and she was glancing around as if looking for the exit.

'Well,' she said, 'I really have no idea.'

'Oh,' said Felix. 'No matter then.'

'Why don't you call Geoffrey? I'm sure he'll take care of everything.'

'Yes. Good idea. I'll do that,' said Felix miserably.

'I should be going,' said Delia, getting up. 'Don't want to hit rush hour.'

It was two thirty.

'Of course,' he said, standing politely. He didn't try to reason with her or stop her. She wanted to go and he wanted her gone. He wished he'd never called her and felt dreadfully exposed and vulnerable.

'Thank you for coming, Delia,' he said. 'You've been a big help.'

She flapped him back down into his seat, and Felix imagined it was because she didn't want to risk a maniac walking her to her car.

Following her to her car.

He demurred and sat – even though he'd only have to get up again in a minute or two – and watched Delia bustle past the big windows and hurry across the car park, head down and bulldog legs working overtime to get away from him.

So much for all for one and one for all . . .

Felix was on his own.

The Funeral

Two weeks after the death of Albert Cann, DCI King, Pete Shapland and Calvin Bridge walked from the police station along Nunnery Walk to St Mary's Church and filed in separately. They sat with strangers. Possibly with killers. Hoping for a twitch, a flush, a furtive glance – anything that might indicate guilt beyond that which everybody felt on the death of a loved one that they hadn't visited enough, or spent enough on, or cared enough about.

It was a long shot, but Calvin had learned that this job was a combination of methodical slog and ridiculous chance.

He looked around at the sombre gathering of mostly middle-aged people in their Sunday best. Reggie was in the first pew, alone. Old Charles Cann wasn't here. Skipper. Poor old boy must be too sick to come to his own son's funeral.

There were thirty or forty people in attendance, but they were lost in the church, which was big on the outside and seemed even bigger on the inside, with towering pillars and arches and vast dark recesses where the light from the tall thin windows could not reach – filtered as it was through a stained-glass Jesus and his many colourful miracles.

The congregation huddled at the front of the church, which only accentuated how many pews remained unfilled. Albert Cann's coffin was laid alongside the ornate wooden font, which somehow felt either very wrong or very right – the cradle-to-grave circle of life summed up in a simple, sobering diorama. Like *The Lion King*, but with songs that were thinly sung and started late. *Rise up! Rise up!* they all sang loudly, then tailed off into *lalalala something something lala something LORD.*

Calvin only mouthed the hymns, and used them as an opportunity to look around him at people reading the words they didn't know. Everybody seemed to be behaving the way they should if they hadn't killed Albert Cann.

The vicar was a large, blue-nosed man in his sixties, with lustrous grey hair in a bouffant unbecoming to his humble calling. He started off talking about Albert Cann in conventional, if impersonal, terms – his long years of service to carpets and his later ill health – but with surprising ease he worked his way up to the coming of the Beast.

Calvin was taken aback but nobody else seemed perturbed by the apocalyptic turn of events. Most people were examining their fingernails or flicking through the order of service for coming attractions. Spoiler alert: there were none.

But even pestilence and famine couldn't outweigh the need to eat free food off paper plates at the Royal Mail, and they all mumbled their last hymn and then filed past the coffin and out of the door, where Reggie stood beside the vicar to shake hands with mourners.

Thank you for coming. Thank you for coming. So nice to see you. Thank you for coming.

Calvin joined the queue behind a woman who was so short that he could have leaned an elbow on her head. It was only when she stepped forward to take Reggie Cann's hand that he was stunned to see that it was Old Greybeard – brushed, plucked, scrubbed and de-anorakked for the occasion. She wore a flowery dress under a long navy jacket. She wore shiny blue court shoes with a tiny heel. She wore white gloves, like the Queen, or the Queen's fussy butler.

She gripped Reggie's hand and stared up into his eyes, but

Calvin saw no flicker of recognition from him. *Thank you for coming*, he said, and was already sliding his eyes to the left to see who was next in this awkward line-up.

But Old Greybeard didn't let go of his hand and move on to the vicar. She said something that Reggie had to bend to hear. Then he straightened up and looked uncomfortable, and Calvin could tell that their hands were connected now only because Old Greybeard was holding on tight. She put up a hand as if she might touch Reggie's face and he blinked and swayed away from the contact. She finally released him and moved on – passing the vicar without a glance and walking haphazardly down the drive, like someone who'd forgotten where she'd parked her car. Calvin broke away from the line and started to go after her, but he slowed quickly and stopped. He couldn't rush in blindly. He hadn't heard enough to question her as a police officer, and couldn't call her a friend.

He turned back towards the church. Mourners were passing him now, heading round the corner to the pub. Kirsty King and Pete Shapland went with them. Listening. Learning . . .

Calvin walked against their tide and found Reggie standing alone at the church doors, looking grim.

'Reggie?'

His frown dissolved and he shook Calvin's hand warmly.

'You OK?'

'Yeah. You know. Thanks for coming. All of you.'

Calvin felt bad that Reggie didn't seem to know they were working. 'It's the least we could do,' he said, so as not to shatter the illusion of caring. 'Nice turnout,' he added, even though it was one of the smallest he'd seen.

'Yeah,' Reggie said. 'Some people I haven't seen for years. From school and stuff . . .'

'Funerals are like that.'

'I suppose so,' Reggie said with a nod.

'Skipper couldn't make it?'

Reggie shook his head. 'He hasn't been downstairs in months.'

'Who'll look after him now while you're at work?'

'Dunno.' Reggie shook his head. 'I'll sort something out.'

'What about the cleaner? Is she flexible?'

'What do you mean?'

'With the hours she can work.'

'Oh, yeah. I think so.'

'Good,' said Calvin. 'Hey, who was the old woman in the flowery dress?'

Reggie shrugged. 'God knows.'

'I thought she was leaning in for a kiss!' said Calvin.

Reggie laughed. 'Me too!'

'What did she say?'

'She asked if Dad gave us the slip.'

Calvin frowned. 'By dying?'

'I suppose so.' He shrugged and squinted towards the pub. 'But she's right. He gave us all the bloody slip.'

Calvin detected an edge of bitterness in his voice.

'Whatever,' said Reggie. 'She's probably just here for a free sandwich.'

Calvin smiled, but he couldn't see Old Greybeard taking off her anorak and wellies for a free sandwich. 'You going to the pub?'

'Yep. You?'

'Just got to have a word with the vicar,' said Calvin. 'Be there in a bit.'

'Right,' said Reggie. 'See you later. Thanks again.'

They shook hands once more and Calvin went into the church and found the vicar putting his Bible back in the pulpit.

'Nice service,' he said.

'Glad you enjoyed it.'

Calvin wondered if he was being sarcastic as well, but went on, 'Can I ask you, Vicar, all that fire and brimstone stuff – is that standard? Or specially for Albert Cann?'

The vicar didn't look at Calvin. He busied himself with his Bible and notes. 'I always say that people take from a service whatever it is they need to hear. I merely channel the word of God. *He* ensures it reaches the right ears.'

'Did you know Albert?'

'I knew *of* Albert.'

'In what way?'

'In the way people in small towns know of other people in small towns,' said the vicar.

There was an uncomfortable silence while Calvin wondered how much the vicar knew about *him*. Then he thanked him and went outside.

There was nobody there now, not even in the car park. Calvin walked past Reggie Cann's little red Mazda. Reggie hadn't lied about the bump – the Mazda's offside wing mirror was hanging by wires alone.

Calvin continued to the pub, where, despite the free sandwiches, Old Greybeard was nowhere to be seen.

The Stick

The vacuum cleaner was loud, the TV even louder.

'Look!' Hayley shouted proudly. 'I'm cleaning!'

'Well done,' Felix shouted back. 'Looks marvellous.' It didn't really, but at least she wasn't sitting on the sofa, crying into her crisps.

She turned the vacuum off and Felix said, 'I brought Charles a new stick.'

'Skipper!' she said. 'Nobody calls him Charles.'

'Right,' said Felix. 'Is he in?'

'Yep. In bed.'

The vacuum roared back into life as Felix went upstairs. Mabel trotted into the bedroom ahead of him.

Skipper Cann looked around from his bed at the window and said weakly, 'And who are you?'

Felix stopped nervously at the door. 'I'm Felix.'

'I was talking to the dog,' Skipper said, and Felix relaxed a little. 'Her name is Mabel.'

Mabel wagged at the sound of her own name, and the little black-and-tan dog jumped off the bed to greet her.

'Hello, Mabel,' the old man said. 'That there's Toff and I'm Skipper.'

'Hello, Skipper. I was here the other day. When you fell.'

'I didn't fall. Bloody stick broke.'

'That's why I brought you a new one.'

Felix crossed the room and held out the stick. It was Margaret's, and had been next to the front door since she'd died. Felix hadn't moved it because sometimes when he saw it, for a fleeting moment he could fool himself that his wife was still in the house, and that if he only walked into the front room he might find her there, reading or doing cross-stitch. He'd miss those moments now, but he felt sure that Margaret would want Skipper Cann to have her stick, because it was part of making things right.

Skipper took it from him and examined it suspiciously. 'Do I have to pay for it?'

'No,' said Felix.

'Who pays for it then?'

'Nobody pays for it,' said Felix. 'Social services.'

'Well, which is it? Nobody? Or social services?'

'Social services. I only meant, *you* don't have to pay for it.'

Skipper observed him with an icy blue eye from under a frosted brow, then glared at the stick, as if he might not want it if it was free. He looked at it from all angles and banged it on the side of the bed several times and finally he nodded and held out his hand, and Felix went to shake it.

But instead of shaking his hand, Skipper gripped it like a vice and dragged him closer so he could look him square in the face.

'I *thought* it was you,' he hissed, and hit him with the stick.

Felix lurched backwards, trying to yank his hand free.

'Wait!' he cried. 'Wait!'

But Skipper didn't wait and Skipper didn't let go. Skipper stumbled awkwardly out of bed, helped by his wincing grip on Felix's hand, and when he'd achieved his feet, he hit him again. Harder this time, and on the head.

'You killed my boy!' he yelled, while Toff and Mabel yapped and circled them. 'You killed Albert!'

'The gas was in the wrong place!' cried Felix. 'It was a mistake!'

'A mistake?' hissed Skipper hoarsely. 'You killed my son!'

Felix shielded his head and the man hit him in the elbows while he tried to grab the stick, but without any luck. He had never been in a fight before and knew he was making a very bad job of the one he was in now. He could have pushed Skipper Cann over, but even through the fog of war, he didn't want to hurt him. However, that kindness was doing him no favours. Skipper was older than him and terribly frail. But he was also *enraged* – whereas Felix was only sorry he'd ever come.

He finally gripped the business end of the walking stick and tried to wrestle it away from his assailant in a series of jerks that only succeeded in unbalancing them both and – after an odd, tottering tango around the end of the bed – they both fell over and hit the floor with matching grunts.

Felix lay breathless, looking at the yellowing ceiling, while Mabel panted foully on his face and the sound of the TV and vacuum cleaner leaked loudly through the floor. Felix turned his head fractionally, grimacing at a dart of pain in his neck, to see the old man lying beside him, staring blankly upwards. For a dreadful moment Felix thought he'd killed him this time, but then Skipper blinked, and he breathed a long sigh of relief.

'I came to say I'm sorry.'

'Bollocks to your sorry,' wheezed Skipper. 'You can take your sorry and shove it up your arse.'

Felix nodded at the ceiling. It was stippled Artex, with thousands of tiny meringue stalactites dripping from it.

'We should get up,' he sighed. 'Can you get up?'

Skipper said nothing.

'I hope *I* can,' Felix muttered. It had been a long time since he'd got up off the floor. It took him a few goes but he finally rolled on to his side and then his elbows, and from there he managed to lever himself up on his hands and get one knee, and then one foot, underneath him and, using the chest of drawers, hauled himself to his feet like an infant.

'Made it,' he panted with satisfaction. He turned and reached a hand out to Skipper, who slapped it away, but then made no effort to get up under his own steam – just lay there with his pyjama top popped open from the struggle, showing his pale, bony chest.

Felix put out his hand again. 'Come on,' he said. 'Let me help you.'

Skipper Cann ignored his hand. 'I fell asleep,' he said. 'I don't know why. I was waiting for you and then I just . . . fell asleep.'

Felix slowly withdrew his hand. The older man went on tentatively, as if he was discovering all this for the first time.

'I should've heard you come in for the gas. Could've stopped you. But I fell asleep and now . . . now they're burying Albert . . .' Skipper started to cry – a hoarse, dry sound that betrayed years of neglect in the machinery of weeping.

Felix sat down on the bed.

Toff crept over to his prone master and lay pressed against his ribs while he wheezed and rattled. Tears oiled his eyes, drained away through the ancient wrinkles, and dripped from his cheeks on to the swirly green rug. Felix wished he would stop sobbing because he was starting to feel the pressure in his own eyes that he remembered so well from Jamie's funeral, and beyond.

Not now, he told himself fiercely. *Not now*.

'I understand,' he said. 'I lost my son too.'

'I don't care about *your* son,' said Skipper. 'I care about *my* son.'

Of course he did – and Felix felt ashamed that he'd thought it might help to tell him about Jamie. Of course it wouldn't help. Nothing would help. Not even time, whose billing as a great healer was vastly overrated, in his experience. So he said nothing more – just stared through the window at the fuzzy fields and the misty sky beyond them while behind him Skipper Cann cried himself down to a sniff and a sigh.

When all was finally still once more, Felix held out his hand again to his fallen foe. 'Come on,' he said. 'Don't be daft.'

This time Skipper lifted his hand and Felix helped him to sit and then – with grunts and staggers from the pair of them – grappled him upright and steered him back to his bed, where they both plumped down, catching their breath. Toff jumped up between them and looked from one to the other like a nervous umpire, alert to transgressions.

Felix took out his hanky and blew his nose, while Skipper hung his head over his own flaccid chest. His pyjamas hung open off the knives of his shoulders. He took for ever to find a button and then a buttonhole and then to fumble one through the other.

'I'm outta shape,' he wheezed, 'or I'da ripped you apart.'

Felix nodded as if that were true. Then he said gently, 'You've done those up wrong.'

Skipper stared down at his lopsided pyjamas for a long, long time, chewing his gums.

'I used to be something,' he whispered. 'Now I'm nothing.'

Felix felt jolted by the familiar.

Without you I am nothing . . .

They were both nothing. Two old men who'd outlived their usefulness. Often Felix wondered how useful he'd ever been.

Fixit Felix.

He could fix a fence, but he couldn't fix Jamie; couldn't stop Margaret's descent into hell . . .

'I brought this to show you.' Felix retrieved Skipper's broken walking stick from where he'd dropped it in the fracas.

Felix held it out to him but Skipper made no move to take it.

'See the break? Here? It looks to me as if it's been sawn through.'

Skipper glanced at it and looked away. 'So?'

'I just thought . . .' Felix stopped and sighed. 'I'm only trying to help.'

Skipper shrugged. 'You got any more of that gas with you?'

'No.'

'Then you're no help to me.'

Skipper looked out of the window at the near horizon of hills that blocked his view of the sea. 'Get me back in bed.'

Felix picked up the older man's featherlight legs, and pivoted him slowly on his backside until he was propped back on his pillows, then covered him with the rumpled blankets. He held on to the footboard to steady himself as he folded over to pick up Margaret's walking stick for the last time. He laid it on the bed and Skipper gripped the handle and Felix didn't flinch. If the old man hit him again, well . . . he probably deserved it.

'Come on, Mabel.'

She trotted to the door and Felix followed her and reached for the handle.

'He said it'd be quick.'

Felix turned. 'Pardon?'

The old man chewed his gums for a moment, then found the words. 'Geoffrey said. With that gas . . .'

Felix felt ashamed again. He wasn't the only one who needed answers to important questions. 'Very quick,' he said. 'And completely painless.'

Skipper didn't look at him. He jerked his chin almost imperceptibly at the sky. 'Still . . .' he said.

Felix understood. *Still* the son was dead. *Still* the father was alive, and both of those things were still his fault.

'I'm truly sorry,' he said, but Skipper just kept looking out of the window. The rage in him had burned off, and left behind only sad, grey ashes.

'Get out,' he said wearily. 'If you come here again, I'll kill you.'

When he got home, Felix studied the lump on his head in the bathroom mirror. It was just where his hairline used to be, and had a nasty cut in the middle.

He pressed the lump and winced, and didn't press it again.

You should see the other guy, he thought ruefully. That was what men said, wasn't it? When they'd won a fight? Felix had never said it, of course, but he thought it was something that every man *ought* to get the chance to say, just once in his lifetime.

But there was nobody who cared enough about him to ask what had happened to his head.

And even if there had been, Felix would never have said *you should see the other guy.*

Not when the other guy had been lying on the floor, crying for his dead son.

Suspicion

Skipper Cann woke in the darkness, tingling with fear.

There was somebody in his room. A scuff on the floor. A shadow in the corner. A creak.

His hand closed around his stick. 'Who's there?'

'It's only me, Skip.'

'Where have you been?'

'Sorry I'm late.'

Skipper reached for the lamp and switched it on. 'What time is it?' He peered at the clock. Twelve fifteen. When had he gone to sleep? *How?* On the day they'd buried his son . . .

'Just gone midnight,' said Reggie. 'Did you eat?'

Skipper waved the idea of it away. He was never hungry these days. Hayley had made him a cheese sandwich at lunchtime but he hadn't touched it. The cancer was the only hungry thing about him now, eating him from the inside out, and it had had nearly all it could get.

'What are you doing?'

Reggie was at the open wardrobe, beyond the puddle of light under the bedside lamp.

'I was just putting away the tie you lent me.'

'In the dark?'

Reggie shrugged. 'Yeah, sorry. I should have just waited till morning, but I came in to make sure you were all right, so . . .'

Skipper struggled into a sitting position against his pillow. The day just gone was coming back to him, but from very far away.

This was how it happened lately, like his brain took a while to remember the way the world was.

Even when he'd rather not remember . . .

He rubbed his eyes. 'Been asleep for ages. Always bloody sleeping. Sleep for England.'

'I'll make some tea,' said Reggie.

'I'll come down,' said Skipper.

'Down*stairs*? What? Now?'

He hadn't been downstairs for a long time.

'Gimme a hand.'

Reggie helped Skipper into his slippers and a ratty old robe. Skipper smelled beer on his breath.

'You been to the pub?'

'Yeah.'

'You already bumped the car once.'

'I know, I know.'

Skipper let it go. Reggie had had a rough day.

He let his grandson help him downstairs, slowly and full of old aches and new. They stopped once and just sat on the stairs with the little dog between them, eager to go anywhere as long as it was where his master was going.

'I remember when you were small enough, I had to hold *your* hand going down these stairs.'

'Yeah?'

'Remember the sled?'

Reggie laughed. 'Yeah!'

They'd called it the sled but it was just a bit of thick cardboard from the box the washing machine had been delivered in. With a clear run Reggie could hit the front door. He'd had a clear run often enough to leave a mark, which Skipper had never painted over.

He was glad his grandson remembered it.

Good times.

They continued the descent.

In the kitchen, Reggie lowered him on to a chair and filled the kettle and put it on the hob, and Skipper smelled that winter-kitchen smell of the gas, and the tiny hiss that *just like that* made him feel like a boy again, with his mother at the stove; his socks drying on the grill; the bare bulb reflected in the black, school-morning window.

Like it was yesterday. *Better* than yesterday. Yesterday could be a bit of a blur.

Skipper cleared a space for his elbow among the detritus on the table next to the phone. 'How was the funeral?'

'Fine. It was fine.'

They didn't look at each other. Reggie cracked two eggs into a pan and they both watched them spit and splutter.

'What the vicar say?'

'Nice things.'

'Yeah?' said Skipper.

Reggie put bread in the toaster and pushed the handle down hard.

'Did the blokes from the shop go?'

'No.'

Skipper nodded.

'Why would they?' shrugged Reggie.

Skipper chewed his gums. 'Albert done the best he could, Reg.'

'His best was rubbish.'

'Bought you that car.'

'That he couldn't afford! So we're left paying his bills, as usual. Like *mugs*. You on a pension and me with a crap job. He was a shitty father, Skip, and that doesn't change just because he's dead.' Reggie rattled open a drawer. 'Where's the fucking forks? *Shit!*'

He found a fork and slammed the drawer shut. The toast popped up. He tossed it on to a plate and squashed it roughly under butter.

Skipper just watched him. Toff jumped on to his lap and he stroked the dog's ears. 'Fella came to see me today.'

'Yeah? Who?'

'The one who done it.'

'Done what?'

Skipper jerked a thumb at the ceiling. 'The Exiteer.'

Reggie stopped. 'He came *back*?'

Skipper nodded. 'Said he were sorry. Said it were a mistake. Then we had a fight.'

'You *what*?' Reggie was aghast. 'You had a *fight*? What *kind* of a fight?'

'A fight fight. I were going to make a citizen's arrest. I woulda had him too, 'cept I'm out of shape from being stuck in bed for so long. But I got him a couple of good whops with my new stick!'

'What new stick?'

'He brung me a new stick.'

Reggie frowned. 'Why?'

'Old one broke. He says it were deliberate.'

'Did you call the police?'

'About the stick?'

'About the fight! About the man who killed Dad!'

Skipper shook his head. 'I took a pill after. Knocked me out till just now. You do it, Reg. My teeth are upstairs.' He held out the telephone.

Reggie took it. 'That woman copper said that right off the bat, you know? That it might have been a mistake. Can't believe the cheeky bastard came back though.'

Skipper nodded. 'Are you calling or what?'

'Yeah.' Reggie patted his pockets. 'I've got that card she gave me somewhere. It's got a direct line on it. What did he look like?'

'Taller than me. Big fella. And a lot younger too!'

'How young?'

'Oh, I don't know,' said Skipper with a dismissive wave. 'But he had a dog.'

'A *dog*?'

'Called Mabel.'

An uneasy silence descended on Reggie Cann. 'Mabel?' he said.

'You don't believe me!' said Skipper.

'I *do*.'

'Call then!'

'I *will*.' Reggie put a card on the counter and peered at it as he dialled. He asked for DCI King but she wasn't there, so he asked for Detective Constable Shapland instead and recounted the story while Skipper watched him closely.

'Did he say his name?' Reggie asked him.

'No.'

'What colour hair did he have?'

'Grey,' said Skipper.

'Grey,' Reggie told Shapland.

'Balding.'

'Balding where?'

'On his head.'

'No, from the front or a patch in the middle or what?'

'The front. And tell him about the stick.'

'Yeah, apparently Skipper's stick broke and this bloke said it had been sawn through. No, I haven't seen it . . . Where's the stick now, Skip?'

'I think he took it with him.'

Reggie rolled his eyes before relaying that information, then he said goodbye and thank you and rang off.

'What did he say?' said Skipper.

'Said it was really helpful. He said the description's so specific that if he's in their files they're sure to find him.'

'*If* he's in their files,' said Skipper warily. 'And if he's not?'

'They'll get him, Skip, don't you worry. Best to leave it to the police now. They've got all the details.' He handed Skipper tea in his favourite mug:

FISHERMEN HAVE MUGS <u>*THIS BIG*</u>*!*

Then he slid the eggs out of the pan and on to the toast. 'You want me to take you back to bed?'

'I'm all right for a bit,' said Skipper. 'Thank you.'

'I'm going to watch telly. You coming?'

Skipper shook his head. 'I'll sit for a bit.'

Reggie stood for a long moment, staring at his eggs.

'Are you going to try again, Skip?'

'What?'

'You know what.'

Skipper thought about it hard, then shook his head. 'Not before I find out what happened to Albert.'

Reggie nodded again, then disappeared, and Skipper heard the TV go on. Canned laughter.

He sat and sipped his tea.

When he'd finished his tea, he just sat.

Looked at the phone. Looked at the card.

Finally he picked up both. He tilted the card to the light and held it at arm's length.

BIDEFORD POLICE

DCI KIRSTY KING

DS PETER SHAPLAND

01237 908809

Skipper peered at the phone and then hit REDIAL.

There was a brief tone, three rings . . .

And then the speaking clock told him it was twelve thirty-eight precisely.

The Bad Apple

The morning after the fight, Felix knocked on Miss Knott's door.

He couldn't remember the last time he'd done that. It might have been Christmas nine or ten years ago. Margaret had asked him to take round some mince pies because she'd used an old recipe and made too many for the two of them. Felix remembered he'd protested. Why would Miss Knott want their mince pies? Wouldn't she have her own mince pies? She wasn't a charity case! But Margaret had ignored every argument and piled a cake tin full of pies in his arms and bustled him out of the door in the sleet, and – of course – Miss Knott had been very pleased. Felix hadn't gone in, even though she'd asked him to have a sherry – but he had glimpsed a tree and a hallway festooned with lights and old-fashioned paper chains, of the kind they'd made too, when Jamie was small. They didn't make them now. Why would they? They only had a tree because Margaret insisted – even though each bauble was a memory of their son. The snowman, the reindeer, the elf. The only chocolate coin Jamie had ever managed not to eat . . .

Miss Knott opened the door with a smile. Then her eyes widened. 'Oh my goodness! What happened to you?'

Felix touched the lump on his head and reddened. 'Oh,' he said. 'It's nothing.' But before he could stop her, Miss Knott had him sitting at the kitchen table and was dousing his head with Dettol, while keeping up a running commentary of exactly what was coming next. The Dettol stung like billy-o but she kept dabbing at the cut even after Felix told her he'd washed it (which wasn't true), and then she covered it with gauze and a big square Elastoplast and it turned out she'd been an A&E nurse, which Felix had never known, but for which he was very grateful.

'Better?' asked Miss Knott.

'Yes, thank you,' said Felix.

Now she said, 'Did you get that mark out of your nice jacket?'

Felix was thrown. 'Mark?'

'The, um, mascara.'

'Actually, no,' he said. 'It's quite stubborn.'

In fact the beige jacket had come out of the wash looking just the same as it had going in. He had no idea whether it could be saved.

'Mustard powder and vinegar,' said Miss Knott. 'Make a paste and rub it in before washing. Or bring it round and I'll see what I can do.'

Felix wasn't sure about that. He'd always thought of laundry as rather an intimate thing. Certainly too familiar to share with a neighbour.

'I'll give it a go, thank you, Miss Knott. Now, in the meantime, I wondered whether I might use your telephone?'

'Of course,' she said. 'Is yours broken?'

'No,' said Felix, 'but I'm in a rather odd situation. I have to call somebody but I don't want them to know that it's me who is calling them, so it occurred to me that I might call them from another telephone.'

Felix feared Miss Knott would ask all sorts of awkward questions that he wouldn't want to answer, but she didn't ask a single one. Instead she led him through to the front room and patted the back of a big wing chair.

'You sit yourself down. The phone's right there. I'll leave you in peace and make us a nice cup of tea. How do you take it?'

Felix didn't want a cup of tea, but what could he say? 'Just a dash of milk, thank you, Miss Knott.'

She left the room and he sat down. The wing chair was remark-
ably comfortable. There was a little table either side of the
chair – one with a lamp and the television remote control on it,
and the other with the phone and a little pad, not unlike the one
he had in his own hallway, except without the tasselled pencil.
Instead there was a cheap biro. There was a paperback book, open
and face down, which almost made Felix have palpitations. He
always used a bookmark and it pained him to see a book treated so
shabbily – even a Clive Cussler. It was lucky that Margaret had
respected a book, or it could have been a very rocky fifty years.

From the kitchen he could hear Miss Knott singing. Not loudly
or showily, but almost under her breath, and missing a few words
and even some notes, as if she were singing to herself. Margaret
used to do that sometimes – sing old numbers they'd danced to
when they were courting – 'Bewitched' or 'The Way You Look
Tonight'. Miss Knott was nothing like the singer that Margaret had
been but, still, it was a cheerful sound.

He'd better call before she came back. He patted his pockets and
unfolded the paper on which he'd written Amanda's number.

Felix took a deep breath. He was very nervous. His hand shook
so hard that he had to concentrate to dial – carefully, and with
much peering. There was a clicky silence before the first ring, during which Felix noticed that Miss Knott had placed the tulip he'd
given her in a little crystal bud vase on the windowsill, and that it
had opened into a wonderful bloom. It made him feel just a little
bit less anxious.

'Hello?'

'Hello!' Felix sat upright in surprise. 'Amanda?'

'Yes, hi?'

He was flummoxed. He hadn't expected her to answer, or to
answer so quickly, or to answer to the name Amanda. He should
have prepared better. Too late now.

'Hello,' he said again.

'Who is this?' she said.

'John,' he said. 'From Abbotsham.'

There was a short silence and so he ploughed on. 'Amanda, I know I told you I would take care of everything, and I will, but before I do, I just wanted to check a few facts with you.'

This time the silence was longer.

'I . . .' she said. 'What do you want? To check?'

Relief swamped Felix. She *wasn't* a bad apple! A bad apple would have simply hung up on him. A bad apple wouldn't have stayed on the line and asked him what he wanted to check. Poor girl was probably set up too!

He spoke quickly and quietly. 'Well, something rather strange is going on. The police apparently feel that the death we . . . *attended* . . . was caused deliberately—'

'Deliberately?'

'Well, there seem to have been some . . . discrepancies . . . For instance, Mr Cann used oxygen and the police say there was an oxygen tank in the poor man's room. I don't recall that being the case at the time, you see, and I wondered whether you did?'

'No . . . I . . . no.'

'Oh good!' he hurried on. 'And the will and the waiver were next to his bed, weren't they? I mean, I'm ninety-nine per cent sure they were, but are *you*? Because I want to make sure I'm remembering things *right*, you see? Given my age. Haha!' He could hear Amanda breathing. 'I've even been thinking of checking with a member of the family . . .'

He let it hang there, inviting her to admit that she had already done that very thing. That, however foolish it seemed, she had met Albert Cann's son and apologized and that he had explained what had happened and that *somehow* it wasn't their fault . . .

She said none of this.

'You see, Amanda, I'm a little bit concerned because, well, to be honest, this is all starting to feel a little bit like . . . a set-up.'

Felix attempted a chuckle but it was so tight and mirthless that he turned it into a little exercise in throat-clearance.

'Amanda?'

Silence.

'Hello?'

Silence.

'Hello? Amanda?'

She had hung up on him.

Felix put down the phone and dabbed at his brow with a fresh handkerchief, then looked up as Miss Knott came through the doorway with a tray laid for tea. Pot, cups, saucers, milk, biscuits . . .

He felt hot and panicky. He didn't want to be here. He needed to be somewhere else, somewhere he could think. He hauled himself out of the wing chair to take the tray from Miss Knott, but she was adept and made it to the coffee table with barely a rattle of teaspoons.

He looked at his watch. 'I can't be long,' he said, although he had no idea of what he was going to do after he left, other than panic in his own house.

'Of course,' she said. 'Now you sit down and I'll be mother.'

Felix sat and sweated while she fussed with the pot and a sieve, and then poured a cup of tea and handed it to him. It was beautifully red and thin, just the way he liked it.

'Biscuit?'

'Excuse me?'

'Biscuit?'

'Oh. Yes. Sorry, Miss Knott. Miles away.'

They were good biscuits too. From a tin, rather than a packet, and covered in chocolate or bright foil wrap. Felix had to make a huge effort to concentrate on appearing normal, even if inside he was in turmoil. He reached for the least ostentatious of the biscuits.

'Have one with foil on,' ordered Miss Knott. 'It's such fun to unwrap them.'

Ridiculous, thought Felix, but took a biscuit in purple foil and *did* rather enjoy unwrapping it – however silly that felt.

Miss Knott cleared her throat. 'Mr Mabel, I don't like to pry, but it sounds to me as though you might be in a spot of bother.'

'No, no, no!' Felix flushed and spilled a little tea into his saucer. He put down his cup, ashamed of the lie, and quickly amended it to, 'Well, yes.'

Miss Knott said nothing.

That gave him time to collect his thoughts, smoothing the purple biscuit foil over his knee, taking all the creases out of it with his careful thumb while he wondered what he should tell her and what he should not. Then he got worried about how many lies he could keep straight in his head, and so – finally – he just told her the truth.

Miss Knott didn't interrupt him. She topped up her cup, and his, and listened until he had brought her right up to date.

'And this Amanda is the person you've just spoken to?'

'Yes.'

'The one who hung up the phone?'

'Yes,' said Felix.

Miss Knott was silent for so long that Felix started to wish he hadn't told her. This wasn't lying low. This was blabbing, pure and simple. He'd exposed himself and the Exiteers. He'd shown himself to be an incompetent at best – a killer at worst. No wonder Miss Knott looked so sombre.

'I should leave,' he said, and put his cup back on the tray.

'Don't go, Felix,' said Miss Knott. 'I'm surprised, that's all. Who wouldn't be? To think that all this time you've been leading this double life, going into people's houses in secret, supporting them through their hour of need, destroying the evidence . . . And all at great risk to yourself. So daring! But so kind too . . .' Miss Knott eyed him appraisingly. 'I always suspected you had hidden depths.'

'Did you?' Felix was surprised because it was certainly more than *he*'d ever suspected.

'Of course,' she said, 'everybody has hidden depths. Some are just better hidden than others. And deeper.'

'Well, I appreciate that, Miss Knott, but now I see that I've been trying to rectify a situation that is impossible to rectify. Very foolish of me. And cowardly. I should have gone straight to the police, but I delayed – first because of my own panic and then Geoffrey telling me to lie low, and then by thinking that speaking to Amanda might help me untangle things. But now I've spoken to her and it hasn't helped at all, so I must hand myself in.'

'I don't see why,' said Miss Knott, unexpectedly. Again.

'Because it's the right thing to do!'

'Says who?'

Felix was taken aback. 'Well . . .' he said, 'it's what *Margaret* would do.'

'Pfft!' said Miss Knott with a breezy wave of her orange cream. 'Margaret was never accused of murder, so who knows *what* she'd have done?'

Felix wasn't used to questioning Margaret – or having anybody else question her. This was virgin territory for him, but he could see that Miss Knott had a point.

She went on, 'The thing is, I'm sure police officers are all very decent and hardworking and they only want to charge the right people. But once somebody *confesses* to a crime, then I think it's only natural that they might not have the time or the motivation to go on investigating that crime quite as hard as they should. Or even as hard as *you* would.'

This was not something that had occurred to Felix.

'Because, you see, once they've got *you*, they might just stop looking for anyone else.'

Felix nodded slowly.

'And then this poor old man could be left in terrible danger with nobody to protect him.'

Felix examined his own shiny knuckles while Miss Knott

frowned into the biscuit tin as if all the answers were in there, wrapped in coloured foil.

Then she looked up and said firmly, 'I think you should go back.'

Felix was startled. '*Go back?*' he said. 'To the house?'

'Yes.'

'But he'll kill me!'

'I'm sure he was just *saying* that,' said Miss Knott with a dismissive wave that was becoming a little familiar to Felix. 'After all, he must have been terrified.'

Felix pointed to his lump. '*I* was terrified!'

'Oh, but imagine this poor man – what's his name?'

'Skipper Cann.'

'Skipper's weak and sick and lying in bed, and the man who killed his son suddenly appears in his room. With a stick! He probably thought you'd come to kill him again.'

'I didn't go to kill him the first time!' said Felix, not a little vexed. 'He was going to kill *himself*, remember? He *wanted* to die.'

'Maybe so,' said Miss Knott firmly. 'But nobody wants to be *murdered*.'

The words hung in the air.

Undeniable.

Felix didn't care. He folded his arms. He wasn't going back to Black Lane. He'd done all he could and got nowhere. He'd apologized to Skipper Cann and fixed his fence and shown him the broken stick – and the man had threatened to kill him! As far as he was concerned, he'd done all he safely could to make amends. Margaret would agree with that, he was sure. Miss Knott was too impulsive. Too sentimental. And her expectations of him were completely unrealistic.

'I'll go back tomorrow,' somebody said.

But it was only when Miss Knott looked at Felix with her eyes all proud and shiny that he realized that that *somebody* must have been him.

The Attic

After supper Felix pulled down the loft ladder in a series of squeaky jerks, and ascended carefully to the attic to look for his old chess set.

He had always enjoyed playing chess. It was his abiding memory of his father. Ambrose Pink had been a taciturn man who smelled of pipe tobacco, and who was more an observer of his children than a father to them. Felix remembered the way he would clamp his pipe in his teeth so that his hands were free to applaud something Felix's sister or brother had achieved. Felix had never done anything to compare, but he and his father *had* played chess. Mostly on gloomy Sunday afternoons when the only restless sounds were the rain and the tick of the clock. Still, they'd been alone and together, while his spectacular siblings were off somewhere else, doing something that was doubtless more clap-worthy than losing at chess.

Felix had never beaten his father, but he had come close on two occasions. Unacknowledged both times. In the years since his father's death, Felix had come to understand that the lack of acknowledgement was nothing personal. It mattered not to his father who won. To him, *checkmate* was merely his cue to sit back in his chair and refill his pipe from a soft leather pouch, while his hunched son examined his king from all angles to make sure it was true.

It always was.

But while they'd played, they'd talked. Not about much. Egypt. Hockey. The best route from Barnstaple to Newton Tracey. Sturmey-Archer gears. Nothing, really.

It didn't matter: the point was that talking to his father had always seemed easier when it was done across a chequered board . . .

Now Felix had a sense of where the chess set should be and within ten minutes he was sliding open the lid of the little plywood box. Inside were the old wooden Staunton pieces that he had learned on as a boy – smooth with use – and the same ones he'd used to teach Jamie.

Felix was blindsided by nostalgia.

These chessmen had been here for thirty years. Waiting. Undisturbed. Just as Jamie must have put them away the last time they'd played. What had he been? Sixteen? Seventeen maybe? What had *they* talked about? Nothing, really, but definitely *something* . . .

Felix touched a pawn, as if the residue of his son might linger there. He held a white knight up to the dim bulb and remembered guiding Jamie's pudgy hand in an L across the squares as it clutched this very piece.

Accompanied by soft wooden clicks he rummaged through lovely memories, and found a king.

Checkmate.

Sometimes in his voice and sometimes in Jamie's. Like his father before him, Felix had never let his son win. But unlike *his* father before *him*, Jamie had won anyway.

Jamie was a fighter. A scrapper. Never down for long and always ready to come back for more. He'd been devoted to a game – any game – however silly or serious. He was a good loser and a gracious winner, but it was in the taking part that Jamie had really excelled. He gave his all to everything he did – even if he wasn't much good at it. Jamie *tried*. They'd spent years driving him to football and then driving him home, muddy and happy and shouting in the car with his ruddy-faced friends – always the same, win or lose. And that time when he was twelve and he'd missed the false-start whistle at the county gala and swum a whole length alone. He'd touched the side and looked across the empty lanes in amazement that he'd won by so far . . .

Everybody had laughed at him.

Hundreds of people, with the sound bouncing off the walls of the watery venue in waves. But when Jamie had started to laugh too, they'd cheered – and clapped him as he'd walked all the way back to the blocks – and then cheered him again when he'd finished a tired last. Felix's hands had been sore for two days from clapping so hard, and Margaret was so proud she had cried.

He smiled again now at the memory. Jamie's life hadn't been long, but while it had lasted, *my God,* it had been wonderful.

Wonderful.

Felix stared at the blurred chessmen.

What an ungrateful old bastard he was! Nineteen years of love and happiness, and two of Hell. What a terrible injustice he did to Jamie, to think of him now only with pain and bitter sorrow, when he'd achieved so much wonder to remember him by.

Felix wiped his eyes and touched the pawn again.

All these years the chessmen had been waiting for him.

He was so glad he'd come looking for them now.

Old Greybeard

'Calvin, you said you knew the old lady at the funeral?'
Calvin looked up from the Exiteer database. It was taking for ever and driving him mad. 'Don't really *know* her, ma'am.'

'But you know where to find her?'

He did. So he headed to Ladbrokes in a rare official capacity.

It was the hottest day of the year so far and Calvin rolled up his sleeves and loosened his tie as he climbed the High Street. He nodded curtly at Shifty on the step and went inside.

The shop had no air con, relying on its deep interior to provide a cooling gloom, but the sun was at just the right angle today to make it an oven instead. Dennis Matthews was spreadeagled across two seats at the front of the shop so the air could find his armpits, while Sylvie had loosened her scarf and her chins just a notch in deference to the heat. Old Greybeard, however, was bundled up in her anorak and wellies, as always. Calvin could almost feel his core temperature rising just looking at her.

He went over and stood near her.

She was writing out a bet with a careful hand.

'Can I sit?'

Her nod was almost imperceptible. He waited for a little while, watching the horses and the dogs on the screens.

'How did you know Albert Cann?'

She didn't pause in her work. 'Friend of the family.'

'Yes? For how long?'

Old Greybeard scratched out one of the runners. Wrote in another one.

'A while.'

It was possible, he supposed. Nonetheless, Calvin felt uncomfortable. It was plain Old Greybeard didn't want to talk to him about it, and without a formal interview he had very tenuous grounds on which to press her.

But they needed a break in the case . . .

'What did you say to Reggie afterwards?'

She shrugged. 'Condolences.'

Calvin blinked in surprise. Old Greybeard was lying. To *him*. To the *police*. He was astonished. And a little bit amused. But mostly just astonished.

Old Greybeard picked up her betting slip and studied it as if it were the Rosetta Stone. It certainly had enough writing on it but Calvin could see that the total stake was only 50p – the ticket minimum. Any less than that and they wouldn't even ring it through the till.

He chose his next words carefully. 'I thought the vicar was a bit harsh.'

'Idiot!' she muttered with unexpected anger. 'He din't know Albert. All his life people let him down.'

Calvin sat up straighter with interest. 'Who let him down?'

Old Greybeard looked away and shrugged one mottled hand. 'I were only trying to put things right.'

Calvin was on high alert now. She knew something. Maybe a lot. She might be the key to the whole case.

'How?' he asked. 'And why?'

But she didn't answer. Instead she got up awkwardly and took a single step towards the bet counter.

Calvin looked up at her urgently. 'What were you trying to put right?'

Old Greybeard frowned at the counter.

Then at him.

'I'm going,' she said, and toppled over backwards, betting slip still in hand, and hit the floor with a cushioned thud.

'Shit!' Calvin slithered over the plastic chairs and dropped to his knees at her side. 'Mike, call an ambulance!'

Old Greybeard was conscious. Staring straight up at the ceiling. All the training said to use the patient's name. Keep them focused on you. But Calvin didn't know her name.

'Don't worry,' he said, 'you'll be fine.'

Her rheumy eyes turned his way. They looked sceptical.

'Do you have angina or anything like that?'

She shook her head.

'Taking any medication?'

She shook her head.

'Well, hold on,' he said. 'An ambulance is coming.'

'I'm going,' she whispered through bluing lips.

'No, you're not,' he said sternly, 'you're waiting for the ambulance.' He glanced at the counter, where Dead Mike gave him the thumbs-up. 'It's on its way.'

Legs were all around them. The other punters. Watching. Murmuring. Calvin felt angry with them for no good reason.

'I'm dying,' Old Greybeard said faintly. 'It's my time.'

'It's *not* your time,' he snapped. 'Don't be such a big baby!'

She laughed soundlessly – her lips tight on antique teeth. But her breathing was shallow and Calvin realized that at any minute now she could pass out and stop breathing and he might have to do CPR. He'd never done it in real life, only on a dummy, and the dummy hadn't been bundled up in an anorak. He should take it off her. She'd probably collapsed because of the heat, and it would give her some relief. But she was an old lady and Calvin thought of his Nana Curley, and how she'd rather have died than had her vest exposed to a circle of strangers. Her *spencer* she'd called it, he remembered uselessly. So he didn't take Old Greybeard's coat off.

He just held her hand and tried to remember how many compressions per minute . . .

Sylvie bustled from behind the counter with a glass of water, and Dennis Matthews bent down and gently slid his piles cushion under the old woman's head.

'Not long now,' said Calvin. 'Everything's going to be fine.'

He wished he knew her name. He couldn't ask now.

Old Greybeard suddenly turned her head and looked straight at him. 'What that girl done to you was wrong.'

He was confused. 'What girl?'

'With that box of porn,' she said.

Calvin froze.

But her eyes suddenly filled with tears and she squeezed Calvin's hand hard, pulling him down to hear her better. He lowered himself with dread and she breathed into his ear. 'We all do things we're ashamed of.'

Then her hand slackened in his.

Shit.

He shook her arm. Shouted *HELLO!* in her face. *Hello! Hello!*—

She's gone, said somebody Calvin could have punched. He felt for her pulse. There was none. He yanked down the zip on her big winter coat and pushed it off her chest, relieved to see – not a vest, but an unexpectedly pretty blue blouse. He put his fingers on her sternum to measure the correct distance, feeling bra wires, then put one hand on top of the other and started compressions, pumping the blood for her stilled heart so that her brain wouldn't die before the ambulance arrived.

Pump pump pump

'Let's give her some privacy,' Sylvie said, and the legs started to move, to shuffle away towards the door.

Pump pump pump

Pump pump pump

And then the paramedics were there. So fast! Calvin hadn't even heard the siren. He stood up and stood aside. He knew them. Maria and Dan. They nodded briefly.

What's her name?

I don't know.

Anyone?

Nobody knew, but nobody said *Old Greybeard* either.

Calvin said, 'She got up and just keeled over. Talked for a bit and then boom, out like a light. She doesn't have angina. Isn't taking any medication.'

They nodded grimly and got to work. Smooth and fast. Airway check. Compressions. Oxygen. Compressions. Maria prepared a drip. Calvin looked around. Sylvie had ushered everybody out of the shop and was guarding the door. Calvin could see their backs through the window. Waiting to go on with their lives. Dead Mike was sat nearby on a plastic chair. Ashen-faced and looking even deader than usual.

'You all right?' asked Calvin, and he nodded.

'Give me a hand to sit her up,' said Dan and Calvin helped him to do that. They pulled her coat right off. Dan sliced through her shirtsleeve and the three of them exchanged surprised looks.

Old Greybeard's left arm was covered in tattoos.

All words – many, many words – winding their way around her arm, blurry blue as they emerged from what remained of her sleeve, getting sharper, darker, newer, as they spiralled down towards her wrist and disappearing around the back of her arm, which wobbled with every compression.

Pump pump pump

Calvin could pick out words here and there: AIRBORNE MY LOVE . . .

The words meant nothing to him.

PSIDI . . . UM . . . ?

That wasn't even a word.

Maria couldn't see a vein among the blue ink. She cut off the right sleeve and started again.

Calvin held the old woman's hand and read on: LARKSPUR MERCHANT VENTURA SIR IVOR BLAKENEY

He thought that rang a bell, and frowned to better remember. . . Sir Ivor. Hadn't he won the Derby? Back in the sixties maybe?

As Dan pumped Old Greybeard's chest and Maria blew air into her from a rubber balloon, Calvin searched Old Greybeard's arm with new purpose.

RANKIN THEATRICAL NASHWAN

Nashwan had won the Derby, for sure.

These were horses!

Intrigue turned to triumph at a mystery solved. Partly solved, anyway . . . Calvin craned his head to see better, lifting the woman's limp arm a little now and then to see more of the words.

'We've got a pulse.'

Calvin read faster. Raised and lowered her arm. Craned his neck as much as he could without making it obvious, and, as the list trickled down the old woman's wrinkled arm, the names of the horses became fresher to his memory. TEENOSO and, a few lines later, REFERENCE POINT. Both Derby winners. TERIMON had famously finished second in the race at 500–1. MASTEROFTHE-HORSE had never stood a chance against the sublime SEA THE STARS. And only last year RIDEOUT had run second at 33–1. Calvin knew because he'd backed him. To win, of course. The last name on the list – only an inch above Old Greybeard's bony wrist – was SEASPEAK. Calvin frowned. That made no sense. Seaspeak was in *this* year's Derby field, but the race was still a week away . . .

'Calvin?'

He looked up. 'Sorry?'

'We need to move her.' Maria was looking at him and he

realized they must have already asked him once, and that he was in the way. He stood up and moved aside as they raised the trolley and wheeled her towards the door.

'Will she be OK?'

Dan gave a brief shrug of one shoulder. 'You coming with her?'

Because he was a policeman.

'Yes.'

Because of her arm. He couldn't lie to himself.

And so Old Greybeard was carried out of the bookies on her shield. As he hurried after her, Calvin bent and picked up the crumpled betting slip she had dropped, and put it on the counter with a pound coin.

'That's hers,' he said to Sylvie. Then he went through the door and past the punters who were waiting to be allowed back inside. There weren't as many as there had been. Calvin imagined some had gone to the pub or down the road to William Hill. Others back home, to speak to their wives of how life is short, and to turn over new leaves, which would fast turn into old rotten leaves. Calvin knew. It had taken him years to lose that aching sense of destiny every time he dealt with death.

The journey to the hospital was fast and swaying, and the siren was too loud for proper conversation. He just held on to a hand-grip that looked to be there for the purpose. He sat near the doors and watched Maria work on the old woman, admiring her skill and quiet efficiency.

'You think she'll be OK?' he leaned forward to shout.

Maria glanced at the unconscious woman before shaking her head. *No.* Then she turned away and busied herself with a beeping monitor.

Calvin was sorry Old Greybeard was going to die, but it was not a tragedy. She'd lived a long and apparently good life, and died in a place she'd spent more time in than home, and with somebody holding her hand. Even managed a few final words, although

Calvin couldn't imagine *how* she'd found out about the box of porn. Thank God nobody else had heard her.

They swung hard left and then right, and then lurched to a halt.

The doors opened and he stepped down and watched Dan and Maria wheel Old Greybeard into A&E, then went into the waiting room and sat down.

He wondered how far back the list of Derby horses went. How old she'd been when she'd had her first tattoo. The scandal it must have caused! He wondered why she'd done it and what those horses had meant to her that she'd had them marked for ever on her own skin. There were winners among them, but losers too. And why include Seaspeak, when this year's Derby hadn't even been—

Calvin's jaw dropped.

The names on Old Greybeard's arm were not a record of random Derby runners. They were her *tips*!

The sheer boldness of it took Calvin's breath away.

Punters lied like fishermen. They minimized their losses and inflated their winnings.

But not Old Greybeard.

What was it she'd said?

Have the courage of your own convictions. And she wore hers right there on her arm every day of her life.

Calvin felt new respect for Old Greybeard. Win or lose, those were her choices, and she stood by them.

He took out his phone and checked the Derby market. Seaspeak had attracted little support. No surprise there – the trainer was small, the horse by a jumps sire, and the two-year-old form muddled. A single placed run in a nine-furlong race at Lingfield was the only real point of interest, but it was in the mud, and the form was questionable. Seaspeak's Derby price reflected his chance, at 25–1 in a ten-horse race.

Rumbaba, however, was now 4–1 joint favourite with the Dewhurst winner, and Calvin felt the familiar flutter of panic that came every time he saw the horse's name. Tipping it to Dennis Matthews had drained every bit of joy from the anticipation of pulling off a massive coup.

Ego and ignorance . . .

Maria tapped him on the shoulder.

'I'm sorry,' she said. 'She didn't make it.'

Calvin stood up.

'Looked like a major coronary event. Nobody could have saved her.'

'That's a shame.'

'You OK?'

'Yes,' he said. 'Thanks.'

'Do you know her name? For the paperwork.'

'No. Sorry.'

'Well, I have her personal possessions here. Can I give them to you?'

He wondered why, then remembered he was a police officer. 'Of course,' he said. 'I'll make sure they're handed over to her next of kin when we track them down.'

He took a big plastic ziplock bag from her, of which only one small corner had anything in it, and signed a form saying he'd received whatever it was.

'Thanks, Maria.'

'No problem,' she smiled. 'See you around, Cal.'

He said goodbye and watched her walk away. He didn't know that she knew his name. Nobody called him Cal.

He could get used to it.

On the bus back to Bideford, he looked through Old Greybeard's stuff. There wasn't much. A gold St Christopher medal with BD77 engraved on the back. A little blue leather purse containing a ten-pound note and some loose change. A handful of small brown nuggets that smelled faintly of fish, and a creased Morrisons receipt for cat food and milk. No ID. Not even loyalty cards.

Nothing with a name on it.

And without a name, he couldn't find out who she was, or where she lived or what she'd meant by what she'd said to Reggie at the funeral – or a hundred other things that Calvin now had to add to the long list of stuff that they didn't know about the death of Albert Cann.

'Bad break,' said DCI King.

'Yes, ma'am,' said Calvin. 'Specially for her.'

She turned the St Christopher over and frowned. 'What's BD77?'

'Don't know, ma'am. All I can find on Google is a silicone transistor code.'

'Probably initials. And a birthdate maybe?' She handed the medal back to him and scooped an olive from her jar. 'Have you checked the supermarket?'

She meant the receipt from Morrisons. 'Yes, ma'am.'

He'd watched CCTV of Old Greybeard going through the till with her milk and her cat food, but nobody had remembered her. Just another old person hidden by her age. Her story untold.

King nodded ruefully. 'Someone will report her missing sooner or later.'

'Hope so.'

'What was it she told you again?'

'That people had let Albert down and she was trying to put things right.'

'Did she seem lucid?'

'She *did* . . .' said Calvin, 'but that was right before she collapsed and died, so . . .' He shrugged and wound the fine gold chain through his fingers and studied the medallion. St Christopher brandished a key, and it felt like a teasing symbol for the mystery of Old Greybeard.

He wished he'd known her better.

Known her at all, really.

Too late now.

Calvin got up and switched off his computer and pulled on his jacket. He put Old Greybeard's possessions into an evidence bag.

Then, on impulse, he took the St Christopher out and looped it over his head.

When he found Old Greybeard's next of kin, he'd return it. Until then, he'd wear it. Calvin wasn't religious. He felt no need for the protection of the patron saint of travellers. And he should be putting it with her other belongings in an evidence bag in a forgotten corridor of Bideford police station.

But this just felt . . .

Kinder.

Chess

Skipper Cann glared at Felix. 'I told you, if you came here again I'd kill you.'

Felix stayed near the bedroom door. Nearly backed out of it. But he didn't.

He'd prepared his opening gambit. Now he cleared his throat and delivered it. 'I thought you might like to play chess.'

'I don't play chess.'

Felix edged into the room. 'I can teach you,' he said. 'You'll love it.'

He walked to a little wooden chair and pulled it over to the bed. Then he fetched the wastebasket that was behind the door, and started to clear the bedside table of used tissues and empty pill bottles and all sorts of bits and bobs: a barely nibbled sandwich, medications, a box of dog treats. All he left were Skipper's teeth in a glass of water, another glass of water without any teeth in it, and various medications. Then he opened the board and set up the pieces.

All the time he could feel Skipper Cann's eyes burning into him.

'Right,' he said, 'the aim is to protect your king—'

'Din't say I *can't* play.'

'Oh, good. You go first then. It's only fair.'

'Because you killed my son, I can go first?'

Felix flushed. 'I'm sorry. I didn't mean that.'

Skipper Cann turned his head to look out of the window and

the atmosphere chilled like low cloud sinking down the side of a mountain. Toff shivered as if he could feel it too. The walking stick lay along the shallow hump of Skipper's leg and Felix eyed it warily, thinking of Margaret propping it in the corner of the hallway as they came in. Of him handing it to her as they went out. Of always asking, *Got your stick, old girl?* as he locked the front door behind them.

Perhaps he should leave. But if he left now and Miss Knott asked him how it had gone, what could he say?

'White goes first anyway,' Skipper said, and banged a pawn down defiantly.

Felix moved his own pawn.

Skipper looked around the room as if for a waiter and muttered, 'I need a drink.'

'Shall I make some tea?'

'Pfft!'

Felix frowned at his watch. 'It's only just gone ten.'

'I've got cancer, you know!' said Skipper triumphantly.

Felix demurred. 'I'll see what I can find.'

At the end of the landing the back bedroom filled his vision – the solitary oxygen tank accusing him.

He was pleased to wind around the banister and turn his back on Albert's room.

Toff and Mabel followed him downstairs and into the front room, where Felix looked around without success for a drinks cabinet. The room had very much reverted to the shambles it had been when he'd first spoken to the cleaner.

All I want to do is cry and eat crisps.

Poor girl. Still, she really ought to be doing the job for which she was being paid. Even the brick was still there, although now half hidden by a fresh onslaught of red bills and junk mail. Felix started to gather up the obvious rubbish, before an insistent banging overhead made him remember that Skipper was expecting something to drink. He hurriedly opened and closed cabinets and cupboards which only revealed more clutter.

He went through to the kitchen, where Hayley was drying dishes.

'Skipper wants a drink,' he said tentatively, but she seemed unsurprised.

She nodded at a cupboard and said, 'In there.'

It wasn't a drinks cupboard, it was a condiments cupboard. There was an old tin of mustard powder that reminded Felix he had to buy some to try to get the mascara out of his beige jacket. There was also a half-full bottle of Captain Morgan and two bottles of supermarket-brand gin.

In consideration of Skipper's name and presumed history, Felix chose the rum. He splashed a good inch of it into a tumbler from the drying rack and carried it carefully upstairs.

'Here you go,' he said, and put it on the windowsill within easy reach.

'Is that it?'

'Is what it?'

'That little dribble?'

'I thought I'd been quite generous,' said Felix. 'Given the hour.' He jumped his knight over his pawns.

Skipper countered with another pawn, then downed the rum in one. He stared into the glass as if it might refill by magic.

'Another?' he said.

Felix opened his mouth to protest, but then didn't. He just went downstairs and fetched the bottle.

'Thought you'd be back,' laughed Hayley.

Skipper poured another nip.

'Join me?'

'No, thank you.' Felix's bishop swept across the board and Skipper parried with a pawn to block his queen.

'Sun's over the yardarm somewhere, you know.'

Felix sighed. Fetched a glass. That was four times he'd been up and down the stairs now and his hip was starting to notice. He poured himself a drop and touched the liquid to his lips, feeling the burn. He'd never been much of a drinker and wasn't keen on spirits, but the aroma of the rum made even this dingy room seem a little exotic, as if they were in a cabin in a worn-down old ship, with its creaking wooden floor and simple furniture, and its grizzled old captain surveying the sky – now with a bit more spark about him and some colour in his cheeks.

He looked quite chipper for a man who should be dead.

'Rain.'

'I beg your pardon?'

'Rain,' Skipper said again. 'Can't you smell it?'

Felix followed his gaze. The sky was a bland white. 'Really?'

Skipper nodded at the clouds over the cliffs. 'Them speaks of rain. And I'd tell you when exactly if I could only see the water.' His pale blue eyes searched the clifftops keenly as if they might yet see over them and swoop down across the big grey pebbles to the ocean.

'Did you work at sea?'

'Near enough every day for seventy year,' nodded Skipper, and his tone softened with memories. 'Began when I were twelve on my father's boat, the *Megan*. Till her went down off Hartland.'

'She sunk? My goodness! Was anyone hurt?'

'Only Duffy Braund.'

'What happened to him?'

'Drowned.'

Felix was aghast. 'How awful.'

But Skipper smiled, 'No fisherman wants to die on land! Lost at sea – them's the lucky ones. Like Manny Tithecott. Fishing off the rocks down Bude with his brother and a wave knocked him off. Warn't even on a boat, but it were his time, so the sea come and found him. And Billy Cole. Got a lobster line wrapped round his leg while the other bays on the *Charmain* was asleep. When 'em pulled in the line, there's Billy halfway down, and two big old pinchers in the pot at the end of it!' He laughed, then added respectfully, 'Give 'em to Billy's wife, o' course.'

'Of course,' Felix said faintly.

But Skipper was warming to his subject. 'And there's Chiggy Sleeman what fell out a dinghy over by Instow and he warn't even over the bloody Bar!'

'Which bar?' asked Felix.

'The *Bar*,' said Skipper impatiently, as if *everybody* knew. 'Sand-bar between the river and the sea. Bideford Bar's most dangerous in England, but Chiggy weren't nowhere near it. He were only just off the beach. His wellies filled with water, they said, and that pulled him under, but I don't believe it.'

'What do you believe?' asked Felix, enthralled.

Skipper cocked an eye at him. 'Had a maid with him, see? Noreen, from down the White Hart – you know Noreen?'

'I don't think so,' said Felix. He'd never been in the White Hart or any other Bideford pub.

'Well, she's a nice maid, but thin, see? And they'd gone through near enough a flagon of scrumpy before they set off, so I reckon that's why he's gone over the side, *and* what's stopped him getting back in the boat. Chiggy were a vool, but even drunk, he knew enough to kick his boots off. I reckon Noreen were just too skinny to help him, and he were too squiffy to help himself!'

Skipper cackled so hard that Felix laughed too, even though it was terrible. But he couldn't help it. Being terrible only made it funnier. He could imagine it. The shock of the water. The giggles at first – at the silliness of it all. At Chiggy's comical struggle to haul himself over the side. The growing concern when it was clear he couldn't. Then the creeping fear . . . Felix wondered what they'd said to each other; whether either had acknowledged what was happening. Or if they were too drunk to work it out until it was too late. Maybe that would be the best way to go – drunk and stupid.

So he laughed, and Skipper laughed until it turned to coughing and Felix looked at him anxiously as he thumped his own chest. But the coughing slowed and stopped in a wheeze.

'You all right?'

'If I'm not sleeping, I'm corking,' snorted Skipper dismissively and wiped his eyes, took a gulp of rum and went on.

'What happened after the *Megan* sunk?' said Felix, who was starting to feel the way he had as a child at suppertime, thrilling to tales of his big brother's athletic exploits. The starting gun, and the cheering crowds and the breaking tape and the handshakes. All the more romantic for having been missed.

'After that my father had the *Megan II* for nigh on twenty year before *he* died.'

'Lost at sea?' ventured Felix.

'In bed.' Skipper tapped his heart. 'Ticker. Give my mother the shock of her life. Thing is, a fisherman's *expected* to die at sea. That's why he names his boat for his lover, so they're together at the end, see? Then when it comes, she knows what to do. How to *be*. But this . . . ? Right besides her?' He shook his head sadly. 'And then all the stirrage with the doctor and the undertaker and the funeral with some blasted vicar going on and on, when all a man wants is a bit about Jonah and off to the pub!' He flapped a hand at all the fuss that *not* being lost at sea occasioned.

'What did you do after that?' said Felix.

'Worked the *Megan II* for a year or so,' he said. 'Got married. Had Albert. Then came *Susanna* . . .'

He stopped talking and got a faraway look in his eyes.

'Did that sink too?'

'What's that?'

'Did the *Susanna* sink too?'

'Not yet – far's I know, anyway. Han't seen her for a year. She'd still be there, I reckon. Tied up down the Quay. Rotting, most likely. Last time I seen her was before I got sick . . .' He twisted around and pointed at the wall next to his bed.

'That's her,' he said tenderly.

Felix got up to look. It was one of the few photos that had been professionally framed, and a calligraphic hand had inscribed the boat's name on a faint pencil line on the pale green mount. The *Susanna* hardly deserved the attention. She was a stout little trawler like dozens he'd seen over the years, tied up at Barnstaple, Bideford and Ilfracombe, with a bright-white-painted deck and a hull of sky blue.

'You ever been to sea?'

Felix shook his head. 'I got sick once on a pedalo,' he said ruefully. 'Shaped like a swan.'

Skipper laughed again and Felix joined him, although the truth was that the ocean scared him. The water was too deep; too dark. He'd lived by the sea all his life and never been more than knee-deep at Westward Ho!

He refilled their glasses. Took Skipper's rook. 'Check.'

Skipper huffed at the board, then sacrificed a knight to escape. 'I fished till I were eighty-two year old. Always feared if I stopped it would be the end of us both. Me *and* the *Susanna*. And I were right.' He swirled the rum around his glass. 'Nobody wants her. There's no living in it now. Not here. Not for small boats. Them's just for grockles and history now.'

The chessmen observed a minute's silence, while the past kept watch from the wall. Felix looked at all the pictures of people and places and dogs and boats and boats and boats. None was hung straight, and all in different frames. Next to the *Susanna* was a sepia couple in their Sunday best; then a print of St Peter wading to Christ across the waves; a boy in a dinghy. Probably Albert, Felix thought with a pang. Then the same child alone on a dodgem car. Not smiling, and looking abandoned in a sea of happy people and bright lights.

'Is this Albert?'

'That's him,' said Skipper. 'Poor kid. Always sad . . . My wife left me when he were just a nipper, see . . .' The old man chewed his gums.

'Is she still alive?'

'Who?'

'Your wife. Susanna.'

'My wife died a while back,' said Skipper carefully, 'but her name was not Susanna.'

Felix was flustered. 'Oh, pardon me—'

Skipper sighed his apology away. 'I were a shitty husband and a shitty father and so were Albert. One follows the other, I reckon. *My* father were too free with his fists and his favours . . .'

He looked at the sky and stroked Toff. 'But people change, don't they? Otherwise what's the point? I always tried to do right by Reggie, but by the time I come to my senses it were too late for Albert.

'So when I bin sick for a while and he says I might like to . . . *hurry things along* . . . I couldn't hold it against him, could I? He were only being the man I made him.'

Skipper glanced at Felix, as if to gauge his opinion, but Felix stayed silent.

'It's a hard thing . . .' Skipper's voice wavered. 'To live long enough to know all the hurt you done.'

Felix looked down at the man's big hand on the silky fur of the dog, then put out his own hand and stroked the dog too.

'It's your move,' he said quietly, and Skipper sniffed and sat up straight and took a bishop. Felix slid his rook into position. 'Check.'

Skipper stared at the board for so long that Felix thought he might have fallen asleep, and ducked his head a little to see his face, but Skipper's eyes were open, so he gave him time to make his move.

But Skipper didn't move, and instead he said, 'I'm sorry about your boy.'

Felix was surprised. 'Thank you.'

'What were his name?'

'James,' said Felix. 'Jamie—'

He'd been going to say *he was twenty-one.* He'd been going to say *he was our only child. So funny, so kind, so handsome.* He'd been going to say *he learned to play chess on this very set* – but finally just left it at that. *Jamie* was all that was required.

And Skipper nodded as if he knew *exactly* what Jamie was, and didn't need to be told.

He raised his glass at Felix and they clinked and drank in silent toast to their sons. One because of all he'd been, and the other in spite of it.

Felix cleared his throat. 'Is this your grandson?'

The photo of Reggie Cann next to his red car was new, and tucked into the frame of a much older one.

Skipper nodded. 'That's Reggie. Albert bought him that car last Christmas. Also getting old enough to try to put things right, I s'pose.'

Felix tried to sound casual. 'Does Reggie have a girlfriend?'

'If he has he's not told me. Why?'

Felix spoke tentatively. 'I saw him the other day with this girl. I think her name's Amanda. Do you know her? That might not be her name. Short dark hair. Sensible eyebrows?'

'No. What of it?'

'Well . . .' said Felix, and then paused for a long time while he decided how to go on. *Whether* to go on.

But he'd promised Miss Knott, so finally he said, 'She's an Exiteer.'

Skipper looked steadily into his eyes.

'She was with me . . .' Felix stopped talking. He didn't know what more to say.

Skipper turned to stare out of the window. The knuckles of his hand had gone white and shiny around the glass.

'I don't mean to—'

But Skipper cut across him. 'Reggie wouldn't hurt me.'

'Skipper—'

'Wouldn't hurt *anyone*.'

'But he—'

'No!' Skipper's sudden vehemence made him cough. And cough and cough and cough – and this time he didn't stop. This time it got worse and worse, until he was doubled over his own knees, pink drool swinging from his lips, gasping for air and pressing his chest with an open hand.

'Hayley!' shouted Felix.

Skipper waved at the bedside table and Felix found the bottle of morphine pills.

Skipper grimaced and nodded and held up two fingers.

Felix opened the bottle and tipped out three pills – then frowned and checked the label. *Morphine Sulphate ER 100mg.* But these pills were not like Jamie's. These were round, yellow compressed powder – not the capsules he remembered – and the number on them was 30, not 100.

He got up and limped to the doorway and shouted again. 'HAYLEY!'

There was no response and Skipper whined like a dog at a door. This was no time to quibble.

Felix gave Skipper two pills. He was about to drop the third back into the bottle but put it in his pocket instead. Miss Knott had been a nurse. He'd show it to her.

Skipper tipped the pills into his mouth, then looked around vaguely for his water glass, which was empty, so Felix gave him his rum to wash the pills down. Felix was past caring about safety. He just wanted Skipper to be pain-free and breathing again – even if that was a temporary state.

'Breathe,' he said. 'Breathe.'

'I'm coming!' Hayley shouted, and Skipper gasped, 'Promise me,' and Felix leaned forward to hear him.

'Promise you what?'

Breathe. Breathe.

'Promise me, don't tell the police about Reggie . . .'

'But . . .' said Felix miserably. 'For *your* sake.'

Hayley was coming up the stairs with a heavy tread, and Skipper gripped Felix's arm so hard that it hurt. 'You owe me!' he hissed. '*You owe me!*'

Felix hesitated.

He *did* owe him. He owed them both.

'I promise,' he said.

Paperwork

The colder the body, the colder the case.

It was an old saying but a true one and, by the start of the third week of the investigation, they were all starting to feel the chill.

'Something will turn up,' said King. 'Something always turns up.'

But for the first time since he'd known her, Calvin Bridge could hear a little note of desperation in the DCI's voice.

So he decided to take a flyer. He abandoned HOLMES and just Googled the Canns.

It was an old Devonshire name, and most of the hits were about local councillors, or businesses having sales, or the sponsoring of youth soccer teams, but there had been a fair share of less worthy Canns too, getting drunk, shoplifting and swindling rugby clubs out of their subscription fees. There was even an alleged rape by a Cann near Shebbear, to which he could find no reported resolution.

The only specific reference to the Abbotsham Canns that Calvin could find was a five-year-old photo of Albert. He was being awarded for what the *Bideford Gazette* had called 'thirty years of faithful service' at the carpet shop in Bridgeland Street. Calvin blew the picture up onscreen and looked into the eyes of the man he'd only known as a corpse. In the photo Albert Cann was standing between a colleague and a six-foot plush giraffe, in some apparent joke that the reporter had failed to refer to in either the copy or the caption, so that it would never make sense now. Albert was unrecognizable. Hale and hearty. He was dapper in a suit and tie and sharp white collar, and was holding the carriage clock that Calvin recalled had been on the table beside his bed. It was fake gold and quartz, and he felt suddenly sad for the man who'd obviously treasured it as a symbol of his entire working life.

After a minute's thought, he decided to use Google alongside HOLMES to see what he could discover about the other clients of the Exiteers in life as well as in death. He wasn't sure what he was looking for – or even whether there was anything to find.

Picking out the more unusual names, he started looking anyway.

Raymond Timothy Arlow, IT consultant, showed no police involvement before his death two years ago in Avonmouth after what his family obituary in the *Bristol Evening Post* called 'a short, brave battle against the Big C'.

Julia Jane Barnes, shop manager, had no police record. All Calvin could find on Facebook was a request from her family for donations to the Guide Dogs for the Blind in lieu of flowers.

Tharindu Barraratne had no police record or obituary that he could find. There was a picture on Facebook of Tharindu holding a cocktail at a beach bar. He had lovely teeth.

Jasmine Casper had died of complications of a brain aneurysm. Her obituary made her sound like a saint, and there was no hint of police involvement.

And so it went on. Normal everyday deaths of normal everyday people. Nothing that looked suspicious about any of them, which Calvin supposed was a testament to the discretion of the Exiteers, at least.

Then came Paula Marie Max of Borough Green in Kent. Mrs Max had apparently died of stomach cancer, although of course Calvin knew better now. There didn't seem to be anything remarkable about her life or her death. He found an obituary in the *Kent Messenger*, which stated that she'd worked in a cake shop, and would be missed by all at the badminton club where she'd been a regular member.

That last detail rather depressed Calvin. Paula Max had been a *regular* member. Not a talented member or a popular member – just a regular one. As if her attendance had been noted, and – in the absence of anything else to mark her out as memorable – had been stated for posterity in the obit pages of the local paper.

But Max came up on HOLMES. Not Paula but Leonard Max. Also from Borough Green. Calvin checked Paula's will and found that he was her brother and had inherited a static caravan and five thousand pounds. There was a photo of Leonard, who was in his fifties and looked unshaven and tired. The only familial trait they appeared to share was regular appearances – hers at badminton and his in the local magistrates court.

Petty theft. Common assault. ABH. Cheque fraud.

Who commits cheque fraud any more? thought Calvin idly. *Might as well steal a pig!*

At the end of each court report he found the classic line about taking *x* number of offences into consideration. Over several years, the total of *x*s showed Leonard Max to have been a devoted crook. Calvin wasn't sure what it added to his sum of knowledge about Paula Max, but he put the file to one side.

Then he hit two more in quick succession. Harry Neal had died 'quietly at home, surrounded by family' – which may or may not have included his son, Duncan Neal, who had several convictions for drugs. And Lucy May Powell, who had a niece called Shona who had done eighteen months for fraud.

DCI King came in and ate olives while Calvin told her what he'd been doing.

'So what's the significance of relatives with criminal records?'

'There might be none,' he admitted. 'Maybe blackmail? Or

maybe there's someone who'd . . . you know, *encourage* the death of a relative for personal gain. I was thinking of the tea towel, you know? And after the vicar, I thought there might be more to find out about Albert and then moved on to these others. But it could all come to nothing.'

'Everything does,' she winked at him. Then said, 'Were any of them named in the wills?'

'A few of them, yes, ma'am.'

'Did Albert Cann have a relative with a criminal record?'

'Not one that I can find.'

'Still,' she nodded, 'keep aside the files that show those relatives with criminal records who were also beneficiaries and we'll see if it adds up to a significant number.'

'Will do, ma'am.'

She raised her jar of olives in a toast. 'To Operation Tea Towel.'

Calvin smiled. He was glad DCI King was pleased with him, although it made him think that if he *didn't* want another bite of the cherry, this was a very poor way of showing it.

By lunchtime, Calvin had collated a short pile of eleven slim folders.

Each one represented a deceased client of the Exiteers who had left money or property to somebody who had a criminal record. Now he needed to delve more deeply.

He started at the top. With the big money.

With Bruce Macdonald Bruce. His parents had given him that name, and his wife had given him a stroke.

In July 2014 Vicky Bruce had pleaded guilty to six charges of false accounting totalling over £400,000 – by far the biggest cash amount that Calvin could find connected by blood or marriage to any of the Exiteer clients. Vicky Bruce had spent like a sailor before being caught and sentenced to two years, which Calvin thought seemed lenient. She'd served only twelve months in Askham Grange, as well as being ordered to pay restitution in full to her thirty-two victims who had variously lost between a thousand and forty-five thousand pounds. Near the end of the trial Bruce Bruce had suffered a massive stroke, and was thereafter confined to a wheelchair until his death two years later, from what Calvin could only ascertain had been 'complications'. A coroner had recorded death from natural causes.

But the coroner didn't know about the Exiteers.

The will he'd found in Skeet's file stated briefly that Mr Bruce had left everything to his wife, apart from a twenty-thousand-pound ISA which was to be divided between the two children of his first marriage – Lauren and Sarah.

Calvin thought that seemed unfair, but it wasn't uncommon.

He got Vicky Bruce's number and address from a helpful desk sergeant at Basildon nick, and called her. She answered right away and he introduced himself. He decided not to play games; he didn't have the time.

'I'm calling about your late husband,' he said.

'Are you now?' said Bruce, in a tone that meant she thought he had some nerve.

Calvin glanced at the police file photos. The woman he was talking to was maybe fifty. Stocky and manicured, with bottle-blonde curls and big hoop earrings. Her husband was pictured with her outside Reading Crown Court and looked much older – even before the massive cerebral event that had eventually killed him.

Although it hadn't. They both knew that now.

'He left you almost everything in his will, didn't he?'

'Almost nothing, you mean. Everything he had was swallowed up by his care after his stroke.'

'Oh dear,' he faux-sympathized, 'that can be very pricey. How much was left?'

'After funeral expenses?' She took a breath as if she'd told it many times and knew it off by heart. 'Nine hundred and eleven pounds and seventy-five pence.'

Calvin gave a low whistle. 'Wow. Right down to the wire.'

'Yes,' she said. 'The home care alone cost over a hundred thousand.'

'My goodness,' said Calvin. 'Did his daughters help?'

'Did they *shit*,' she said – still cross about it five years later, even though they'd only inherited a measly ten thousand pounds each.

'I'm assuming you received the house in his will?'

'Of course,' she said. 'It was my home.'

'Right,' said Calvin. 'And how much did you sell it for?'

'I really can't remember,' she said vaguely.

No matter, Google did . . . Calvin quickly found her house on Zoopla and discovered it had been sold the past December for £510,000. It looked worth a lot more than that. Mock Tudor, four bedrooms, nice garden and in Newbury. He looked down the list at nearby property prices. Nothing in the immediate area had gone for under £750,000 in the previous year.

'Did your husband have a life insurance policy, Mrs Bruce?'

'It's Mrs Cornish now,' she said.

'Sorry, Mrs Cornish. Let me amend that here . . .' And while he pretended to amend the file he Googled her new name and searched HOLMES.

Nothing to see there.

'How much did you receive from your husband's life insurance policy?'

'I don't think that's any of your business.'

'I'm a police officer, ma'am,' said Calvin, 'so maybe you should let me be the judge of what's police business and what isn't. If you don't want to talk to me, that is your right, but I can subpoena the insurers and find out that way, so you could save me time and you trouble . . .'

Another grudging silence. 'Two hundred and twenty-five thousand pounds.'

Calvin scribbled the sum along the top of the first sheet of the folder marked BRUCE and glanced at the notes he'd made while on the line to Basildon. In fact Vicky Bruce had paid off her £400,000 restitution in a lump sum a few months before her case had even gone to court. That was unusual but Calvin thought her counsel had probably advised it, and used it to mitigate her sentence. Judges loved crooks who paid up, pleaded guilty, made amends . . . Nothing wrong with that on the face of it, he thought. It was the way these things were *supposed* to work, although they rarely did. A criminal had not only done her time, but also paid back her victims in full.

But *how*? Calvin literally scratched his head. The court report said Vicky Bruce had blown through most of the money she'd stolen.

'Where did you get the money to pay the restitution, Mrs Cornish?'

There was a short pause. 'I borrowed it.'

'From?'

'Family. Friends. People were very kind.'

'People usually are,' he agreed. 'Can you give me their names?'

'Whose names?'

'The names of the people who lent you the money.'

'Absolutely not!' she snapped.

'Why not?'

'Well, because I don't want them dragged into this. Whatever *this* is! People helped me when I needed it and I'm not about to repay them by giving their names to you so you can badger them the way you're badgering me. It's very rude and unpleasant.'

'I'm sorry you feel that way, ma'am.'

'I do! Look, sergeant—'

'Constable.'

'Whatever. Look. I made a mistake and I did my time and I paid back every penny I owed and had to sell my house to do it! I'm not saying I deserve a medal or anything, but I *do* think I deserve to be left alone, thank you very much!'

Calvin was losing her. He wouldn't be able to ask her much more before she clammed up or hung up. His mind raced from one random fact to the next. She'd come out of prison broke and facing big care bills. The longer her husband stayed alive, the bigger the bills got.

Luckily he'd died . . .

'At what point did you contact the Exiteers?' he asked.

There was a gaping silence on the other end of the line, and then she hung up.

Calvin bounced to his feet and punched the vending machine so hard that it shrieked, rocked, and vomited an array of snacks at him.

Vicky Bruce had murdered her husband. And used the Exiteers to do it!

Of course, he couldn't prove it. Wasn't even sure how he'd reached that conclusion. It was all just a game of dot-to-dot and right now Calvin had only the vaguest idea of what picture might emerge. But that didn't mean he didn't *know* it in his gut.

The vending machine alarm howled.

Tony Coral's top half tilted into the doorway – uncommitted to an entire entrance, as was his wont. 'What's all the noise?'

'I punched the machine,' said Calvin, flushed and defiant.

Coral nodded soberly and said, 'Somebody had to,' then tilted out of view again.

Calvin unplugged the machine and in the ensuing silence he scooped out his spoils and dropped them on to the desk in a random pile, then sat and stared at it as he analysed the data he'd just collected from the former Mrs Bruce.

She'd borrowed money immediately after her arrest in order to reduce her sentence. All fine and dandy. She and her husband had probably thought they'd be able to pay it back reasonably quickly. But then he'd had a stroke and instead of bringing in an income, he'd needed round-the-clock care, which would have burned through their savings like wildfire.

By the time he'd died, she was desperate for cash.

Right down to the wire.

It might have been a lucky coincidence that Bruce Bruce had passed away less than a thousand pounds from being too broke to afford further nursing care. But his wife hanging up on Calvin told him a different story. It told him the Exiteers had made it easy for her to dispose of her costly husband before his care started to eat into the life-insurance money. £225,000. Enough to live and to start paying back the friends and family she'd borrowed from.

Calvin frowned. And yet she'd sold the house within a month of inheriting it, and considerably *under* market value. For a woman who was starting over in her fifties, that didn't add up.

Calvin ate a Starbar from the pile while he thought about it.

DCI King appeared. 'What happened here?' she said, nodding at the snacks.

'I got hangry.'

King plucked a Walnut Whip from the motherlode with the reverence of Indiana Jones discovering a relic. She sat down and put her feet on the desk to unwrap it.

'Catch me up, Calvin.'

He did. When he'd finished, she mused: 'Why would she sell the house under market value? It doesn't make sense.'

'Unless whoever lent her the money demanded immediate repayment. Maybe with interest?'

'That doesn't sound like family and friends who'd been *so kind*,' she said, making quote marks in the air.

He nodded. 'Or like a bank or a building society . . .' They looked at each other meaningfully.

'Loan shark,' he said.

'Sounds like it,' she said.

Then she took half the files off his desk, opened the top one, and picked up a phone.

Over the next few hours King and Calvin spoke to a dozen bereaved relatives who fell neatly into two camps – those who had inherited large assets, and those who had not. The responses of the latter group were hurt and angry.

What Dad doesn't realize is that that's our HOME . . . !

What gave her the right to just dispose of a house that belonged to the whole family . . . ?

Sandra would be turning in her grave if she knew what she'd done.

The house had been in the family for over a hundred years. And now it's gone, just like that. Everything inside it too . . .

Those who *had* inherited property had all sold up.

Fast.

Too fast.

King and Calvin hung up on the last relative and looked at each other.

'It's all about the houses,' she said.

'Skipper left the house to Albert in his will,' said Calvin, with a buzz of excitement in his belly. 'Maybe Albert arranged the Exiteers for him . . .'

Kirsty King nodded grimly. 'And then they killed the wrong man . . .'

The Boat

Felix walked Mabel along Bideford Quay. He started at the Old Bridge and passed the big steel vessels with Russian names on their bows that were berthed behind the bus stop – as if you only had to show your pass to get a free return to Vladivostok.

After the Russian ships came the *Oldenburg*, which took supplies to Lundy, and tourists to see the puffins and ponies. After that the boats grew much smaller – a few pleasure boats, but mostly little trawlers with white decks and brightly coloured hulls, and with rust running down from their rivets into the dark green seawater that found refuge here twice a day.

As the rising sun warmed his face, Felix led Mabel all the way along the quay, stepping over ropes as thick as his arm, and alongside the park dotted with municipal marigolds, noting how small the boats became here, and how shabby. Increasingly so, until – just when he thought Skipper must be senile – he finally saw the *Susanna*.

She was the last boat made fast to what might be deemed the quay, although this far downstream it was no longer an obvious thing with a long drop to the water and shiny black capstans, but a grassy bank with a thick wooden post driven into the mud to hold the boat in place. But it was the *Susanna*, all right. Her faded name had been painted in black across her sky-blue stern.

She was a bit of a mess.

Felix knew nothing about boats, but even he could tell she was

no longer seaworthy. Her once-white deck was covered with algae
and streaked with rust, and the windows of her little wheelhouse
were opaque with dirt and cracked in places. There was a puddle
of dirty water in the middle of the deck. There were several coils of
greenish rope, and a bundle of filthy fishing net, but – like everything else on board – they were covered with bird droppings. As if
to drive home the point, a seagull shouted at him from the top of
the mast and spread its wings to warn him off.

Instead Felix climbed on to the boat.

He hadn't planned to, but the tide was low, which meant the
transom was only thigh-high, and he'd only recently climbed a
tree, so he thought he would certainly be able to climb on to a
boat, although even as he did, he had no clear idea of why he would
want to in his brogues. The operation was not completed without
a wobble or two, and a yap from Mabel, who clearly thought the
whole exercise was beyond him. But it wasn't, because before long
Felix was standing on the deck of the *Susanna*.

The shore looked different from here, even though he was roped
to it and had barely moved a yard. He thought he could have had
very much the same view from the bank if he'd just turned around.

But it felt *very* different.

For a start, he now thought of the grassy bank as *the shore*, when
before he'd only thought of it as the grassy bank. The other thing
that was different was that the surface under his feet felt so *hollow*.
It was like standing on a big wooden bubble. He could feel the
slightest vibration of *things* against the hull or passing by in the
water, as if his ears now started in his feet.

Felix walked cautiously across the slippery deck, which creaked
and bowed a little, and made him think of pirates.

Arrrr, me hearties!

He laughed quietly to himself.

There were big drums with nets and floats still attached to
them – frayed and green with algae. He tried the door of the

wheelhouse and was surprised to find it open. Anyone could just come in here and steal anything! He stepped inside. It smelled good in here – and bad too. Salty and fishy and wooden. The dashboard was peeling veneer, with a few basic dials set into it. Along the top, old red and black wires showed where electronic equipment had been removed. Felix touched the wheel, which creaked when he turned it. He touched it again, and imagined life on the high seas. Waves crashing over the bow, and turning the *Susanna* into the wind – or whatever one did in high seas. His entire understanding of seamanship came from Charles Laughton in *Mutiny on the Bounty* and was therefore a little sketchy.

The wheelhouse was so small that he only had to turn around to step back on to the deck, and this he did – feeling more like an old hand now as he observed the now-familiar nets and the puddle. Another boat passed slowly up the river and he watched the wake head towards the shore, and put out a hand to steady himself as it made the *Susanna* bob. The unsteadiness made him feel just a tiny bit drunk. Happy drunk. It was rather fun.

Mabel yapped again, fussing like his mother. *Come OUT of there, Felix! Come DOWN from there, Felix! Get OFF that, Felix!*

When had he stopped doing anything daring? Or had he never done anything daring in the first place? He couldn't remember, so quite possibly not.

'All right, Mabel,' he told her, 'I'm coming,' and he lifted a leg over the side of the boat.

But getting off the *Susanna* was not as easy as getting on it had been. Then he'd stepped *down* from the bank on to the vessel. Now he was trying to step *up* from the boat and on to the slope and, whereas the bank had stayed still as he'd left it, the *Susanna* did not. Another boat passed slowly upstream, and suddenly she was riding little waves up and down and swung a bit away from the land, and the whole affair became fraught with potential disaster.

Felix straddled the transom and thought how silly he must look in his M&S jacket and his brogues, and with his own dog barking at him.

He looked around, but there was nobody watching.

Good.

He waited for the *Susanna* to swing herself back against the bank, and although that took a minute, she finally did start to close the distance between herself and dry land.

Felix licked his lips and waited until he was sure, and then half stepped, half leaned across the divide, but he had no real confidence in the manoeuvre, or commitment to it, and left one leg in the boat while he leaned and leaned and leaned – until he leaned right into the river.

The Torridge closed over his head and the sky turned yellowy-brown . . .

Lost at sea!

Skipper Cann's words rushed back at him like the ocean . . .

Then his feet touched mud and he gathered enough purchase to push himself back up to the light. He surfaced, spluttering, with his face in the grass and the *Susanna* nudging the back of his head. For a horrible second he panicked that she might crush him, but when he put up a hand and pushed her away, she slowed and stopped and then politely withdrew to give him the space to crawl up the bank.

Except he *couldn't* crawl up the bank. It was too steep, and the mud was too soft under his feet, and his hands and arms were those of an old man.

So Felix just stood there, up to his chest in water and holding on to clumps of grass with both hands, while Mabel barked and barked and barked.

'You all right down there?'

Felix lifted his head to see a grizzled old chap wearing overalls and wellington boots at the top of the bank.

'Fell in the water,' he said.

'I see that,' said the man, and spat casually into the grass. 'You happy there? Or you want a hand?'

'A hand would be lovely,' said Felix. 'Thank you.'

The old fellow put down the shopping bags he was carrying and edged down the bank on his bottom. He stopped halfway down to pet Mabel, then reached out for Felix, who took his hand. He managed to scale the bank in a series of slippery pulls and humiliating scrambles until they were both sitting on the slope of grass.

The shore.

'Thank you,' panted Felix at last.

'No trouble,' said the man. 'Trip, did you?'

'No, I was on the boat and then fell in.'

The old chap squinted at the *Susanna*. 'You buying her then?'

'No, no. Just checking on her for a friend.'

'What friend?'

'Skipper Cann.'

'Thought he were dead,' said the man.

'No, no,' said Felix. 'Not yet.'

'Cancer, in't it?'

'I believe so,' said Felix, and the man squinted at the glittering river.

'No way to go,' he said.

'No,' agreed Felix.

'Shoulda died at sea.'

'Yes,' agreed Felix, who now felt better qualified for an opinion on the matter. 'Are you a friend of his?'

The man got a sparkle in his eye. 'Well now, at my age I reckon it's best to be friends with whoever's left alive, don't you?'

'I do,' smiled Felix, and leaned down and tried to wring out his trouser leg, but there was very little point. He just needed to get home and put the whole lot in the wash and himself in a hot bath. 'Well,' he said, 'I should go home and get dry. Thanks for your help, Mr . . . ?'

'Chanter,' said the man. 'Tovey Chanter.'

'Felix Pink,' said Felix, and held the man's hand for the second time in five minutes as they helped each other to their feet.

'All shipshape?'

Felix nodded down at himself. 'Miraculously,' he said. 'I was very lucky you were so close by.'

'Just passing,' said Tovey. He picked up his shopping bags and Felix saw that they didn't contain shopping at all, but were full of odds and sods – old rope, cleats, and pieces of electronics that Felix didn't recognize, although one of them had a picture of a fish on it.

'You have a boat too?'

'No, no,' said Tovey, and nodded vaguely down the quay. 'Working on one for a mate. Doing it up, see? Want to buy a fish-finder?' He held out a chunky apparatus with dangling wires.

Felix smiled but shook his head. Then he nodded ruefully at the *Susanna*. 'This old girl looks past saving.'

But Tovey Chanter winked at him and showed off his gappy brown teeth. 'Nothing's past saving if you got enough money.'

The Pill

Felix got home from Bideford to find that Buttons had claimed the front step as his own and wouldn't budge – even when he waved his arms and hissed.

Felix had seen the cat with a large mouse dangling from its mouth a few days ago. It might have been a rat. Frankly, Buttons gave him the creeps, and the fact that he was obviously well able to take care of himself meant that trying to catch him and put him in a box was becoming an increasingly unattractive proposition.

He decided not to escalate things with Buttons and went around to the back door. That turned out to be a good idea as, rather than traipse muddy river water through the house, Felix emptied his pockets on to the kitchen table and then peeled off his clothes in the kitchen – right down to his underpants – and put them straight in the washing machine. Then he took the beige jacket out again, and looked at the big black mark on it. He had forgotten to get mustard powder, but he had vinegar, so he rubbed some into the mascara stain before feeding it back into the machine and setting it all for a hot wash. He'd be sorry to see the jacket go now, after all they'd been through together. He wondered what Miss Knott would recommend for his brogues, which looked awful. He stuffed them with the *Telegraph* sports section and left them to dry, then went upstairs and had a hot bath.

As he dressed in his bedroom, he could see Miss Knott in her garden, lifting daffodil bulbs in the front border.

On impulse he opened the bedroom window and called, 'Miss Knott?'

'Yes?' She got to her feet and looked up and down the street.

'Up here,' said Felix, and she looked up at the windows of the houses across the street.

'Hello?' she said, with the wariness of a woman who suspects she's being taunted.

Felix was already regretting his boldness. Having flung open the window like Juliet, he was reluctant to give her a clue so familiar as his own name to guide her gaze.

'Next door,' he said, which sounded awkward and impolite, but at least Miss Knott turned his way and shaded her eyes against the sunlight.

'Oh, hello, Felix!'

'Hello,' he said, and then stalled. He'd planned to ask her around to see the pill, but it would be the first time he'd had anyone actually *in* the house since the undertaker, and he wasn't sure how to ask – or even if he *wanted* to ask – or how to behave if she did come round . . .

'Did you want something?' she said.

'No,' he said, and shut the window.

Then he opened it again and she was still standing there, looking at him, so he said, 'Actually I wonder if you would mind popping round? I have something to show you.'

'I'll just wash my hands,' she said, and five minutes later, she was in the kitchen, sitting at the kitchen table with Mabel on her lap, as if she'd been doing it for years.

'Margaret never let her do that,' Felix observed a little nervously. 'She said it would encourage her to jump up while we were eating.'

'Of course it will.' Miss Knott said. 'But how else is she supposed to reach the table?'

Felix smiled. 'Would you like tea?'

'Thank you,' said Miss Knott, and peered at the table. 'I do like a good jigsaw.'

'I've rather stalled on that one,' said Felix. 'This piece here is the bane of my life.'

'Is it grass?' said Miss Knott, frowning at it.

'I'm not sure any more,' said Felix. 'I'm not even sure it's from this puzzle.'

They'd had a teapot once and nice cups, but he couldn't remember where they were, so he just dropped bags into two mugs.

'I only have custard creams, I'm afraid.'

'Lovely,' said Miss Knott.

By the time he set the mugs down on the table, Miss Knott had put the rogue jigsaw piece into place.

'Oh, bravo!,' he said.

'It looked like grass,' said Miss Knott. 'But it was a reindeer's bottom.'

Felix leaned down to examine it. She was right. 'Marvellous,' he murmured.

'Every little helps,' she said modestly. 'What was it you wanted to show me?'

'Ah yes,' said Felix. 'I found this next to Skipper Cann's bed.' He picked up the pill from the corner of the table. 'Do you know what it is?'

'Looks like Oxycodone,' she said immediately.

'Is that a kind of morphine?'

'Well, it's a painkiller, but it's stronger than morphine in tablet form.'

Felix decided not to tell Miss Knott that Skipper had washed down two with rum and his blessing.

'It can make you very sleepy and muddled,' Miss Knott went on.

'Skipper did say he'd fallen asleep the day I . . . when we . . . went into the house . . .'

'If he was taking these, then I'm not surprised,' she said. 'Have they been prescribed?'

'I don't think so. They were in a bottle marked morphine.'

'That's very worrying,' she frowned.

He nodded. 'I think you were right to be concerned about him.'

'And I think you were brave to go back,' she said, and Felix felt as pleased with himself as a small boy with a finger-painting on the fridge.

'We'll have to go to the police now,' she said. 'They'll protect him.'

Felix fiddled nervously with the puzzle. 'I'm afraid that's no longer an option, Miss Knott.'

Miss Knott pursed her lips. 'Because you promised this girl?'

Felix shook his head. 'Because I promised *Skipper.*'

She nodded slowly. They sat in silence. Their tea cooled, unsipped.

Finally Miss Knott reached out and covered his hand with hers. 'I hope you know what you're doing, Felix,' she said. Then she placed Mabel gently on the floor, and left.

Felix sat at the kitchen table and stared at the jigsaw.

He felt lost.

Alone.

Miss Knott hadn't argued with him – and for that he was grateful, because going back on his promise to Skipper Cann was not an option. But it was plain she felt it was a bad idea – and one she could not support. And, even though she was only a neighbour, he was troubled by that.

Inexplicably.

A knock on the door made him jump, and he got up so fast he banged his knee. He didn't care. 'Out of the way, Mabel!'

Miss Knott had come back with a solution. A compromise. A daring plan.

She'd come back to help him.

Felix threw open the front door to find a pretty young woman there. Her hair was in a neat ponytail and she was dressed in hi-vis. He glanced down to see which charity she was collecting for. He gave regularly to two charities – Hodgkin's Lymphoma and the Alzheimer's Society – but wasn't averse to giving occasional sums to other worthy causes. However, she didn't have a bucket.

'Mr Pink?' she said.

'Yes,' he said. 'Hello.'

'I'm Police Constable Braddick—'

Felix almost fainted.

He swayed precariously, and she quickly stepped over the threshold and caught his arm. 'Are you all right, sir?'

He absolutely wasn't. He'd been expecting this moment for what felt like for ever, but now it had arrived he couldn't catch his breath and his legs were like jelly. Things seemed to slow right down and there was a rushing, roaring noise, as if all the blood in his head was falling past his ears and into his feet.

The officer walked him gently backwards into the hallway with the yellow woodchip on the walls and lowered him on to the telephone seat. He bumped it and the memo pad fell to the floor, and she trod on the pencil with the little gold tassel and broke it in two.

'Pencil,' Felix whispered feebly.

'Pardon?' she said, bending to hear him, but he couldn't repeat it. Couldn't even think about it properly, as everything jumbled together in his head. The woodchip and the tassel and *You took your time*, and *I'll take care of everything* and the rough sway of the apple tree under him – all while Mabel barked and wagged at the same time to show she was friendly, yet capable of extreme violence.

PC Braddick left him and he didn't know where she had gone until she came back with half a glass of water, which he sipped only because she wanted him to.

'Are you all right, Mr Pink?' she was saying. 'Do you have pills I can get for you?'

Yes, back-in-time pills would be lovely, thank you.

He didn't say that. Just shook his head and then realized he'd indicated 'no' to one question when the other one required a 'yes' and so he nodded his head too, then shook it again, then stopped moving it altogether because he thought he must look like the little wooden Bambi on a spring that they'd bought for Jamie in Austria many moons ago. He'd sit and play with it for hours, pressing the base into the wooden plinth with his tiny thumb, to make the jointed fawn bend this leg or that leg, or to bow or to sit or to waggle its little leather ears. Jamie's eyes had shone with happiness every time he got it just right, and Felix was suddenly glad that Jamie hadn't lived to see the internet. Then all his memories of his son would be of the back of his head . . .

The young woman was crouched down in front of Felix now, looking anxiously into his face. She reached up and gently touched the lump on his head. 'Oh dear,' she said. 'What happened here?'

'You should see the other guy,' Felix whispered, and then he started to cry.

Part Two

That Meeting at the Café

His father had only been dead for two days, but Reggie's heart still skipped a beat when he saw Amanda waiting for him at the café.

He bent and kissed her cheek and sat down opposite her at the little wooden table.

'I'm so sorry, Reggie.'

'Thanks, Manda.'

'Are you OK?'

'Yeah.'

'How about your granddad?'

Reggie made a face. 'It's harder for him, I think. He lost his son. Plus, he's still alive when apparently he expected to be dead, so you know,' he shrugged, 'he's confused and angry.'

They'd spoken on the phone, of course, but now they were together Reggie could see how genuinely upset she was for him. He was lucky to have her. The three months since they'd met had been the happiest of his life.

'Reggie,' she said softly, 'I have to tell you something.'

'What, Manda?' He took her hands in his, but she didn't look at him. Then she withdrew her hand – and a little alarm bell started to ring in the back of his head.

'What is it?' he said. 'What's wrong?'

He watched in confusion as a tear plopped off her nose and on to the table.

'*What?*'

'I was there,' she said, so low that he had to lean forward again to hear her.

'Where?'

'I was *there*,' she repeated. 'At your house.'

'What do you mean?'

He was confused. Amanda had never *been* to his house. What was she talking about? He didn't know what she—

And then – suddenly – he did know.

'You mean . . . ?'

Her lower lip wobbled and she nodded.

'You're an Exiter?'

'Exiteer.'

Reggie felt sick. Dazed. He sat back in his chair. Someone had released a swarm of hot bees inside his head. 'You never told me.'

'It's not . . .' she started. 'You're not supposed to . . . you know . . . like Fight Club.'

He shook his head. Couldn't look at her. He picked up a fork from the cutlery jar and slowly worked the tines between the slats of the little wooden table.

'What happened?' he said.

'Reggie, I—'

He didn't look at her. 'What *happened*?'

'It was my first time,' she said, 'and . . . we . . . made a mistake.'

A mistake.

'I felt terrible, Reggie. I mean, I didn't even know because I'd never *been* there . . . And I understand why, of course, what with your granddad being so sick and stuff, and I'm not making excuses, I'm just saying, if I'd been to your house before and *met* him . . .'

But she hadn't. Because he hadn't let her. Because he was a coward and a liar.

Reggie levered the fork backwards and forwards, minutely

widening the gap in the slats. Amanda went on talking, even though he wished she wouldn't.

'When I heard his name I got such a shock, but then I just assumed it was Skipper because I knew Skipper was sick. And I was with this old man called John, and I just did what he said because he's experienced. He's killed loads of people. Well, not *killed* but, you know, *helped*—'

'Albert didn't want to be *helped*.'

Amanda nodded miserably and Reggie wanted to hold her. Wanted to hug her and tell her it wasn't her fault because it was *his* fault. *He* was to blame. Wanted to tell her that it would be all right. That *they* would be all right. But he couldn't. Because it wasn't. And they wouldn't.

His silent fork widened the gap.

'Don't do that, please!'

They both looked up at a woman holding a dishcloth and a teapot.

'Sorry,' he said, and put the fork down.

'Would you like to order something?'

'Er, no. Thank you.'

'OK,' said the waitress, 'but you can't just sit here.'

Reggie stood up. Amanda started to rise but he stopped her halfway.

'No,' he said. 'I don't want you . . . with me.'

She looked up at him, blinking tears down her cheeks. 'Please, Reggie,' she begged him. 'I made a mistake—'

She was getting up anyway. Wasn't going to let him go. He had to stop her.

'My father's dead,' he said flatly. 'And *you* killed him.'

The waitress stood open-mouthed, teapot akimbo. *Excuse me?* said someone behind her. *In a minute*, she said, without turning around.

'Just . . . *stay here*,' said Reggie. 'Have a hot chocolate.' He fumbled in his pocket for change.

'Reggie—'

'*Look!*' He slapped the table and she flinched. He softened his tone. 'I don't want to get you in trouble or anything, all right? But I just . . . I really can't see you any more.'

'But, Reggie!' Amanda's voice shook. 'I *love* you!'

'Manda . . .' he started brokenly – as if he might tell her that he loved her too.

But he didn't.

Instead he dropped a random handful of coins on the table and walked away.

The Wing Mirror

Reggie was so disorientated that he'd passed the post office before he remembered that he was parked in the Town Hall car park. He turned around and headed back past the café, but Amanda had gone. She hadn't stayed. Hadn't had another hot chocolate. From here he could still see his money, and the waitress stopping again to watch him pass.

He put his head down and headed for his car with keys in hand. Wanting to be home; wanting never to be home again. Wanting to be able to think and to stop thinking. Still reeling from the shock and the shame—

'This your car, mate?'

'What?' The man standing next to his car was big. Tall. Heavy. Low brow, thick lips, with bright blue eyes and ridiculously yellow curls. He was pointing at the little red MX5 his father had bought him for Christmas. His father, who was so tight he squeaked.

'Someone broke your mirror.'

'*What?* You're joking!'

'See?'

That's what he was pointing at. The mirror, dangling against the driver's door.

'*Bastard!*' It never rained but it poured. Reggie looked around as if some passer-by might put their hand up and admit responsibility. 'This is all I fucking need.'

'You Albert Cann's son, yeah?'

Reggie was confused. 'Yes. Sorry, do I know you?'

'Knew your dad a bit.'

'Oh.' Reggie expected the man to offer his condolences, but he didn't.

'He owes people money.'

'Pardon?'

'Albert. He owes people money.'

'What money? What people?'

'My boss. Terry. Albert owes him forty grand.'

'Forty grand!' Reggie laughed because it was laughable, and shook his head. 'You've got the wrong person, mate.'

He stepped around the man and unlocked the car door. The mirror swung against it, coloured wires bulging from the casing.

The man didn't move aside.

Reggie squeezed past him into the car and tried to pull the door shut, but the man had a hold of it. Put his elbow on it and leaned into the car.

Reggie felt a warning chill pass through him. 'Let go.'

But the big man didn't let go. Instead he propped the door open with his vast buttock. He opened a grubby little notebook and poked a big sausagey finger at the page.

'Albert Cann. Borrowed thirty. With interest it's forty. You don't pay up, Terry owns your house.'

'Bullshit,' said Reggie. 'I don't believe you.'

The man sighed and pulled a piece of paper from another pocket. He unfolded a flyer and Reggie flinched—

CRASH! And they'd all ducked. A brick through the window! Only the curtain had stopped it landing on the table. And for an instant he'd seen it on the floor. A brick with a flyer wrapped round it, secured by an elastic band.

NEED MONEY?

And then he'd run – run into the cold Christmas dark to find the

*vandal, the kids, the drunk. But there was nobody there. And when
he'd got back the brick was on the coffee table, holding down bills,
and the leaflet was gone.*

Threw it away, Albert had said . . . Tore it up and threw it away . . .

Now Reggie knew he hadn't. The *idiot*.

He shook his head, as if to clear it. 'The house isn't even his,' he
said, 'so the joke's on you.'

The big man carefully refolded the flyer and put it in his pocket.
'Terry wants his money.'

'Well, my father's dead,' said Reggie, 'so tell Terry he can fuck
right off. And you can fuck right off too, before I call the police.'

But the big man didn't fuck right off. Instead he straightened up
and stared slowly around the car park. Then he bent down again
and rested his beefy hands on his knees so he could look into the
car.

'Sorry, mate,' he sighed, 'but I have to beat you up.'

'You *what*?'

'It's my job,' he shrugged.

'*What?*' Reggie laughed, because this was surreal.

'Cover your mouth so you don't lose your teeth.'

'Don't be—'

The man hit him hard on the nose. He fell backwards on to the
passenger seat and looked up at the headlining and had no thoughts
at all.

Nothing.

Then a fist gripped his jacket and lifted him back up.

'Cover your mouth.'

Reggie covered his mouth and the punch snapped his head back
and he tasted blood and his arms went all floppy at his sides, but
the man held on to his jacket – held him in place. Then he leaned
right into the car. His huge curly head filled Reggie's blurred vision
and he couldn't cover his mouth again because of his spaghetti

arms, but the man didn't hit him again. Instead he held up his phone and took photographs. *One. Two.*

'Turn your head this way a bit. That's it.'

Three.

'Forty grand,' he said. 'I'll be in Ladbrokes. You got a week.'

'How'm I s'posed to get forty grand in a week?' slurred Reggie.

'Not my problem,' he said. 'But if you go to the cops you'll be sorry.'

Then he let go of Reggie's jacket and walked away.

For a long time Reggie sat there with his chin on his chest and couldn't think of much except to wonder how long the pain would last. Eventually he lifted his head and looked in the rear-view mirror. His eyes streamed with tears and there was blood coming from his nose, his mouth, his left cheek. All down his jacket and shirt.

Slowly, slowly his arms began to work again. He touched his nose and winced. He felt his teeth with his tongue and none was loose, although they all ached. He waited for his breathing to return to normal.

Finally Reggie wiped his hands on his jeans and started the car. *Shit.*

He just sat there while it all sank in.

Forty grand.

Forty *grand.*

The idiot. The selfish fucking idiot.

Happy Christmas, Reg. Been meaning to get you a nice car for a long time.

Reggie's fury at Albert couldn't stop his eyes filling as he thought of that moment. His father had not been a sentimental man – or a generous one – so the little red Mazda had felt like a lot more than a gift.

It had felt like *sorry.*

Sorry for leaving and sorry for coming back. Sorry for the chaos and the anger. Sorry for the lack of interest in schoolwork or hobbies. The lack of interest in *him*. Sorry for the slaps. All the casual slaps. Back of the legs, back of the head. Sorry for not caring, not calling, until he'd got sick and moved in with Skipper – and needed somebody else to pay the bills.

The car hadn't made any of it right. But it *had* made it better. Just the thought of his father saving for years, denying himself maybe, with this one goal in mind – a peace offering, a balm for wounds finally acknowledged.

But now Reggie knew it wasn't that at all. The car was just a way to show off at the Pig on the Hill, where he had driven Albert – in the Mazda – twice a week so he could get drunk and belligerent.

See that car? Bought that for my lad for Christmas. Twenty-five grand! Top of the range. And I paid cash.

Somebody else's cash. He'd borrowed thirty grand and blown almost all of it on the car. And if that wasn't stupid enough, he'd put up the *house* as collateral. *Skipper's* house! The house where Skipper had been born and grown up and got married and raised his baby son alone after his wife had left them both . . .

Albert probably thought he was being clever. Conning the loan shark. Not caring whether he paid the money back, or what would happen if he didn't. Not caring who was dragged into his bullshit. Never thinking of the consequences.

Reggie looked at his battered face in the mirror.

Well, *these* were the consequences . . .

He should drive to the police station right now. Before the blood even dried. Give them a description. The big man wouldn't be hard to find. Get his fat arse in a jail cell before the day was out . . .

But Reggie met his own eyes in the mirror.

Who was he kidding? He couldn't tell *anyone* about this.

Least of all the police.

The Will

The solicitor peered at Reggie's face through wire-rimmed spectacles.

'Oh dear, that looks painful.'

She was right. It had been a week, but his nose still hurt and his eye had turned yellow.

'Had a bump in the car,' he said, which was not entirely a lie.

Mrs Boucher showed him a seat and he took it, while she sat down at her desk.

'I'm sorry for your loss.'

'Thank you,' said Reggie.

'It must have been a terrible shock.' Mrs Boucher stared at him as if it might elicit further information. But Reggie was here for the bottom line and didn't need the niceties, so he only nodded.

She must have been used to people wanting to cut to the chase, because she simply cleared her throat and got down to business. 'Normally probate takes much longer than this to sort things out, but obviously after your call I put it on top of my pile.'

'Thank you.'

'Not at all,' she nodded. 'Actually this turned out to be quite speedy, for reasons that will become clear.'

'Great,' he said.

'So,' Mrs Boucher said, placing her palms on her big wooden desk, either side of a thin sheaf of papers, 'the will!'

She picked up the top sheet and perused it with what Reggie

imagined was her will-reading face – as if she was seeing it for the first time. He wondered whether she practised that face in front of the mirror. It made him want to yank the will from her hands and scour it for the nitty-gritty.

How much? How much howmuchhowmuchhowmuch?

But she took her time.

'He didn't cut me out of it, did he?' he laughed nervously.

'No, no, on the contrary,' she said, and his heart blipped with hope.

Mrs Boucher read slowly, '*I, Albert Charles Cann, leave all my worldly goods to my only son, Reginald Albert Cann, with love.*'

'That's nice, isn't it?' said Mrs Boucher.

Reggie nodded. He felt choked by relief. Losing the house – or even just having to tell Skipper what Albert had done – had been unthinkable to Reggie. And now he didn't have to think about it. His father had been a petulant drunk but he had worked all his life and lived low on the hog. He had a pension. He had life insurance. And now it would pay off, thank God! There might even be a bit left over after the forty grand was paid off.

'So what does that mean?' he asked. 'In real terms.'

'Well,' she said, and put down the will and picked up the next sheet of paper. 'In real terms, unfortunately, not a lot.'

'I don't understand,' said Reggie, because he didn't. 'I don't understand.'

'Well,' said Mrs Boucher with a brittle-bright smile, 'obviously the house is your grandfather's, which just leaves any personal and monetary assets.'

Reggie nodded.

'I'm sure you know that your father liked a . . . *flutter.*'

'Sure,' said Reggie. His father had loved the horses and the dogs and, when he couldn't make it down to William Hill any more, he'd opened a little online account.

'But he didn't bet much,' he told her. 'I mean, he bet pennies!'

'Well,' said Mrs Boucher, 'he lost pounds.'

'How many pounds?'

'A lot of them.'

'How much is a lot?'

Mrs Boucher paused perilously and then said, 'All the pounds he had.'

'You what?'

'He lost everything,' she said. 'I'm very sorry to tell you.'

'*Everything?*'

'Yes. Everything. All the money he had.'

Reggie couldn't grasp it. *He'd lost everything.* It sounded like the start of a stupid movie. 'But,' he said. 'I . . .' He shook his head to clear his ears. '*Everything?* What about life insurance? He had life insurance!'

'He did,' she nodded, but Reggie's relief was curtailed as she went on, 'However, two years ago he cashed in his policy to release those funds, and – given he transferred almost the entire amount to his online gambling account – I can only assume he lost that too.'

'How much was that?'

Mrs Boucher checked the paperwork. 'After early withdrawal fees it came to thirty-three thousand pounds.'

Reggie's jaw dropped open. 'And he lost *thirty grand*? In *two years*? On the *horses*?'

Miss Boucher blanched nervously. 'I did advise him against withdrawal, of course, but he was quite adamant.'

It was impossible. Albert had *stuff*. He paid for *things*.

'How much is left?' said Reggie faintly.

'Well, I had to go through quite a process to—'

'How much is *left*?'

'Forty-five pence.'

'I'm sorry?'

'Forty-five pence.'

'*Pence?* Forty-five *pence*?'

She nodded, not meeting his eyes, and Reggie felt punched in the face all over again.

They'd never been rich people and he hadn't expected to inherit much from his father.

But *nothing*?

Mrs Boucher was talking again and Reggie slowly caught up: '. . . current account with the HSBC which was overdrawn by sixteen pounds and seventy-two pence, and a savings account with the same bank that did have ninety-two pounds and twenty pence in it. I took the liberty of paying off the overdraft, including fees, with the money from the savings account, which leaves a total monetary legacy of . . .' she picked up a cheque . . . 'thirty-six pounds and ninety-three pence.' She turned the paperwork around and slid it across the desk at him. Reggie stared down at it as if it were a magic trick. As if any minute now Mrs Boucher would abracadabra the shit out of this whole mess and reveal that actually his father had left a few thousand quid. A few hundred even.

Something!

But Mrs Boucher wasn't magic.

Thirty-six pounds and ninety-three pence.

'And, of course, anything of his is now automatically yours, as per the terms of the will.'

Reggie nodded mutely and looked at his watch with a rising sense of panic. The big man would be waiting for him right now at Ladbrokes. What would he say when he told him there *was* no money? What would he *do*? Break his legs? Did people still do that? Reggie touched his nose and could believe that they did.

'Did he have much of value?' Mrs Boucher asked kindly, and Reggie tried to think of all the things his father had valued. A stuffed pigeon in a glass dome. A horse-hoof inkwell he claimed had come off Nijinsky. That fucking carriage clock.

'No,' he said, and heard the shock in his own voice. 'I don't understand it. He bought me a car. I thought he was doing OK.

And all the time he had nothing? I mean . . . Jesus! I mean, what the *fuck* was he thinking? The *fucking fucking arsehole*!'

Mrs Boucher flinched and tentatively gathered the papers back into a pile and self-consciously squared off the corners. 'I'm very sorry, Mr Cann,' she murmured, and put the papers into a clear plastic folder for him.

Reggie didn't answer. What could he say? *It's all right?* It *wasn't* all right. But there also wasn't anything he could do about it. There was no money. Not even enough to pay for the funeral – let alone forty thousand pounds to keep some thug from taking their home. It would kill Skipper—

'Mr Cann?'

Mrs Boucher tentatively slid another piece of paper towards him. 'I tried my best to keep it low,' she murmured.

It took Reggie a long moment of stupid staring before he realized it was a bill for her legal services.

Seven hundred pounds.

Felix's Confession

'I'm so sorry about this,' said PC Braddick.

She looked so glum that Felix almost patted her hand.

'Between you and me,' she went on, 'I don't think this is the kind of thing that should be treated as a police matter at all.'

'You're very kind,' he said.

'Still, it's my job,' she sighed.

Felix nodded. Of course it was. He had killed a man. Whether it was deliberate murder or tragic mistake, it was only right and proper that he be interviewed formally by police. Frankly, he'd have been disappointed if this *hadn't* happened. He would have lost a bit of confidence in the system.

'Can I get you anything before we get started?' she said. 'Nice cup of tea?'

'That would be lovely, thank you.'

'Well, actually it's a horrible cup of tea from a machine,' she said, 'but it is free. You wait here and I'll be right back.'

She went out of the interview room, leaving Felix with a Formica table, four plastic chairs and – on the table – a thing that looked like a shortwave radio. Felix assumed it was some kind of tape recorder. He recognized it from the TV crime shows that Margaret had loved. There was a TV mounted on the wall in one corner of the room and a camera pointing straight at him from the other. Felix flinched and looked away and thought of countless grainy clips of suspects in rooms just like this one, all over the world. People not like him.

Except now they were *just* like him.

Criminals.

His hands trembled. He clasped them together on the table to try to control the shake. He wasn't cold – PC Braddick had gone upstairs and fetched him a cardigan – so it would look like exactly what it was: guilt and fear.

He felt very alone. But he had promised Skipper he would not tell the police about Reggie. And if he told them about Amanda, he felt sure she would lead them to Reggie, which would amount to the same thing.

Fair or unfair, right or wrong, Felix was on his own – and was determined to keep it that way.

PC Braddick came back in and put a paper cup in front of him.

'Thank you,' he said, looking at the watery grey tea, and sipped it to please her. It tasted exactly the way it looked.

'Shall we start?' she said.

'Just us?'

PC Braddick seemed very young to be handling a murder investigation by herself.

'Just us,' she nodded. 'Unless you'd like me to call a lawyer for you? It's no trouble. As I told you earlier, you are legally entitled to have one present.'

Felix couldn't recall her saying that, but assumed she must have done so while an ocean was pounding inside his ears. But what was the point of a lawyer? All it would do was prolong the agony and make him look as if he was trying to hide something, when he just wanted to tell the truth and get out of here as soon as possible.

'No, thank you,' he said. 'Unless you think I'll be here overnight?'

'Oh, I very much doubt that,' she smiled, and Felix felt enormous relief that they were not going to treat this like anything more than the terrible mistake that it was.

'Right,' said PC Braddick, and fiddled with the recorder for a bit. One lock of hair kept falling from behind her ear and bothering her. Finally she sat up and blew out her cheeks and said *Right!* again, and corralled her hair back into a grip.

Then she spoke to the machine instead of to Felix, saying his name and age and address, before looking at him and giving an encouraging nod.

'Now, Mr Pink, could you confirm for the record that you have been read your rights and that you understand those rights?'

Felix was sure she had read him his rights even if he hadn't actually heard them, so he nodded.

'Verbally please, Mr Pink.'

Felix leaned into the recorder and said, 'Yes.'

'You don't have to lean in, Mr Pink,' said PC Braddick kindly. 'The microphone is very sensitive.'

'Oh, sorry,' said Felix and cleared his throat and said it again without leaning in.

'Good. Now, before I ask you anything, is there anything you'd like to tell me about the incident?'

'Well . . .' said Felix, 'only that I admit it fully. Put my hands up. I acted alone and can only apologize sincerely to that poor man and his family for what happened.'

PC Braddick looked surprised. Felix imagined she didn't get many quicker confessions.

'So . . .' she said, and then frowned – as if now that he'd confessed he'd negated her entire line of questioning, '. . . so . . . you've made a full and frank confession. Thank you, Mr Pink. That makes everything simpler. Can you explain what happened and why?'

'Not really. I mean, I've thought about it so much, and asked questions, but I haven't been able to . . . *ascertain* exactly what went wrong. All I can say is that it was an honest mistake and I'm terribly sorry about it. Truly, it will haunt me until—'

He couldn't finish. Suddenly he was too choked up.

PC Braddick took out a little pack of tissues and gave one to him, just the way he'd once offered his hanky to Amanda. That memory only made his tears flow harder. He'd liked Amanda. He'd trusted her. He must be a terrible judge of character. Margaret would have spotted something amiss with Amanda, he was sure. Miss Knott had and she hadn't even met her! But Felix hadn't had a lot of experience of friendship.

He blew his nose and slowly calmed down.

'Is there anything else, Mr Pink?'

Felix hesitated.

'No,' he said firmly. 'That's all.'

PC Braddick bent over her paperwork again, then said, 'OK. If you wouldn't mind waiting here for a few minutes, I'll try not to keep you.'

She scooped up her papers and left the room.

Despite the tears, despite the tiredness, Felix breathed properly for the first time since the death of Albert Cann.

Mr Martin had a face like a lemon.

That's what Jackie Braddick thought as she watched him mentally searching for a loophole that would allow him to reject Felix Pink's apology without looking like a complete arse. He couldn't find it, of course, and eventually his sour little face puckered in concession.

'It's just very upsetting,' he said for about the millionth time since walking into the police station and demanding action.

'Of course, Mr Martin. But I can assure you that Mr Pink is truly sorry. He's an elderly gentleman and—'

'Elderly *thief*!' Mr Martin interjected.

'Well, he's got a nasty bump on the head and seems a little confused. I imagine he just wasn't thinking straight.'

'Are you saying he's off his rocker? Because if he's off his rocker, how do I know he's not going to do it again?'

'I didn't say he was off his rocker, sir,' said Jackie sharply.

'Well then, what the *hell* is he doing leaning over my wall and picking my flowers?' His voice became loud and Jackie put her hands on her hips.

'Calm down, please, Mr Martin.'

She waited until he had done that to her satisfaction.

'Now, if you're prepared to accept Mr Pink's apology, and if he'd be prepared to be bound over, then I think that would be a good way of handling it, don't you?'

'What about my losses?'

'What losses?'

'He picked my tulips!'

'One tulip.'

'That I know of! And even if it *was* only one, I paid for that bulb and I dug it in and I watered it and tended it. That was *my flower*. And then he comes along and just *steals* it.'

'So what are you saying, Mr Martin?

'I think compensation would be fair.'

They glared at each other, unblinking.

'Right,' sighed Jackie finally. 'And how much do you think would be fair for picking one tulip?'

'Fifty pounds.'

'*Fifty pounds?*'

'Yes.'

Jackie gave him a look that would have withered an oak, but Mr Martin was made of more lemony stuff.

'Wait here,' she said, and banged away through the double doors.

Calvin Bridge poked his head into the corridor. 'You all right?'

She stopped and put her hands on her hips – always a sign of impending meltdown. 'Effing people!' she hissed. 'Worst job *ever*!'

'Not so fast!' Calvin put up an imperious hand to stop her. 'I'm having to go through the Exiteer database *again*, so I'm still in the running. Want a crisp?'

'I guarantee you lose.' She stomped in and took a crisp. 'Get this. I've just had to arrest a lovely old man after this utter git comes in accusing him of picking his flowers.'

'Did he do it?'

'Yeah.'

'I hate to break it to you, Jacks, but that's theft.'

'But he didn't pick a *bunch* of flowers. He picked *one bloody tulip!*'

'All right,' laughed Calvin, 'that's pretty mean. But technically . . .'

'Wait for it . . .' she said. 'You haven't heard the worst bit yet. When I arrested the old man he . . . *cried*.'

'Shit!' Calvin threw up his hands. 'Take the whole packet.'

Jackie grinned and swiped the crisps off the table and stuffed a handful into her mouth. 'Want to see the crime of the century?'

'It's on CCTV?' he said, and – when she laughed and nodded – pulled out the chair so that she could sit at the desk and bring up the footage on the screen.

There it was: an old man walking a little white dog into frame . . .

'Watch now,' said Jackie. 'He stops and his dog has a wee, and then he leans over and . . . *there*. A tulip, m'lud! Plucked in its prime and carried off in broad daylight! Lock him up and throw away the effing key!'

She giggled, but Calvin didn't.

Calvin was frowning very hard at the screen. At the tall, thin man with a vague limp and a short beige zip-up jacket.

'Bloody hell,' he said. 'I think that's the bloke who killed Albert Cann.'

Felix's Other Confession

'Sorry to keep you waiting so long, Mr Pink. I'm DCI Kirsty King and this is Acting DC Calvin Bridge. PC Braddick you already know.'

'Yes. Thank you. How do you do?'

'I'm sorry?'

'How do you do?'

'Oh, right. Thank you. How do *you* do? Now, before we get started, are you all right for food and drink and a bathroom break?'

'Yes, thank you, Inspector King. Sergeant Coral . . . ?'

'Yes, Sergeant Coral.'

'He brought me a cup of tea and a piece of fruit cake.'

'Well, apologies for those.'

'Ha! Yes, well, it's the thought that counts.'

'Indeed. So, Mr Pink . . .'

'Felix. Please.'

'So, Felix, I've listened to the recording PC Braddick made earlier and it appears you've made a full and frank admission.'

'I have.'

'Good. That's good. Well, thank you, Felix.'

'Not at all. When one has made a terrible mistake, one must take responsibility for it.'

'I agree. But there's something I have to check.'

'Oh yes? What's that?'

'Given you declined the assistance of a lawyer, I just want to make absolutely sure you know what's going on.'

'Right ho.'

'Can you tell me why you were arrested, Felix?'

'Well, I'm not sure of the actual *charge*, but it was for . . . for being . . . *responsible* . . . for the, um . . . death of Albert Cann.'

'Ah. OK. I thought as much. The trouble is, Felix, you weren't actually arrested in connection with the death of Mr Cann.'

'Oh?'

'No. You were arrested for stealing flowers from one of your neighbours.'

'Oh!'

'Yes. A Mr Andrew Martin.'

'Oh. Um. I see. Well, how embarrassing.'

'It's only because Acting DC Bridge here saw the CCTV footage of that incident that he recognized you as the man who went into the Cann home on the morning of the second that we realized there may well have been a misunderstanding.'

'Oh.'

'PC Braddick actually arrested you for the crime of common theft. She says she read you your rights in relation to *that* crime.'

'Did she?'

'She says she did, but if you're disputing that . . . ?'

'No, no, that's probably my fault. I'm a little deaf anyway and it was a shock to be arrested, and Mabel was barking, and Jackie stood on my pencil, so you can imagine I was quite upset all round.'

'Your pencil?'

'The one with the tassel. In the hallway. She didn't mean to break it.'

'Jackie?'

'I didn't realize I'd broken anything, ma'am. I'm very sorry if I did.'

'We will of course replace anything that was broken during your arrest, Mr Pink. We have a form you can fill in. Jackie, if you can—'

'I can't replace it. It came with the address book and it's attached by a gold cord. It belonged to my wife, you see? She died a few years ago . . . But that's neither here nor there. I'm not complaining, just *explaining* why I was distracted.'

'So you don't want to claim compensation?'

'Of course not. It's just a pencil. Worse things happen at sea.'

'That's very good of you, Felix. Thank you. Now, the more pressing issue we have is this . . . because you did not know why you were being arrested, the confession you made with regard to the death of Albert Cann is actually inadmissible.'

'Inadmissible?'

'Yes. We can't use it. It's like it never happened.'

'Oh.'

'Do you understand?'

'Not really.'

'Well, you've confessed to a crime we haven't arrested you for. And *haven't* yet confessed to the crime for which you *were* arrested.'

'Oh dear. I'm sorry if I've complicated things.'

'Don't worry about it. I'm sure we can sort it out now.'

'Excellent.'

'So, Felix, the good news is that Mr Martin is willing to accept your apology and some compensation, if you are prepared to be bound over, which means that you must promise to keep the peace and not to touch his property again—'

'Oh, I won't be doing *that* again, believe me!'

'Good, so if you're happy to make an apology, and to be bound over and to pay Mr Martin fifty pounds compensation, then we can put that whole matter to bed.'

King smiled, but then tapped the file on the table.

'The *bad* news is that we're going to have to arrest you on the charges relating to the death of Albert Cann. You'll have another opportunity to call a lawyer, of course, and we'll go back to the start, as it were, and do things properly, all right?

'. . . Mr Pink?'

'. . . Felix . . . ?'

'Fifty pounds?'

'Sorry?'

'Fifty pounds?'

'That's the sum Mr Martin feels is fair for the theft of his tulip.'

'Well . . . *he* might feel it's fair, but I certainly don't! Whatever happened to accepting an apology? I'll shake his hand like a gentleman and I'm more than happy to buy him a whole *bag* of bulbs, but fifty pounds? For one measly flower? And his garden wasn't even a ten. It was only an eight – and then I had to reduce that to a seven because of the grass, so it's not as if his tulips are winning any medals at Chelsea, is it? I'll give him five pounds and that's *that*.'

'O . . . K . . . um. Well, then . . . Jackie, would you mind letting Mr Martin . . . ?'

'Yes, ma'am.'

'Thank you. PC Braddick leaving the room. Right, Felix. While Jackie's speaking to Mr Martin, would you like me to call a lawyer?'

'For what?'

'So that we can take a statement from you about Albert Cann.'

'Oh yes, of course. Sorry – I'm still thinking about the tulip.'

'So do you have a lawyer you'd like us to call?'

'No, no, let's just get on with it, shall we? I want to get it off my chest.'

'Felix, I really do advise having a lawyer. Especially in a case of this potential gravity.'

'If you don't mind, Inspector, I've been here several hours already and I'm tired. I just want to get it off my chest and make sure Skipper's all right and then have a rest.'

'Why would Skipper not be all right, Felix?'

'Just . . . No. No reason. It's just, he fell recently when his stick broke. And – you know – he's very unwell . . .'

'Of course. We understand. As part of the investigation we have already informed his doctor and health visitors that he needs more regular monitoring now that Albert is no longer . . . in the home. However, his grandson still resides in the house and is used to caring for Skipper, and I understand the cleaner helps out too, when she's there, so there's no need to worry about him, all right?'

'Well . . . I suppose so.'

'OK. Again, for the record, Mr Pink has been advised of his right to have a lawyer present and has declined. Mr Pink states his desire to continue unrepresented. Are you ready, Felix?'

'Yes. Well, nearly. I wonder if someone might ask my neighbour, Miss Knott, to look after my dog?'

'Of course. We'll take care of it.'

'Thank you. Mabel's good for about six hours, you see, but after that she will widdle on the floor.'

Mr Martin stood up and glared at Jackie Braddick. 'You took your time!'

'I'm sorry to keep you waiting, Mr Martin, but things became rather complicated.'

'Complicated how?'

'I'm afraid Mr Pink says no.'

The man was plainly surprised. 'No, what?'

'No, he doesn't agree to your terms,' she said. 'He says he's happy to apologize and pay what he considers to be reasonable compensation or to replace your tulip, but he's not paying you fifty pounds.'

Martin's face became a walnut of confusion. 'What does that mean?'

Jackie Braddick took a deep breath. 'He says he'll give you a fiver.'

'A *fiver*?'

'And an apology, of course.'

'But that's ... totally unacceptable! And anyway, surely *he* doesn't get to decide this?'

'Well, that's not strictly true,' she told him. 'Mr Pink has to agree to the terms of any binding over. If he doesn't agree to be bound over, then he can be charged with theft, but he doesn't *have* to do anything.'

'Fine then,' he said petulantly. 'You'll be charging him with theft, I assume?'

'I'm not sure that's going to happen, Mr Martin. Events have rather overtaken us and Mr Pink is likely to be charged in connection with a more serious crime.'

'More serious than theft?' He laughed sarcastically. 'Like what? Murder?'

'That's the allegation.'

Mr Martin stopped laughing and blinked rapidly several times instead. 'Oh my God. Murder? Really?'

Jackie nodded.

'Jesus,' said Martin, and he slumped down on to the bench. 'You never think it's going to happen to you, do you?'

'To be fair,' she said, 'it *didn't* happen to you.'

'But it *could* have! I mean, all this fuss about the flowers! Who knows where that could have gone?'

'That's true,' Jackie nodded. 'I suppose things might have ended quite differently.'

Mr Martin nodded. 'Maybe I've had a narrow squeak there.'

'Maybe you have.'

Martin looked around the dingy reception area as if in need of somebody else to bear witness to the narrowness of his squeak, but there was nobody, so he looked at Jackie again.

'I assume he'll be kept in custody?'

'Unlikely,' said Jackie. 'Mr Pink's very old and he's not a flight risk.'

'You mean he could be let *out*? On *bail*?'

'Very likely, yes. Prisons are bursting at the seams, Mr Martin, and judges aren't encouraged to send people there – especially vulnerable people.'

'What about *this* vulnerable person?' he shouted and poked himself in the chest several times.

'Please don't feel concerned, Mr Martin. The circumstances of the allegations against Mr Pink are very specific. He has no reason to feel aggrieved with anyone.'

'He has reason to feel aggrieved with *me*!'

'Well, I mean *really* aggrieved.'

'How do you know?' he said. 'Maybe he only has to be aggrieved *enough*.' He ran his hand through his hair anxiously, and Jackie gave him no words of comfort.

Instead she clapped her hands together to show she was getting on with business. 'Now, sir, do you want me to go back to Mr Pink with a counter-counter-offer?'

'No!' said Martin. He got up and started towards the door. 'No, thank you.'

'Are you sure, sir? It's no trouble.'

'You said Mr Pink was confused and vulnerable. So I think on balance it would be more . . . compassionate . . . to leave it, don't you?'

'I think it would,' she agreed.

'Thank you,' he said, and pulled open the door.

'Thank *you*, Mr Martin.'

The door swung shut behind him and Jackie Braddick headed back to the interview room with a grin on her face.

Best job ever.

The Terrible Liar

Felix Pink was a terrible liar.

When he'd finished confessing to killing Albert Cann, DCI Kirsty King simply sat back in her seat, gave him a long hard look, and said, 'I don't believe you.'

Felix was briefly offended, but then remembered she was right, and that his natural propensity to tell the truth was a very poor platform on which to construct an elaborate scaffold of lies. He thought of how ashamed Jamie would be if he could see him now, and shrivelled a little inside.

DCI King sighed heavily. 'However, there are some things I do believe.'

'Oh, good,' he said encouragingly.

'I do believe you were in the house.'

Felix nodded eagerly. Finally a truth he could agree with.

'I do believe you went there to oversee the death of Skipper Cann.'

He nodded again.

'I do believe that Albert Cann's death was as a result of a mistake on your part.'

He nodded sadly.

'But what I *don't* believe,' said DCI King, 'is that you did all this alone, and without help from either someone in the Cann family or another Exiteer.'

He said nothing.

DCI King looked at him steadily for a long, uncomfortable moment, then seemed to make an important choice. 'We have information which indicates that you and your colleague may have been set up.'

Felix flinched and looked at his hands, clasped together on the table in front of him.

'We think you may have been used, Felix. None of this may be your fault. And if that's the case then your silence may be protecting the very person who set you up.'

Felix held fast.

DCI King changed tack. 'And you're concerned for Skipper. But if you don't tell me who else was involved in all of this, then how can I protect him? When I don't know who I should be protecting him *from*?'

Felix sighed. He liked DCI King, and he understood and supported what she was trying to do. He just couldn't help her *do* it. He had made a promise to Skipper Cann and would die before breaking it.

Kirsty King reached urgently across the table – her small hands almost touching his. 'Felix,' she said, 'this could be a matter of life and death.'

But Felix knew it was much more important than that.

It was a matter of integrity.

After two hours with Felix Pink, DCI Kirsty King came into the office in such a rare bad mood that even the vending machine dared not dally with her. She punched the buttons hard and got exactly what she asked for.

'I've never heard a confession that made me *less* convinced of somebody's guilt,' she fumed. 'CPS are never going to go for a charge on the basis of him saying he acted alone when we have him on camera with an accomplice.'

'Makes no sense,' said Pete. 'Why would he protect this woman if he doesn't even know her?'

'Maybe he *does* know her,' said Calvin. 'Maybe she's his daughter. He'd want to protect her then, wouldn't he? Or a granddaughter.'

'Or maybe he's shagging her,' said Pete.

'I didn't get that vibe from him *at all*,' said King.

Pete shrugged. 'Everybody's shagging *somebody*.'

Pete's wife had moved in with her gym instructor. Everybody knew it.

'What do you think about his concern for Skipper Cann, ma'am?' asked Calvin.

King scooped her items from the vending bin. 'It feels like a distraction.'

'The old tea towel?' Calvin said, and King smiled – albeit briefly.

'Can we get Geoffrey Skeet back in?' Calvin asked.

King shook her head. 'We'd need hard evidence to do that now.'

For a moment she stood and frowned at her sandwich, then made up her mind.

'We're going to have to go back to basics,' she said decisively. 'Did you call the neighbour about the dog, Calvin?'

'Not yet, ma'am.'

'Then go over there instead. You two get a warrant and search the house. Find good hard evidence. We'll forget the confession and build a case from the ground up. It's not impossible; it's just a pain when we thought we were so far ahead of the game.'

'Yes, ma'am!' said Pete, and picked up the phone.

King started for the door, but stopped halfway. 'Pete?'

'Ma'am?'

'Don't tear the place apart. Jackie already stepped on his pencil.'

Calvin Bridge had to lean over a large ginger cat to open the front door. It hissed menacingly.

'Ignore it,' said Pete. 'The thing is to show no fear. Watch this.' Fearlessly, he worked the toe of his boot under the cat's bottom.

It whipped around, dug its claws into his leg and bit him hard through his trousers.

'Shit!' He had to kick out several times before it let go – and then re-took its place on the doormat to lick its own shoulders.

'Did you see that?' Pete rolled up his trouser leg. Little rivers of blood snaked through the hairs on his shin.

'Little *bastard*! You think it's got rabies?'

Calvin thought that was nigh-on impossible, but he shrugged and said something about the Channel Tunnel anyway.

Then he opened the door and they edged around the cat.

Inside, a little white dog wagged and barked.

'I'll have a look upstairs,' said Pete.

Calvin went through to the kitchen and let the dog out into the garden, then looked around him as he pulled on a pair of latex gloves.

There was a jigsaw on the table. Reindeer. It looked like a tough one with all that snow. Next to the puzzle was a collection of random objects. A few coins. A tablet. A crumpled receipt. It reminded him of the little pile that emerged when he emptied his pockets on to the top of the chest of drawers in his bedroom every night.

But why would Felix Pink empty his pockets on to the kitchen table?

Unless . . .

Calvin looked around the room. His eyes came to rest on the washing machine. A little green light flashed to show the cycle had finished. Calvin switched it off and opened the door.

The first thing he pulled from the machine was a short beige zip-up jacket.

He held it up to the light from the window. The jacket was wet and streaked with black, but it was so like the one on the CCTV footage that Calvin felt almost sure it was a match.

Pete came in, waving an address book. 'Hey, this was in the hall-way and guess who's under D for Dentist? A Mr D. Williams in Tiverton!' He smiled triumphantly. 'Who the hell goes thirty miles to a dentist? Must be the supplier of the laughing gas.'

'Nice going,' said Calvin. 'And look at this. That's the jacket he was wearing in the CCTV, isn't it?'

'Maybe.' Pete frowned at it. 'What's all that black muck?'

'Maybe he's tried to dye it.'

'*Dye* it?' said Pete. 'Why not just chuck it?'

'He's old,' shrugged Calvin. 'Waste not, want not. Hey, look at this . . .'

He put the jacket on the counter and turned to the little clus-ter of random pocket-items. He picked up the tablet. It was a round, yellow pill with the letters *OC* stamped on one side and *30* on the other. It looked innocuous, but Calvin only had to meet Pete's eyes to confirm that it was Oxycodone – the drug found in Albert Cann's system, even though it had not been pre-scribed for him.

With a surprisingly heavy heart, Calvin put down the pill and smoothed open the receipt. It was a return bus ticket from Bide-ford Quay to Abbotsham. The date on it was May 2 – the day Albert Cann was killed.

'Hey, Pete. Looks like he went to the murder on a bus after all.'

'Jesus,' said Pete softly. 'Who needs a bloody confession?'

He called DCI King to give her the good news, while Calvin gazed around the room. There really was an embarrassment of evidence. Too much, really. So much unhidden . . .

Was it another tea towel?

Pete hung up. 'She's happy. She's coming out and we're all off to the dentist. Doesn't want to call first and give him the chance to destroy any records.'

Calvin nodded and looked at the clock. It was nearly four now. 'We'd better take the dog next door and get going then.'

He opened the back door and yelped in surprise.

'Can I help you?' said the old woman standing there.

'DC Bridge, ma'am. Bideford Police.'

'And what are you doing in there?'

'We have a warrant to search Mr Pink's house.'

'So why are you unloading the washing machine?' she said a bit crossly.

She walked in as if Calvin wasn't there, took the jacket from the counter and held it up to study it. Then she frowned and hung it neatly on the back of a kitchen chair.

Calvin should have stopped her, of course, but she was an old lady, so what could he do?

She hasn't asked where Felix is, thought Calvin. *Isn't surprised we're searching his house. She knows what's going on . . .*

'Are you Miss Knott?' he said, and when she nodded curtly, he said, 'Felix asked if you might look after his dog, ma'am. Would that be OK?'

She softened a little. 'Of course,' she said and – right on cue – the dog trotted in from the garden and made a fuss of her.

While she did, Calvin picked up the pill and swapped glances with Pete.

'Does Mr Pink take any medication?' Pete asked.

Immediately Miss Knott looked concerned. 'Not that I'm aware of, no. Why? Is he unwell? I was a nurse . . .'

'Maybe you can help then,' said Calvin. 'Do you know what this is?' He held the pill out to her.

'It looks like Oxycodone,' she frowned. 'But Felix shouldn't be taking anything that strong. He has a bit of a hip, but nothing too serious.'

'Do you know why he'd have it in his possession?'

She frowned and then shook her head warily.

'Have you heard him mention a man named Albert Cann?' said Pete.

'Look, young man,' she said briskly, 'I'm old and I can't stand here all day answering questions. I need to get Mabel some food and get home.'

And with that she shouldered between them and opened a few cupboards until she found one stacked with little metal trays of dog food. She piled half a dozen on to the counter and looked around for something to carry them in. 'Could you pass me that bag, please?'

She pointed at the string bag hung on a hook. But Calvin just stared past her into the open cupboard full of dog food. He walked over and shone his torch into the back of the cupboard. There, exposed by Miss Knott's raid on the dog food, were four steel cylinders – each with a mask and rubber tubing coiled neatly beside it.

Either Felix Pink wanted to make absolutely sure of killing himself, or he was planning a slow, funny massacre.

'So much for not providing the instrument of death,' said Pete grimly.

'But he didn't do it!'

They both looked at Miss Knott.

'Didn't do what?' said Calvin, heart thudding.

'Felix didn't kill that poor man,' she blurted out. 'It wasn't his fault. He was set up by that girl he was with. He promised to keep her out of it because she's young and he's old, which is all very noble of course, but I tell you, I think she's a bad apple! And now Felix is taking the blame for something that he didn't do!'

She stopped talking and shut her mouth tightly, as if she hadn't meant to say *any* of that, and *certainly* wouldn't be saying any more.

'This girl who was with Felix,' said Calvin, 'you don't happen to know her name, do you?'

Miss Knott wrestled gallantly with her mouth for a moment or two, and finally lost.

'I most certainly do,' she said. 'It's Andrea.'

Amanda

MAN, 75, QUIZZED IN ABBOTSHAM DEATH
'All right, maid?'

Amanda blinked.

She looked away from the *Devon Live* headline scrolling across the TV screen and back at Dickie Richards, who was waiting at the rough chipboard counter for . . . what? She couldn't remember. Had he told her? Also a blank.

Amanda was a parts assistant at LecCo, an electrical supplies firm in Barnstaple. It was a dreadful job, on the face of it. She worked in a gloomy warehouse with ceiling-high shelves filled with big boxes containing smaller boxes containing wire and screws and bulbs and relays. She'd been nervous when she'd got the job a year ago, as she'd turned out to be the only woman in the place. However, instead of being objectified by a bunch of sexist tradesmen the way she'd expected, Amanda had found herself adored and protected. They did tease her, of course, and they'd all – whether married or single – asked her out at first, and she'd had to invent a boyfriend called Mark to rebuff them without hurting their egos. She'd done a good job, though – Mark was not sporty, and was thinning on top. He also was rather tight and bought her very poor gifts: a lumpy woollen scarf, a photo of himself in a plain wooden frame, and a *Grand Tour* box set for Christmas. Once they'd gone for a meal at a mediocre restaurant where he'd embarrassed her by refusing to leave a tip after the

waiter had declined to honour an out-of-date voucher. All of this
allowed her LecCo colleagues and customers to feel superior to
Mark and sympathetic to Amanda, even as it forced them to keep
their distance.

Then, a few months ago, she'd met Reggie. A chance meeting,
but a wonderful chance. They'd gone for coffee and drinks, and
had once seen a movie starring Mark Wahlberg. Despite that,
they'd nearly had sex, before she'd decided she was too old to do it
in a car, especially as his little red coupé didn't even have a back
seat.

But she *would* have sex with Reggie. Amanda had been sure of
that almost from the start. She liked him. She thought she might
love him. And he had his own house, while she still lived with her
parents. The house was a big point in Reggie's favour, even though
she hadn't been there yet. He'd told her it smelled like a hospital
and they'd both agreed that having sex with his grandfather dying
of cancer in the next room would be *a bit weird*.

She totally understood that. She could wait. His grandfather
wouldn't live for ever, and then they'd have the place all to themselves. So, by April, Amanda had felt confident enough in their
future together to invent a girl called Chloe for Mark to cheat with,
and a break-up which she bore with great stoicism at work. Her
refusal to tar all men with the same brush had only endeared her
further to her colleagues. Of course, she'd had to tell them about
Reggie pretty sharpish to avoid any of them trying to move into
the boyfriend vacuum, but Amanda had been grateful for their
very real support of her entirely fictitious predicament.

Now, however, her predicament was only too real, and she wondered just how supportive her friends and colleagues would be if
they knew what she'd done . . .

'Sorry, Dickie. What was it you wanted?'

'Two ten-metre rolls of twin-core.'

'That's right. You said.'

'No, I didn't.'

'Didn't you?'

She glanced back at the TV and Dickie looked at Stevo and Sean, then crossed his arms on the counter and demanded, 'You pregnant, maid?'

'Me? No! Why?'

''Cos my wife gone all mazed when she were pregnant. *Where was I? Where am I? What the eff am I doing married to you?*'

They all laughed. Amanda didn't. The TV was showing a photo of Albert Cann next to a giraffe.

'I need a ride to Abbotsham,' she said.

The three men gave each other confused smiles. Amanda must have made a joke, but it couldn't have been a good one because none of them had really got it . . .

She slapped the counter with a crack like a rifle. 'Right now!'

And before they knew it, Dickie and Stevo were driving her to Abbotsham in the van, while LecCo and the displaced Sean disappeared in the mirrors.

They drove in weird silence. Divided from Amanda by the counter, Dickie and Stevo could banter for England; thigh-to-thigh with her on the bench seat of a Transit van, they were mute.

'Can we go any faster?' Amanda didn't know why speed was critical, but felt instinctively that it must be.

Dickie speeded up.

'This Reggie,' he said carefully, 'he's not done a Mark on you, has he?'

'Mark?'

'Mark,' he nodded.

Mark. Oh, *Mark*! She'd forgotten Mark and how he'd cheated with that girl whose name she couldn't remember. It was so easy to forget imaginary people. How sweet of Dickie to ask, though, and a useful distraction from what had really happened. So she only shrugged, and was touched to see Dickie and Stevo exchange meaningful glances.

She looked at her phone. Four fifteen. Reggie left work at four on Fridays. He should be home by now. She imagined him opening the door . . . Didn't know what she'd say when he did, but she'd say *something* and then *he*'d say something, and they'd take it from there, the way they always did, and everything would be OK. It *would* be. Reggie had been terribly upset at the café, of course, but he was honest and kind and she knew that he'd have perfectly reasonable answers for all the questions the old man had raised in her mind. Then they could work it out *together*, and what had seemed like the end would become no more than a hiccup. A shared tribulation. A bonding experience.

A way back . . .

Amanda felt a little burst of optimism. The truth could be the making of them. But first they'd have to find it.

The van reached Abbotsham and pulled up outside the house in Black Lane.

Stevo jumped out to let her out of the cab but Amanda looked up at the house and faltered.

Reggie's dad, choking and pleading.

'That his car?' said Dickie.

'Mm.'

'Fancy,' said Stevo.

'You want me to come with you?' said Dickie.

'No!' she said. Then smiled. 'Thanks. I'll be fine.'

'We'll wait then,' he said firmly, and suddenly Amanda was at the point of no return. If she'd come alone, she wouldn't have done it. Would have turned around and walked back to the bus stop. But instead she said *thank you* and Stevo put up a hand and helped her down and her numb legs walked her on to the driveway, just the way they had on that morning four weeks ago . . . Then there had been an air of unreality about walking into a house to watch a man die. A still, dreamlike state – like the first snow of winter.

But now the van ticked over loudly, and Stevo's work boots scuffed the pavement and she was only halfway up the drive before she could hear two people arguing. A man and a woman.

The man was Reggie.

Amanda glanced back at the van nervously. Stevo and Dickie were watching her.

Feeling utterly exposed, she could only stand and listen.

Bad Day at Black Lane

Reggie Cann was sitting on the sofa in his underwear playing *Call of Duty*, because war was less stressful than the web of lies that his life had become.

He wondered what a nervous breakdown felt like: he thought he might be having one. The woman he loved had killed his father, thanks to his cowardly deception. And Albert's death had been only the beginning. In the weeks since then he'd lied to Amanda, been punched in the face, and was facing financial ruin – or broken legs. He couldn't go to the police because Amanda would go to jail, and couldn't even ask Skipper for help, because knowing that Albert had risked their home would kill him . . . Which was how they'd got into this mess in the first place.

The whole thing was like juggling jellies.

Without taking his eyes off the screen or his hands off the controls, Reggie lifted his legs up so that the cleaner could vacuum under them.

She said something he didn't catch.

'What?'

She turned off the vacuum cleaner.

'What?' he repeated.

'I'm pregnant,' she said – apparently again – and, for a single blissful moment, Reggie thought she was telling him because she would have to cut back on her hours. That would be great. She'd become terrible at her job and he'd love to pay less for it . . .

But she was looking at him in a way a cleaner wouldn't, and an electric jolt passed through him as he realized she must be telling him for a far more dreadful reason.

'*What?*' he said again anyway, because he never wanted to move on past that point in the conversation.

But she only put a cliché of a hand on her tummy and explained as she might to an idiot, 'I'm going to have a baby.'

Reggie stared at her hand. She wasn't a fat girl but she was no lightweight, and she didn't look any different to him. 'Don't be silly,' he said firmly. He didn't know the cleaner that well – she might have that kind of sense of so-called humour that meant she thought it was funny to tell men she was having their baby, just to see the look on their faces.

'I'm not being silly,' she said, and looked hurt. 'I've missed loads of periods.'

'But we only did it once!'

'But I've only *ever* done it once!' she shouted. 'With *you*!'

And she burst into tears that washed Reggie backwards through time . . . She cleaning and dusting with more cleavage and wiggle each week. A tease here, an innuendo there, and – when he'd driven her home one afternoon with a cut finger and found an empty house – a brief, clumsy shag on a pile of dirty clothes, while a parrot made a noise like a fire engine.

'You said you loved me!' she cried.

'I did not!'

He might have, though. It had been a while since he'd had sex. Certainly long enough to be grateful enough to leave the key under the mat for her every day, so she could get away from the mayhem of her own home even when she wasn't cleaning his. He'd thought it was a *quid pro quo*.

Apparently it wasn't.

It seemed impossible that something so minor could result in something so major when they hadn't even taken their clothes off.

Reggie was dazed. He took her hand. Started to speak. Forgot her name. Hannah. Layla. *Hayley.* Hayleyhayleyhayley. Phew!

'Hayley,' he said cautiously, 'do you want to keep it?'

'Of course! Don't you?'

'Well . . .' He pulled a very reluctant face.

'But you've got a house!'

'That doesn't mean I have to have a *baby*. The two don't go together, you know!'

Her weeping turned to anger. 'Well, I can't stay at my house with a baby! It's mad there. Josie plays her music and Rita already takes up more than half the bedroom with her Harry Potter shit! And you've got a spare room now—'

'Jesus, Hayley, Albert's only just died! And anyway, you can't just *move in*. What about Skipper?'

'What about him?' She shrugged. 'It's your house!'

He might have said that too. He'd let Amanda believe it as well. Little white lies to make himself look richer. More manly. And it *would* be true. Soon! So where was the harm in it?

He was only just beginning to see . . .

Hayley apparently took his hesitation as impending victory. 'We won't be any trouble,' she said eagerly. 'Honest! I won't even ask you to help with the baby 'cos you've already got tons to do, with work and all. And I can look after Skipper and I'll clean the house for free and it'll be no trouble, Reggie, I *swear*.'

It's already trouble! he wanted to yell. It had only been two minutes and it was already a fucking *nightmare*.

He felt like crying. He really did. Hayley meant nothing to him and he was pretty sure he meant nothing to her. They hadn't even talked about the sex since it had happened, and hadn't repeated it because shortly afterwards he'd met Amanda, and had moved forward without any desire to look back. So far the only real consequence of having sex with the cleaner had been that, when her work rate had dwindled to zero, he hadn't fired her.

And now this. After everything else! There had to be a way out.

Reggie squeezed Hayley's hand and said, 'I think you should see a doctor. Just to be sure.'

But she shook him off furiously and shouted, 'I told you! I'm *pregnant!*'

She stormed into the kitchen and Reggie turned to follow her—

And saw Amanda.

Standing in the driveway. Looking at him through the hole in the window.

How?

For an infinite moment their eyes met and Reggie saw in her face all the hurt that the world had to offer. Then she ran.

No!

Nononononononono!

He went after her, out of the door in his socks, across the wet grass. 'Manda!' he shouted. 'Manda, wait!'

There was a van – and a man standing beside it. And Amanda reached the open door. '*I want to go!*' she shouted. '*Please, Dickie!*'

And then the man in the dirty work boots was pushing her into the van like a kidnap victim—

'*Manda, please!*'

The man turned and spread his arms to stop him—

Oi oi OI!

But Reggie was watching Amanda and never saw the punch coming.

Right on his previously punched nose.

The Dentist

The bright, smiley girl on reception was dressed in blue scrubs, as though she needed to be sterile to answer the phone. A big childish badge told them her name was BECKY.

When they said they were police officers, Becky's eyes widened.

'Dr Williams is with a patient right now,' she said. 'Can you wait?'

'No,' said DCI King. 'Please tell him it's urgent.'

The girl disappeared and Pete and Calvin stood looking at the posters of talking teeth, and the overpriced toothbrushes for sale on the counter. Calvin wondered if they ever sold one.

The girl came back and said Dr Williams would be right out.

But he wasn't.

King gave it thirty seconds, then gave them the nod and they barged in to find the dentist trying to climb out of the window, while a horizontal patient with a spit-sucker in her cheek demanded to know 'Wha-go-ah?'

'Excuse us, madam,' said Pete. 'Police.'

Calvin moved quickly to grab Dr Williams, who protested loudly at being manhandled and said he'd been going to buy a sandwich.

Calvin ushered him back to the surgery, where Kirsty King was already going through his accounts with the receptionist.

'Just the nitrous oxide transactions, thank you. Ah. Dr Williams, I presume?'

'He was trying to get out of the window, ma'am,' said Pete.

'I was going for a sandwich,' Williams maintained haughtily.

'Of course,' she said. 'Sorry to interrupt your lunch, Dr Williams, but you could save us all time by telling me if you recall selling cylinders of nitrous oxide to a Mr Felix Pink of Barnstaple.'

'Never heard of him,' he said.

'How about Geoffrey Skeet?'

'No, sorry.'

'There's nothing on the computer in those names,' said Becky helpfully.

'Is that it? Where are your paper files?'

'We don't have them any more,' he said. 'Paperless office.'

'We're very environmentally conscious,' agreed Becky.

'Well, please could you print off records of all the N_2O purchases and sales you have made in the past year? For starters.'

'Do you have a warrant or something?' said Williams.

'We assumed you would cooperate, sir. If you'd rather not, let me know now and I'll be happy to arrest you and lead you out of here in handcuffs so you can sit in a cell while we get a warrant.'

'Obviously I'll co*operate*. I'm a dental surgeon, not a criminal! We just got off on the wrong foot, that's all.'

'We did,' King said drily. 'That whole *window* thing . . .'

'Becky, print off the purchases for the officers, please. You won't find any sales on the system because there *are* no sales of nitrous oxide. N_2O is very tightly controlled.'

'I didn't know dentists even used laughing gas any more.'

'Oh, we do. People like it. No needles.'

'I can see the appeal,' she nodded. 'Well, that clears that up then. If you could show me your N_2O stocks while Becky prints off the purchases and relevant patient records that would be great. Then we can make sure it's all accounted for and be on our way.'

'Excuse me?'

'Well, I assume that when you administer N_2O to a patient you keep a record of that.'

'Yes. Of course.'

'Then you'll have a record of how much N_2O you have bought and how much you've used. All we have to do is check your stocks and do the maths and *voila*.'

'Yes. Except, I'm afraid, patient records are confidential. We can't just *print them off*.'

He smiled, but King did not. 'Patient confidentiality is not a priority here, Dr Williams. We're investigating a murder.'

The dentist paled. 'A what?'

'You heard me.'

A cold silence descended, in the middle of which Becky discreetly slid two sheets of laser-printed paper across the desk.

'Those are the purchase orders.'

'Thank you,' King said, picking them up and studying them. 'I see you order tanks, bottles *and* whippits.'

'Whippits?' said the dentist.

She looked at him curiously. 'Aren't those the little metal cylinders kids take to festivals?'

'You flatter me,' Williams laughed mirthlessly. 'I'm too old for festivals. I have no clue what kids do now.'

But luckily Becky did, and volunteered, 'Yeah, you see loads of people huffing noz at Glastonbury. Not me. Other people.'

'And what do *you* use the whippits for, Dr Williams?'

'I don't. I think that must have been a purchasing error.'

King ran her eye down the list. 'One you've repeated on six occasions in the past year?'

Williams said nothing, and Calvin felt almost sorry for him. They could all see the precipice he was heading for now, even Becky. Calvin always found it hard to watch people realize they were screwed. There were only two options for them. He always hoped they would turn back from the edge and come clean, but lots of people just closed their eyes and ran into the precipice.

'So can we see your N_2O stocks, please, Dr Williams?'

'Umm ... I don't know where the storeroom key is,' he said pathetically. 'You lost it a couple of days ago, didn't you, Becky?'

'No,' said Becky, because she was on minimum wage, and because the blue scrubs made her arse look big, and because Dr Williams had once docked her a day's pay for booking an all-four-corners wisdom-tooth extraction on an afternoon when he'd arranged to play the back nine at Burnham and Berrow.

She handed him his fate on a key ring shaped like a molar.

The Dead Man

Reggie slowly opened his eyes. The sky was a brilliant blue, with puffy little Simpsons clouds.

Amanda!

He tried to sit up to see if she was still there, but it hurt too much to move his head, so he lay back down on the pavement and just waited to recover. He flinched as the shape of a man blocked out the sun.

Dennis Matthews bent over him. 'Not your day, is it?'

Reggie agreed it wasn't his day. It wasn't his *life*. But all he could mumble was, 'Please don't hit my nose.'

Matthews straightened up and looked around him, then walked away.

Out of shot, thought Reggie vaguely. He couldn't move his head; it hurt too much.

Brilliant blue. Cotton-wool clouds sailed gently by.

Then the sky darkened and Matthews was back. Didn't bend down this time, just stood there with a gnome in his hands. The one with a butterfly on its nose.

'We had a meeting.'

Reggie had to frown to remember. *I'll be in Ladbrokes. You've got a week.* That copper had been there, though, and he'd had to make up the story about his ex—

Before he could say this, Matthews threw the gnome through the rear window of the Mazda.

Reggie made a face that shouted *NO!*

Matthews flickered briefly through his peripheral vision, then came back with two gnomes – one in the crook of each elbow, like a proud dad showing off twins.

'Where's Terry's money?'

'I haven't got it.'

The fishing gnome exploded on the boot.

'What about the will?'

'There's nothing left.'

'Nothing?'

'I can't even pay for the funeral.'

The disco gnome shattered the windscreen.

Again Matthews passed him.

Again he came back.

'What about the house?'

'It's Skipper's house, not mine.'

'Then make it yours,' said Matthews. 'Like father, like son.' The gardening gnome hit the bonnet so hard that it stayed there, still clutching a broken spade, and cradled in a metal depression of its own making.

Reggie felt sick.

Not because of the car. Not because of the punch. But because for the first time he understood that Albert had planned to pay off his gambling debts by arranging the death of his own father.

Dennis Matthews bent over one more time and Reggie squeezed his eyes shut, waiting for the pain.

'I feel sorry for you, Reggie,' said Matthews. 'But take care of it by tomorrow, or you're a dead man.'

The first gnome had woken Toff, and Toff had growled and woken Skipper from an unnaturally deep sleep. The second gnome made him roll awkwardly towards the window to see what was going on.

What was going on was so surreal that at first Skipper wondered if he were still asleep and dreaming. Reggie was lying in the road, on his back and with his arms spread out as if he were falling, while a huge toddler threw gnomes at his car.

Skipper sprang into action.

In his head.

In reality he twitched and tried to turn over and got his legs caught in the sheet and kicked feebly to free himself, and by the time he'd admitted he wasn't going to be able to rush downstairs and save his grandson, the big man was bent over Reggie, and Skipper stopped moving and held his short breath, so he could hear what he was saying.

What about the house?

The house is Skipper's, not mine.

Then make it yours. Like father, like son.

Skipper Cann rolled away from the window before the sound of the final crash.

He stared at the ceiling with his old heart beating so hard that it hurt.

Like father, like son.

Now he knew what Albert had done.

But what would Reggie do?

Off the Hook

Felix Pink said he didn't know anyone called Andrea.

They spent an hour after booking the dentist scouring HOLMES, but without finding anything close to being a match.

Pete Shapland finally pushed his chair away from his desk and made a sound like a hard-ridden pony. 'All Andrea'd out, ma'am,' he said, and helped himself to a Mars bar from the stash Calvin had punched out of the vending machine.

DCI King nodded morosely. 'What did he say about the Oxy?' asked Calvin.

'I haven't got into that with him. I'll do that first thing tomorrow. We have to be mindful of his age, particularly as he's not being represented. I had to ask him about Andrea, but I can't push him too hard.'

Calvin nodded, but shared her frustration. Even allowing for the couple of hours when this was still about the tulips, their right to hold Felix Pink in custody would run out just before midday tomorrow. After that they'd have to charge him with what they could or let him go.

Jackie Braddick had already brought in a duvet and pillow — both covered with Transformers.

'What's that?' Calvin had said.

'I popped home and got them for Felix,' she'd answered. 'He's too old to be sleeping on that crappy bench.'

Tony Coral's top half leaned into the office. 'Young lady for you at the desk, ma'am,' he said. 'About Mr Cann.'

It was well past the end of their shifts, but none of them even looked at their watches before hurrying out of the office.

The girl in reception had sensible eyebrows but was so nervous that Calvin's heart started to beat faster just looking at her.

They led her through to the cramped interview room and King closed the door behind them. 'Have a seat. I'm DCI King. This is DC Shapland and Acting DC Bridge.'

The girl sat, but perched on the very edge of the chair, as if she might be getting up again any minute now. King asked her name.

'I'm Amanda,' she said, as if it were an announcement. She looked around as if they might know her. 'Didn't John mention me?'

'Who's John?'

'We were together,' she said, 'when Reggie's dad . . . died.'

'Hold on,' said King. 'You were there when Albert Cann died?'

'Yes,' Amanda said, and looked as if she might cry, but caught herself.

'Then I think I should caution you,' said King, 'that anything you say—'

'But it was a *mistake*,' said Amanda in a rush. 'I gave him the instrument of death and I felt terrible and Reggie broke up with me when he found out, and I didn't blame him, but then John called me and said we were set up and I didn't believe him because I know *I* didn't set him up so he must have meant Reggie, and I was, like, *Reggie would never hurt anyone, and why would he set me up?* but then I saw on the news that John had been arrested and I couldn't let him take all the blame even though he said he would, but I wanted to talk to Reggie about it first, but when I went there I saw him having a row with this . . . *girl* . . . who's *pregnant* . . . so now I'm thinking maybe it *was* a set-up. Maybe he knew what was going on and decided to get rid of me *and* his dad all in one go!'

She burst into tears, and they all took a long moment to digest.

Then DCI King asked her, 'So you're an Exiteer?'

'Yes,' she sobbed. 'Well, *was*. They probably won't let me do it again.'

King found a photo on her phone and held it out to Amanda. 'Do you know this man?'

'Yes. That's John.'

'His real name is Felix Pink.'

'Oh. Felix. I didn't know.'

'Is Amanda your real name?'

'Yes. Amanda Bell.'

Calvin slapped the table and made them all jump. 'Oh, *Andrea*!'

They all exchanged looks of illumination, but Amanda looked confused and King waved it away. 'Ignore that,' she said. 'Exiteers apparently use pseudonyms to protect themselves, and somebody threw Andrea into the mix.'

'Oh,' she sniffed, 'I didn't think to use a fake name. I just used mine.'

'Amanda,' said King, 'do you have any evidence of a set-up? Apart from Felix Pink telling you there might have been one.'

She'd stopped crying now. 'Like what?'

'Like witnesses, or text messages, or something Reggie said?'

She frowned. Thought. Shook her head. 'No. Just the girl . . . At least now I know why he never took me to his house. He said it was because his granddad was sick, but really it was because *she* was there.' She started crying again.

'Tissues, Calvin,' said King. 'Do you mind?'

Calvin went into reception to find a box of tissues, just as Jackie Braddick was arriving with Tovey Chanter in handcuffs.

'All right, Tovey?'

'All right, Calvin?'

'What news?'

'Drunk and disorderly,' he said with a shrug, 'but I'm not even drunk.'

'Just disorderly then?' said Calvin.

'He was peeing on Tarka the Otter,' said Jackie brusquely.

A bronze of the celebrated otter had been recently installed near the old bridge. There'd been quite a fuss about it being so low, and hence vulnerable to vandalism, but if it had been much taller, nobody could have seen the otter.

It often wore a hat.

'Bit low, in't it?' said Calvin.

Tovey nodded gravely. 'Temptingly.'

Calvin grinned, then beckoned Jackie over to him and lowered his voice so he could tell her about Amanda.

'You mean Andrea?'

'No, the neighbour got it wrong. And now this Amanda just waltzes in here and coughs to killing Albert Cann!'

'So Felix is off the hook?'

'I don't know. This literally happened five minutes ago. But she came right out and said she thinks Reggie set them both up.'

'Oh, this is such *bollocks*!' Jackie glared furiously at Tovey, who was helping himself to fruit cake. 'You solve a murder and I'm washing piss off an otter.'

Calvin conceded with a shrug: 'Worst job ever.'

Amanda Bell was arrested on suspicion of conspiracy to murder just after eight p.m. When DCI King said *murder*, she cried again and said, 'But I was set up! We both were!'

'You believe her, ma'am?' asked Calvin afterwards.

'It's possible. There's a lot of circumstantial evidence building up against Reggie. Now we've got Amanda's testimony, we'll speak to him again.'

'You want me to go and get him, ma'am?' said Pete keenly.

King glanced at the clock and shook her head. 'No. We'll speak to him tomorrow at the shop. Don't want to bring him in and give him time to think.'

Also conscious of the time, Calvin asked, 'What about Felix, ma'am?'

King pursed her lips.

'He's hardly a flight risk,' said Pete.

'I hate to keep an old man in a cell overnight,' agreed King, 'even *with* a Transformers duvet.' She thought and then nodded. 'If you two don't mind sticking around to do the paperwork . . .'

Neither of them minded, and shortly after nine o'clock, Felix Pink was released on police bail.

Taking Care of Skipper

Felix had to sign a lot of papers saying that he understood a lot of things – including that he couldn't go to Abbotsham or contact the Cann family. He also had a nine o'clock curfew, which was handy, as that was his bedtime anyway.

As he left, Jackie gave him a big hug and Calvin shook his hand, and Tony Coral patted his shoulder and handed him a paper bag so heavy that it might have contained gold, but which Felix feared contained cake.

Then Pete Shapland drove him home and refused to take any petrol money.

It was too late to wake Miss Knott to retrieve Mabel, but he did call Geoffrey.

'John! Are you home?'

'Yes. I've just been released on bail.'

'Have you been charged?'

'No.'

'Wonderful! You must let me know what you told them so we're on the same page.'

'I'll explain everything later, Geoffrey, but right now I need your help.'

'Of course!' said Geoffrey without hesitation.

'One of my bail conditions is that I can't go to Abbotsham.'

There was a confused pause. 'Do you *want* to go to Abbotsham?'

'Well, I'm rather worried about Skipper.'

'Skipper Cann?' said Geoffrey. 'What's wrong with him?'

'I think he's in danger, Geoffrey. I think somebody might be trying to kill him.'

'You mean apart from us?'

'Well, yes. But not suicide. I'm talking *murder*.'

'Murder!' Geoffrey was shocked. 'Are you sure?'

Felix thought about the question very seriously. 'Ninety per cent sure,' he said. 'I think somebody sawed through his walking stick and replaced his morphine with Oxycodone.'

'Have you told the police?'

'No.'

'Why on earth not?'

Felix was embarrassed. 'Well, it's a long story, Geoffrey. I promised Skipper I wouldn't.'

'*You what?*'

'Yes. Well. Things got a bit out of hand after the initial . . . incident. I went back to the house and Skipper and I became friendly—'

'Good God, Felix!'

'I know. I'm sorry. But the point is, I'd been sort of keeping an eye on him, but now I can't and I fear he's in danger, and – as you know – he wouldn't *be* in danger if we'd done our job properly in the first place.'

'You mean if he was dead?'

Felix didn't know how to respond to that, and finally Geoffrey sighed. 'All right,' he said, 'how can I help?'

Felix was so relieved he could have hugged him. Geoffrey hadn't berated him, hadn't told him he'd been stupid, even though he'd been exactly that; he also hadn't told him he wanted nothing to do with his mess and slammed down the phone. He was just being Geoffrey – practical and supportive, working to help others despite his own illness. A proper Exiteer.

Felix felt moved almost to tears. He cleared his throat. 'I hoped you might send somebody round there to keep an eye on him. I'd hate anything to happen to him.'

There was a short silence and then Geoffrey said simply, 'Leave it with me, Felix. I'll take care of Skipper.'

After he hung up on Felix Pink, Geoffrey Skeet sat for a long moment, just thinking.

Then he picked up a screwdriver, got up from his wheelchair, and walked quickly to the bottom of the stairs.

He crouched beside the stairlift, unscrewed the motor compartment plate, and swung it open. Inside there was no motor. The space where a motor should have been was stuffed with dozens of tightly wadded bricks of fifty-pound notes, and a smartphone.

Geoffrey withdrew the phone and settled down on the second stair, elbows on his knees, and made a call. A small black-and-white cat wound its way around his legs and he scratched its head gently and murmured, 'Hello, Buttons.'

When his call was answered, the voice that came out of Geoffrey's mouth was quite different. Less cultured. Less kind. More . . .

'Shifty?' he said. 'It's Terry.'

Old Salt

Skipper Cann always slept with the curtains open so that he could see the moon.

Sometimes when he woke at night he would half open his eyes on the stars and think himself still at sea, dozing at the wheel of the *Susanna* while the waves slapped gently at her clinker sides.

This night the ropes strained at the cleats, making them *creak creak creak . . .*

Skipper opened his eyes.

The moon was thin and the room was dark and it took him a moment to understand that he was not on a boat, but in bed – where he'd been for months, and would be now until the end.

creak . . . creak . . .

He moved his eyes but not his head.

creak . . . creak . . .

Closer. Closer.

Toff quivered against his leg as a shadow arrived at the bedside. There was so little light that if he hadn't been fifty years at sea and used to the shapes of the night, Skipper would never have made out Reggie – or the pale pillow he clutched to his chest.

'Skipper?'

Slowly Skipper closed his eyes.

'Skipper?'

Reggie wasn't whispering. It was as if he wanted him to wake up and say *yes*.

But Skipper said nothing.

He knew what was coming and, although his heart was jumbled, his head was very clear.

Don't fight it, his head said. *This is what you wanted before. You were ready then. Let it happen now. Better somebody who loves you than strangers. Better here than a hospital bed where they never turn the lights off. It'll all be over soon. Out of this life, out of this pain, and on to . . . what? Everybody goes, but nobody knows. Terrifying and magical. Don't fight it. Let it come. Don't fight it . . .*

But it took all his willpower not to sit up and cry out that he was awake and alive – and planned to remain so for ever!

'Skipper?' Reggie said more softly, and this time there was a catch in his voice that made the old man's heart break.

His boy. His boy's boy. Little Reggie. Who'd needed him so badly for so long. They'd needed each other, him and Reggie. Wife gone, mother gone; Albert no help. Alone together. Life had been tough for the two of them. And continued that way. But they'd always loved each other, hadn't they?

They had.

They did.

They *still* did – Skipper was sure of it, even as he waited for the boy he loved to kill him . . .

Tears rolled silently from his closed eyes and down the ravines of his crow's feet and into his ears, where they pooled and cooled, and down his cheeks to his lips. He would never be lost at sea, but at least he would die with salt on his face, and the flavour of oceans would comfort him as he drifted away.

One last glimpse of the moon . . .

He opened his eyes a slit, and flinched.

Reggie was gone.

But he was still here.

And Skipper Cann lay back on his damp pillow and wept with relief and disappointment.

Derby Day

Reggie Cann woke early on Derby Day, and with the weight of the world off his shoulders.

When Dead Mike arrived at Ladbrokes to open up, he was already on the doorstep, and when Dennis Matthews came in around nine thirty, Reggie got up and went straight over to him in the middle of the shop.

'I couldn't do it,' he said defiantly, 'and I'm *not* doing it. So do your fucking worst!'

He was shaking like a leaf, but he wasn't ashamed of that. Wasn't ashamed of not killing his grandfather so he could steal his house to pay off a crook. Let the curly-headed bastard beat the shit out of him if he wanted to. *Fuck him.*

But Matthews just stood there and frowned at him – as if there was a simple solution to Reggie's problem and he'd offered that solution to him, but Reggie hadn't taken it. His big furrowed face said that made no sense to him, and now he looked at Reggie as if he were a crazy street-person and he was debating whether to give him a fiver or set him alight.

'Won't wash with Terry,' he said at last.

Then fuck Terry, thought Reggie.

'And I've got a reputation to think of.'

And fuck you too, Reggie thought, and he trembled, but he didn't blink. Didn't speak. Didn't back down. *This* was his line in the sand.

And it held.

Dennis Matthews broke eye contact first. Looked at the wall of screens. Then shrugged and said, 'I wouldn't normally do this, but I feel sorry for you . . .' He sighed. 'You owe me one.' Then he held out his hand, and Reggie shook it out of sheer surprise.

'Thank you,' he said. 'I do! *Thank* you.'

Reggie left the shop and walked up the hill to work.

He'd been so scared! So scared that he'd nearly killed Skipper. It didn't seem real now.

Thank God it was over.

When the front door opened, Toff growled and woke Skipper up.

'Hayley?'

She didn't answer. No matter – she'd be up soon. Maybe she'd make him breakfast. *Breakfast!* He couldn't remember the last time he'd actually wanted anything to eat. But today he'd make himself. Today he needed the energy. Marmite on toast maybe.

Skipper turned on the radio.

So he never heard Dennis Matthews creak across the wooden floor of the front room to the kitchen – pause briefly – and then creak out of the house again.

He never heard the door clicking gently closed behind him.

And he never heard the gas hissing from the hob, where all four knobs had been turned to FULL.

Shifty Sands had been cursed with just enough intelligence to know he was not quite smart enough. Hence, he was a bitter young man.

He'd drifted through life, angry about his underachievements but too lazy to work any harder than he already was. Which was hardly at all. Sometimes he cut grass, sometimes he built walls, sometimes he did odd jobs. Sometimes he did *very* odd jobs. And sometimes he was too drunk to do anything at all, which was nice while it lasted.

He'd started smoking at twelve, taking a chance that it would kill him by thirty and he might start the next life over with better gifts, more money, and in a warmer place. But he was thirty-six now, and was just starting to worry that – unless he did something uncharacteristically daring – he would soon be a bitter *old* man.

He'd never been married. Never been in love. Never even in *like*. Never had a proper job, and never likely to now. His parents were dull renters with no money. The only person he called 'friend' was Dennis Matthews.

While most of his friendships only lasted till the end of the bottle, the friendship with Matthews had more substance. Shifty was small and Matthews was big. That was good for Shifty. Shifty never had money, while Matthews sometimes had plenty. That was good for Shifty too. And – most importantly – they shared the dream of winning on horses, and the reality of losing on them.

That dim dream of winning – something, somehow – was the only reason Shifty Sands got out of bed most mornings.

But this morning he'd got out of bed to kill a man.

It would be his first.

He'd done jobs for Terry before. Not beatings – those were Den's department – but low-level threats, distributing NEED MONEY? leaflets – that sort of thing. It paid better than walls or grass, but was not what he craved. Not the big score.

This was the big score. Ten thousand pounds. Cash. No tax.

And it was an old man that needed offing. An old man who *wanted* to die. The way Terry told it, it would barely feel like murder at all. It would be like doing the old bloke a favour and getting paid for it.

And, because he was getting paid for it, before he went to Abbotsham Shifty Sands went to Cleverdons in Mill Street as soon as they opened, and treated himself to a full English breakfast.

Shifty took his own sweet time over his eggs and bacon and fried bread, and afterwards he left a pound beside his plate – the first tip he'd ever left anyone – and caught the bus the three miles up the hill to Abbotsham.

He alighted outside the church and walked fifty yards to Black Lane, and another fifty to the last house on the right. Number 3. There was a little red sports car parked in the drive. It was totally wrecked. Someone had really done a number on it and for the first time Shifty began to feel nervous. He hadn't expected to but he couldn't help it. He started to shake, and felt as if he were being watched. He stood at the Canns' front door and looked around.

Across the street a jagged row of gnomes all watched him. Shifty didn't like it. But there was no *human* watching him. No excuse not to jemmy open the door and step inside and close it quickly behind him.

He stood in the hallway and let out a long, wobbly breath. When he drew in the next one, he screwed up his nose. Fucking cats! The place reeked of piss.

Shifty didn't have a weapon with him, so he went into the kitchen to find the knife he would use to kill the old man. It didn't have to be anything special. A point and an edge. A knife was a knife, and this way it meant that it couldn't be traced to him. He would use it, wash it, and put it back in a drawer. That was the sum total of his plan, and he thought it a good one, given the short notice.

But his hands were still shaking a little, and he knew he'd have to stop that if he was going to get this done cleanly.

So Shifty did what came naturally.

He lit a cigarette.

Boom!

CompuWiz was like a time warp. It was exactly as they'd seen it last. Not even the dust had been disturbed, and Daz was wearing his Asteroids T-shirt again. Or still. Calvin shuddered at the thought. Daz fetched Reggie from the back of the shop. He came out still holding a tiny screwdriver.

'We've arrested Amanda Bell on suspicion of murder,' said King bluntly, and Reggie's face went slack with shock.

'His girlfriend?' said Daz. They ignored him.

'Reggie?' said King.

'W–what do you want from me? I don't know anything about it.'

'If you'd like to come with us then we can talk about it at the station.'

'Do I have a choice?'

'Not really,' she said kindly, so he walked through the shop with them.

'This is fucked up, man,' Daz kept saying. 'This is so fucked up.'

Calvin made sure Reggie didn't bump his head as he got into the back of the car. He leaned in to fasten Reggie's seatbelt because Reggie looked so dazed.

Calvin joined King in the front of the car and they did a U-turn on the broad concrete apron of the fire station opposite the computer shop.

'It's not her fault,' Reggie said flatly. 'I think Albert wanted to die.'

King stopped on the apron and turned to look at him. 'What do you mean?'

'He owed people a lot of money. Bad people. He put the house up as collateral for the loan.'

King and Calvin exchanged looks. 'How big a loan?' said King.

'Forty grand,' said Reggie. 'And when they called it in, I'm pretty sure he arranged the Exiteers for Skipper. Probably talked him into it—'

He stopped talking and collected himself before going on. 'He knew I'd be out of the house. Would have been easy for him to take the stuff out of Skipper's room. Skipper was probably asleep. He's *always* asleep these days.'

King and Calvin nodded together. They had a fair idea why. It would have been a simple matter for Albert to give his father the Oxycodone he was obviously using instead of his usual morphine.

'Who are these bad people, Reggie?' said King.

Reggie hesitated, then glanced at Calvin. 'He's from the bookies. Dennis Matthews.'

'I know him,' said Calvin.

'He beat me up,' said Reggie. 'Told me I had to pay back Albert's loan. But there was no money left and that's when he told me to kill Skipper—'

DCI King's eyes widened. 'You didn't, did you?'

Reggie shook his head. 'Like father, like son, he said. Before that I only knew Albert had put the house at risk. But that's when I knew he'd called in the Exiteers.'

'But why would Skipper go along with it?' asked Calvin.

Reggie shrugged. 'He's old and sick and he's always felt guilty. He had an affair when Albert was a baby, and his wife left him and never came back. He's always trying to make it up to Albert. Always defending him. Making excuses for him . . .'

'And why would Albert change his mind and kill himself?'

'I don't know,' Reggie said. 'Maybe so he could give everybody the slip – like that old woman said at the funeral. But I reckon he used the Exiteers to kill himself, so I don't want his death becoming somebody else's fault.'

DCI King nodded slowly. 'A set-up—'

There was a visceral *BOOM*!

'What the hell was *that*?' said King. She picked up her phone, but before she could call anyone about anything, all hell broke loose around them as the fire-station alarm whooped, steel doors opened, and three shiny red engines roared around them with flashing lights and wailing sirens. Without a word, King tossed her phone at Calvin, jammed the car into first, hit the lights and raced after them – up Abbotsham Road and towards a pillar of smoke and dust that rose from the horizon.

The Cann house was gone.

Just . . .

Gone.

In its place was a huge pile of smoking rubble that spread in every direction, turning Black Lane into a rocky moonscape. Every house in the street had lost windows and the gnomes across the road had gone down in a row, like ducks in a shooting gallery.

King parked at the edge of the debris and Calvin turned to look at Reggie. His mouth hung open, but he was so shocked that no sound came out.

Firemen were already hard at work, clearing a path through the rubble.

'Check the neighbours!' King cried, and opened her door. Behind her, Reggie tried to do the same, but the rear locks were on.

'Stay here, Reggie!' she said. 'As soon as they find anything, you'll know. I promise.'

Calvin ran to the Moons' house first. He knocked but there was no answer, so he picked up a flowerpot from the front garden, smashed the glass in the door and let himself in. Despite the sounds of emergency outside, the house felt eerily quiet, and dust darkened the air.

'Mrs Moon?' he called. 'Mr Moon? Donald?'

Several windows had blown in and there was glass everywhere. Calvin crunched and snapped his way down the hall. In the back room Donald Moon sat in the chair he'd occupied last time. Glass in his lap. Glass and blood and dust. The French windows had come in on top of him. He was still holding his binoculars.

'Mr Moon?'

He looked up, dazed. Calvin had never been more relieved to see a man move. 'Mr Moon, it's PC Bridge.'

'Who?'

'PC Bridge,' he repeated. 'Calvin Bridge, from Bideford Police.'

'Calvin,' nodded Donald Moon. 'I was just watching the birds and the window fell in.' He sounded surprised more than anything.

'Right,' said Calvin. 'Where's Mrs Moon?'

'Shopping.'

Thank God.

'Good,' he said. 'You just sit still a minute, Mr Moon, and I'll clear this off you.'

'Thank you.'

He picked slabs of glass off the man until only a single shard remained, buried in his thigh. There was a lot of blood, but it was not pumping, so Calvin discounted the possibility that it had cut through the femoral artery.

'This is good news, Mr Moon. All you've got is this one bit of glass in your leg and it hasn't cut through an artery. I'm going to go and get some towels to mop up the blood, and an ambulance will be here any minute.'

'In the bathroom,' said Donald Moon. 'Is it going to be all right?'

'Yes it is,' he said confidently as he left the room. 'And how lucky that Mrs Moon is out.'

'Yes,' Donald Moon kept rambling. 'She only went for bread and I said not to bother because we've got some in the freezer, but she likes fresh . . .'

Calvin pounded up the stairs and grabbed the towels off the rail in the bathroom. All the time, he called down inane encouragement about buns and rolls. The biggest threat to Mr Moon now was shock, and as long as they were talking about baked goods that was unlikely to kick in. He hurried downstairs, trying to avoid the bigger pieces of glass, to find Donald Moon unconscious in his chair.

Things after that became a blur for Calvin – of no pulse, and lips turning blue, and laying Mr Moon on the carpet, and finding the right place on his sternum and starting to pump, while shouting for help, but nobody came and nobody came and, with Old Greybeard uppermost in his mind, he finally hoisted Mr Moon roughly on to his shoulders and stumbled out into the war zone of flames and smoke and dust and fire engines and ambulances and police cars.

Everybody rushed to help then, and Mr Moon was quickly loaded into an ambulance, which sped out of Black Lane, past Reggie Cann's stricken face pressed against the back window of the police car.

'Are you hurt?' shouted a fireman into Calvin's face, and Calvin looked down at his navy suit and white shirt, covered in blood, and said, *No*, and could only hope it was true.

The firefighter disappeared and Calvin went next door and checked on deaf Mrs Digby. Her windows had shattered, but not come in. Then he crossed the road and met DCI King coming out of Bob Wilson's house.

'Jesus, Calvin, are you hurt?'

'No, ma'am,' he said.

She'd checked that side of the street. Minor lacerations and shock. Three people had been sent to hospital. Bob Wilson was unscathed and already complaining about bricks strewn across his lawn. In the gathering crowd, Calvin saw Hayley Pitt and her sisters, goggle-eyed and giggling.

A team of gas engineers in hi-vis and helmets arrived to secure the main.

Calvin and King stood at the kerb and looked at the the ruin of number 3, where the firefighters had stopped pouring water and started to work through the smoking rubble. The destruction of the house was nearly complete. Here and there was something recognizable – a chair leg, a spatula, a microwave oven – but everything was the same brick-dust colour, which made one lump of something look very like another.

Calvin walked to the edge of the rubble and spoke to a firefighter.

'Did you find anyone yet?'

'Nothing yet.'

'He'd have been in the front bedroom.'

'Thanks. We'll search that as soon as we find it.'

Firefighter sarcasm. He was just in the way. He turned to go.

Body.

Calvin *felt* the word more than heard it. It was a weird thing. A strange undercurrent of information passing through the firefighters around him. Something in their manner, their look, the way they moved, was suddenly subtly different.

All of them staring at one spot.

'Hey!' The sarcastic firefighter beckoned him over. 'You know the resident?'

Calvin's blood ran cold. He nodded. Didn't look at Reggie. Didn't look at anything beyond the dark cloth and hi-vis flashes on the firefighter's trouser legs as he followed them carefully across the rubble. His hands itched with sudden sweat. Would Skipper Cann even look like a man? Or just another *thing* covered in brick-dust? He wished he didn't have to be the one to find out. Wished

he was back at the nick eating bad fruit cake, or cleaning piss off
an otter.

Worst job ever.

He followed the legs until they stopped beside three similar
pairs.

Calvin took a breath and looked down and saw the shape of a
man's torso, covered in brown dust. Face down, thank God. Most
of the body still buried in brick. One arm was gone at the elbow,
but the head was almost intact.

Almost. He tried only to look at the bits that were still there.

'Is it him?'

Calvin looked up. DCI King had brought Reggie to the edge of
the rubble.

'Is it him?'

'No,' he said, and turned to Reggie. 'It's not him, Reggie.'

Reggie's face crumpled. 'Then who the hell is it?'

'Jesus!'

Everybody looked at Calvin in confusion, but he could only
point past them and down Black Lane, where – through the post-
apocalyptic dust and smoke and rubble – came an old man leading
a small black-and-tan dog.

The Loser

Everybody cried. Even the firemen.

Paramedics sat the shaken Skipper Cann down in the back of an ambulance and, between puffs of oxygen, he told them he'd been down to Bouchers in Bideford to put the house in Reggie's name.

'But now there *is* no house,' he said mournfully.

'The house doesn't matter, Skip,' Reggie said huskily, and everyone cried again.

Then Reggie hugged his grandfather and said, *See you soon*, and they closed the doors and took him off to hospital.

Calvin suddenly felt very tired. Very tired and very dirty. He looked down at his suit, which was ruined, and his shirt, which was stuck to his belly with Donald Moon's blood. Old Greybeard's St Christopher medal glimmered through the gore. Calvin picked it up and looked at it. He wasn't religious, but something had protected him today. Something had protected them all . . .

'St Peter,' said Reggie, as if he'd heard Calvin's thoughts.

'Sorry?'

Reggie pointed at the medal. 'St Peter.'

'It's a St Christopher,' said Calvin.

'Nah,' Reggie insisted. 'See, he's holding the keys to the kingdom of heaven?'

Calvin looked down, and he was. 'What does St Christopher do then?'

'Just stares off into the distance, I think.'

'Didn't know you were religious,' Calvin said, and Reggie shook his head.

'I'm not. But Skipper had one just like it when I was little. St Peter's the patron saint of fishermen.'

Calvin turned the medallion over. 'Do you know what this means?'

Reggie squinted. 'BD77? It does ring a bell . . .' But then he shook his head.

DCI King came over. 'I'll take Reggie to the hospital now, Calvin, but I want to know who the hell that dead man is. I've told them to call you as soon as they've got him out so you can check him for ID.'

'Yes, ma'am.' He watched her take Reggie and the dog back to the car.

An alert on his phone sounded and Calvin sat down heavily on the kerb and watched Seaspeak come round Tattenham Corner as if he were on rails, and power up the Epsom hill to win the Derby.

He nearly cried that Old Greybeard wasn't here to see it.

Rumbaba trailed in ninth, so Calvin was a dead man, but he was far too tired to muster any interest in his own fate. He propped his head on his hands and his elbows on his knees, and let the noise and the dirt and the mayhem swirl around him.

A firefighter woke him twenty minutes later to identify the corpse.

It was Shifty Sands.

Calvin knew it the moment he looked down at the fully exposed and water-washed corpse, but he went through the man's pockets too, to confirm his identity. There was only a debit card in another man's name, and a thin sheaf of A5 flyers, folded in half. Calvin opened one out. *NEED MONEY?* it said in bold letters. And, under that: *BIG CASH FAST! Call Terry NOW!* and there was a mobile phone number.

He was still standing over the body when Maria, the paramedic, called to tell him that Donald Moon was going to be OK. 'He lost tons of blood. You saved his life for sure,' she said.

'One out of two ain't bad,' he said. He had no idea where she'd got his number.

'You still at the scene?'

'For a while.'

'Stay safe.'

'That's the aim.'

'When you're free, Dan and I will buy you a drink for doing our job for us.'

Dan. The other paramedic. 'Great,' he said, 'thanks.'

'But Dan can't come,' she said, and – even here in the ruins – Calvin caught the tease in the silence that followed her words.

So he laughed and she said, 'You have my number now, so use it.'

'I will,' he said, and felt like Ryan Gosling.

He hung up and asked the nearest firefighter if they'd need him for anything else.

'Not unless we find another body,' he winked.

Calvin nodded gratefully. It had been a long, rough day and he was ready to go home and get drunk.

He headed back over the rubble. It was a precarious business. He took a bad step, dislodged a chunk of masonry and nearly fell. A glint of gold was exposed under his right foot, and he bent to pick up Albert Cann's carriage clock. The one he had kept beside his bed. It was broken, of course – the face hanging off like a comedy eyeball, and the case buckled. As Calvin turned it over in his hands, the back swung open and two bits of folded paper dropped out.

He bent and picked them up. The first was a flyer that read *NEED MONEY?* Calvin knew what the other was before he even touched it. The size, the colour, the quality of the paper were all instantly, embarrassingly, familiar.

He unfolded the betting slip.

SEASPEAK DERBY £5000 WIN.

He lost his breath. Had to read it twice. Three times. Five *thousand* pounds? To *win*?

Silly money . . .

Old Greybeard's words echoed in his head. First in the bookies – and then at the funeral.

But Albert Cann hadn't given them the slip. He hadn't given *anyone* the slip.

Although he *had* taken a price . . .

50–1.

The betting slip in Calvin Bridge's hand was worth a quarter of a million pounds.

The Big Secret

They broke down Dennis Matthews' front door at dawn the next day so that they had the element of surprise. But Matthews turned out to be a morning person and put up a good fight. He cut Pete's forehead open on a chunky ring, and got Calvin in a headlock before they managed to grapple him to the bedroom carpet and sit on him.

While they were down there, they spotted a holdall under Matthews' bed which turned out to be stuffed with money. Later Jackie Braddick would count it (and take selfies with it) and make it just shy of seventeen thousand pounds.

Despite that, when they finally managed to manhandle Matthews to the car and force his enormous head through the rear door, he growled at Calvin, 'You owe me five hundred quid.'

'That's racing,' shrugged Calvin – but only because Matthews was already cuffed.

On the way back from East-the-Water, DCI King called to say they'd done a reverse directory search on the *NEED MONEY?* flyer and had an address for Terry the loan shark.

'You'll never believe it,' she said, 'but we've been there before . . .'

They all went to Exeter. Two cars. Calvin in uniform, because he'd had to throw away his navy suit and didn't have another one. Before they left, he checked he had the medallion around his neck.

It was stupid. He wasn't even at sea – let alone fishing – but after yesterday, he felt naked without it.

'So Geoffrey Skeet lent money to Albert?' said Pete, on the way.

'Maybe to all of them,' Calvin said grimly, and wondered whether he'd missed something in the Exiteer files that could have got them here sooner.

'So the Exiteer boss lent money to people, then got it back when their wealthy relatives killed themselves . . . as arranged by the Exiteers?'

Calvin nodded ruefully. 'All this time we thought the borrowers were using the Exiteers to hurry things along and inherit more quickly. But now it looks like the Exiteers were using *them* in the first place. Skeet, anyway. Creating demand with the loans and supplying the solution via assisted suicide.'

'Bloody hell,' said Pete. 'I did *not* see that coming.'

Calvin thought that spoke well of Pete, because you'd have to be pretty sick to see that coming.

They parked a street away so as not to tip off Skeet. He was hardly a flight risk, but they didn't want to give him time to destroy the evidence they knew they'd have to work harder to find this time round.

No tea towels.

King knocked and they waited, then knocked again, and they waited again.

The next-door neighbour poked her head out of her door and said, 'He's in there. Keep trying.'

And indeed, as King lifted her hand to knock again, there was a definite noise from inside.

'Probably getting in his chair,' said the neighbour helpfully. 'Has he done something wrong?'

'Go inside, please, ma'am,' said King, and knocked again.

This time there was no sound from inside. 'Mr Skeet?' she called loudly. 'Police. Please open the door.'

Nothing.

'Right, we're going in,' she said.

And they did.

But when they got in, courtesy of a police-issue crowbar, there was nobody home.

Geoffrey Skeet's wheelchair was in the hallway. His crutches against the banister, the house empty, apart from a small, friendly black-and-white cat.

'Weird,' said King. 'Look again. Including the attic.'

Skeet was not there.

King left Jackie and Pete to start the search for evidence, while she and Calvin went back to the car to scout the area. As they got in, Calvin did a double take.

A man had just crossed the far end of a nearby alleyway. A fleeting glimpse, but . . .

'I think that was him, ma'am.'

'In a chair?'

'No,' he said. 'Bloody walking!'

She started the car, while he ran down the alleyway and out the other end.

He was right! It *was* Geoffrey Skeet. Striding down the street! And carrying a bag not unlike the one they'd found under Dennis Matthews' bed that very morning, only bigger.

'Geoffrey Skeet!' Calvin ran after him. He expected a chase. If Skeet could walk, he could probably run. But instead Skeet turned at the sound of footsteps, then headed up a garden path, down the side of a house, and stopped and waited for Calvin to catch up.

'What the hell are you doing? You're *walking*!'

'Miraculous, isn't it?' Skeet laughed. 'Nobody wants to believe a cripple can be a crook. At least, nobody wants to be the first one to say it.'

'Yeah?' said Calvin, 'Well, I'm saying it. Geoffrey Skeet, I'm arresting you for conspiracy to murder. You do not have to say anything, but—'

'You're not arresting me,' Skeet interrupted with such imperious conviction that Calvin stopped mid-sentence. 'If you arrest me, I won't give you half the money in this bag.'

'I don't want money,' snapped Calvin.

'Everybody wants money,' said Skeet. 'And there's half a million quid in this bag. It's very heavy and I'm quite old and – as you know – an invalid . . .' He laughed and Calvin longed to punch him. 'So you'd be doing me a favour taking half off my hands. Or more than half. Please. I insist.'

Calvin shook his head and started again. 'Geoffrey Skeet, I'm arresting you for conspiracy to murder. You do not—'

'Your mother is Cynthia Curley.'

The words hit Calvin like something physical.

Geoffrey smiled at him and went on. 'Thief, low-life and biggest fence in four counties. Spent fourteen of the last nineteen years behind bars – deservedly so, I have to say. Your father is Michael Bridge – since the divorce only the *second* biggest handler of stolen goods in the West Country. Your brother is Louis Bridge, thief, fence, burglar and now sole proprietor of Bridge Fencing and heir to the Bridge family throne of corruption. Your other brothers are junkies and your sister is a *fucking whore.*'

Calvin felt a hole gape open in his chest. Everything he'd done since the age of sixteen had been about keeping this secret. He'd left home, cut ties, broken hearts – his own included – to escape his family. To escape his destiny. He'd made a new life for himself – a different life – somewhere else. He'd started over. Alone. He missed his family but he could never go back, because the Bridges destroyed everything. Everything and everybody. They couldn't help it. It was their curse. And they would destroy him too. Who would trust him once they knew what he was? What he'd come from? Nobody. Neither coppers nor cons. And the job was all about trust. If you couldn't be trusted, you couldn't be in the job – and the Bridges were not to be trusted.

The smile on Geoffrey Skeet's face was that of a man who'd played an unbeatable ace. Calvin didn't know how. It didn't matter. Skeet knew, and there was nothing he could do about that now. If he cared about his job, Calvin had only one option.

He spun Geoffrey Skeet around and shoved him so hard against the side of the house that his dentures fell out on the concrete pathway and – after Calvin had cuffed the dazed, bleeding old man and read him his uninterrupted rights – he accidentally stepped on them.

Twice.

When DCI King caught up with them Calvin had the back of Skeet's jacket bundled tightly in one fist, and half a million quid in the other.

It really *was* heavy.

DCI King and Jackie Braddick drove back to Bideford with the prisoner.

On the way, Geoffrey Skeet told them every bad thing he knew about Calvin Bridge. Every miserable, low-down, scum-of-the-earth detail of his family's criminal past, present and probable future.

He did it even though it wasn't easy for him to talk. The deep cuts to his lips couldn't congeal properly while he struggled to make himself understood, and he had cracked a front tooth. He winced and grimaced throughout, but DCI King was patient, and kept making eye contact in the mirror to encourage him to go on, even when it was hard for her to understand him without most of his teeth and with his torn lips, and when he had to repeat himself four or even five times.

In the passenger seat Jackie Braddick's eyes got rounder and rounder as she listened to Geoffrey Skeet systematically destroy Calvin Bridge. He even revealed that Calvin still met his brother Louis once a year to go camping on Exmoor; that he was therefore turning a blind eye to his brother's flourishing network of crime. For a serving officer, it was a damning indictment.

But even after that point, DCI King wanted more. She nodded eagerly in the rear-view mirror and encouraged Geoffrey Skeet to go on.

And he did. It took him all the way to Torrington to finish spewing all the venom he had in him regarding Calvin Bridge. Finally he stopped, wincing with pain and queasy from all the blood he had swallowed in the telling.

King raised her brows in the mirror, looking disappointed. 'Is that it?'

'That's enough,' he mumbled – because they all knew that it was. Enough to drum Calvin Bridge out of the police force. Possibly even enough for criminal charges.

But Kirsty King only shrugged at him and said, 'Tell me something I don't know.'

And then she and Jackie Braddick laughed so hard all the winding way back to Bideford that Geoffrey Skeet thought several times that they might crash.

He sort of wished they would.

Much later that day – after Geoffrey Skeet had been charged with a litany of crimes that included murder and extortion, with more to follow – a weary-looking DCI King called Calvin into the interview room, sat him down, and relayed what had taken place on the drive back from Exeter.

Calvin was stunned. 'You knew?'

'Of course,' she said. 'It's my job to know who I can trust.'

Calvin's throat got tight. He could only nod.

'I hope you'll stay in plainclothes this time, Calvin. You've got a nose for it.'

'Yes, ma'am. Thank you.'

'Oh, and Calvin,' she said, 'if you want to keep a secret around here, for God's sake don't tell Tony Coral.'

Part Three

The Birds

As he had every morning without fail since Old Greybeard had died, Calvin was going through the latest missing persons reports, when Jackie Braddick came in.

'All right, *DC* Bridge?'

'All right, *PC* Braddick? To what do I owe this interruption?'

'Donald Moon's here to see you.'

'Oh!' Calvin put down his pen and got up. 'That's nice.'

'He's not here to say thank you for saving his life.'

'Oh, that's not so nice,' said Calvin and sat down again.

Jackie laughed. 'I know, right? Grumpy old bastard. Somebody broke his bird feeder and he'll only talk to you.'

Calvin grimaced. 'PC Braddick, did you tell Mr Moon that I'm a detective now, and that bird feeders are beneath me?'

'I *did* tell him that,' she nodded. 'I said, listen, Mr Moon, DC Bridge is a very important man now, who catches killers and clears tall buildings with a single bound, and he can't be bothering with your crappy little sparrows. But he's insisting, so . . .'

In reception Mrs Moon gave Calvin a big hug, but Donald just nodded in silence under a flat cap. He was using a stick, but wasn't moving badly, considering.

In the interview room, he unpacked what looked like an entire CCTV system from a Morrisons bag – much of it covered in bird shit.

Worst job ever, Calvin sighed to himself.

But he didn't hurry Mr Moon. He let him say his piece. And gleaned a certain satisfaction from the fact that the man was still alive to bore the tits off him.

When all the hardware was on the table, Calvin explained to Donald Moon that all he really needed was the memory card, and once he'd found that and popped it into the office computer, it was the work of a minute to find the huge interruption to the near-stationary picture caused by a giant intruder.

He reversed it a few seconds and started to watch.

Calvin guessed the camera was mounted on a branch of the apple tree, because it pointed at a nesting box on the trunk. Everything in the apple tree was calm. Then there was a shaking and a pitching and a fuzzy pink ear and a tuft of grey hair and a seventeen-second shot of something big and beige moving across the screen, and then another bump and, after that, just leaves and sky.

'That's it,' said Donald, in case Calvin had missed it.

Calvin played it again. 'So someone climbs along the branch . . . ?'

Donald Moon nodded.

'And hits the camera with his head . . . He passes through the frame, because that's his jacket there . . .'

'Broke the feeder,' said Donald Moon, 'and I missed the blue-tits fledge 'cos of him.'

'Late for babies, in't it?'

'This were a few months back.'

Calvin sighed. This crime wasn't even recent. He was being asked to investigate a broken bird feeder that had been damaged *how* long ago?

He checked the date on the screen and the hair on his forearms prickled upright.

The footage was from May 4 – two days after Albert Cann had died.

He played the clip again. But this time he reversed a bit further to thirty seconds before the camera was knocked askew.

What was he looking at? The nesting box. The tree. And beyond that the house.

The *houses*.

He realized he could see part of the back of the Cann house! The back door and, above that, Reggie Cann's bedroom window. Not Albert's, annoyingly, but even so. The back door might be critical . . .

'How far back does this recording go, Mr Moon?'

Donald shrugged. Calvin hit reverse and started to pray. Not to God but to something, somebody, somewhere who held the purse strings to luck. *Please let it go back two more days,* he prayed. *Please . . .*

He held his St Peter as he watched time run backwards . . .

A flash of hi-vis.

That was him! On Donald Moon's birdcam – coming out of the back door and disappearing around the corner of the house.

Then Felix Pink walked comically backwards up the garden to the house. He'd missed him by seconds. Felix must have been leaving the garden as he checked the back door.

Calvin reversed the recording at x16 speed. Felix again. Frenetic pixels moving through one corner of the still picture. And then just the birdbox, the houses and occasionally a bird blurring by.

'You going to watch it all backwards?' said Donald.

'Just give me a moment, Mr—'

He stopped because there was somebody else moving across the screen.

It took great willpower to reverse through the action at speed, but that's what Calvin did next, so he could watch events unfold in real time.

He stopped it again at 09.15.

At 09.18 a window opened in the Cann house. Upstairs, but not Albert's room. The bedroom next door. Reggie's, he thought from memory. What time had Daz said Reggie got to work that morn-ing? Eight thirty? Did this tell a different story?

The footage showed nothing for several minutes. Birds flapping, squabbling, shitting in the tree.

Then—!

The cleaner came out of the back door.

'*Shit!*'

'What?' said Marion Moon, who'd been sitting quietly along-side her husband all this time.

'Excuse me,' said Calvin. 'Would you mind waiting in reception while I watch this? I won't be long.'

The Moons shuffled out and Calvin hit play again.

It was Hayley Pitt all right. Distant and grainy, but he was sure of it. She came out of the back door at 09.28, picked up a ladder at the edge of the overgrown lawn, and propped it against the back wall of the house, under the open window.

'Shit shit shit!'

Calvin paused the footage and went to find DCI King and Pete Shapland. Brought them back with him. Reversed to 09.18 and they watched the footage together.

The window opening. The ladder against the wall. Hayley went back inside.

10.11 – they knew the Exiteers had arrived at the front door. 'She's still in the house!' whispered King, as if Hayley might hear them and spook.

10.20.

'Here she comes.'

Hayley climbed awkwardly out of the window and down the ladder. She let it drop down in the grass outside the back door, and hurried down the garden towards the camera, disappearing out of shot.

'Must have gone over the fence,' murmured Calvin.

At 10.33, Felix Pink came out. The dog came out. Felix picked up the dog, put it inside, then came out again and hurried towards the camera, disappearing out of shot in almost the same place Hayley had nearly fifteen minutes before.

At 10.35 Calvin appeared round the side of the house and tried the back door.

He froze the picture.

For a moment they all sat in stunned silence.

'So they *were* set up,' said King. 'By a jealous rival.'

'Oldest tea towel in the book,' said Calvin.

Pete Shapland crossed his arms. 'I told you so,' he said. 'Everybody's shagging somebody.'

At first, when she was arrested and interviewed, Hayley Pitt seemed not to understand that what she'd done was really that wrong.

She freely admitted giving Oxycodone to Skipper. Her mother worked at the hospice and always nicked a few around Christmas to sell for turkey and presents.

'Albert gimme a tenner a pill,' she said with impressed eyes. 'Made Skip right woozy,' she giggled.

'You didn't think it was wrong to give someone a powerful drug without them knowing it?' asked DCI King.

Hayley shrugged. 'It's only a sleeping pill, in't it? My mum takes 'em all the time. And Skipper was going to kill himself anyway!'

'How did you know that?'

'Albert said. Weren't a secret. Not to me, anyway. Albert had to pay for the gas online and he was shit with computers so I done it for him. But then—'

'But what?'

Hayley frowned angrily. 'This is all Reggie's fault. He told me the house was his, but when I read Skipper's will I seen it's *not* his. It's Skipper's!'

'What difference does that make to you, Hayley?'

'Well, I wouldn't have shagged him otherwise, would I? And now I've got a baby coming, so I *need* a house. More than *any* of them! I can't have a baby at my house! My mum'd go nuts. But I'm like, when Skipper goes, I'll move in and no harm done. But then I seen in the will that Skipper's not even *leaving* the house to Reggie, he's leaving it to bloody *Albert*!'

She looked outraged at the injustice of it all.

'So what did you do about it?' said King neutrally.

Hayley shrugged. 'Just switched things around a bit. Gave Oxy to Skipper *and* Albert and put the gas and the other bits in Albert's room instead and moved his oxygen behind the door so they wouldn't see it. Then I just shut all the doors apart from Albert's and they walked straight in. They were so stupid, so it weren't hard.'

'You made the tip-off call?'

Hayley nodded. 'I wasn't going to. Was just going to put it all back and go. But then I seen *her* through a crack in the bedroom door.'

'Amanda?'

'Whatever.' Hayley pursed her lips. 'I seen her picture before on Reggie's phone. Texting him and stuff. But I'm the one having his baby, so she can fuck right off!' She looked at DCI King defiantly.

'And what about after Albert was dead?' asked King. 'Did you keep giving oxy to Skipper?'

'A bit.'

'And sawed through his walking stick?'

'Reggie had tools in the shed, so . . .' Hayley shrugged as if that were self-explanatory.

King nodded sombrely. 'And you did all this so that Reggie would inherit the house more quickly?'

'Course.' Hayley nodded sincerely. 'I mean, Skipper'll be dead soon anyway. But Albert could've lasted *years*.'

Calvin Bridge Grows Up

A month or so after Hayley Pitt was charged with murder, Calvin Bridge grew up.

The change was so sudden that he could almost feel things rearranging themselves within him, like the mysterious transformation that takes place inside a chrysalis.

He'd bought a new suit for work. Dark grey wool from Banbury's and two hundred and sixty quid, which was nearly three times what he'd paid for the navy one. He'd also bought three pale blue shirts and two straight knitted wool ties. One black, one navy. He hadn't needed the shirts and ties but he also hadn't wanted to wear the same things any more. Hadn't wanted to look the same way.

Like a kid.

Suddenly Calvin no longer wanted to behave like a kid, or be treated like one.

But checking his cuffs in the mirror on the first morning he was officially in plainclothes, Calvin could still see the boy lurking inside.

The suit was not going to be enough.

The trouble was, Calvin didn't know what else there could be. He was twenty-seven, so numerically a man. He had a manly job and had done several manly things. He'd very nearly married a woman. Technically, he *was* a man.

It just felt like he was faking it.

He toyed several times with calling Maria. Got as far as dialling her number, then didn't press call. He didn't know why. He wanted a girlfriend. A girlfriend would be great. Especially one as attractive as Maria. He missed sex. He missed sharing. And yet, he didn't call.

A man would have called.

But Calvin didn't, and over the next few days a restlessness built up inside him that left him anxious and frustrated, just when he needed to be shining.

What was *wrong* with him?

He didn't know.

Then one morning Calvin Bridge woke early and made coffee, and then sat at his kitchen table in just his shorts, and wrote a letter to Shirley.

He wrote it several times. It started quite long and rambling and got shorter and shorter and shorter. Really he *un*wrote a letter to Shirley.

Dear Shirley, it finally said, *I hurt you and I'm truly sorry. We all do things we're ashamed of. Calvin.*

He felt better for writing it.

Much better.

Next time he saw Shirley in town, he wouldn't hide. Next time he saw her, he'd smile and say hello.

He put on his new suit and Old Greybeard's St Peter and walked to work.

He'd never felt more like a man.

'What's the occasion?' said Jackie Braddick at his suit.

'The occasion of me asking you to dinner.'

'You buying?'

'Of course. Otherwise it wouldn't be a date.'

'A date?' Jackie smiled uncertainly, waiting for the joke.

'Yes,' he said seriously. 'Do you want to go on a date?'

Jackie hesitated, but Calvin didn't panic. If she said no, he'd take her out to dinner anyway, because they were good mates and she deserved it and they always had a laugh together.

But she said yes.

A New Start

The window next to Skipper's new bed looked out on a long back garden that was patrolled by a big ginger tomcat, and where Mabel and Toff chased each other like fat old puppies across a well-mown lawn.

Felix did his best, and Skipper was grateful, but it wasn't home. Nowhere was home now.

The insurance wouldn't pay up on Black Lane because its destruction had been ruled a criminal act. So they were suing Geoffrey Skeet, although Skipper doubted he'd live to see any payout. Sometimes he doubted he'd live to see breakfast.

But he *had* lived to see Reggie engaged.

You hardly know each other, he'd grumbled.

But we've already been through a lot together, Reggie had replied, and Skipper knew that was true and secretly he thought they'd be happy.

Amanda had sensible eyebrows.

They were buying a cottage in Pilton. Mortgage free. God alone knew what had possessed Albert to stake silly money on a 50–1 shot in the Derby, but he'd finally given his son a worthy gift.

Skipper *had* been a bit worried about Hayley, but then it turned out she'd had a fibroid instead of a baby, which was all for the best. Having a baby in prison would have been dreadful.

And now he had nothing to look forward to except death.

Death had never held any fears for Skipper, but now he had

nothing to think about other than the sad ebbing of a once-powerful tide. Too much time to reflect on what he had lost.

And whom.

That was the trouble with living too long and dying in bed.

'It's your move,' said Felix.

Skipper looked down. Felix wasn't a bad player but he'd left his queen wide open at the back. Two moves and he'd have her. He took a pawn with his bishop to manoeuvre into place.

Felix moved his king and said, 'We're going on a trip.'

'What kind of trip?'

'A day trip.'

Skipper wouldn't go. He'd have to get dressed. It would be tiring. It would be to somewhere with flowers, or antiques, or a model village, and he'd have to pretend to be grateful they'd arranged it. Much easier to refuse to go now. Nip it in the bud.

'I'm not going,' he said, with a decisive move of his rook.

'You'll have fun,' said Felix.

'I won't.'

'You will. We all will.' Felix castled.

Skipper banged a knight down firmly. 'I'll stay here with the dogs.'

Felix sighed. The clock ticked. Toff ran in from the garden and jumped on the bed, all happy and lolling, and Skipper rubbed his silky little ears.

'We can take the dogs.'

'I'm not coming.'

'Winner decides,' said Felix.

The queen was still wide open at the back. 'Right you are,' said Skipper.

'Checkmate,' said Felix.

Skipper glared at the board to make sure it was true.

It bloody was.

*

'There she is,' said Felix.

Skipper Cann's heart skipped a beat – and then almost burst out of his chest.

'*Susanna*,' he whispered, and lifted himself out of the wheelchair they'd borrowed from the Red Cross.

Felix grabbed his arm to steady him.

'What do you think?' he said anxiously, but Skipper couldn't tell him. Couldn't speak. Not for a bit. He just nodded. Kept nodding. Kept looking.

He thought he'd never see her again. And he'd forgotten how beautiful she was. She looked sleek. Cleaned up. De-rusted. New ropes, new cables, even new brass cleats. The cracked glass in her wheelhouse replaced and polished. Her hull repainted in the same sky blue, with her name across the stern – *Susanna* – and her registration on the bow in bold black letters.

BD77.

'You want to go aboard?'

Stupid bloody question!

Felix went ahead of him and Miss Knott behind. They all helped each other and the dogs down the grassy bank and across the new gangplank.

Skipper's feet touched the deck and a great surge of energy ran up his old legs like electricity. Suddenly he was no longer part of the land, but was part of the sea. And he knew the sea in a way he'd never known the land or wanted to know the land. The thought that from this very spot he could go anywhere in the world. Anywhere! And the *Susanna* would carry him there . . .

He felt young again. Alive again. In love again. And he stood on the fresh white deck and had to blow his nose with happiness.

Miss Knott hugged him, and Felix tried to shake his hand, but Skipper ignored it and hugged him too.

He strode into the wheelhouse. The wooden interior was freshly sanded and varnished but still as familiar as his own face in a mirror. The wheel with the one repaired spoke, the compass he'd taken off the *Megan II*, his trusty old fish-finder. All just as he'd left it, but better now for having been lost to him.

The key was in the ignition. He turned it and the engine chugged into life. He laughed like a child.

Then switched off and the silence felt louder.

'You did this?'

'Not personally. I found a local chap who did her up. Tovey.'

'Tovey Chanter?'

'Yes. You know him?'

'I do,' nodded Skipper. 'Know him well.' He hesitated, then smiled and looked around at the *Susanna* again more carefully. 'He done a proper job, Felix. And this is a proper day out.'

Felix beamed, as pleased as punch, and Miss Knott squeezed his arm, and Skipper could see they were going to be in love, even if Felix didn't know it yet.

What he wouldn't give to be seventy-five.

'Are you going to take her out?' said Felix.

Skipper looked across the river and scratched his chin. The day was bright and sunny, but it was blowy and the tide was on the turn, and there was a chop on the Torridge that was quite daunting. Not for an old salt like him, of course – he knew the river like a lover – but even before the treacherous Bar that had to be crossed before reaching the sea, there were sandbanks and gullies and cross-currents to catch out the unwary.

'Not today,' he said. 'But another day, we must all go together.'

They both looked a little disappointed. Probably thinking he might not last till another day, thought Skipper, with no little amusement.

'Bring the dogs too,' he smiled. 'And a picnic.'

'Oh, that would be lovely,' said Miss Knott. 'Wouldn't it, Mabel?'

'*Grrrreat*,' growled Felix, and they both laughed.

'Can you take a picture, Miss Knott?' said Skipper. 'Me and Felix?'

She had bought a small disposable camera. One with real film in it, for added expense and inconvenience.

Felix stood beside him at the wheel and Skipper put his arm around his shoulder and Miss Knott took a little while to work out how to press the button, but got there in the end.

'And one from the shore? Get the *Susanna* in?'

They helped Miss Knott on to the gangplank and then Felix shepherded her and Toff and Mabel carefully up the grassy bank so they could get the whole boat in the picture.

By the time they turned around at the top, Skipper had cast off and the *Susanna*'s bow was already swinging lazily away from the shore.

'Skipper!'

He started the engine and turned the wheel and adjusted the choke, and the deck throbbed like a heart under his feet. He looked out of the wheelhouse door. Watched them grow smaller. Miss Knott clinging to Felix – worried for him – as if he didn't know what he was doing.

But he knew the *Susanna*.

And he knew Tovey Chanter.

Skipper didn't know how much Felix had paid Tovey, but it was sure to be too much. And it was just as sure that Tovey had done a horrible job where it mattered most – in all the places Felix would never see.

And all those places were under the water.

Yes, Tovey had been most liberal with the paint, but paint was not planking or caulking. Paint didn't hold a boat together . . .

Skipper opened the little porthole, the better to hear the gulls arguing overhead. A swan made way for him with a bow. A Bideford Blue slid past in a single scull, working hard to get home, and a man and his boy in a dinghy made jagged little turns in the eddies near the slipway over East-the-Water.

Learning the ropes.

Skipper looked back at the grassy bank. Felix and Miss Knott and Mabel and Toff were still easy to see with his seafarer's eyes. Miss Knott was animated. Waving her arms a bit. Wanting to go for help, most likely.

But Felix just stood.

Stood and watched him steer the *Susanna* down the Torridge and under the new bridge and towards the open ocean.

Skipper felt an unexpected lump in his throat.

Felix knew what he was doing. He knew. Had probably known for a while.

Maybe right from the start . . .

The first proper wave slapped the boat sideways. Skipper snatched at the fish-finder to steady himself and it came away in his hand. He looked at it and started to laugh. That was so Tovey! It wasn't even wired up! The lazy old bastard had just glued it to the dash! He'd probably nicked it and then charged Felix a fortune to put it back where he'd found it. Skipper doubled over with laughter.

The *Susanna* would never make it over the Bar.

Lost at sea.

The wind freshened and blew salt spray into his face. He licked his lips and smiled.

As they passed through the towering portal of the new bridge, he stepped out of the wheelhouse and looked back at the riverbank one last time.

Miss Knott had gone for help, but Felix still just stood.

Skipper Cann waved goodbye, and his friend waved back.

Acknowledgements

Thanks to Jim Maxwell and other Bideford police officers who were helpful during the writing of *Exit*, and to Richard Harris at the British Dental Association.

As always, I'm grateful to the whole team at Transworld, who work with unflagging enthusiasm to make each book the best it can be. Special mention to my lovely publicist, Becky Short, who makes being on the road so much easier for me, and to Richard Shailer for his beautiful book covers, and to the World's Greatest Driver, Bradley Rose. Thank you all.